THE
WANDERING
EARTH

CIXIN LIU is the leading science fiction
writer in the People's Republic of China.
He has won the China Galaxy Science
Fiction Award nine times and the Nebula
(Xingyun) Award twice. Before becoming
a writer, he was a computer engineer in a
power plant in Yangquan.

ALSO BY CIXIN LIU

The Three-Body Problem

The Dark Forest

Death's End

THE WANDERING EARTH

Cixin Liu

TRANSLATED BY
Ken Liu
Elizabeth Hanlon
Zac Haluza
Adam Lanphier
Holger Nahm

Originally published by Beijing Guomi Digital Technology Co., Ltd
on June 17, 2013.

First published in the UK in 2017 by Head of Zeus Ltd.

9 7 5 3 1 2 4 6 8

A catalogue record for this book is available from
the British Library.

HB 9781784978495
XTPB 9781784978501
KINOKUNIYA EDITION 9781786696717
E 9781784978488

Typeset by e-type, Aintree, Liverpool

Printed and bound in Great Britain by
CPI Group (UK) Ltd, Croydon CRO 4YY

Head of Zeus Ltd
First Floor East
5–8 Hardwick Street
London EC1R 4RG

WWW.HEADOFZEUS.COM

Contents

The Wandering Earth 1

Mountain 49

Sun of China 103

For the Benefit of Mankind 155

Curse 5.0 209

The Micro-Era 235

Devourer 273

Taking Care of God 325

With Her Eyes 371

Cannonball 393

With Her Eyes
China Galaxy Science Fiction Award of the Year 1999

The Wandering Earth
China Galaxy Science Fiction Award of the Year 2000

Sun of China
China Galaxy Science Fiction Award of the Year 2002

Cannonball
China Galaxy Science Fiction Award of the Year 2003

For the Benefit of Mankind
China Galaxy Science Fiction Award of the Year 2005

The Wandering Earth

Chapter 1

The Braking Era

I have never seen the night. I have never seen the stars. I have never seen spring, fall or winter. I was born as the Braking Era ended, just as the Earth stopped turning.

It had taken forty-two years to halt the Earth's rotation, three years longer than the Coalition had planned. My mother told me about the time our family watched the last sunset. The Sun sank very slowly, as if stuck on the horizon. It took three days and three nights to finally set. Of course, afterward there was no more 'day' or 'night'. The Eastern hemisphere was shrouded in perpetual dusk for a long time, maybe a decade or so. The Sun lay just below the horizon, its glow filling half the sky. During that endless sunset, I was born.

Dusk did not mean darkness. The Earth Engines brightly illuminated the whole Northern hemisphere. They had been installed all across Asia and North America – only the solid tectonic plate structure of these two continents could withstand the enormous thrust they exerted. In total, there were twelve thousand engines scattered across the Eurasian and North American plains.

From where I lived, I could see the bright plasma beams of hundreds of engines. Imagine an enormous palace, as big as the Parthenon on the Acropolis. Inside the palace, countless massive columns rise up to the vaulted ceiling, each one blazing with the blue-white light of a fluorescent tube. And you, you are just a microbe on the palace's floor. That was the world I lived in. Actually, that description was not totally accurate. It was the tangential thrust component generated by the engines that halted the Earth's rotation. Because of this, the engine jets needed to be set at a very precise angle, causing the massive beams to slant across the sky. It was like the grand palace that we lived in was teetering on the verge of collapse! When visitors from the Southern hemisphere were exposed to the spectacle, many of them suffered panic attacks.

But even more terrifying than the sight of the engines was the scorching heat they produced. Temperatures reached as high as seventy or eighty degrees Celsius, forcing us to don cooling suits before we stepped outside. The heat often raised torrential storms. When a plasma beam pierced the dark clouds, it was a nightmarish scene. The clouds would scatter the beam's blue-white light, throwing off frenetic, surging rainbow halos. The entire sky glowed as if covered in white-hot lava. My grandfather had grown senile in his old age. One time, tormented by the implacable heat, he was so overjoyed to see a downpour arrive that he stripped to the waist and ran out the door. We were too late to stop him. The raindrops outside had been heated to boiling point by the superheated plasma beams, and his skin was scalded so badly that it sloughed off in large sheets.

To my generation, born in the Northern hemisphere, all of this was perfectly natural, just as the Sun, stars, and Moon had been natural to the people who lived before the Braking Era. We called that period of human history the Ante-solar Era – and what a captivating golden age it had truly been!

When I started primary school, as part of the curriculum, our teachers led our class of thirty children on a trip around the world. By then, Earth had completely stopped turning. Except for maintaining this stationary state, the Earth Engines were only being used to make small adjustments to the planet's orientation.

Because of this, during the three years from when I was three until I turned six, the plasma beams were less intensely luminous than when the engines were operating at full capacity. It was this period of relative inactivity that allowed us to take a trip to gain a better understanding of our world.

First, we visited an Earth Engine up close. The engine was located near Shijiazhuang, by the entrance to the railway tunnel that ran through the Taihang mountains. The great metallic mountain loomed over us, filling half the sky. To the west, the Taihang mountain range seemed like a series of gentle hills. Some children exclaimed that it must be as tall as Mount Everest. Our head teacher was a pretty young woman named Ms Stella. She laughed and told us that the engine was eleven thousand meters tall, two thousand meters taller than Mount Everest.

'People call it "God's Blowtorch",' she said. We stood in its massive shadow, feeling its tremors shake the earth.

There were two main types of Earth Engines. Larger engines were dubbed 'Mountains', while smaller ones were called 'Peaks'. We ascended North China Mountain 794. It took a lot longer to scale Mountains than Peaks. It was possible to ride a giant elevator straight to the top of a Peak, but the top of a Mountain could only be reached via a long drive along a serpentine road. Our bus joined an endless procession of vehicles creeping up the smooth steel road. To our left, there was only a blank face of azure metal; to our right, a bottomless chasm.

The traffic mostly consisted of massive, fifty-ton dump trucks, laden with rubble from the Taihang mountains. Our bus quickly reached five thousand meters. From that height, the ground below appeared blank and featureless, washed out by the bluish glare of the Earth Engine. Ms Stella instructed us to put on our oxygen masks. As we drew closer to the mouth of the plasma beam, the light and heat increased rapidly. Our masks grew shaded, and the micro-compressors in our cooling suits whirred to life. At six thousand meters, we saw the fuel intake port. Truckload after truckload of rocks tumbled into the dull

5

red glow of the gaping pit, consumed without a sound. I asked Ms Stella how the Earth Engines turned stones into fuel.

'Heavy element fusion is a difficult field of study, too complex for me to explain it to you at this age,' she replied. 'All you need to know is that the Earth Engines are the largest machines ever built by humankind. For instance, North China Mountain 794 – where we are now – exerts fifteen billion tons of thrust upon the earth when operating at full capacity.'

Finally, our bus reached the summit. The mouth of the plasma beam was directly above us. The diameter of the beam was so immense that, when we raised our heads, all we could see was a glowing wall of blue plasma that stretched infinitely into the sky. At that moment, I suddenly recalled a riddle posed to us by our philosophy teacher.

'You are walking across a plain when you suddenly encounter a wall,' our haggard teacher had said. 'The wall is infinitely tall and extends infinitely deep underground. It stretches infinitely to the left and infinitely to the right. What is it?'

A cold shiver washed over me. I recited the riddle to Ms Stella, who sat next to me. She teased it over for a while, but finally shook her head in confusion. I leaned in close and whispered the riddle's dreadful answer in her ear.

Death.

She stared at me in silence for a few seconds, and then hugged me tightly against her. Resting my head on her shoulder, I gazed into the far distance. Gargantuan metal Peaks studded the hazy earth below, stretching all the way to the horizon. Each Peak spat forth a brilliant jet of plasma, like a tilted cosmic forest, piercing our teetering sky.

Soon after, we arrived at the seashore. We could see the spires of submerged skyscrapers protruding above the waves. As the tide ebbed, frothing seawater gushed from their countless windows, forming cascades of waterfalls. Even before the Braking Era ended, its effects upon the Earth had become horrifyingly apparent. The tides caused by the acceleration of the Earth Engines engulfed two-thirds of the Northern hemisphere's major cities. Then, the rise in global temperatures melted the polar ice caps, which turned the flooding into a catastrophe that spread to the Southern hemisphere. Thirty years ago, my grandfather witnessed giant hundred-meter waves inundating Shanghai. Even now, when he described the sight, he would stare off into space. In fact, our planet had already changed beyond recognition before it even set out on its voyage. Who knew what trials and tribulations awaited us on our endless travels through outer space?

We boarded something called an 'ocean liner' – an ancient mode of transportation – and departed the shore. Behind us, the plasma beams of the Earth Engines grew ever more distant. After a day's travel, they disappeared from view altogether. The sea was bathed in light from two different sources. To the west, the plasma beams still suffused the sky with an eerie bluish glow; to the east, rosy sunlight was creeping over the horizon. The competing rays split the sea in two, and our ship sailed right along the glittering seam where they met on the surface. It was a fantastic sight. But as the blue glow retreated, and the rosy glow strengthened, unease settled over the ship. My classmates and I were no longer to be seen above deck. We stayed hidden away in our cabins, blinds pulled tight across the portholes. A day later, the moment we most dreaded finally arrived. We all gathered in the large cabin that we used as a classroom to listen to Ms Stella's announcement.

'Children,' she said solemnly, 'we will now go to watch the Sun rise.'

No one moved. Every pair of eyes was fixed in a glassy stare, as if abruptly frozen to the spot. Ms Stella tried to urge us from the cabin, but everyone sat perfectly still. One of the other teachers remarked, 'I've mentioned it before, but we really ought to schedule the Global Experience trip before we teach them modern history. The students would adapt more readily.'

'It's not that simple,' Ms Stella replied. 'They pick it up from their surroundings long before we teach them modern history.' She turned to the class monitors. 'You children go first. Don't be afraid. When I was young, I was nervous about seeing my first sunrise, too. But once I saw it, I was just fine.'

Finally, we stood up and, one by one, trudged out through the cabin door. I suddenly felt a small clammy hand clasp my own, and looked back to see Linger.

'I'm scared...' she whimpered.

'We've seen the Sun on TV before. It's the same thing,' I assured her.

'How can it be? Is seeing a snake on TV the same as seeing a real live one?'

I did not know how to reply. '... Well, we have to go look anyway. Otherwise we'll be marked down!'

Linger and I gripped hands tightly as we gingerly made our way to the deck with the other children. Stepping outside, we prepared to face our first sunrise.

'In fact, we only began to fear the Sun three or four centuries ago. Before that, humans were not afraid of the Sun. It was just the opposite. In their eyes, the Sun was noble and majestic. The Earth still turned on its axis back then, and people saw the Sun rise and set every single day. They would rejoice at sunrise and praise the beauty of sunset.' Ms Stella stood at the bow of the ship, the sea breeze playing with her long hair. Behind her, the first few rays of sunlight shot over the horizon, like breath expelled from the blowhole of some unimaginably colossal sea creature.

Finally, we glimpsed the soul-chilling flame. At first, it was just a point of light on the horizon, but it quickly grew into a blazing arc. I felt my throat close up in terror. It seemed as if the deck beneath my feet had suddenly vanished. I was falling into the blackness of the sea, falling... Linger fell with me, her spindly frame quivering against mine. Our classmates, everyone else – the entire world, even – all fell into the abyss. Then I remembered the riddle. I had asked our philosophy teacher what color the wall was. He told me that it was black. I thought he was wrong. I always imagined the wall of death would be bright as fresh snow. That was why I had remembered it when I saw the wall of plasma. In this era, death was no longer black. It was the glare of a lightning flash, and when that final bolt struck, the world would be vaporized in an instant.

Over three centuries ago, astrophysicists discovered that the conversion rate of hydrogen to helium in the interior of the Sun was accelerating. They launched thousands of probes straight into the Sun to investigate, and eventually developed a precise mathematical model of the star.

Using this model, supercomputers calculated that the Sun had already evolved away from the main sequence on the Hertzsprung-Russell diagram. Helium would soon permeate the Sun's core, triggering a violent explosion called a helium flash. Afterward, the Sun would become a massive, cool-burning red giant, swelling until its diameter encompassed the Earth's orbit.

But our planet would have been vaporized in the preceding helium flash long before then.

All of this was projected to occur in the next four hundred years. Since then, three hundred and eighty years had passed.

This solar catastrophe would not only raze and consume every inhabitable terrestrial planet in the solar system – it would also completely transform the composition and orbits of the Jovian planets. After the first helium flash, as heavy elements re-accumulated in the Sun's core, further runaway nuclear explosions would occur repeatedly for a period of time. While this period represented only a brief phase of stellar evolution, it might last thousands of times longer than all of human history. As long as we remained in the solar system, humanity stood no chance of surviving such a catastrophe. Interstellar emigration was our only way out. Given the level of technology available to humanity at the time, the only viable target for this migration was Proxima Centauri. It was the star closest to our own, a mere 4.3 light-years away. Reaching a consensus on a destination was enough, the real controversy lay in how to get there.

In order to reinforce the lesson, our ship doubled back twice on the Pacific, giving us two sunrises. By then we were accustomed to the sight and no longer needed to be convinced that children born in the Southern hemisphere could actually survive daily exposure to the Sun. We sailed on into the dawn. As the Sun rose higher in the sky, the cool ocean air of the past few days retreated, and temperatures began to rise. I was drifting off to sleep in my cabin when I heard a commotion outside. My door opened and Linger stuck her head in.

'Hey, the Leavers and Takers are at it again!'

I could not have cared less. They had been fighting for the last four centuries. Even so, I got up to take a quick look. Outside, a group of several boys were fighting. One glance told me Tung was up to his usual tricks again. His father was a stubborn Leaver, and he was still serving a prison sentence for his part in an uprising against the Coalition. Tung was a chip off the old block.

With the help of several brawny crewmen, Ms Stella managed to pull the boys apart. Despite a bloody nose, Tung still raised a fist and shouted, 'Throw the Takers overboard!'

'I'm a Taker. Do you want to throw me overboard, too?' asked Ms Stella.

'I'll throw every single Taker overboard!' Tung refused to yield. Global support for the Takers had been rising of late, and they had grown unruly again.

'Why do you hate us so much?' asked Ms Stella. Several Leaver children immediately shouted in protest.

'We won't wait to die on Earth with you Taker fools!'

'We will build spaceships and depart! All hail spaceships!'

Ms Stella pressed the holographic projector on her wrist. An image immediately materialized in the air before us, arresting our attention. We quieted down for a moment. The hologram showed a crystal-clear glass sphere. The sphere was about ten centimeters in diameter and two-thirds full of water. It held a small shrimp, a branch of coral, and a bit of green algae. The shrimp swam languidly around the coral.

'This is a project Tung designed for his natural science class,' said Ms Stella. 'In addition to the things you can all see, the sphere also contains microscopic bacteria. Everything inside the sphere is mutually interdependent. The shrimp eats the algae and draws oxygen from the water, and then it discharges organic matter in its faeces and exhales carbon dioxide. The bacteria break down the shrimp's waste into inorganic matter. The algae then use the inorganic matter and carbon dioxide to carry out photosynthesis under an artificial light source. They create nutrients, grow and reproduce, and release oxygen for the shrimp to breathe. As long as there is a constant supply of sunlight, the ecological cycle in the glass sphere should be able to sustain itself in perpetuity. This is the best design by a student I have ever seen. I know that this sphere embodies Tung's dream and the dreams of all Leaver children. It is the spaceship you long after, in miniature! Tung told me he designed it according to the output of rigorous mathematical models. He modified the genes of every organism to ensure their metabolisms would be perfectly balanced. He firmly believed that the little world inside the sphere would survive until the shrimp reached the end of its natural life span. The teachers all adored this project. We placed it under an artificial light source at the required intensity. We were persuaded by Tung's predictions, and we silently wished the tiny world he had created would succeed. But now, less than two weeks later...'

Ms Stella carefully withdrew the real glass sphere from a small box. The shrimp floated lifelessly at the surface of the murky water. The decaying algae had lost any hint of green and had turned into a dead, woolly film that coated the coral.

'The little world is dead. Children, who can tell me why?' Ms Stella raised the lifeless sphere so that everyone could see it.

'It was too small!'

'Indeed, it was too small. Small ecosystems like this, no matter how precisely designed, cannot endure the passage of time. The spaceships of the Leavers are no exception.'

'We will build spaceships as large as Shanghai or New York City,' Tung objected, his voice much quieter than before.

'Yes, but anything larger is beyond the limits of human technology, and compared to Earth, those ecosystems would still be much too small.'

'Then we will find a new planet!'

'Even you Leavers don't really believe that,' replied Ms Stella. 'There are no suitable planets in orbit around Proxima Centauri. The nearest fixed star with inhabitable planets is eight hundred and fifty light-years away. At present, the fastest spaceship we can build can only travel at 0.5 per cent of the speed of light, which means it would take us one hundred and seventy thousand years to get there. A spaceship-sized ecosystem would not last for even one-tenth of the voyage. Children, only an ecosystem the size of Earth, with its unstoppable ecological cycle, could sustain us indefinitely! If humanity leaves Earth behind,' she proclaimed, 'then we would be as vulnerable as an infant separated from its mother in the middle of a desert!'

'But...' Tung paused. 'Ms Stella, it's too late for us and too late for Earth. The Sun will explode before we accelerate and get far enough away!'

'There is enough time,' she replied firmly. 'You must believe in the Coalition! How many times have I told you? Even if you don't believe, at the very least we can say, "Humanity dies with pride, for we have done everything that we could!"'

Humanity's escape was a five-step process. First, the Earth Engines would generate thrust in the opposite direction of the Earth's movement, halting its rotation. Second, operating at full capacity, the engines would accelerate the Earth until it reached escape velocity, flinging it from the solar system. Third, the Earth would continue to accelerate as it flew through outer space toward Proxima Centauri. Fourth, the engines would reverse direction, restarting the Earth's rotation and decelerating gradually. Fifth, the Earth would enter into orbit around Proxima Centauri, becoming its satellite. People called these five steps the 'Braking Era', the 'Deserting Era', the 'First Wandering Era' (during acceleration), the 'Second Wandering Era' (during deceleration), and the 'Neosolar Era'.

The entire migration process was projected to last 2,500 years, over one hundred generations.

The ocean liner continued its passage toward the part of the Earth shrouded in night. Neither sunlight nor the glow of the plasma beams could be seen here. As the chilly Atlantic breeze nipped at our faces, for the first time in our young lives we saw the stars in the night sky. God, it was a heartbreakingly beautiful sight! Ms Stella stood with one arm around Linger and I. 'Look, children,' she said, pointing to the stars with her other hand. 'There is Centaurus, and that is Proxima Centauri, our new home!' She began to cry, and we cried along with her. All around us, even the captain and the crew – hardened sailors all – began to well up. With tearful eyes, everyone gazed in the direction in which Ms Stella pointed, and the stars shimmered and danced. Only one star held steady; it was the beam of a distant lighthouse over dark and stormy seas, a flicker of fire beckoning to a lonely traveler freezing on the tundra. That star had taken the place of the Sun in our hearts. It was the only pillar of hope for one hundred future generations as they navigated a sea of troubles.

*

On our voyage home, I saw the first signal for Earth's departure. A giant comet appeared in the night sky – the Moon. Because we could not take the Moon with us, engines had been installed on the lunar surface to push it out of Earth's orbit, ensuring that there would be no collision during the acceleration period. The sweeping tail of the Lunar Engines bathed the sea in blue light, obscuring the stars. As it moved past, the Moon's gravitational pull raised towering breakers. We had to transfer to a plane to fly home to the Northern hemisphere.

The day of departure had finally arrived!

As soon as we disembarked, we were blinded by the glare of the Earth Engines. They blazed many times brighter than before, no longer slanted but pointing straight toward the sky. The engines were running at maximum power. The planet's acceleration created thunderous, hundred-meter waves that battered every continent. Blistering hurricanes howled through the towering columns of plasma, whipping up boiling froth and uprooting whole forests... Our planet had become a gigantic comet, its blue tail piercing the darkness of space.

Earth was on its way; humanity was on its way.

My grandfather passed away just before departure, his burnt body ravaged by infection. In his final moments, he repeated one phrase over and over: 'Ah, Earth, my wandering Earth...'

Chapter 2

The Deserting Era

Our school was scheduled to relocate to an underground city, and we were among its first inhabitants. Our school bus entered a massive tunnel, which sloped gently downward into the earth. After driving for half an hour, we were told that we had entered the city, but nothing outside the bus windows resembled any city I had seen before. We whipped past a labyrinth of smaller side tunnels and countless sealed doors set back into cavities in the walls. Under the row of floodlights mounted to the tunnel ceiling, everything assumed a leaden blue tinge. We could not help but feel dejected at the realization that, for most of the remainder of our lives, this would be our world.

'Primitive humans lived in caves, and now so will we.' Linger said this quietly, but Ms Stella still caught her words.

'It can't be helped, children,' she sighed. 'The surface will soon become a terrible, terrible place. When it is cold, your spit will freeze before it hits the ground. When it is hot, it will evaporate even as it leaves your lips!'

'I know it'll be cold because Earth is traveling away from the Sun, but why will it get hot?' asked a little girl from one of the lower grades.

'Idiot, haven't you studied transfer orbits?' I snapped.

'No.'

Linger launched into a patient explanation, as if to dispel her sorrowful thoughts. 'It's like this: the Earth Engines aren't as powerful as you think. They can accelerate Earth a little bit, but they can't just push it out of its solar orbit straight away. Before Earth escapes the Sun, we still need to orbit it fifteen times! Through these fifteen orbits, Earth will gradually accelerate. Right now, Earth's orbit around the Sun is pretty much circular, but as it speeds up, it will become increasingly elliptical. The faster we move, the flatter the ellipse grows, and the more the Sun will be shifted toward one end of the orbit. So when Earth is furthest from the Sun, naturally it will be very cold—'

'But... that's still not right! It will be cold when Earth is far away from the Sun, but on the other end of the ellipse, its distance from the Sun will be... Hmm, let me think.' The girl chewed on her lip. 'Orbital dynamics says Earth won't be any closer to the Sun than it is now, so why would it get hotter?'

She truly was a little genius. Genetic engineering had made this type of exceptional memory the new norm. Humanity was quite fortunate in this respect. Otherwise, unimaginable miracles like the Earth Engines could not have been realized in the span of four centuries.

'Don't forget about the Earth Engines, dummy,' I chimed in. 'Over ten thousand of those giant blowtorches are on full blast. Earth is basically just a ring to hold the rocket nozzles. Now be quiet. I'm getting annoyed.'

*

We began our new lives underground. Located five hundred meters below the surface, our city had space for over one million residents. Many others just like it were scattered across every continent. Here, I finished primary school and entered secondary school. My schooling concentrated on science and engineering. Art, philosophy, and other subjects deemed inessential had been minimized or removed from the curriculum. Humanity had no time for distractions. It was the busiest era in human history. Everyone had work to do, and the work was never finished. Interestingly, every world religion had vanished without a trace overnight. People finally realized that if God truly existed, he was a real bastard. We still studied history, but to us, the Ante-solar Era of human history seemed as mythical as the Garden of Eden.

My father served in the Air Force as an astronaut. He frequently flew low-Earth orbit missions and was rarely at home. I remember in the fifth year of orbital acceleration, when Earth was at aphelion, we took a family trip to the seashore. Aphelion Day was a holiday like New Year's Eve or Christmas. As Earth entered the part of its orbit furthest from the Sun, everyone basked in a false sense of security, though. We still needed to wear special thermal suits to go to surface. Instead of cooling suits, we donned sealed heating suits powered by nuclear batteries. Outside, we were nearly blinded by the Earth Engines' towering plasma beams. The harsh light eclipsed our view of the surface world, and it was difficult to tell if the landscape had changed at all. We had to fly for a long time in our car before we escaped the glare and we could actually see the shore. The Sun had shrunk to the size of a baseball. It hung motionless in the sky, surrounded by a faint, dawn-like halo. The sky was the deepest blue we had ever seen, and the stars were clearly visible. Looking around, I fleetingly wondered where the ocean had gone. There was now only a vast, white, icy plain stretching to the horizon. A large crowd of revelers had gathered atop the frozen sea. Fireworks whistled through the darkness. Everyone was carousing with unusual abandon. Drunken party-goers rolled across the ice, while others belted out the words to a dozen different songs, each trying to drown out the competing voices around them.

'Despite it all, everyone is living their own lives. No harm in that,' my father said approvingly. He paused, suddenly remembering something. 'Oh, I forgot to tell you – I've fallen in love with Stella Li. I want to move out to be with her.'

'Who is she?' my mother asked calmly.

'My primary school teacher,' I answered for him. I had started secondary school two years ago, and had no idea how my father knew Ms Stella. Maybe they had met at my graduation ceremony?

'Then go,' said my mother.

'I'm sure I'll grow tired of her soon enough. I'll come back then. Is that okay by you?'

'If you want to, certainly.' Her voice was as calm and even as the frozen sea. But a moment later, she bubbled with excitement. 'Oh, that one is beautiful! It must have a holographic diffractor inside!' She pointed to a firework blossoming in the night sky, genuinely moved by its beauty.

Movies and novels produced four centuries ago were baffling to modern audiences. It was incomprehensible to us why people in the Ante-solar Era invested so much emotion into matters that had nothing to do with survival. Watching the hero or heroine suffer or weep for love was bizarre beyond words. In this day and age, the threat of death and the desire to escape overrode everything else. Nothing but the most current updates on the solar state and position of Earth could hope to move us or even hold our attention. This hyper-focus gradually changed the essence of human psychology and spirituality. Humans paid scant attention to affairs of the heart, like a gambler taking a swig of water, unable to tear his eyes from the roulette wheel.

Two months later, my father returned from his jaunt with Ms Stella. My mother was neither happy nor unhappy to see him.

'Stella has a good impression of you,' my father told me. 'She said you were a very creative student.'

'Who said that?' My mother asked with a puzzled expression.

'My primary school teacher, Ms Stella,' I replied impatiently. 'Dad was living with her for the last two months!'

'Oh, I remember!' She shook her head and laughed. 'Not even forty yet, and my memory is already shot.'

She looked up at the holographic stars on the ceiling and the forest on the walls. 'It's good to have you home. Now you can switch up these images. Your son and I are sick of looking at them, but we don't know how to work the darn thing.'

By the time Earth began its fall back toward the Sun, we had all entirely forgotten the episode.

*

One day, the news reported that the ocean had begun to thaw, so we took another family trip to the seashore. Earth was just passing through Mars' orbit. The available sunlight should not have significantly raised temperatures, but the Earth Engines ensured the surface was warm enough to thaw the sea ice. It felt delightful to step outside without the encumbrance of a thermal suit. The Earth Engines still lit up the sky in our hemisphere, but on the other side of the planet people could really feel the Sun's approach. Their sky was clear and pure blue, and the Sun was as bright as it had been before departure. But from the air, we spotted no signs of a thaw. We saw only a white expanse of ice. Disappointed, we got out of our car. Just as we closed the doors, we heard an earthshaking rumble that seemed to rise from the very depths of the planet. It sounded like the Earth was about to explode.

'That's the sound of the ocean!' my father shouted over the noise. 'The sharp rise in temperatures is heating the thick ice unevenly – it's like an earthquake on land!'

Suddenly, a sharp noise like a thunderclap pierced the low rumble, eliciting cheers from the people watching the sea behind us. I saw a long crack appear, shooting across the frozen ocean like a black fork of lightning. The rumbling continued as more fissures appeared in the ice. Water gushed from the cracks, forming torrents that rushed across the icy plain.

On the way home, we looked out over the desolate land below and saw broad tracts of wild grass sprouting from the earth. All kinds of flowers had burst into full bloom, and withered forests were mantled in tender green leaves. Life was throwing itself into the business of rejuvenation as if there was no time to lose.

Every day the Earth drew closer to the Sun, dread knotted itself tighter in our stomachs. Fewer people made the trip to the surface to admire the spring scenery. Most of us retreated into the depths of the underground city, not to avoid the approaching heat, torrential rains, and hurricane-force winds, but to escape the creeping terror of the Sun. One night, after I had already gone to bed, I overheard my mother tell my father in hushed tones, 'Maybe it really is too late.'

'The same rumor was going around during the last four perihelions,' he replied.

'But this time it's true,' she insisted. 'I heard it from Dr Chandler. Her husband is an astronomer on the Navigation Commission. You all know him. He told her that they have observed accelerated rates of helium concentration.'

'Listen, my dear, we mustn't give up hope. Not because hope is real, but because we have to conduct ourselves nobly. In the Ante-solar Era, nobility required wealth, power, or talent, but now one just needs hope. It is the gold and jewels of this age. No matter how long we live, we must hold on to it! Tomorrow, we'll tell our son the same thing.'

Like everyone else, I felt restless and uneasy as the perihelion approached. One day after school, I found myself in the city's central plaza. I stood by the round fountain in the middle of the plaza, looking down at the glittering water in the pool and then up at the ethereal ripples of light reflected on the domed ceiling. Just then I noticed Linger. She was holding a little bottle in one hand and a short length of tubing in the other. She was blowing soap bubbles, her eyes blankly following each string of bubbles as they drifted away. She watched them vanish one by one, only to blow another stream.

'You still like blowing bubbles at your age?' I asked, walking over.

Linger looked pleased to see me. 'Let's take a trip!'

'Take a trip? Where?'

'To the surface, of course!' She swept her hand through the air, using the computer on her wrist to project a hologram of a beach at sunset. A gentle breeze stirred the palm trees, and white surf lapped at the shore. Pairs of lovers dotted the yellow sand, black silhouettes against the gold-flecked sea. 'Mona and Dagang sent me this. They've been traveling all over the world. They said it's not too hot on the surface. It's so nice out. Let's go!'

'They were just expelled for cutting class,' I objected.

Linger sniffed. 'That's not what you're really afraid of. You're afraid of the Sun!'

'And you're not? You had to see a psychiatrist because of your heliophobia.'

'I'm a different person now. I've been inspired! Look,' said Linger, using the tube to blow another stream of soap bubbles. 'Watch closely.' She pointed to the bubbles.

I singled out a bubble, examining the waves of light and color surging across its surface, the iridescent patterns too complex and intricate for humans to process. It was as if the bubble knew it would lead a short life and was frantically broadcasting the myriad dreams and legends of its prodigious memory to the world. A moment later, the waves of light and color vanished in a silent explosion. For a half-second, a tiny wisp of vapor remained, but then that, too, was gone, as if the bubble had never existed at all.

'See? The Earth is a cosmic soap bubble. One pop, and it's gone. So what is there to be afraid of?'

'But it won't happen like that. It's been calculated that after the helium flash it will take one hundred hours before the Earth is completely vaporized.'

'That's exactly the scariest part!' Linger cried. 'Five hundred meters underground, we're like meat stuffing in a pasty. First we'll be slowly cooked through, and then we'll be vaporized!'

A cold shiver ran down my entire body.

'But it won't be like that on the surface. Everything will be vaporized in the blink of an eye. Anyone up there will be like soap bubbles: one pop and...' She trailed off. 'So I think it would be better to be on the surface when the flash hits.'

I couldn't say why, but I did not go with her. She went with Tung instead, and I never saw either of them again.

But the helium flash never happened. Earth swept past perihelion and climbed toward aphelion for the sixth time. Humanity breathed a collective sigh of relief. Because Earth no longer rotated, at this point in its orbit around the Sun the Earth Engines installed in Asia faced into the planet's direction of flight. As a result, the engines were completely powered down, save for occasional adjustments to the Earth's orientation. We sailed into a quiet, endless night. In North America, however, the engines were operating at full capacity, the continent securing the rocket nozzles to the planet. Because the Western hemisphere also faced the Sun, the heat there was devastating. Grass and trees alike went up in smoke.

Earth's gravity-assisted acceleration progressed like this year after year. When the planet began its ascent toward aphelion, we unwound proportionally to the Earth's distance from the Sun; at the new year, when the planet began its long fall toward the Sun, we grew tenser with each passing day. Each time Earth reached perihelion, rumors swirled that the helium flash was imminent. The rumors would persist until Earth climbed again toward aphelion. But even as people's fears subsided as the Sun shrank in the sky, the next wave of panic was already brewing. It was like humanity's morale was dangling from a cosmic trapeze. Or perhaps it was more accurate to say that we were playing Russian Roulette on a planetary scale: every journey from perihelion to aphelion and back was like turning the chamber, and passing the perihelion was like pulling the trigger! Each pull was more nerve-wracking than the last. My boyhood was spent alternating between terror and relaxation. Come to think of it, even at aphelion, Earth never left the danger zone of the helium flash. When the Sun exploded, Earth would be slowly liquefied, which was a fate considerably worse than being vaporized at perihelion.

In the Deserting Era, disaster followed disaster in quick succession.

The changes in velocity and trajectory generated by the Earth Engines disturbed the equilibrium of Earth's iron-nickel core. The turbulence passed through the Gutenberg discontinuity and spread to the mantle. As geothermal energy escaped to the surface, volcanic eruptions ravaged every continent, which posed a lethal threat to humanity's underground cities. Beginning in the sixth orbital period onward, catastrophic magma seepage events occurred all too frequently in cities around the world.

On the day it happened, I was on my way home from school when the sirens sounded. It was quickly followed by an emergency broadcast from city hall.

'Attention citizens of City F112! The city's northern barrier has been breached by crustal stress. Magma has entered the city! Magma has entered the city! Magma flows have already reached Block Four! Highway exits have been sealed off. All citizens should report to the central plaza and evacuate by lift. Please note that the evacuation will be conducted in accordance with Article Five of the Emergencies Act. I repeat, the evacuation will be conducted in accordance with Article Five of the Emergencies Act!'

Looking around the labyrinth of tunnels, our underground city seemed eerily normal. But I was aware of the immediate danger: of the two subterranean highways that led out of the city, one of those routes had been blocked off last year by necessary fortification work on the city's barriers. If the remaining route was also blocked, we could only escape through the vertical elevator shafts that led directly to the surface.

The carrying capacity of the lifts was very limited. It would take a long time to move all three hundred and sixty thousand residents to safety, but there was no need to scramble for a place on the lifts. The Coalition's Emergency Act had made all necessary arrangements for the evacuation.

Past generations once grappled with an ethical dilemma. A man is faced by rising floodwaters and can only save one other person. Should he save his father or his son? In this day and age, it was unbelievable that the question had ever been raised at all.

When I arrived in the plaza, I saw that people had already begun to arrange themselves in a long line according to age. At the front of the line, closest to the lifts, stood robotic nurses, each cradling an infant. Then came the kindergartners, followed by the primary school students. My place was in the middle of the line, still rather close to the front. My father was on duty in low-Earth orbit, leaving only my mother and myself in the city. Unable to see her, I began to run along the unending line of people but did not get far before I was stopped by soldiers. I knew she stood at the very back. Our city was primarily a university town, with only a few families, so she was grouped with the city's oldest residents.

The line inched forward at an excruciating pace. After three long hours it was finally my turn, but I felt no relief as I boarded the lift. There were still twenty thousand university students standing between my mother and survival, and I could already smell the strong odor of sulfur.

Two and a half hours after I made it to the surface, magma inundated the entire city five hundred meters beneath my feet. A knife twisted in my heart as I imagined my mother's final moments. Standing alongside eighteen thousand others who could not be evacuated in time, she would have watched magma surge into the plaza. The city's power supply would have failed, leaving only the dreadful crimson glow of the magma. The intense heat would have blackened the lofty white dome over the plaza. The victims likely never came into contact with the magma before the thousand-plus-degree temperatures proved fatal.

But life went on, and even in this harsh, terrifying reality, sparks of love still flew from time to time. During the twelfth climb toward aphelion, in an attempt to ease public tension, the Coalition unexpectedly revived the Olympic Games after a two-century hiatus. I competed at the Games in the snowmobile rally. Beginning in Shanghai, athletes raced their snowmobiles across the frozen surface of the Pacific to New York.

At the sound of the starting gun, more than a hundred snow-mobiles shot off across the frozen ocean, blazing across the ice at two hundred kilometers per hour. At first, there was always a competitor in my sights. Two days later, however, having fallen behind or surged ahead, they had all disappeared over the horizon.

The glow of the Earth Engines was no longer visible behind me, and I sped into the darkest part of the planet. My world was the boundless starlit sky and the ice that stretched in all directions to the ends of the universe – or perhaps *this* was the end of the universe. And in this universe of infinite stars and endless ice, I was alone! As an avalanche of loneliness overwhelmed me, I wanted to cry. I drove as if my life depended on it. Whether or not I placed on the podium was beside the point: I needed to get rid of this terrible loneliness before it killed me. In my mind, the opposite shore no longer existed.

At that moment, I saw a figure silhouetted against the horizon. As I grew closer, I realized it was a woman. She was standing next to her snowmobile, her long hair fluttering in the icy wind. The moment our paths crossed, it was clear that the rest of our lives had been decided. Her name was Yamasaki Kayoko, and she was Japanese. The women's team had set off twelve hours before us, but her snowmobile had been caught in a crack in the ice, snapping one of the skis. As I helped her repair her sled, I shared with her the feeling that had gripped me earlier.

'I felt exactly the same way!' she exclaimed. 'It was like I was alone in the universe! You know, when I saw you appear in the distance, it was like watching the Sun rise.'

'Why didn't you call a rescue plane?' I asked.

She raised her small fist. 'This race embodies the human spirit,' she declared with the tenacity so characteristic of the Japanese. 'We must remember that Earth cannot call for help as it wanders through the cosmos!'

'Well, now we have to call. Neither of us has a spare runner, so your snowmobile is beyond repair.'

'Why don't I ride on the back of yours?' she suggested. 'If you don't care about placing, that is.'

I really did not care, so Kayoko and I made the rest of the long journey across the frozen Pacific together.

As we passed Hawaii, we saw a glimmer of light on the horizon. On this boundless expanse of ice, illuminated by the tiny Sun, we submitted an application for a marriage license to the Coalition Department of Civil Affairs.

By the time we reached New York City, the Olympic referees had grown tired of waiting and had packed their things and left. But an official from the municipal Bureau of Civil Affairs stood waiting for us. He congratulated us on our marriage and then began to perform his official duty. With a sweep of his hand, he summoned a hologram that was neatly lined with tens of thousands of dots. Each dot represented a couple that had registered for marriage with the Coalition in the last few days. In light of harsh environmental conditions, by law only one out of every three newly married couples was permitted to procreate. This right was awarded by lottery. Faced with thousands of dots, Kayoko hesitated for a long time before picking one in the middle.

When the dot turned green, she jumped for joy. I was not sure how I felt about the prospect of starting a family. If I brought a child into this era of suffering, would it be a blessing or a calamity? The official, at least, was over the moon. He told us it was always a happy occasion when a couple got their little green dot. He pulled out a bottle of vodka, and the three of us took turns drinking from it, toasting the continuation of the human race. Behind us, the faint light of the distant Sun gilded the Statue of

Liberty. Before us, the long-abandoned skyscrapers of Manhattan cast long shadows over the quiet ice of New York Harbor. Feeling tipsy, I realized tears had begun to stream down my cheeks. *Earth, my wandering Earth!*

*

Before we parted ways, the official handed us a set of keys and hiccupped, 'These are for your newly allotted house in Asia. Run along home, now. Run to your wonderful new home!'

'Just how wonderful is it?' I asked coldly. 'Asia's underground cities are fraught with danger – but of course you Westerners wouldn't know that.'

'We are about to face our own unique hazard,' he replied. 'Earth is about to pass through the asteroid belt, and the Western hemisphere is facing right toward it.'

'But we passed through the asteroid belt on the last few orbits. It's no big deal, is it?'

'We just swiped the edges of the asteroid belt. The Space Fleet could handle that, of course. They have lasers and nukes to clear small rocks from the Earth's path. But this time...' He paused. 'Haven't you seen the news? This time, Earth will pass straight through the middle of the belt! The fleet will deal with the small rocks, but the large ones...'

On the flight back to Asia, Kayoko turned to me and asked, 'Are those asteroids very big?'

My father was one of the Space Fleet officers tasked with asteroid diversion and destruction. Therefore, though the government had imposed the usual media blackout to prevent mass panic, I still had some idea of what was about to happen. I told Kayoko that some of the asteroids we faced were the size of mountains; even fifty-megaton thermonuclear bombs would only pockmark their surfaces.

'They'll have to use the most powerful weapon in the human arsenal,' I added mysteriously.

'You mean antimatter bombs?' she asked.

'What else could it be?'

'What is the fleet's cruising range?'

'Currently their strength is limited. My dad told me it extends out to about one and a half million kilometers,' I answered.

Kayoko gave a little squeal. 'Then we'll be able to see it!'

'Best not to look.'

But Kayoko did look, and she did so without protective glasses. The first flash of an antimatter bomb arrived from space shortly after we took off. At that exact moment, Kayoko had been admiring the starry sky outside the window. The flash blinded her for over an hour, and her eyes were red and watery for more than a month afterward. In the bloodcurdling moments that followed the flash, the antimatter shells continued to bombard the asteroid. Ruinous flashes pulsed across the pitch-black sky, as if a horde of colossal paparazzi had descended upon the planet and were frenziedly snapping away.

Half an hour later, we saw the meteors, dragging streaming tails of fire across the sky, mesmerizing in their terrible beauty. More and more meteors appeared, each streaking further into the atmosphere than the last. Suddenly, a deafening roar shook the plane, immediately followed by more rumbling and shaking. Thinking that a meteor had struck the plane, Kayoko screamed and threw herself into my arms. Just then, the captain's voice came on over the intercom.

'Ladies and gentlemen, please do not be alarmed. That was merely the sonic boom created by a meteor breaking the sound barrier. Please put on your headphones to avoid permanent hearing loss. Because the safety of the flight cannot be guaranteed, we will make an emergency landing in Hawaii.'

As the announcement ended, my eyes fastened on a meteor much larger than the others. I became convinced it would not burn up in the atmosphere like the ones before it. Sure enough, the fireball hurtled across the sky, shrinking as it fell, and smashed into the frozen ocean. Seen from ten thousand meters above, a small white spot appeared at the point of impact. The spot immediately spread into a white circle and rapidly expanded across the ocean's surface.

'Is that a wave?' asked Kayoko, her voice trembling.

'Yes, it's a wave over a hundred meters high. But the ocean is frozen solid. The ice will soon dampen it,' I replied, mostly to comfort myself. I did not look down again.

We landed in Honolulu not long after. The local government had arranged to take us to an underground city. The drive along the coast afforded us a clear view of the meteor-filled sky. It was as if a legion of fiery-haired demons had burst all at once from a single point in space.

We watched as a meteor struck the surface not far from the coast. There was no visible plume of water, but a white mush-room cloud of water vapor bloomed high overhead. Beneath the frozen surface, roiling seawater surged toward the shore. The thick layers of ice groaned as they splintered apart, rolling like waves, as if a school of giant, sinuous sea monsters was swim-ming beneath the surface.

'How big was that one?' I asked the official who had met us at the airport.

'Less than five kilograms, no bigger than your head. But I have just been informed that a twenty-ton meteor is splashing down eight hundred kilometers north of here.'

His wrist communicator began beeping. He glanced at it and immediately told the driver, 'We won't make it to Gate 204. Head for the nearest entrance!'

The van turned a corner and pulled to a stop in front of an entrance to the underground city. As we got out, we saw that several soldiers guarded the entrance. They stared unblinkingly into the distance, eyes filled with terror. We followed their gaze to the horizon and saw a black barrier. At first glance, it looked like a low bank of clouds, but its height was too uniform for clouds – it was more like a long wall stretching across the hori-zon. Closer inspection revealed that the wall was edged in white.

'What is that?' Kayoko asked an officer timidly. His answer made our hair stand on end.

'A wave.'

The tall steel gates to the subterranean city grated shut. Ten minutes later, we felt a deep rumble emanate from the ceiling, as if a titan were rolling about on the surface up there. We gazed at each other in speechless despair, for we knew at that moment hundred-meter waves were rolling over Hawaii and on toward the mainland. But the quakes that followed were even more terrifying. It was as if a giant fist were pummeling Earth from outer space. Underground, the assault was faint, but we felt each tremor keenly in our souls. It was the barrage of meteors against the surface.

The brutal bombardment of our planet continued on and off for a week. When we finally left the underground city, Kayoko cried, 'My God, what happened to the sky?'

The sky was a muddy gray. The upper atmosphere was filled with the dust that had been kicked up by the asteroid collisions. The Sun and stars were lost in this endless gray, as if the entire universe was blanketed in thick fog. On the ground, the sea-water left in the wake of the monstrous waves had frozen solid. The surviving high-rises stood isolated above the ice, cascades of ice spilling down their sides. A layer of dust had settled on the ice, draining all color from the world except for that all-pervading gray.

Kayoko and I soon resumed our voyage back to Asia. As the plane crossed the International Date Line, which had long since ceased to matter, we witnessed humanity's darkest night. The plane seemed to cruise silently through the inky depths of the ocean. As we gazed through the windows, searching in vain for a glimmer of light in the gloom, our moods turned equally black.

'When will it end?' Kayoko murmured.

I did not know if she meant our journey or this lifetime of misery and suffering. I was beginning to think there was no end to either one. Indeed, even if Earth sailed beyond the blast radius of the helium flash, even if we escaped with our lives – then what? We stood on the bottom rung of an immeasurably tall ladder. In a hundred generations, when our descendants reached the top and glimpsed the promise of new life, our bones would have long turned to dust. I did not imagine the suffering and hardships yet to come, much less consider leading my lover and my child down that endless, muddy road. I was so tired, too tired to go on...

Just as sorrow and despair threatened to suffocate me, a woman's scream rang through the cabin: 'Ah! No! Darling, you can't!'

I turned and saw a woman wrest a gun from the hands of the man sitting next to her. He had just attempted to put the muzzle of the gun against his own temple. The man looked wan and emaciated, his eyes staring listlessly into the distance. The woman buried her head in his lap and broke into little chirping sobs.

'Be quiet,' the man said coldly.

The sobbing stopped, leaving only the low hum of the engines, like a steady funeral dirge. In my mind, the plane was stuck in the vast gloom, motionless. There was nothing else left in the entire universe except for the plane and the enveloping darkness. Kayoko pressed herself tightly into my embrace. Her entire body felt ice-cold.

Suddenly, there was a commotion at the front of the cabin and people began whispering excitedly. I looked out the window and saw a hazy light in front of the plane. The dust-filled night sky was uniformly suffused with a formless blue glow.

It was the light of the Earth Engines.

One-third of the Western hemisphere's engines had been destroyed by meteoroids, but Earth had sustained less damage than the calculations had projected before departure. The Earth Engines in the Eastern hemisphere, sheltered on the reverse side of the impact surface, had suffered no losses. In terms of power, Earth remained well equipped to make its escape.

When I laid eyes on the dim blue light ahead, I felt like a deep-sea diver finally seeing the sunlit surface after a long ascent from the abyss. I began to breathe steadily again.

From a few rows away, I heard the woman's voice. 'Darling, pain, fear – we can only feel these things while we are alive. When we die, there is nothing at all. Only darkness. It is better to live, don't you think?'

The emaciated man did not reply. He was staring at the blue light up ahead, tears rolling down his face. I knew he would live through this. Just as long as that hopeful blue light still shone, we would all live through this. I remembered my father's words of hope.

When we touched down, Kayoko and I did not go directly to our new underground home. Instead, we went to look for my father at the Space Fleet's base station on the surface. When we arrived at the station, however, I found only a medal of honor, posthumously awarded and ice-cold. The medal was presented to me by an air vice-marshal. He told me that my father had lost his life during the operation to clear the asteroids from the Earth's path. An antimatter explosion had blasted an asteroid fragment straight into his single-seater craft.

'When it happened, the rock was traveling at one hundred kilometers per second relative to his ship. The cabin was vaporized on impact. He felt no pain,' said the air marshal. 'I assure you, he felt no pain at all.'

When Earth began its fall back toward the Sun again, Kayoko and I traveled to the surface to see the spring scenery. We were sorely disappointed.

The world was still a monochromatic gray. Under the overcast sky, frozen lakes of residual seawater dotted the landscape. There was not a single sprig of green to be seen. The great pall of dust in the atmosphere blocked the light of the Sun, preventing temperatures from rising again. The oceans and continents did not thaw even at perihelion. The Sun remained a faint, dim presence, like a specter lurking behind the dust.

Three years later, as the dust in the atmosphere dissipated, humanity made its last pass through perihelion. As we reached it, those living in the Eastern hemisphere were privileged to witness the fastest sunrise and sunset in Earth's history. The Sun leapt up from the sea and streaked rapidly across the sky. Shadows changed directions so quickly that they looked like second hands sweeping across the faces of countless clocks. It was the shortest day Earth had ever seen, over in less than an hour.

When the Sun plunged below the horizon and darkness fell across the planet, I felt a twinge of grief. This fleeting day seemed like a brief summary of Earth's four-and-a-half-billion-year history in the solar system. Even until the end of the universe, Earth would never return.

'It's dark,' Kayoko said sadly.

'The longest night,' I replied. In the Eastern hemisphere, this night would last twenty-five hundred years. One hundred generations would pass before the light of Proxima Centauri illuminated this continent anew. The Western hemisphere was facing its longest day, but even so, it would last just a moment compared to our age-long night. On that side of the world, the Sun would quickly rise to its zenith, where it would remain motionless, steadily shrinking. Within half a century, it would be difficult to distinguish from any other star.

The Earth's intended trajectory called for a rendezvous with Jupiter. The Navigation Commission's plan was as follows: the Earth's fifteenth orbit around the Sun would be so elliptical that its aphelion would enter Jupiter's orbit. Earth would brush past Jupiter on a near-collision course. Harnessing the gas giant's enormous gravitational pull to assist its acceleration, Earth would finally attain escape velocity.

Two months after Earth passed perihelion, Jupiter became visible to the naked eye. At first, it appeared as a dim point of light, but it soon flattened and became disk-shaped. After another month, Jupiter had grown as large as the full Moon, reddish-brown with faintly visible banding. Then some of the Earth

Engines' plasma beams, which had remained perpendicular for fifteen years, began to shift. Final adjustments were being made to Earth's orientation before the rendezvous. Jupiter sank slowly below the horizon, where it stayed for the next three months. We could not see it, but we knew the two planets were converging upon each other.

It almost came as a surprise when we heard that Jupiter was visible again in the Eastern hemisphere. Everyone thronged to the surface to take a look. When I passed through the airlock of the underground city, I saw that the Earth Engines, after running continuously for fifteen years, had been powered down. We could see the stars in the sky once again. Our final rendezvous with Jupiter was in progress.

Everyone peered nervously toward the western sky, where a dim red glow was beginning to show above the horizon. The glow swelled until it filled the entire skyline. I soon realized that the red expanse had formed a neat border against the stars; it was an arc so massive that it spanned from one end of the horizon to the other. As it slowly rose, the sky beneath it turned red, as if a velvet theater curtain were being drawn across the rest of the universe. I let out a gasp, reeling from the realization that the curtain was Jupiter. I knew that Jupiter was thirteen hundred times the size of Earth, but only when I saw its immense splendor did I truly take in its colossal size.

It was difficult to describe in words the fear and oppression that accompanied the behemoth as it reared above the horizon. One reporter later wrote, 'I did not know if I was in my own nightmare, or if the whole universe was just a nightmare in the enormous, twisted mind of that deity!' As Jupiter continued its terrible ascent, it gradually came to occupy half the sky. We then had an unobscured view of the storms raging in its cloud layers, which whipped the gasses in the atmosphere into chaotic, disorienting lines. I knew that beneath those thick decks of clouds lay seething oceans of liquid hydrogen and liquid helium. The famous Great Red Spot appeared, still raging across Jupiter's surface after hundreds of thousands of years. The maelstrom was large enough to swallow three Earths. Jupiter now filled the entire sky. Earth was like a balloon floating on Jupiter's boiling red sea of clouds. The Great Red Spot climbed to the middle of the sky and stared down upon our world like a cyclopean eye. The entire landscape was shrouded in its ghastly light. It was impossible to believe that our tiny planet could escape the gravitational field of this colossus. From the ground, it even seemed unimaginable that Earth might become a satellite of Jupiter – no, we would certainly plummet into the hell concealed beneath that unending ocean of clouds.

But the navigational engineers' calculations were faultless, and the bewildering ruddy sky continued to drift past us. After some time, a black crescent appeared on the western horizon and swiftly widened to reveal the twinkling stars. Earth was breaking free from Jupiter's gravitational clutches. Just then, sirens began to wail, announcing that the gravitational tide Jupiter had raised was rushing back inland. We were told later that giant waves, reaching over one hundred metres high, had again swept across the continents. As I ran toward the gates of the underground city, I stole one last glance at Jupiter, which still occupied half the sky. Distinct scoring marred the gas giant's cloud layer, which I later learned was the trail left by the gravitational pull of Earth on Jupiter's surface. Our planet, too, had left mountainous breakers of liquid helium and hydrogen in its wake. At that point, the Earth, accelerated by Jupiter's mighty gravity, was hurled into deep space.

As it departed Jupiter, Earth reached escape velocity. It no longer needed to return toward the Sun, where only death lurked. As it hurtled toward the open reaches of space, the endless Wandering Era began.

And under the dark red shadow of Jupiter, deep within the earth, my son was born.

Chapter 3

Rebellion

After we left Jupiter behind, Asia's ten thousand Earth Engines roared to life again. They would operate at full capacity for the next five hundred years, constantly accelerating the planet. During those five hundred years, the engines would consume half of the mountains on the Asian continent as fuel.

Freed at last from the fear of death after four centuries, humanity breathed a collective sigh of relief. But the expected revelry never took place, and what happened next was beyond anyone's imagining.

After our subterranean city's celebratory rally concluded, I donned my thermal suit and ascended to the surface alone. The familiar mountains of my childhood had already been leveled by mega-excavators, leaving only bare rock and hard, frozen soil. The bleak emptiness was broken by patches of stark white covering the land as far as the eye could see: the salt marshes left behind by the great ocean tide. Before me, the city in which my father and grandfather had lived out their days – a city once home to ten million – lay in ruins. In the blue light of the Earth Engine's plasma beams, the exposed steel skeletons of skyscrapers dragged long shadows behind them, like the fossilized remains of prehistoric beasts. The chronic floods and meteor strikes had destroyed virtually everything on the surface. All that humankind and nature had wrought over millennia lay in ruins; our planet had been rendered as barren and desolate as Mars.

Around this time, Kayoko grew restless. She often left our son unsupervised while she took the car on long flights. When she returned, she would say only that she had gone to the Western hemisphere. Finally, one day she dragged me along with her.

We drove for two hours at Mach 4 before we caught a glimpse of the Sun. It had just risen above the Pacific Ocean. No bigger than a baseball, it cast a faint, cold light over the frozen surface.

At an elevation of five thousand meters, Kayoko shifted the car into hover. She then pulled a long package from the backseat. After she removed its cover, I saw that it was an astronomical telescope of the sort favored by hobbyists. Kayoko opened the car window, pointed the telescope at the Sun, and told me to look.

Through the tinted lens, I could see the Sun, magnified hundreds of times. I could even clearly see the light and dark sunspots slowly drifting across its surface and the faint prominences at the edges of the solar disk.

Kayoko linked the telescope to the onboard computer and captured an image of the Sun. She then pulled up a different solar image and said, 'This is from four centuries ago.' The computer proceeded to compare the two images.

'Do you see that?' Kayoko asked, pointing to the screen. 'Luminosity, pixel arrays, pixel probabilities, layer statistics – every parameter is exactly the same!'

'What does that prove? A toy telescope, a cheap image-processing program, and you, an uninformed amateur.' I shook my head. 'Pay no attention to those rumors.'

'You're an idiot,' she snapped, retracting the telescope and turning the car toward home. In the distance, I noticed a few other cars both above and below us. They hovered in the air just as we had, a telescope trained on the Sun through every car window.

Over the next few months, a terrible allegation swept like wildfire across the world. More and more people made it their business to observe the Sun with the assistance of larger, more sophisticated instruments. An NGO even launched an array of probes toward the Sun, which passed through their target three months later. The data transmitted by the probes finally confirmed the fact:

The Sun had not changed at all in the past four centuries.

On every continent, the situation in the underground cities was volatile, like bubbling volcanoes building toward eruption. One day, heeding a decree from the Coalition, Kayoko and I placed our son into a Foster Center. On the way home, we both sensed that the only tie that held us together was gone. As we neared the central plaza, we saw a man addressing a crowd. Others were distributing weapons to the citizens who had gathered around the speaker.

'Citizens! Earth has been betrayed! Humanity has been betrayed! Civilization has been betrayed! We are all the victims of a tremendous hoax! The sheer scale of this hoax would shock God himself! The Sun is entirely unchanged! It will not explode, not then, not now, not ever! It is the very symbol of eternity! What is explosive is the wild and insidious ambition of those in the Coalition! They fabricated all of it, just so they could establish their own tyrannical empire! They have destroyed Earth! They have destroyed human civilization! Citizens, citizens of conscience! Take up arms and rescue our planet! Rescue human civilization! We will overthrow the Coalition! We will seize control of the Earth Engines and steer our planet from the cold depths of outer space back to its original orbit! Back to the warm embrace of the Sun!'

Without a word, Kayoko stepped forward to accept an assault rifle from one of the people handing out weapons, joining the column of armed citizens. She did not look back as she disappeared into the haze of the underground city alongside the ranks of her neighbors. I just stood there. In my pocket, the medal for which my father had traded his life and loyalty was clenched in my hand, so tightly that its points drew blood.

Three days later, rebellion broke out on every continent.

Wherever the rebel army went, the people rallied to its call. Few citizens still doubted that they had been deceived. Even so, I still joined the Coalition army. It was not that I had any real faith in the government, but my family had served in the military for three generations. They had sown the seeds of loyalty deep in my heart, and to betray the Coalition was simply unthinkable, no matter the circumstances.

One after another, the Americas, Africa, Oceania, and Antarctica fell to the rebels as the Coalition army drew back to defensive lines around the Earth Engines in Eastern and Central Asia, ready to defend them to the death. The rebel army quickly surrounded these lines. Their forces overwhelmingly outnumbered the Coalition forces, but because of the close proximity of the engines the offensive made no progress for a long time. The rebel army had no desire to destroy the engines, and thus refrained from deploying heavy weapons, giving the Coalition a stay of execution. The two sides remained locked in a stalemate for three months. But after twelve field armies defected in succession, the Coalition defenses crumbled along all fronts. Two months later, with things looking bleak, the last hundred thousand government troops found themselves besieged on all sides at the Earth Engine control center on the coast.

I was a major in what remained of the army. The control center was the size of a mid-tier city, built around the Earth Navigation Bridge. A dead arm, seared by laser fire, had landed me in a cot in the combat casualty ward. It was there that I learned Kayoko had been killed in action in the Battle of Australia. Like the others in the ward, all day, every day, I would drink myself blind. We lost all track of the war raging outside, and we were indifferent to it. I do not know how much time had passed when I heard a voice bellow across the ward.

'You know why you have been reduced to this? You blame yourselves for standing against humanity in this war! So did I!'

As I turned my head to look, I saw that the speaker wore a general's star on his shoulder. 'No matter,' he continued. 'We have one last chance to save our souls. The Earth Navigation Bridge is only three blocks away. We will take it and hand it over to the sane humans outside! We have done our duty to the Coalition, and now we must do our duty to humanity!'

With my good arm, I drew my pistol and followed the frenzied mass of able-bodied and wounded soldiers surging through the steel corridors toward the bridge. To my surprise, we met almost no resistance along the way. In fact, more and more people emerged from the complex maze of passageways to join us. Finally, we arrived before a metal gate so tall that I could not see the top of it. It rumbled open and we charged into the Earth Navigation Bridge.

Even though we had seen it countless times on television, everyone was still floored by the bridge's grandeur. It was difficult to judge the size of the space, as its dimensions were hidden by the huge holographic simulation of the solar system that dominated the room. The entire image was essentially black space that stretched infinitely in all directions. As soon as we came in, we were suspended in this blackness. Because the simulation was designed to reflect the true scale of the solar system, the Sun and the planets were minuscule, like fireflies in the distance, but still distinguishable. A striking red spiral expanded out from the distant point of light that represented the Sun, spreading like concentric red ripples on the surface of a vast black ocean. This was the Earth's route. At a point on the outer edge of the spiral, the route turned bright green, indicating the distance Earth had yet to travel. The green line swept over our heads. We followed it with our eyes until it vanished into the depths of a brilliant sea of stars, its end beyond our sight. Numerous specks of glittering dust floated through the black expanse. As a few of these motes drifted closer, I realized they were virtual screens, filled with scrolling streams of digits and curves.

Then my gaze fell upon the Earth Navigation Platform, known to every human on the planet. It looked like a silvery white asteroid floating in the blackness. The sight made it even harder to grasp the size of the place – the Navigation Platform itself was a plaza. It was now densely packed with over five thousand people, including the leaders of the Coalition, most of the Interstellar Emigration Committee that was responsible for implementing the voyage plan, and the last remaining loyalists. The voice of the Chief Executive rang out in the darkness.

'We could fight to the last, but we might lose control of the Earth Engines. If that were to happen, the excess fissile material could burn through the entire planet or evaporate the oceans. Instead, we have decided to surrender. We understand the people. Humanity has endured forty generations of bitter struggle and must endure one hundred generations more. It is unrealistic to expect everyone to remain rational throughout it all. But we ask the people to remember that we, the five thousand who stand here, from the Chief Executive of the Coalition to the ordinary privates, kept our faith until the end. We know we will not see the day the truth is verified, but if humanity survives future generations will weep over our graves! This planet called Earth will be an everlasting monument to our memory!'

The massive gate of the control center rumbled open again, and the last five thousand Takers emerged. They were then herded to the shore by rebel forces. Both sides of the road were jammed with people. The onlookers spat at the prisoners and pelted them with ice and rocks. A few of the masks on their thermal suits were shattered, exposing the faces beneath to temperatures more than a hundred degrees below freezing. But even as they were numbed by terrible cold, they trudged on, fighting for every step. I saw a little girl pick up a chunk of ice and hurl it with all her might at an old man, the wild rage in her eyes searing through her mask.

When I heard that all five thousand of the prisoners had been sentenced to death, I felt it was too lenient. One death? Could one death repair the evil they had done? Could it make amends for the crime of perpetrating an insane hoax that destroyed both the Earth and human civilization? They should die ten thousand times over! I suddenly recalled the astrophysicists who had forecast the explosion of the Sun and the engineers who had designed and built the Earth Engines. They had passed away a century ago, but I truly wanted to dig up their graves and make them die the deaths they deserved.

I felt truly thankful that the executioners had found a suitable method for carrying out the sentence. First, they confiscated the nuclear batteries that powered the thermal suits of every person sentenced to death. Then, they deposited the prisoners on the frozen ocean and let the subzero conditions sap the life from their bodies.

The most insidious, most shameful criminals in the history of human civilization stood clustered together, a dark mass atop the ice. Over one hundred thousand people had gathered on the shore to watch. Over one hundred thousand jaws clenched in anger, over one hundred thousand pairs of eyes burned with the same rage I had witnessed on the face of that little girl.

By now, all the Earth Engines had been powered down, and the stars had blinked majestically into view over the ice. I could imagine the cold piercing their skin like daggers, the blood freezing in their veins, the life draining bit by bit from their bodies. A pleasant warmth ran through my body at the thought. As they watched the prisoners slowly succumb to the agonizing cold, the mood of the crowd on the shore began to lift and they began to sing a cheerful rendition of 'My Sun'.

As I sang along, I gazed in the direction of a star that was slightly larger than the rest, its tiny disk shining with yellow light – the Sun.

Oh, Sun, my Sun
Mother of life
Father of creation
Bright spirit, a god above!

Constant and eternal
We are but star dust in your orbit
and yet like fools
we dared dream your doom.

An hour passed. Out on the ice, those enemies of humanity still stood, but not one among them remained alive. Their blood had frozen in their veins.

All at once, I lost my sense of sight. Several seconds passed before my vision began to recover, and the ice, the shore, and the crowd of onlookers gradually sharpened into focus. Finally everything was clear again – even clearer than it had been before, in fact, because the world was enveloped in an intense white light. It was this abrupt glare that had blinded me a moment ago.

The stars, however, did not reappear, their radiance swallowed up, as if the cosmos had melted under the harsh light. The glare burst forth from a single point in space. That point had now become the center of the universe, and I had been staring right at it as it did so.

The helium flash had occurred.

The chorus of 'My Sun' froze mid-song. The crowd on the shore stood transfixed; like the five thousand corpses on the ice, they seemed frozen, as stiff and still as stone.

The Sun shed its light and heat upon the Earth for one last time. On the surface, the dry ice melted first, rising in plumes of white steam. Then the sea began to thaw, and the layers of ice began to creak and groan as they were heated unevenly. Gradually, the light softened and the sky took on a tinge of blue. Later, generated by the fierce solar winds, auroras appeared in the sky, great prismatic curtains of light fluttering across the heavens.

The last Takers stood firm atop the ice, five thousand statues thrown into clear relief by the sudden dazzling sunlight.

The solar explosion lasted only a short time. After two hours, the light rapidly weakened until it was extinguished altogether.

A dim red sphere had replaced the Sun. From our vantage point, it slowly swelled until it reached the size of the Sun of old, a strange memory from Earth's original orbit. It was so voluminous that its diameter exceeded the orbit of Mars. Mercury, Venus, Mars – Earth's constant companions – had been reduced to wisps of smoke by the intense thermal radiation.

But it was no longer our Sun. No longer emitting light and heat, it resembled a cold piece of red paper pasted onto the firmament, its muted glow merely a reflection of the surrounding starlight. This was the evolutionary fate common to all mid-sized stars: transformation into a red giant.

Five billion years of majestic life were now a fleeting dream. The Sun had died.

Fortunately, we still lived.

Chapter 4

The Wandering Era

As I recall all of this now, half a century has passed. Twenty years ago, Earth sailed past Pluto's orbit and out of the solar system, continuing its lonely voyage into the vast, cold reaches of space.

My last visit to the surface was a dozen or so years ago. I was accompanied by my son and my daughter-in-law, a blonde-haired, blue-eyed girl. She was pregnant at the time.

When we arrived on the surface, the first thing I noticed was that I could no longer see the Earth Engines' massive plasma beams, even though I knew the engines were still operating at full capacity. The Earth's atmosphere had vanished, leaving nothing to scatter the plasma's light. The ground was covered with strange translucent yellow-green crystals. They were made of solid oxygen and nitrogen, the remnants of our frozen atmosphere.

Interestingly, the atmosphere had not frozen evenly across the surface. Instead, it had formed irregular mounds, like hills. The frozen surface of the sea, once flat and smooth, now rose up into a fantastic crystalline landscape. Overhead, the Milky Way stretched motionless across the sky, as if it, too, had frozen. But the stars were bright, too bright to look at for long.

The Earth Engines would operate without interruption for the next five hundred years, accelerating the planet to 0.5 percent of light speed. Earth would cruise at this incredible speed for thirteen hundred years. After it had completed two-thirds of its voyage, we would reverse the direction of the Earth Engines and Earth would enter a five-hundred-year deceleration period. After twenty-four hundred years of travel, Earth would finally reach Proxima Centauri. In another hundred years' time, it would lock into stabilized orbit around the star, becoming one of its satellites.

I know I have been forgotten
This voyage wanders on and on
But call me when the time comes
When the East sees another dawn

I know I have been forgotten
Our departure is long past
But call me when the time comes
When men see blue skies at last

I know I have been forgotten
Our solar story is over now
But call me when the time comes
When blossoms hang from every bough

Every time I hear that song, warmth floods this stiff, aging body of mine, and these dry old eyes fill with tears. In my mind's eye, the three golden suns of Alpha Centauri rise above the horizon one after another, bathing everything in their warm light. The solid atmosphere has melted, and the sky is clear and blue again. Seeds planted two thousand years ago sprout from the thawed soil, breathing new life into the earth. I see my great-grandchildren, one hundred generations removed, playing and laughing on green grass. Clear streams flow through the meadows, filled with small silver fish. I see Kayoko, bounding toward me across the green earth. She is young and beautiful, like an angel...

Ah, Earth, my wandering Earth...

Mountain

Chapter 1

Where There's a Mountain

'Today is the day I'm finally going to get you to tell me why you never go on land,' the Captain declared, arching an eyebrow. 'It's been five years, and the *Bluewater* has docked in heaven knows how many ports in more countries than I can count, yet you have never gone ashore. Not even when we docked back in China. And not even last year, back in Qingdao when we were in for overhauls. You're the last person I'd need to tell that the ship was a complete mess, and noisy, and still you stayed put, holed up in your cabin for two months,' the Captain continued, eying Feng Fan intensely as he spoke.

'Do I remind you of that guy Tim Roth played in *The Legend of 1900*?' Fan asked in return.

'Are you insinuating that if we ever scuttle the *Bluewater* you plan on going down with the ship like he did?' the Captain countered, unsure if Fan was joking or not.

'I'll change ships. Oceanographic vessels always have a place for a geological engineer who'll never leave ship,' Fan replied.

The Captain returned to his original point. 'That naturally begs the question: is there something on land that keeps you away?'

'On the contrary,' Fan answered. 'There is something that I yearn for.'

'And what's that?' the Captain asked, curious but now a bit impatient.

'Mountains,' Fan uttered, his gaze dissolving into a thousand-yard stare.

They were standing portside on the geological oceanographic research vessel *Bluewater*, looking out onto the equatorial waters of the Pacific. The *Bluewater* had crossed the equator for the first time only a year ago. Back then, they had given in to whimsy and marked the occasion with the ancient rite of the line-crossing ceremony. Their discovery of a manganese nodule deposit in the seabed, however, had left them crisscrossing the equator more times than any of them could possibly remember. By this point, they had all but forgotten about the existence of that invisible divide.

As the sun slowly set beyond the sea's western horizon, Fan noticed that the ocean was unusually calm. In fact, he had never seen it so quiet. It reminded him of the Himalayan lakes, perfectly still to the point of blackness, like the eyes of the Earth. One time, he and two of his team mates had sneaked a peek at a Tibetan girl bathing in one of those lakes. A group of shepherds had spotted them and given chase, blades drawn. When they failed to catch them, the shepherds had resorted to slinging stones. The disconcertingly accurate bombardment had left Fan and his cohorts no other option than to surrender. The shepherds had sized them up and finally let them go.

Feng Fan recalled that one of them had muttered in Tibetan: 'As outsiders, they sure couldn't run quickly up here.'

'You like the mountains? So that's where you grew up then?' The Captain interrupted Fan's reminiscing.

'No, not at all,' Feng Fan explained. 'People who live their entire lives surrounded by mountains usually care nothing for them. They end up seeing the mountains as the things that stand between them and the world. I knew a Sherpa who scaled Everest forty-one times, but every time his team would get close to the peak he'd stop and watch the others climb the final stretch. He just couldn't be bothered to reach the top. And make no mistake about it: he could have easily pulled off both the northern and southern ascent in ten hours.

'There are only two places where you can really feel the true magic of the mountains: on the plains from far away and standing on a peak,' Feng Fan continued. 'My home was the vastness of the Hebei Plain. In the west I could see the Taihang Mountains, but between them and my home lay an immense expanse of perfectly flat land without obstructions or markers. Not long after I was born, my mother carried me outside the house for the first time. My tiny neck could barely carry my head, but even then I turned to the west and babbled my heart out. As soon as I learned to walk, I took my first tottering steps toward those mountains. When I was a bit older, I set out early one morning and walked along the Shijiazhuang–Taiyuan Railway. I walked until noon when my grumbling stomach made me turn back, yet the mountains still seemed endlessly far away. In school, I rode my bicycle toward the mountains, but no matter how fast I pedaled the mountains seemed to withdraw just as quickly. In the end, it never felt as if I had gotten even an inch closer to them. Many years later, distant mountains would again become a symbol of my life, like so many things in life that we can clearly see but never reach – a dream crystallized in the distance.'

'I visited there once,' the Captain noted, shaking his head. 'The mountains are very barren, covered with nothing but scattered stones and wild grasses. You were doomed to be disappointed.'

'I wasn't. You and I feel very differently about these things. For me, all I saw was the mountain, and all I wanted was to climb it. I really wasn't looking for anything on the mountain. When I climbed those mountains for the first time and I saw the plain stretch out below me, I felt like I had been reborn.' As Feng Fan finished, he realized that the Captain was paying no heed to his words; instead, he was looking to the sky, staring at the scattered stars.

'There,' the Captain said, pointing skyward with his pipe. 'There shouldn't be a star there.'

But there was a star. It was faint, barely visible.

'Are you sure?' Fan turned his gaze from the sky to the Captain. 'Hasn't GPS done away with sextants? Do you really know your stars that well?'

'Of course I do,' the Captain answered. 'It is a basic element in the craft of sailing.' Turning back to Fan, he returned to their previous topic. 'But you were saying...'

Feng Fan nodded. 'Later, in university, I put together a mountaineering team, and we climbed a few seven-thousand-footers. Our final climb was Everest.'

The Captain carefully studied Feng Fan before finally saying, 'I thought so! It really is you! I always thought you looked familiar. Did you change your name?'

'Yes, I used to be called Feng Huabei,' he admitted.

'Some years ago, you caused quite the stir. Was what the media said about you true, then?' the Captain asked.

'The gist of it. In any case, those four climbers are certainly dead because of me,' Fan said glumly.

Striking a match to re-light his pipe, the Captain continued. 'I reckon that being the leader of a mountaineering team is not that different from being a captain: the hardest part is not learning when to fight on but understanding when to back down.'

'But if I had backed down then, it would have been very hard to get another shot at it,' Fan immediately replied. 'Mountain climbing is a very costly undertaking, and we were just college students. It had not been easy for us to find sponsors.' He paused, taking a deep breath. 'The guides we hired had refused to go on, and so it took much longer than anticipated before we set up the first base camp. The forecast predicted a storm, but we studied the images and maps and came to the conclusion that we still had at least twenty hours before it would hit. By then, our team had already set up the second camp at twenty-six thousand feet, and so we thought that we could make it to the peak if we set out immediately. You tell me, how could we have backed down then? We never even contemplated giving up, and so we continued our ascent.'

'That star is getting brighter,' the Captain said, looking up again.

'Of course it is. The sky is getting darker,' Fan retorted dismissively.

'This seems different,' the Captain noted. 'But go on.'

'You probably know what happened next: when the storm hit, we were close to the so-called "Chinese Ladder" of the Second Step on a vertical rock face that rises from 28,500 feet. The peak was almost within reach, and, save for a strand of cloud rising from the other side of the summit, the sky was still perfectly blue. I can still clearly remember thinking that the peak of Everest looked like a knife's edge cutting open the sky, drawing forth its billowing, pale blood.' Fan paused at the memory before returning to his tale. 'It only took a few moments before we lost all visibility; when the storm hit us out of nowhere, it whipped up the snow. Everything was shrouded in an impenetrable white that left behind only murky darkness. In a heart-stopping instant, I felt the other four members of my team blown off the cliff. They were hanging by my rope, and all I was clinging to was my ice axe wedged into a crack in the wall. It simply could not have held the weight of five people. I acted on instinct, cutting the buckle strap that held the rope. I let them fall.' He hesitated, swallowing hard. 'They still haven't found the remains of two of them.'

'So four died instead of all five,' the Captain noted dryly.

'Yes, I acted according to the mountaineering safety guidelines. Even so, it remains my cross to bear.' Fan paused again, this time distracted by something other than his memories. 'You're right. There's something strange about that star. It's definitely getting brighter.'

'Never mind,' the Captain said. 'Does your current...' he

paused, pursing his lips '... shall we say, "condition", have anything to do with what happened then?'

'Do I have to spell it out? You must remember the overwhelming condemnations and the crushing contempt the media heaped on me back then,' Fan reminded him. 'They said I acted irresponsibly, that I was a selfish coward, that I sacrificed my four companions for my own life.' He was clearly still pained. 'I thought I could at least clear myself of that last accusation, so I donned my climbing gear and put on my mountain goggles. Ready for a climb, I went to my university's library and scaled a pipe straight up to its roof. I was just about to jump when I heard the voice of one of my teachers; I hadn't noticed him come up to the roof behind me. He asked me if I was really willing to let myself off the hook that easily, if I was just trying to avoid the much harsher punishment awaiting me. When I asked what he meant, he told me that it would entail a life as far away as possible from mountains. To never again see a mountain – would that not be a harsher punishment?

'So I didn't jump. Of course, I attracted even more ridicule, but I knew that what my teacher had told me was right: this would be worse than death for me. To me, mountain climbing had been my life. It was the only reason I studied geology. To now live a life eternally separated from the object of my passion, tormented by my own conscience – it felt just. That was the reason why I applied for this job after graduation, why I became the geological engineer of the *Bluewater*. On the ocean,' he said with a sigh, 'I'm as far as I can be from mountains.'

The Captain stared blankly for a long moment, at a loss for words. Finally, he came to the conclusion that it would probably be best to just leave it be. As if on cue, something in the sky above abruptly forced a change of topic. 'Take another look at that star,' he said, an edge in his voice.

'Heavens!' Fan exclaimed as he, too, looked up. 'It's turning into something!'

The star was no longer a dot but now a small, yet rapidly expanding, disc. In the blink of an eye, it turned into a striking sphere in the sky, glowing blue.

A flurry of rapidly approaching footsteps drew their gazes back down to deck. It was the First Mate, running straight towards them.

He was barely within earshot when he breathlessly called to the Captain, 'We have just received a message: an alien ship is approaching Earth! We can clearly see it from our position at the equator! Look, there it is!'

The three of them looked up, only to see that the small sphere had continued its rapid expansion. It had already ballooned to the size of the Moon.

'All stations have ceased their regular broadcasts and are now reporting on it!' the First Mate rattled on. 'The object had been spotted earlier, but they have just now confirmed its true nature. It is not responding to any of our attempts to hail it, but its trajectory shows that it is being propelled by some immense force, and it is hurtling straight toward Earth! They say it is as big as the Moon!' He held an earpiece to his head, listening intently.

Above them, the alien sphere was no longer the size of the Moon; it was now easily ten times as big, looming large in the heavens and appearing much closer than the Moon. With a finger firmly on his earpiece, the First Mate continued, 'They say that it has stopped. It is now in geosynchronous orbit twenty-two thousand miles above the Earth. It has become a geostationary satellite.'

'A geostationary satellite? Are you saying it is just going to hang above us?' the Captain shouted.

'It is! Over the equator, right above us!' the First Mate confirmed.

Feng Fan stared at this huge sphere in the sky; it seemed almost transparent, suffused with an unfathomable blue light. Looking at it left Fan with the strange impression of staring right up at an orb of seawater. A feeling of profound mystery, of intense anticipation, would grip him every time the sampling probe was raised from the seabed; looking up now, he experienced a very similar sensation. It was as if some long-forgotten remnant of time immemorial had returned to the surface.

'Look, the ocean!' the Captain shouted, wildly thrusting his pipe aftward. 'What is happening to the ocean?' He was the first to break free from the hypnotic power the giant sphere seemed to exert over all of them.

Where he pointed, the ocean's horizon had begun to bend, curving upward like a sine wave. This huge swell of rising water rapidly grew taller and taller. It was as if a gigantic, albeit invisible, hand was reaching down from space to scoop up the ocean.

'It's the spaceship's mass! Its gravity is pulling at the ocean!' Feng Fan exclaimed, rather surprised that he still had enough of his wits about him to understand what was happening. The ship's mass was probably equivalent to that of the Moon, but it was ten times closer! It was fortunate that the ship had entered a geosynchronous orbit; the water it was pulling would be held in one spot. If the spaceship moved, it would send a gravitational tidal wave across the world so large that it could easily ravage continents and destroy cities.

This colossal wave had by now swelled up to the heavens, rising as a flat-topped cone. Its mass shone with the blue glow of the ship above, even as its edges burned with the bright crimson fire of the setting sun, now hidden behind the towering waves. The stark, cold air at the cone's summit chilled the froth, sending forth streams of misty clouds that quickly bled away in the night sky, as if the dark heavens had been cut open. Feng Fan felt his heart stir with memories as he took it all in. His mind drifted back toward the day of the climb…

'Give me its height!' the Captain shouted, jerking him back to the here and now.

A minute later, someone called out, 'Almost thirty thousand feet!'

Before them was the most terrifying, most awesome and most magnificent sight humanity had ever seen. Everyone on deck stood transfixed by its spell.

'It must be destiny...' Feng Fan mumbled, mesmerized more than most by its grandeur.

'What did you say?' the Captain demanded loudly, his eyes still fixed on the rising waters.

'I said that this must be destiny,' Fan repeated.

It was – it had to be – destiny. He had gone to sea to avoid mountains, to put as much distance between them and himself as humanly possible; and now he was in the shadow of a mountain that eclipsed even Everest by almost a thousand feet. It was the world's tallest mountain.

'Port five! Full ahead! We need to get out here now!' the Captain commanded the First Mate.

'Out of here? Is it dangerous?' Feng Fan asked, confused.

'The alien spaceship has already created a huge area of low pressure. Right now a gigantic cyclone is taking form. I tell you, this could be the greatest tempest the world has ever seen. If it catches the *Bluewater*, we will be ripped straight out of the water and tossed about like a leaf in a storm. I just pray we will be able to outrun it,' the Captain explained, sweat clearly visible on his brow.

Just then the First Mate signaled them all to be quiet. Covering his earpiece with one hand, he listened intently and then said, 'Captain, the situation is much worse than that! They are now saying that the aliens have come to destroy Earth! With nothing but its enormous mass, their ship is doing much, much worse than just raising a storm; it is about to gash a hole in Earth's atmosphere!'

'Hole? Hole to where?' the Captain asked, his eyes wide.

The First Mate explained what he had just heard over the radio. 'The spaceship's gravity will puncture the upper layers of the atmosphere. Earth's atmosphere will be like a pricked balloon, its air escaping through that puncture, right into space! All of Earth's atmosphere will disappear!'

'How long do we have?' the Captain asked, confronted with horror after horror.

'The experts say that it will only take a week or so for the atmospheric pressure to fall to a lethal level.' The First Mate reported mechanically, but his wild eyes betrayed his panic. 'They say that when the pressure falls to a certain point, the oceans will begin to boil,' he continued, his voice beginning to break. 'Heavens, that would be like…' He trembled as he heard further news. 'All of Earth's major cities have fallen into chaos. Humanity has lost all semblance of sanity. Everywhere people are rushing into hospitals and factories, pillaging all the oxygen they can get their hands on.' His eyes continued to widen. 'Wait, now they are saying that Cape Canaveral is being overrun by a crazed mob trying to get its hands on the liquid oxygen used in the rocket fuel.' The First Mate's spirit appeared to slump along with his body. 'Oh, it's all over!'

'A week? That doesn't leave us enough time to make it home,' the Captain said steadily. It seemed that his composure had returned. With a quick flick of his fingers, he re-lit his pipe.

'Right, there's no time to make it home…' the First Mate echoed, his voice now emotionless.

'If that is what it's going to be, we might as well get on with it and make the best of the time we have left,' Feng Fan noted, a sudden edge of enthusiasm in his voice. His entire body was readying to the occasion, flushed with excitement.

'And what is it that you want to do?' the Captain asked.

'Climb a mountain,' Fan answered with a smile.

'Climb a mountain? Climb…?' The First Mate's face suddenly twisted from puzzlement to outright shock. 'That mountain?' he gasped, pointing at the mountain of water looming above them.

'Yes. It's now the world's tallest peak. Where there's a mountain, there will always be someone to climb it,' Fan replied calmly.

'And how do you plan to climb it?' the First Mate asked.

'Isn't it obvious? Mountain climbing is something one does with hands and feet, so I will swim,' Fan said with a smile.

'Are you crazy?' the First Mate shouted. 'How are you going to swim up a thirty-thousand-foot slope of water? It looks like a forty-five degree incline to me! That is going to be very different from climbing a mountain. You'll have to swim nonstop; and if you stop, even for a moment, you'll slide down the side!'

'I want to try.' Fan would not be dissuaded.

'Let him go then,' the Captain said flatly. 'What better time than now to embrace our passions? How far is it to the foot of that mountain?'

'About a dozen miles,' someone answered.

'Take one of the lifeboats,' the Captain told Feng Fan. 'Remember to take enough food and water.'

'Thank you!' Fan expressed his heartfelt gratitude.

'It looks like today fortune smiles upon you,' the Captain said with a wry smile, giving Feng Fan a clap on the shoulder.

'I believe so,' Fan replied. 'Captain, there is one thing I haven't yet told you: one of the four climbers on Everest was my girlfriend. A single thought flashed through my mind when I cut that rope: I don't want to die. There's still another mountain to climb,' he said, pain and bright enthusiasm merging in his eyes.

The captain nodded. 'Go.'

'And,' the First Mate said, looking lost, 'what do we do?'

'Full speed ahead away from the coming storm. One more day to live is one more day to live,' the Captain answered thoughtfully.

Feng Fan stood in the lifeboat, his gaze following the *Bluewater* as it sailed into the distance. Soon, the ship he had once seen as his home for life was well and truly out of reach.

Behind him, the mountain of water towered serenely under the blue glow of the alien sphere. Had he not seen it form, he could have easily been tricked into thinking that it had been there for millions of years. The ocean was very calm, its flat surface unruffled by waves. Feng Fan, however, could feel a breeze brush his face; it was weak, but it was blowing toward the looming waters. Raising the lifeboat's sail, he began his journey to the mountain. The wind soon picked up, and his vessel's sail filled in its wake. The lifeboat's prow now cut the ocean's surface like a knife as it sped toward Fan's goal.

In the end, the twelve-mile journey took no longer than forty minutes. As soon as Feng Fan began to feel the hull of his boat climb the slope of water, he leapt off the side of his vessel into the shining blue waters that were aglow with the light of the alien vessel above.

A few strokes later, he became the first person to swim a mountainside.

From his position, he could no longer see the summit. Lifting his head out of the liquid mountain, all he saw was an unending expanse of sloping water. He could almost imagine a titan beyond the horizon, lifting the ocean like a vast, watery blanket.

Feng Fan began to swim the breaststroke, conserving as much energy as possible. The First Mate's warning was still fresh in his mind. A quick calculation told him that it would be about eight miles to the summit. On level water, his endurance would have allowed him to easily cover the distance, but here he would have to deal with the slope. If he stopped moving upward, he would slip down. That alone would make reaching the summit almost impossible. It did not matter; the very act of attempting to climb this watery Everest was a greater achievement than he had ever dared hoped for in all of his mountaineering dreams.

As these emotions washed over him, Fan became aware of more physical sensations. He felt his body gradually being pulled up along the slope. Swimming up seemed to demand no additional effort. Looking back, he could see the lifeboat that he had abandoned at the mountain's foot. Before leaving the vessel he had lowered its sail, yet it remained floating on the slope, strangely stationary. Fan decided to try something.

He ceased his strokes and began to carefully observe his surroundings. He was not sliding. On the contrary, he was floating on the slope as if it did not exist at all! Fan slapped his forehead as he cursed his and the First Mate's foolishness: if the ocean's water on the slope did not flow downward, why would a person? Or a boat, for that matter?

The gravitational pull down the incline was being neutralized by the giant sphere's mass. The further up he climbed, the less he would feel of Earth's gravity. This meant that the slope's angle would not matter one bit. As far as gravity was concerned, there was neither a watery slope nor a mountain in the ocean. The forces acting on him would be no different from those on the level ocean.

He knew now that this mountain would be his.

He continued to swim upward. As he climbed, he felt his strokes gradually require less and less exertion. In large part, this was due to his body growing lighter, making it easier and easier to come up for air. Around him, Fan could see another sign of the reduced gravity: the higher he got, the slower the ocean's spray fell. This phenomenon was mirrored in the undulations and movements of the waves. They, too, grew ever slower the higher he swam. The harshness of the open sea had all but left them, leaving the waves softer and gentler than normal gravity would ever allow.

It was by no means calm, however. The wind was picking up, and bands of waves had begun to rise on the watery slope. Freed from much of Earth's gravity, these billows rose to considerable heights. However, they did not roll up the slope as full-bodied waves; instead, they were thin slices of water that twisted in on themselves as they gently collapsed. In a strange way, they reminded Fan of exquisitely thin wood shavings sliced from the ocean by an invisible planer. The waves did nothing to hinder his progress. In fact, it was quite the opposite; sweeping toward the summit, they actually pushed him along as he continued his climbing swim.

As the pull of gravity grew weaker, even stranger things happened: instead of pushing him, Fan was now being gently thrown along by the waves. In the blink of an eye, he felt himself leaving the water and flying over the ocean's surface, only to be caught by another wave a moment later, and then he was up in the air again. The gentle yet powerful hands of the ocean carried him along, rapidly passing him upward and onward. He soon discovered that under these strange conditions the butterfly stroke was best suited to expediting his already rapid ascent.

Around him, the wind had picked up even more strength. Gravity's grip on Feng Fan, on the other hand, was becoming weaker and weaker. The waves up here easily reached thirty feet in height before falling in slow motion. These huge billows were also gentler than they had ever been, softly rolling into one another; they did not even make a sound as they fell. The only remaining noise was the howling of a growing cyclone.

Fan's ever-lighter body was leaping from wave crest to wave crest. As he jumped again, he suddenly realized that he was spending more time in mid-air than he was in the water. Up here, he could hardly tell if he was swimming or floating. Time and again, the thin waves would come to completely envelope him, rolling him into a tunnel formed by the slowly tumbling waters. The gently roiling roof of these tunnels glowed in a blue light. Through the thin, watery roof he could see the light's source – the giant alien sphere hanging in the sky. The wave tunnel distorted the ship's form; to Feng Fan, it was as though he were seeing it through teary eyes.

He glanced at the waterproof watch he wore on his left wrist. He had only been climbing for an hour, and at this hope-defying speed it would only take another hour for him to reach the summit.

Fan thought of the *Bluewater*. Considering the current wind speeds, the tempest was only moments away from unleashing its fury. There was no way that the ship would be able to outrun the coming cyclone. In a flash, it occurred to Fan that the Captain had made a grave mistake: he should have turned the *Bluewater* straight toward the water mountain. Since gravity exerted no pull down the slope, the ship could have sailed up to the peak just as easily as it sailed the level ocean, and the peak would be at the eye of the storm – safe and calm! No sooner had he realized this than he pulled the walkie-talkie from his lifejacket. He tried to reach her, but the *Bluewater* did not respond.

By now, Feng Fan had mastered the skill of leaping from crest to crest. He had been climbing like this for twenty minutes, making it two-thirds of the way to the top. From here, the perfectly round summit already seemed within reach. It glittered in the softly glowing light of the alien spaceship above. To Fan, the summit looked like an alien world waiting for him. At that moment, the whistling of the wind suddenly turned into a sharp howl. This terrifying noise came from all directions, accompanied by a sudden increase in the wind's strength. Fifty-foot waves – even one-hundred-foot waves – thin as sheets rose high; but they never fell, torn apart by the cyclone's gale in mid-air. Looking up, Feng Fan could see that the slope above him was covered in the spray of broken wave crests dancing a crazed, wind-whipped dance over the ocean's surface. Illuminated by the glow of the alien sphere, the chaotic splashes shone with dazzling white light.

Finally, Feng Fan made his last leap. A thin, hundred-foot wave carried him into the air. It was torn to slivers by the powerful wind the moment he left its crest, and he found himself falling toward a band of waves slowly rolling in front of him. The waves looked like giant, transparent wings slowly unfurling to embrace him. Just as Fan's outstretched hands reached the waves, the waves shattered into white mist, their glittering crystal film ripped apart by the violent winds. A strange noise that sounded disturbingly like laughter accompanied the bizarre spectacle. This was also the very moment when Feng Fan stopped falling; his body was now light enough to float. The manically twisting ocean below slowly began to grow more distant as he was thrown into the air like a feather in a hurricane.

Almost weightless, Fan was tossed and turned in the twisting air. Dizzy, he felt as if the glowing alien sphere was spiraling around him. When he was finally able to steady himself, he realized with a start that he was actually swirling through the air above the summit of the water mountain.

From up here, the bands of giant waves rolling up the mountain looked like nothing more than long lines. Spiraling toward the peak, they made the mountain look like a titanic watery whirlwind. Feng Fan felt the circles he was making above the peak grow smaller and smaller while his speed accelerated. He was being carried directly into the heart of the cyclone.

When Fan arrived at the exact eye of the storm he felt the wind suddenly weaken. The invisible hand of air that had been holding him suddenly let go, and he fell toward the water mountain, straight into the faint blue glow of the summit.

He plummeted deep into the mountain before he felt himself floating upward again. He was surrounded by darkness, and in a matter of moments the fear of drowning beset him. With mounting panic, Fan suddenly realized that he was in mortal peril: the last breath he had gulped before he fell had been at thirty thousand feet! At that height, he would have hardly breathed in any oxygen at all, and in the minimal gravity here he would only rise very slowly. Even if he swam up with all his strength, he feared that the air in his lungs would not be enough to carry him back to the surface.

Feng Fan was gripped by an eerie sense of *déjà vu*. He felt himself returned to Everest, completely in the dark, enshrouded by the swirling snow of the storm, utterly overwhelmed by mortal fear. Within this darkest moment, Fan found a light: several silvery spheres were floating upward next to him. The largest of these spheres was about three feet in diameter. Looking at them, he suddenly realized that they were air bubbles. The weak gravity had allowed giant bubbles of oxygen to form in the ocean. With all the strength he could muster, he thrust himself at the largest bubble. No sooner had his head pierced the silvery shell than he was able to draw breath again. As he slowly recovered from the dizziness oxygen deprivation had induced, Fan found himself enveloped by the air bubble. He was in a sphere of air completely surrounded by water, and, looking up, he could see the ripple of the surface shimmer through the top of his bubble. Floating upward, he noticed a sudden drop in the water pressure, causing his bubble to rapidly expand. As the bubble grew, Feng Fan could not shake the impression that he was caught in a crystalline party balloon, floating into the sky.

The blue shimmer of the waves above slowly grew brighter and brighter, until finally their glare was so strong that he was forced to avert his gaze. Just then, the bubble burst with a soft pop. Fan had reached the surface; and he was going higher, the weak gravity launching him a good three feet into the air. His drop back to the surface was not a sudden but a gentle descent.

As he fell, Feng Fan noticed countless beautiful watery orbs gently dropping alongside him. These orbs greatly varied in size, the largest being roughly the size of a soccer ball. All of them shone and glittered with the blue light from the gigantic sphere above. As Fan looked more closely, he saw that they, in fact, contained layers upon layers, which made them sparkle with crystal light. These orbs were splashes of water that had been cast from the ocean as he had broken its surface. The low gravity had allowed their surface tension complete freedom to shape themselves like this. Reaching out, Fan touched one of the orbs. The sphere shattered with a strange metallic ring that was wholly unlike any sound he had ever imagined water producing.

Except for the orbs, the summit of the water mountain was altogether tranquil, the waves rushing in from all sides merging into nothing but broken swell. This was, beyond all doubt, the eye of the storm, the only place of quiet in a chaotic world. The calm was offset by a tremendous background howl – the screaming of the cyclone. Looking into the distance, Feng Fan found himself, along with the entire mountain of water, to be in a massive 'well'. The walls of this well were made of the swirling, frothing waters of the cyclone. These impenetrable masses of water and wind slowly turned around the water mountain. Looking upward, Fan saw that they appeared to reach straight into space. Shining through the mouth of the well was the alien sphere. Like a giant lamp hanging in space, its light illuminated all within the well. Gazing up, Fan could see strange clouds forming around it. They looked like fibers, trailing a loose net around the alien vessel. These strands of cloud shone brightly, appearing to glow from within. Fan could only guess that they were made of ice crystals formed as the Earth's atmosphere escaped into space. Even though they appeared to surround the spaceship, there actually had to be a good twenty thousand miles between the web and the blue sphere. If his guess was right, the atmosphere had already begun to leak and the mouth of this giant, swirling well was nothing other than the fatal hole in Earth's shell.

It doesn't matter, Fan thought to himself. I have reached the summit.

Chapter 2

Words on the Mountaintop

Suddenly, the all-pervading ambient light changed. Flickering, it began to dim. Looking up again, Feng Fan saw that the alien sphere's blue light had disappeared. It suddenly occurred to him what that light had been. It was the background light of an empty display; the entire body of the huge alien sphere was one gigantic screen. Just then, this massive screen began to display an image. It was a picture taken from a great height, and it revealed a person floating in the ocean, his face turned skyward. That person was Feng Fan. Thirty seconds ticked past, then the image disappeared. Fan had immediately understood its meaning; the aliens had shown that they could see him. It made Fan feel like he was truly standing on the roof of the world.

Two lines of text appeared on the screen. They contained all the characters in every alphabet Fan had ever seen. Recognizing the words for 'English', 'Chinese' and 'Japanese', he surmised that they must spell out the names of all the world's languages. He also spotted a dark frame quickly moving between the different words. It all appeared rather familiar. His guess was soon proven right, as he discovered that this frame actually did follow his gaze. He fixed his eyes on the characters for 'Chinese', causing the dark frame to stop over them. He blinked once, but there was no response.

Maybe it needed a double-click, Fan thought, blinking twice. The dark frame flickered, and the giant sphere's language menu closed. In its stead, a huge word appeared in Chinese.

>> Hello!

'Hello!' Fan shouted his response into the sky. 'Can you hear me?'

>> We can hear you; there is no need to shout. We could hear the wings of a mosquito anywhere on Earth. We picked up the electromagnetic waves leaking from your planet and thereby learned your languages. We want to have a little chat with you.

'Where do you come from?' Fan asked, his voice now considerably quieter.

A picture appeared on the surface of the giant sphere, showing a dense cluster of black dots. These dots were connected by a complicated web of lines. The sheer intricacy of the picture made Fan's head swim. It was obviously some sort of star map. Sure enough, one of these dots began to glow in a silver light, growing brighter and brighter. Unfortunately, Feng Fan could not really make heads or tails of it, but he was confident that it had already been recorded elsewhere. Earth's astronomers would be able to understand it. The sphere soon displayed characters again, but the star map did not disappear. Instead, it remained in the background, almost like some sort of alien desktop.

>> We raised a mountain. You came and climbed it.

'Mountain climbing is my passion,' Fan answered.

>> It is not a question of passion; we must climb mountains.

'Why?' Fan asked. 'Does your world have many mountains?' He realized that this was hardly humanity's most pressing issue, but he wanted to know. Everyone he knew considered mountaineering an exercise in foolishness, so he might as well talk about it with aliens. After all, they had just stated that they were prone to climb; and after all, he had gotten this far all by himself.

>> There are mountains everywhere, but we do not climb as you do.

Feng Fan could not tell if this was meant as a concrete description or an abstract analogy. He had no choice but to express his ignorance. 'So you have lots of mountains where you come from?' It was more a question than a statement.

>> We were surrounded by a mountain. This mountain confined us, and we needed to dig to climb it.

This answer did nothing to alleviate Fan's confusion. For a long time he remained silent, contemplating what the aliens where trying to tell him.

Then they continued.

Chapter 3

Bubble World

>> Our world is a very simple place. It is a spherical space, somewhat more than 3,500 miles in diameter, according to your units of measurement. This space is completely surrounded by layers of rock. No matter what direction one chooses to travel in, the journey will always end with a solid wall of rock.

>> Naturally, this shaped our first model of the cosmos: we assumed that the universe was made of two parts. The first was the 3,500 space in which we lived; the second was the surrounding layers of rock. We believed the rock stretched endlessly in all directions. Therefore, we saw our world as a hollow bubble in this solid universe, and so we gave our world the name Bubble World and we call this cosmology the Solid Universe Theory. Of course, this theory did not deny the possibility of other bubbles existing in these infinite layers of rock. However, it gave no indication as to how near or far away those other bubbles might be. That became the impetus for our later journeys of exploration.

'But infinite layers of rock cannot possibly exist; they would collapse under their own gravity,' Feng Fan pointed out.

>> Back then we knew nothing of gravitational forces. There was no gravity inside the Bubble World, and so we lived our lives without ever experiencing its pull. We only really came to understand the existence of gravity many thousands of years later.

'So these bubbles were the planets of your solid universe? Very interesting,' Fan commented. 'Density in our universe is entirely the inverse. Your universe must be an almost exact negative of the real universe.'

>> The real universe? You are ignorantly considering the universe only as you know it right now. You have no idea what the real universe is like, and neither do we.

Chastened, Fan decided to continue his line of enquiry. 'Was there light, air and water in your world?'

>> No, none; and we needed none of them. Our world was made entirely of solids. There were no gases or liquids.

'No gases or liquids. How did you survive?' Fan asked.

>> We are a mechanical life form. Our muscles and bones are made of metals, our brains are like highly integrated chips, and electricity and magnetism are our blood. We ate the radioactive rocks of our world's core, and they provided us with the energy we needed to survive. We were not created; we evolved naturally from extremely simple, single-celled mechanical life forms when – by pure chance – the radioactive energies formed p–n junctions in the rocks. Instead of your use of fire, our earliest ancestors discovered the use of electromagnetism. In fact, we never found fire in our world.

'It must have been very dark there then,' Fan remarked.

>> Actually, there was some light. It was generated by the radioactive activity within our world's walls. Those walls were our sky. The light of that 'sky' was very weak, and it constantly shifted as the radioactivity fluctuated. Yet it led us to evolve eyes.

>> Since our world's core lacked gravity, we did not build walls. Instead, our cities floated in the dim, empty space that was our world. They were about as big as your cities, and seen from afar they would have looked to you like glowing clouds.

>> The evolutionary process of mechanical life is much slower than that of carbon-based life, but eventually we reached the same ends by different means; and so one day we, too, came to contemplate our universe.

'That sounds like it must have felt cramped. Was it like that for you?' Fan asked, mulling over the sphere's strange revelations.

>> 'Cramped'... That is a new word. We came to experience an intense desire for more space, much stronger than any similar longing that might affect your species. Our first journeys of exploration into the rock layers began in earliest antiquity. Exploration for us meant tunneling into the walls in an attempt to find other bubbles in our solid universe. We had spun many fascinatingly alluring myths around these distant spaces, and almost all of our literature dealt with the fantasy of other bubbles. Soon, however, exploration was outlawed – forbidden on pain of death by short-circuiting.

'Outlawed? By your church?' Fan assumed.

>> No, we have no church. A civilization that cannot see the sun and stars will be without religion. There was a very practical reason for our senate to forbid tunneling: we were not furnished with the near-infinite space you have at your disposal. Our existence was limited to that 3,500-mile bubble. All the debris that the tunneling produced ended up within this space. As we believed in infinite layers of rock stretching in all directions, those tunnels could have become very long indeed – long enough even to fill the entire bubble space at the core of our world with rubble! To put it another way: we would have transformed the empty sphere in the core of our world into a very long tunnel.

'There could have been a solution to the problem: just move the newly mined rubble into the already excavated space behind the diggers,' Fan suggested. 'Then you would have only lost the space needed by the explorers to sustain themselves and dig.'

>> Indeed, later explorers used the very method you just described. In fact, the explorers would only use a small bubble with just enough space for themselves and their mission. We came to call these missions 'bubble ships'. But even so, every mission meant a bubble ship-sized pile of debris in our core space, and we would have to wait for the ship to return before we could place those rocks back into the wall. If the bubble ship failed to return, this small pile would mean another small piece of space lost to us forever. Back then we

felt as if the bubble ship had stolen that piece of space. We therefore came to call our explorers by another name – Space Thieves.

>> In our claustrophobic world, every inch of space was treasured, and later a significant area of our world had been lost in the wake of the far-too-many bubble ships that had failed to return. It was because of this loss of space that bubble ship exploration was outlawed in antiquity. Even without legal censure, life in the bubble ships was fraught with hardships and dangers beyond imagining. A bubble ship crew usually included several diggers and a navigator. At the time, we did not have mining machinery and so had to rely on manual excavation, comparable to rowing on your early vessels. These early explorers had to dig tirelessly with the simplest of tools, pushing their bubble ship through the layers of rock at a painfully slow pace. Working like machines in those tiny bubbles surrounded by solid rock – confined in every way, in search of an elusive dream – doubtlessly shows an incredible strength of spirit.

>> As the bubble ships tended to return the same way they departed, the journey back was usually a good deal easier. The rock in their path would have already been loosened. Even so, a gambler's hunger for discovery often led the ships to go well beyond the point of safe return. These unfortunate explorers would run out of strength and supplies and remain stranded mid-return, their bubble ship becoming their tomb. Despite all of this, and even though the extent of our exploratory efforts was greatly scaled back, our Bubble World never gave up on the dream of finding other worlds.

Chapter 4

Redshift

>> One day, in the year 33,281 of the Bubble Era – this is expressed in your chronological terms, as our world's reckoning of time would be too alien for you to understand – a tiny hole began to open in the rocky sky of our world. A small pile of rocks drifted out of this hole, their weak radioactive light sparkling like stars. A unit of soldiers was immediately dispatched to fly to this crack and investigate. (Now keep in mind that there is no gravity in the Bubble World.) They discovered an explorer's bubble ship that had returned. This ship had set out eight years before, and the world had long given up hope that it would ever return. The ship's name was the *Needle's Point*, and it had dug 125 miles deep into the rock. No other ship had ever made it as far and returned.

>> The *Needle's Point* had set out with a crew of twenty, but when it returned only a single scientist remained. Let us call him Copernicus. He had eaten the rest of the crew, including the captain. In ancient times, this means of sustenance had, in fact, proven to be the most efficient method for explorers going into the deep layers of rock.

>> For breaking the strict laws against bubble ship exploration, and for cannibalism, Copernicus was sentenced to death in the capital city. On the day the sentence was to be carried out, more than a

hundred thousand gathered in the central square of the capital to witness his execution. Just as they were waiting for the awesome spectacle of Copernicus being short-circuited in a beautiful shower of sparks, a group of scientists floated onto the square. They were from the World Academy of Science, and they had come to announce a groundbreaking discovery: researchers had discovered some-thing in the density of the rock samples that the *Needle's Point* had retrieved. To their great surprise, the data indicated that the rock density had steadily decreased the further the ship had dug.

'Your world had no gravity. How did you ever measure density?' Fan interjected.

>> We used inertia; it's somewhat more complicated than your methods. No matter, in those early days our scientists thought that the *Needle's Point* had merely chanced upon an uneven layer of rock. However, in the following century, legions of bubble ships journeyed forth in all directions, penetrating deeper than the *Needle's Point* ever had, and they, too, returned with rock samples. What they found was incredible: Density decreased in all directions, and it did so con-sistently! The Solid Universe Theory that had reigned supreme in the Bubble World for twenty millennia was shaken to its core. If the den-sity of the Bubble World continually decreased as one dug outward, then it stood to reason that it would eventually reach zero. Using the gathered data, our scientists were easily able to calculate that this would happen at about twenty thousand miles.

'Oh, that sounds very much like how Hubble used the redshift!' Fan exclaimed, recognizing the concept.

>> It is indeed very similar. Since you could not conceive of the redshift velocity exceeding the speed of light, you concluded that it denoted the edge of the universe; and it was very easy for our ances-tors to comprehend that an area with a density of zero is open space. Thus a new model of the universe was born. In this model, it was assumed that density decreased in proportion to distance from the Bubble World, eventually declining to the point of opening into a space that would continue into infinity. This is known as the Open Universe Theory.

>> The Solid Universe Theory, however, was deeply ingrained in our culture, and its supporters dominated the discourse. Soon they found a way to salvage the Solid Universe Theory, coming to the conclusion that all the decreasing density meant was that a spherical layer of looser rock encircled the Bubble World. Were anyone to pass through this layer, they theorized, they would find no further decrease. They calculated the thickness of this loose layer to be two hundred miles. Testing this theory was, of course, not difficult; one merely needed to dig through two hundred miles of rock. It did not take long for ships to reach this distance, but the decrease of density continued unabated. The supporters of the Solid Universe Theory then declared that their previous calculations had been mistaken and that the true thickness of the layer of loose rock was three hundred miles. Ten years later, a ship crossed this distance, and again the decrease in density was shown to continue beyond the calculated point. In fact, the speed of decrease accelerated. The Solid Universe purists then expanded the layer of loose rock to nine hundred miles...

In the end, an incredible, epochal discovery forever sealed the fate of the Solid Universe Theory.

Chapter 5

Gravity

>> The bubble ship that crossed the two hundred-mile mark was called the *Saw Blade*. It was the largest exploration vessel we had ever built, outfitted with an extremely powerful excavator and an advanced life-support system. Its cutting-edge equipment enabled the ship to travel farther than anyone had ever gone before, changing the course of our history.

>> As it passed a depth – or one might say height – of two hundred miles, the mission's chief scientist – we shall call him Newton – reported an utterly baffling observation to the ship's captain: whenever the crew went to sleep floating in the middle of the bubble ship, they would wake up lying on the tunnel wall closest to the Bubble World.

>> The captain did not think it meant anything; he concluded that it was the result of homesick sleep floating and nothing more. In his mind, the crew wanted to return to the Bubble World, and so they would always find themselves floating toward home in their sleep.

>> Consider, however, that there was no air in the Bubble World, and therefore no air in the bubble ship. This meant that there were only two ways to move: either by pushing off from the wall – something that could not possibly happen while the crew was floating in the middle of the ship, or by discharging their bodies' excrement to

propel themselves. Newton, however, never found any trace of the latter happening either.

>> Even so, the captain would not put stock in Newton's claims. He should have considered otherwise, as it was this indifference that would soon leave him buried alive. On the day it happened, the crew was particularly exhausted after having completed the latest stage of the dig, and so they did not immediately move the day's debris to the back of the ship. The plan was to move the rocks first thing after they had rested. The ship's captain joined the diggers, and they went to sleep in the center of the ship. They all woke with a start, buried alive! In their sleep, they, as well as the rocks, had all moved toward the rear of the bubble ship, closer to the Bubble World. Newton very quickly realized that all things in the ship had a certain tendency to move toward the Bubble World. This movement was very gradual and barely noticeable under normal conditions.

'So your Newton did not need an apple to discover gravity,' Fan quipped.

>> Do you really think it was that easy? For us, the discovery of gravitation was a much more involved process than it ever could have been for your kind; it had to be, considering the environment in which we lived. When our Newton discovered the directionality of attraction, he had to assume that it originated from the 3,500-mile empty space of the Bubble World; and so our early theory of gravity was marred by a rather silly assumption. We had concluded that it was vacuums that produced gravity, not mass.

'I can see how that happened. In an environment as complex as yours, it would of course be much more difficult for your Newton to figure things out than it had been for ours,' Fan said, nodding.

>> Indeed. It took our scientists half a century before they began to unravel the mystery. Only then did we begin to truly understand the nature of gravity, and soon we were able – by using instruments not unlike those you used – to measure the gravitational constant. Even so, it was a painfully slow process before the theory of gravity found widespread acceptance in our world. As it spread, however, it became the final nail in the coffin of the Solid Universe Theory.

>> Gravity did not allow for the existence of an infinite, solid universe around our bubble. The Open Universe Theory had finally triumphed, and the cosmos it described soon came to exert a powerful attraction on the inhabitants of our world.

>> Beyond the conservation of energy and mass, Bubble World physics was also bound by the law of the conservation of space. Space in the Bubble World was a sphere roughly 3,500 miles in diameter. Digging tunnels into the layers of rock did nothing to increase the amount of available space; it merely changed the shape and location of the existing space. Furthermore, we lived in a zero-gravity environment, and so our civilization floated in space at the core of our world. We affixed nothing to the walls of our world, which would have been comparable to the way you live on your planet. Because of this, space was the most treasured commodity in the Bubble World. The entire history of our civilization was one long and bloody struggle for space.

>> Now we had suddenly learned that space was quite possibly infinite. How could it not have whipped us into a frenzy? We sent forth an unprecedented number of explorers, waves upon waves of bubble ships digging forward and outward. They all did their utmost to reach that paradise of zero density that the Open Universe Theory predicted could be found beyond 19,900 miles of rock.

Chapter 6

World's Core

>> From what has been said, you should now, if you have grasped it, be able infer the true nature of our Bubble World.

'Was your world the hollow center of a planet?' Fan gave his best guess.

>> You are correct. Our planet is about the same size as Earth; its radius measures roughly five thousand miles. Our world's core, however, is hollow. This space at its center is approximately 3,500 miles in diameter. We are the life inside that core.

>> Even after the discovery of gravity, it still took us many centuries before we finally came to understand the true nature of our world.

Chapter 7

The War of the Strata

>> After the Open Universe Theory had fully established itself, the quest for the infinite space outside became our only real concern. We no longer cared about the consumption of space inside the Bubble World. Massive piles of rock, dug out by the fleets of bubble ships, soon came to fill the core space. This debris began to drift around our cities in vast, dense clouds. It got so bad that merely floating across the city was no easier a task than navigating an obstacle course. And because the cities themselves moved about, the denizens of the core also suffered devastating downpours of stone rain. Only half of the space these rocks stole was ever recovered.

>> At the time, a World Government had come to replace our senate. Its politicians took on the responsibility of overseeing and safeguarding the core space. They attempted to crack down harshly on the frenetic explorers, but this had very little effect. Most of the explorers' bubble ships had already dug into the deep layers of our planet.

>> The World Government soon realized that the best way to stop bubble ships would be with bubble ships. Following this logic, the government began building an armada of gigantic ships designed to intercept, attack and destroy the explorers' vessels deep within the rock. The government's ships would then retrieve the space that

had been stolen. This plan naturally met with the resistance from the explorers, and so the prolonged Strata War broke out, fought in the vast battlefield of layers of rock.

'That sounds like a very interesting way to fight a war!' Fan called up to the sphere, intrigued.

>> And very brutal, even though at first the pace of the fighting was languid at best. The excavation technology of the time only allowed our bubble ships to move at a pace of less than two miles per hour through the rock.

>> Large ships were the most highly valued asset on both sides in the Strata War. There was a simple reason for this: the larger the bubble ship, the longer it could go without refueling; also, the ships' offensive capabilities were in direct proportion to their size.

>> Regardless of how big they were, the ships of the Strata War were all built to have the smallest bow width possible. Again, this was for a very simple reason: the slenderer the bow, the smaller the area of rock that the ship would need to dig through and the faster the ship would be able to move. As a result, almost all of the warships looked very similar when seen from the front. On the other hand, their bodies and lengths varied widely. In extreme cases, our largest ships ended up looking like very long tunnels.

>> The battlefields of the Strata War were, of course, three-dimensional, and so the combat was fought somewhat like your forces engaging in aerial warfare, even if things were a good deal more complicated for us. When a ship encountered an enemy, its first course of action was to hastily broaden its bow width. The ships did so to bring the largest possible front of weaponry to bear; in this new configuration, a ship could transform into a shape similar to that of a nail.

>> When necessary, the bow of a bubble ship could also split into multiple sections, like a claw ready to strike. This configuration would allow the ship to attack from multiple directions at once. The raw complexity of the Strata War also revealed itself in another tactic: every warship could separate at will, transforming into multiple smaller ships. Ships could also band together, quickly combining to form a single, giant ship. Whenever opposing battle groups met, the

question of whether to link up or split up was an object of profound tactical analysis.

>> Interestingly enough, the Strata War did little to hinder the drive for further exploration. In fact, the war spurred a technological revolution that would play a critical part in our future endeavors. Not only did it bring about the development of extremely efficient excavators, but it also led to the invention of seismoscopes. This technology could be used for communication through the layers of rock and could also be employed as a form of radar. Powerful seismic waves were also used as weapons. The most sophisticated seismic communication devices could even transmit pictures.

>> The largest bubble battleship we ever built was called the *World-of-the-Line*. It was commissioned by the World Government. In its standard configuration, the *World-of-the-Line* was more than ninety miles long. It was just as its name suggested: a small, very elongated world, self-contained. For its crew, serving on the *World* was much like it would be for you to stand in the English–French Channel Tunnel; every few minutes a high-speed train rushed by, delivering tunneled debris to the aft of the ship. The *World-of-the-Line* could of course break up into an armada all by itself, but for the most part it operated as a single vessel of war. Naturally, it did not always remain in its 'tunnel' configuration. In motion, its stretched hull could be bent impressively, forming a closed loop or even crossing its own path to create intricate shapes of destruction. The *World-of-the-Line* was equipped with our most advanced excavators, allowing it to travel twice as fast as ordinary bubble ships, reaching a cruising speed of up to four miles per hour. In combat, it could even maneuver at speeds exceeding six miles per hour! Furthermore, an extremely powerful seismoscope was installed in its hull, allowing it to pinpoint bubble ships at ranges eclipsing three hundred miles. Its seismic wave weapon had an effective range of 3,300 feet, and anything and anyone within a bubble ship it targeted would be shattered to pieces or crushed. Every once in a while the *World-of-the-Line* returned to the Bubble World, carrying onboard its booty of space recovered from the explorers.

>> It was the devastating blows struck by the *World-of-the-Line* that finally pushed the explorer movement to the brink. It seemed the age of exploration was about to come to a sudden end.

>> Throughout the duration of the Strata War, the explorers continually found themselves outmatched. Perhaps most importantly, they were prevented from building or forming a ship longer than five miles. Any ship larger than that would be quickly detected by the seismoscopes installed on the *World-of-the-Line* and the walls of the Bubble World. Once they were spotted, destruction would be swift. And so, if exploration was to continue in earnest, it became imperative to destroy the *World-of-the-Line*.

>> After extensive planning and preparation, the Explorer Alliance, founded by the outmatched explorers, encircled and attacked the *World-of-the-Line* with over one hundred warships. Not one of the explorers' ships was longer than three miles in length. The battle was fought one thousand miles outside the Bubble World and became known as the Thousand-Mile Battle.

>> The Alliance first assembled twenty ships, combining them to form a single twenty-mile-long ship one thousand miles outside the Bubble World, daring the *World-of-the-Line* to attack. The *World* took the bait, rushing in for the kill in its tunnel configuration. Just as it was speeding toward its prey, the Alliance sprang its ambush. Over one hundred ships dug forward, simultaneously attacking the flanks of the *World-of-the-Line* from all directions. The mighty ninety-mile ship was split into fifty sections. Each of these sections, however, could carry on the fight as a powerful warship in its own right. Soon, more than two hundred ships from both sides were engaged in fierce battle, tunneling through the rock in a brutal and chaotic melee. Warships were constantly combining and separating, eventually blurring into an amorphous cloud of vessels and violence. In the final phase of the battle, the 150-mile battlefield became honeycombed beyond recognition by the loosened rock and empty space left behind by the destroyed ships. The Thousand-Mile Battle had created an intricate three-dimensional maze, 2,250 miles beneath our planet's surface.

>> The jarring rumble of vicious, tight combat reverberated all throughout this bizarre battlefield for what seemed like an eternity. Located so far from the core of the planet, gravity produced very noticeable effects on the action – effects that the explorers were far more familiar with than the government forces. In this great maze battle, it was this difference that slowly swung the battle in favor of the Explorer Alliance. In the end, their victory was decisive.

Chapter 8

Under the Ocean

>> After the battle, the Explorer Alliance gathered all the space left over by the battle into a single sphere sixty miles in diameter. In this new space, the Alliance declared its independence from the Bubble World. Despite this declaration, the Explorer Alliance continued to coordinate its efforts with the explorer movement in the Bubble World from afar. A constant stream of explorer ships left the core to join the Alliance, bringing considerable amounts of space with them. In this way, the territory of the Explorer Alliance continually grew, in effect allowing them to turn their territory into a fully stocked and equipped forward-operating base. The World Government, exhausted by the long years of war, found itself unable to stop any of this. In the end, they were left with no other option than to acknowledge the legitimacy of the explorer movement.

>> As the explorers reached higher altitudes, they came to dig through ever more porous rock. This was not the only benefit these heights offered; the strengthening gravity also made dealing with the excavated debris that much easier, and this newly discovered environment led to success after success. In the eighth year after the end of the war, the *Helix* became the first ship to cross the remaining 2,250 miles, completing the five-thousand-mile journey from the planet's center, 3,250 miles from the edge of the Bubble World.

'Wow! That was all the way to the surface! It must have been so exciting for you to see the great plains and real mountains!' Fan exclaimed, fully absorbed in the visitors' story.

>> There was nothing to be excited about; the *Helix* reached the seabed.

Fan stared up at the alien sphere in shocked silence.

>> When it happened, the images from the seismic communicator began to shake and suddenly stopped appearing altogether. Communication had been lost. A bubble ship tunneling through the rock beneath it could only catch one strange sound on its seismoscopes; a noise that in the open would have sounded like something being peeled. It was the sound of tons upon tons of water bursting into the vacuum of the *Helix*. Neither the machine life forms nor the technology of the Bubble World had ever been designed to come into contact with water. The powerful electric current produced by short-circuiting life and equipment almost instantly vaporized everything the water touched. In the rushing waves, the crew and instruments of the *Helix* exploded like a bomb.

>> Following this event, the Alliance sent more than a dozen bubble ships to fan out in various directions, but all met a similar fate when they reached that apparently impenetrable height. Not one crew was able to make their sacrifice worthwhile by sending back information that could have led us to understand that mysterious peeling sound. Twice a strange crystalline waveform could be seen on the monitors, but we were completely incapable of comprehending its nature. Subsequent bubble ships attempted to scan what lay above with their seismoscopes, but their instruments produced only mangled data; the returning seismic waves indicated that what lay above was neither space nor rock.

>> These discoveries shook the Open Universe Theory to its core, and academic circles began discussing the possibility of a new model. This new model stipulated that the universe was bound to a five-thousand-mile radius. They came to the conclusion that the lost explorer ships had come into contact with the edge of the universe and had been sucked into oblivion.

>> The explorer movement was faced with its greatest test yet. Before the *Helix* incident, the space taken by lost explorer ships had always remained, if only in theory, recoverable. Now, however, our people were faced with the edge of the universe. The space it eagerly devoured appeared to be lost forever. Considering this, even the most steadfast explorers were shaken. Remember that in our world, deep within layers of rock, space – once lost – could never be regain. With this in mind, the Alliance decided to send a final group of five bubble ships. As they reached an altitude of three thousand miles, these ships proceeded with extreme caution. If they were to suffer the same fate as the previous missions, it would mean the end of the explorer movement.

>> Two bubble ships were lost. A third ship, the *Stone Cerebrum*, however, made groundbreaking progress. At an altitude of three thousand miles, the *Stone Cerebrum* was slowly digging upward, every foot of rock tunneled with the utmost caution. When the ship reached the seabed, the ocean's waters did not gush through the entire ship and so did not instantly collapse the vessel, as had happened in all previous attempts. Instead, the seawater spurted through a small crack, forced into a powerful but minute stream by the immense pressure above. The *Stone Cerebrum* had been designed with a beam width of 825 feet. By the standards of the explorer ships, this was considered large, yet it turned out to be an unbelievable stroke of luck. Because of the ship's size, the rising seawater took nearly an hour before it filled the ship's interior. Before coming into contact with the bursting water, the ship's seismoscope had recorded the morphology of the ocean above, and numerous data and images had been successfully transmitted back to the Alliance. It was on that day that the People of the Core saw a liquid for the first time.

>> It is quite imaginable that there might have been liquid in the Bubble World in ancient times, but it would have been nothing but searing magma. Once the violent geology of our planet's formation had finally come to rest, this magma must have completely solidified. In our planet's core, nothing remained but solid matter and empty space.

>> Even so, our scientists had long since predicted the theoretical possibility of liquids, but no one had really believed that this legendary substance could actually exist in the universe. Now, however, in those transmitted images, the scientists clearly saw it with their own eyes. And what they saw left all of them in shock: shocked at the white, bursting jet, shocked at the slow rise of the water's surface and shocked at seeing that demonic substance warp itself into any form, clinging to every surface in complete defiance of all laws of nature. They saw it seep into even the tiniest cracks, and they witnessed how it seemed to change the very nature of rock, darkening it with but a touch, even as it seemed to make it shimmer like metal. However, what fascinated them most was that while most things disappeared into this strange substance, some shattered remains of the crew and machinery actually came to float on its surface! There was nothing that seemed to distinguish those things that floated from those that sank. The People of the Core gave this strange liquid substance a name; they called it 'amorphous rock'.

>> From that point on, the explorers could again celebrate a long string of successes. First, engineers from the Explorer Alliance designed a rudimentary drainpipe. In essence, it was a 650-foot-long, hollow, drilling pole. After it had drilled through the final layers of rock, the drill bit of this pole could be opened like a flap valve, drawing the ocean's waters down the pipe. A second valve was attached to the bottom of the drainpipe.

>> Another bubble ship rose to an altitude of three thousand miles. Then it began drilling the drainpipe through the final layers into the seabed. Nothing could have been easier; drilling was, after all, a technology with which the People of the Core were abundantly familiar. There was another piece to the puzzle, however, and that required technology of which we had never even conceived: sealing.

>> As the Bubble World had been completely devoid of liquids or gases, sealing technology had never been necessary, or even imaginable, to the People of the Core. As a result, the valve at the bottom of the drainpipe was far from watertight. Before it was even opened, it allowed water to leak out and into the ship. This accident, however,

proved to be very fortunate indeed; had the valve ever been opened fully, the power of the onrushing water would have been much greater than the spray through the rock crack encountered by the *Stone Cerebrum*. It would have burst forth in a concentrated beam of water powerful enough to cut through everything in its path like a laser. Now, instead, the water seeped through the porous valve at a much more controllable drip. You can imagine just how fascinating it was for the crew of the bubble ship to see that thin stream of water trickling before their very eyes. This liquid was completely unknown territory to them, much as electricity had been to early humanity.

>> After carefully filling a metal container with the strange liquid, the bubble ship retreated to the lower layers, leaving the drainpipe buried in the rocks. As the ship descended, the explorers took great precautions, keeping their strange sample as still and safe as possible in its container. Carefully observing it, they soon made their first new discovery: the amorphous rock was actually transparent! When they had first seen the seawater shoot through the cracked rock, it had naturally been heavily laden with sediment and mud. The People of the Core had accepted this as the amorphous rock's natural state. Following this discovery, the ship continued to descend, and as it did the temperature on board began to rise.

>> It was with a deep fear that the explorers suddenly came face to face with the most horrible realization yet: the amorphous rock was alive! Stirring, its surface had begun to roil with anger, its terrifying form now covered with countless bursting bubbles. But this monster's surging life force seemed to consume its very being, its body dissolving into a ghostly white shadow. Once all the amorphous rock in the container had transformed into this new phantasmal state, the explorers began to feel a strange sensation grip their bodies. Within moments, the sparks of shorting circuits erupted from within their bodies, ending their lives in agonizing fireworks.

>> Seismic waves transmitted this terrible spectacle live to the Explorer Alliance, right up until the monitors, too, went dark. A quickly dispatched relief ship suffered the same fate. As soon as it made contact with the doomed vessels, its crew also erupted into

terrible sparks, dying in pain. It seemed as if the amorphous rock had become a specter of death, looming over all of space. The scientists, however, noticed that the second series of short circuits was nowhere as violent as the first explosive deaths. This led them to a conclusion: as the area of space increased, the density of that amorphous shadow of death decreased.

>> It took many lives and countless horrible deaths, but in the end the People of the Core finally discovered another state of being they had never encountered before: gas.

Chapter 9

To the Stars

>> These momentous discoveries even moved the World Government, and they reunited with their old enemies, the Explorer Alliance. The Bubble World now also committed its resources to the cause, heralding a period of intense exploration marked by rapid progress. The final breakthrough was within reach.

>> Even though we came to an ever greater understanding of water vapor, we still lacked the sealing technology that would have allowed the core's scientists to protect our people and machinery from harm. Nonetheless, we had come to learn that at an altitude above 2,800 miles, the amorphous rock remained dead and inert, unable to boil. To study the strange new states, the World Government and the Explorer Alliance constructed a laboratory at an altitude of 2,900 miles. They equipped this facility with a permanent drainpipe. Here experts began to study the amorphous rock in earnest.

'Only then could you begin to undertake the work of Archimedes,' Fan chimed in.

>> You are quite correct, but you should not forget that our earliest forebears had already done the work of Faraday.

>> As a byproduct of their work in the Laboratory for Amorphous Rock Research, our scientists came to discover water pressure and buoyancy. They also managed to develop and perfect the sealant

technology necessary to deal with liquids. Now we finally understood that sealing the amorphous rock would be an incredibly simple undertaking, much simpler in fact than drilling through layers of rock. All that would be required was a sufficiently sealed and pressure-resistant vessel. Without excavators, this ship would be able to rise at speeds that seemed almost incomprehensible to the People of the Core.

'You built a Bubble World rocket,' Fan noted with a smile.

>> More of a torpedo, really. This torpedo was a metallic, pressure-resistant, egg-shaped container with no drive or propeller whatsoever. It was designed for a crew of one. We shall call this pioneer 'Gagarin'. The torpedo's launch pad was set up in a spacious hall excavated at an altitude of three thousand miles. One hour before the launch, Gagarin entered the torpedo, and the entire vessel was hermetically sealed. After all instruments and life-support systems had been checked and determined to be functional, an automatic excavator began digging its way through the mere thirty feet of rock separating the launch hall from the seabed above. With a mighty roar, the ceiling collapsed under the pressure of the amorphous rock. The torpedo was immediately and completely submerged in a sea of liquid. As the chaos began to subside, Gagarin could finally catch a glimpse of the outside world through his transparent steel–rock porthole. With a start, he realized that the launch pad's two searchlights were casting beams of light through the amorphous rock. In the Bubble World, which lacked air, light could not scatter and emit beams. This was the first time any of us had ever seen light this way. Just then seismic waves communicated the launch order, and Gagarin pulled the release lever.

>> The anchor hinges holding the bottom of the torpedo to the rock sprang open, and the torpedo slowly began to rise from the seabed. Engulfed by the amorphous rock, it soon began to accelerate, floating upward.

>> Given the pressure at the seabed level, it was very easy for our scientists to calculate that roughly six miles of amorphous rock covered the ocean's floor. If nothing unexpected happened, the torpedo

would float to the surface in roughly fifteen minutes. What it would encounter there, no one could know.

>> The torpedo shot up unimpeded. Through his porthole, Gagarin could see nothing but fathomless darkness. Only the occasional glimpse of dust zipping past in the lights outside his porthole gave him any indication of how rapidly he was ascending.

>> All too soon panic began to well in Gagarin's heart. He had lived all his life in a solid world. As he now entered, for the first time, a space filled with amorphous rock, a feeling of utterly helpless emptiness threatened to drown the very core of his being. Fifteen minutes seemed to stretch into infinity as Gagarin did his best to focus on the hundred thousand years of exploration that had led to this moment...

>> And just as his spirit was about to break, his torpedo broke the surface of our planet's ocean.

>> The inertia of the ascent shot the torpedo a good thirty feet above the water's surface before it came crashing back down toward the sea. Looking through his porthole as he fell, Gagarin could see the boundless amorphous rock, stretching into forever, shimmering with strange sparkles. But he had no time to see where the light was coming from; the torpedo slammed heavily into the ocean with a great splash, sending amorphous rock splashing in all directions.

>> The torpedo came to rest, floating on the ocean's surface like a boat, gently rocking with the waves.

>> Gagarin carefully opened the torpedo's hatch and slowly raised himself out of the vessel. He immediately felt the gust of the ocean breeze, and, after a few perplexed moments, he realized that it was gas. Tremors of fear shook his body as he recalled a flow of water vapor he had once seen through a steel–rock pipe in the laboratory. Who could have ever foreseen that there could be this much gas anywhere in the universe? Gagarin soon understood that this gas was very different from the gas produced by boiling amorphous rock. Unlike the latter, it did not cause his body to short circuit.

>> In his memoirs he later wrote the following description of these events:

>> I felt the gentle touch of a giant invisible hand brush by my body. It seemed to have reached down from a vast, boundless, and completely unknown place; and that place was now before me, transforming me into something wholly new.

>> Gagarin lifted his head, and then and there he finally embraced the reward of one hundred thousand years of our civilization's exploration: he saw the magnificent, sparkling wonder of the starlit sky.

Chapter 10

Of the Universality of Mountains

'It really wasn't easy for you. You had to explore for so many years, just to reach our starting point!' Fan exclaimed in admiration.

>> That is the reason why you should consider yourselves a very lucky civilization.

Just then, the size of the ice crystal clouds formed by the escaping atmosphere dramatically increased. The heavens shone with a sparkling light, a brilliant rainbow wreath blooming as the alien vessel's glow scattered in the ice. Below, the gigantic cyclonic well continued its rumbling turns. It made Fan think of a massive machine pulverizing the planet bit by thundering bit. On top of the mountain, however, everything had become completely still. Even the tiny ripples had disappeared from the summit's surface. The ocean was mirror-still. Again, Feng Fan was reminded of the mountain lakes of North Tibet...

With a jolt, he forced his mind back to reality.

'Why did you come here?' he asked the sphere above.

>> We are just passing by, and we wanted to see if there was intelligent life here with which we could have a chat. We talk to whoever first climbs this mountain.

'Where there's a mountain, there will always be someone to climb it,' Fan intoned, nodding.

>> Indeed, it is the nature of intelligent life to climb mountains, to strive to stand on ever higher ground to gaze farther into the distance. It is a drive completely divorced from the demands of survival. Had you, for example, only been concerned with staying alive, you would have fled from this mountain as fast and as far away as you could. Instead, you chose to come and climb it. The reason evolution bestows all intelligent life with a desire to climb higher is far more profound than mere base needs, even though we still do not understand its real purpose. Mountains are universal, and we are all standing at the foot of mountains.

'I am on the top of the mountain,' Feng Fan interjected. He would not stand for anyone, not even aliens, challenging the glory of his having climbed the world's tallest mountain.

>> You are standing at the foot of the mountain. We are all always at the foot. The speed of light is the foot of a mountain; the three dimensions of space are the foot of a mountain. You are imprisoned in the deep gorge of light-speed and three-dimensional space. Does it not feel... cramped?

'We were born this way. It is what we are familiar with,' Fan replied, clearly lost in thought.

>> Then the things that I will tell you next may be very unfamiliar. Look at the universe now. What do you feel?'

'It is vast, limitless, that kind of thing,' Fan answered.

>> Does it feel small to you?

'How could it? The universe stretches out endlessly before my eyes; scientists can even peer as far as twenty billion light years into space,' Fan explained.

>> Then I shall tell you: it is no more than a bubble world twenty billion light years in radius.

Fan had no words.

>> Our universe is an empty bubble, a bubble within something more solid.

'How could that possibly be? Would this larger solid not

immediately collapse in under its own gravity?' Fan asked, bewildered.

>> No, at least not yet. Our bubble is still expanding in this super-universal solid. Gravitational collapse is only an issue for a bounded, solid space. If, however, the surrounding solid area is actually limitless, then gravitational collapse would be a non-issue. This, of course, is no more than a guess. Who could know whether this solid super-universe has its own limits?

>> There is so much space for speculation. For example, one could theorize that at its immense scale, gravity is offset by some other force, just like electromagnetism is largely offset by nuclear forces on the microscopic scale. We are not aware of such a force, but when we were inside the Bubble World we remained unaware of gravity. From the data we have gathered, we can see that the form of the universe's bubble is much like your scientists have surmised. It is just that you do not know what lies beyond it yet.

'What is this solid? Is it...?' Fan hesitated for a moment. 'Rock?' he finally asked.

>> We do not know, but we will discover that in fifty thousand years, once we reach our destination.

'Where exactly are you going?' Fan asked.

>> The edge of the universe. Our bubble ship is called the *Needle's Point*. Do you remember the name?

'I remember,' Fan answered. 'That was the ship that first discovered the law of decreasing density in the Bubble World.'

>> Correct. We do not know what we will find.

'Does the super-universe have other bubbles in it?' Fan enquired.

>> You are already thinking very far ahead, indeed.

'How could I not?' Fan responded.

>> Think of the many small bubbles inside a very big rock. They are there, but they are very hard to find. Even so, we will go and look for them.

'You truly are amazing.' Fan smiled, feeling a deep admiration for the adventurous aliens.

>> Very well, our little chat was most delightful, but we must make haste; fifty thousand years is a very long time, and we are burning daylight, so to speak. It was a pleasure meeting you; and remember, mountains are universal.

The sheer density of the ice crystal clouds made the last few words indistinct, blurred behind the clouds. And with those final words, the giant sphere, too, began to slowly dim, its form fading smaller and smaller into the heavens. Soon it had shrunk to a mere dot, just another star in an endless sky. It left much faster than it had arrived, and within moments it had disappeared altogether across the western horizon.

Everything between sky and ocean was restored to deep black. Ice crystal clouds and the cyclonic well were swallowed by the darkness, leaving only a trace of swirling black chaos, barely visible in the skies above. Feng Fan could hear the roar of the encircling tempest rapidly diminish. Soon, it was no more than a soft whimper, and before long, even that had died. All that remained was the sound of the waves.

Feng Fan suddenly became aware of the sensation of falling. Looking around, he could see the ocean slowly begin to change. The perfectly round summit of the water mountain had begun to flatten like a giant parasol being stretched open. He knew that the water mountain was dissolving and that he was plummeting a good thirty thousand feet. Within minutes, the water he was floating on stopped falling, having reached sea level. The inertia of his fall carried him down deep below the surface.

Luckily, he did not sink too far this time and quickly bobbed up to the surface.

As he surfaced, he realized that the water mountain had completely disappeared into the ocean, leaving not even the slightest trace, appearing just as if it had never been there. The cyclone, too, had spun itself out of existence, even though he could still feel the hurricane-force winds batter him as they whipped up large waves. Soon, the ocean's surface would be calm again.

As the ice crystal clouds scattered, the magnificent starry heavens again spanned the sky.

Feng Fan looked up at the stars, thinking of that distant world so very, very far away – so remote that even the light of that day must have been reeling from exhaustion before reaching Earth. There, in that ocean long ago, Gagarin of the Bubble World had raised his head to the stars as Fan did now; and through the vast barrenness of space and the desolation of time, he felt a deep bond of kinship unite their spirits.

In a sudden a burst of nausea, Feng Fan retched. He could tell from the taste that it was blood. Miles above sea level, on the summit of the water mountain, he had suffered altitude sickness. A pulmonary edema was hemorrhaging. He instantly realized the severity of the situation. The sudden increase in gravity had left him too exhausted to move. Only his life jacket was keeping him afloat. He had no inkling as to the fate of the *Bluewater*, but he was almost certain that there could be no boats within at least half a mile of him.

When he was atop the summit, Feng Fan had felt his life fulfilled. Up there, he could have died in peace. Now, suddenly, there was no one on the planet who could have been more afraid to die than he was. He had climbed to the rocky roof of our planet, and now he had also climbed the highest watery peak the world had ever known.

What kind of mountain was left for him to climb?

He would have to survive; he had to find out. The primal fear of the Himalayan blizzard returned. Once, this fear had made him cut the rope connecting him to his companions and his lover. He had sealed their fate. Now he knew that he had done the right thing. If there had been anything left for him to betray to save his life, he would have betrayed it.

He had to live. There was a universe of mountains out there.

Sun of China

Prologue

Shui Wah took the small parcel from his mother's trembling hands. It contained one pair of thick-soled shoes she had sewn herself, three steamed buns, two heavily patched coats and twenty yuan. His father squatted by the roadside, sullenly smoking a long-stemmed pipe.

'Our son is leaving home. Would it kill you to put on a good face?' Ma scolded Pa. When she met with stony silence, she added, 'Fine, don't let him go. Can you afford to build him a house and find him a wife?'

'Go, then! East, west, they all leave in the end! I'd have been better off raising a litter of puppies!' Pa bawled, without looking up.

Shui lifted his eyes to the village in which he had been born and raised. Condemned to perpetual drought, the villagers scraped by on what little rainwater they could collect in cisterns. Shui's family had no money to build a cistern out of cement and had to make do with an earthen one instead. On hot days, the water stank. In years past, the foul water had been safe to drink after boiling, just a little bitter, a bit astringent. This summer, however, even the boiled water gave them diarrhea. They had heard from a local military doctor that some toxic mineral had leached into the water from the ground.

With one last glance at his father, Shui turned and walked

away. He did not look back. He did not expect Pa to watch him go. When Pa felt miserable, he would crouch over his pipe for hours, unmoving, as if he had become a clod of dirt on the yellow earth. But he still clearly saw Pa's face, or perhaps it was better to say he walked upon it. Northwestern China stretched around him, a vast expanse of parched ocher, lined with cracks and gullies carved by erosion. Was the face of an old farmer any different? The trees, the soil, the houses, the people – everything was blackened, yellowed, wrinkled. He could not see the eyes of this face that stretched toward the horizon, but he could feel their presence, staring toward the sky. In youth, that gaze had been filled with longing for rain; in old age, it had grown glassy.

In fact, this giant visage had always been dull and impassive. He did not believe this land had ever been young.

There was a sudden gust of wind, and the path out of the village was swallowed in yellow dust. Shui followed this road, taking his first step toward his new life. It was a road that would lead him to places beyond his wildest dreams.

Life Goal #1:

Drink some water that is not bitter, make some money.

'Oh, there are so many lights!'
Night had fallen by the time Shui reached the cluster of many small, unauthorized coal pits and kilns that constituted the mining district.

'Those? Hardly. Now in the city, that's a lot of lights,' said Guo Qiang, who had come to meet him. Guo was from the same village as Shui, but he had left many years before.

Shui followed Guo to the workers' bunkhouse for the night. At dinnertime, he was delighted to discover that the water tasted pleasantly sweet. Guo told him a deep well had been drilled in the district, so naturally the water was good. 'But go to the city,' he added, '*that's* sweet water!'

Before bed, Guo handed Shui a hard, wrapped bundle to use as a pillow. He opened it and saw round sticks covered in black plastic. Peeling back the plastic, he saw that the sticks were yellowish, like soap.

'Dynamite,' Guo mumbled before he rolled over and started snoring. Shui noticed that his head rested on the same sort of 'pillow'. There was a stack of dynamite beneath the bed, and a cluster of blast caps dangled above his head. Later, Shui learned that there were enough explosives in the bunkhouse to blow his whole village sky-high. Guo was the mine's blast technician.

Work at the mine was hard and tiring. Shui ran back and forth, digging coal, pushing carts, erecting props and doing other odd jobs. He was dead tired at the end of each day. But Shui had grown up with hardship, and he did not fear it. What did frighten him were the conditions in the pit. The descent felt like burrowing into a dark anthill. At first, it felt like a waking nightmare, but later he grew accustomed this, too. He was paid a piece rate, and he could make 150 yuan every month. He could even earn 200 when the work was good. He was quite content with this.

But what satisfied Shui most of all was the water. After his first day of work, his entire body was blackened with soot, so he followed his fellow miners to the showers. When he entered, he watched as they used washbasins to ladle water from a large pool. They then rinsed themselves, letting the water stream down from head to toe, black rivulets running across the earth. He was utterly astounded. *Ma, how can they waste such sweet water like this?* In Shui's eyes, it was that sweet, fresh water that made this dusty, blackened world beautiful beyond comparison.

Guo, however, urged Shui to move to the city. He had previously worked as a laborer there, but because he had stolen from a construction site he had been labeled a vagrant and sent back to his registered home. He assured Shui that he could earn more money in the city. Moreover, he could do so without having to work himself to death, as in the mine.

Shui hesitated, but as he struggled to make up his mind, Guo met with an accident in the pit. He was removing a dud stick of dynamite when it exploded. He had to be carried from the pit, his body riddled with shards of rock. Before he died, he turned to Shui and rasped, 'Go to the city... there are more lights there ...'

Life Goal #2:

Go to a city with more lights and sweeter water, make more money.

'Night here is as bright as day!' exclaimed Shui. Guo had not been mistaken. There really were many more lights in the city. At that moment, he was following Junior, carrying a shoeshiner's trunk on his back. They were walking along the main thoroughfare of the provincial capital toward the train station. Junior was from a village that neighbored Shui's home, and he had once worked together with Guo in the provincial capital. Despite Guo's directions, it had taken Shui a while to track him down. Junior, it turned out, no longer worked in construction; he had switched to shining shoes. But luck was on Shui's side: not only did he find the shoeshiner but one of Junior's flatmates, who plied the same trade, had just returned home to attend to a personal matter. Junior quickly walked Shui through the polishing process and then told him to pick up the other guy's trunk and follow behind.

As he walked, Shui decided he had very little confidence in his new trade. He could see the use in repairing shoes. But shining shoes? Anyone who spent one yuan on a shine – three yuan for the good polish – surely had a screw loose. In front of the station, however, their first customer arrived before they had even finished setting up their stall. To his surprise, by eleven o'clock that night, Shui had earned fourteen yuan!

Junior, on the other hand, wore a surly expression on his face as they returned home. He griped that business had been bad that day, and Shui did not miss the implication that he had stolen Junior's business.

'What are those big metal boxes under the windows?' Shui asked, pointing at a building up ahead.

'Air-conditioning units. It feels like early spring in there.'

'The city is incredible!' Shui exclaimed, wiping the sweat from his face.

'Life here is tough. It's easy to earn enough money for a bowl of rice, but if you want to marry and settle down, forget about it,' Junior said, gesturing with his chin toward the building. 'An apartment in there costs two, three thousand per square meter!'

'What's a square meter?' Shui asked innocently.

Shaking his head in disdain, Junior did not reply.

*

Shui split the rent on a small makeshift apartment with a dozen other men. Most of them were migrant laborers or farmers peddling their produce in the city. But the man who occupied the mattress right next to Shui was a proper city-dweller, although he did not come from this city. He was really no different from the other men. He ate no better than anyone else, and at night he, too, would strip to the waist to enjoy the cool evening air. Every morning, however, he would don a sharp suit and leather shoes. As he walked out the door, he seemed to become a different person. It was like watching a golden phoenix soar out of a chicken coop.

The man's name was Zhuang Yu. The others did not resent him, mainly because of something he had brought with him. It looked liked a large umbrella to Shui, only it was made from mirrors. The inside was very bright and reflective. Zhuang first placed the upturned umbrella on the ground beneath the sun. Then, he set a pot of water on a bracket where the handle should be. The reflected glare heated the bottom of the pot and the water quickly came to a boil. Later, Shui learned it was called a solar cooker. The men used it to boil water and cook food, which saved them quite a bit of money. On overcast days, however, it was useless.

The so-called 'solar cooker' umbrella had no ribs; it was just a very thin sheet. Shui looked on with fascination when Zhuang collapsed the umbrella. A long thin electrical wire ran from the top of the cooker into the apartment. To close it, Zhuang simply pulled the plug from the socket. The umbrella drooped to the ground with a small puff of air, suddenly transformed into a length of silver cloth. Shui picked up the cloth and inspected it carefully. It was soft and smooth and so light that it hardly seemed to weigh anything all. His own distorted likeness was reflected on its surface, glinting with the iridescent sheen of a soap bubble. As soon as he relaxed his grip, the silver cloth slipped through his fingers and fell to the ground without a sound, like an airy handful of quicksilver. When Zhuang reinserted the plug into the power socket, the cloth lazily unfurled like a lotus in full blossom. After a short time, it reverted to its round, upside-down umbrella shape. When he touched the surface again, it was thin and firm. Giving it a light tap, he was rewarded with a pleasant, metallic ping. In this state, it was extremely strong, able to support a full pot or kettle once fixed to the ground.

'It's a type of nanomaterial,' Zhuang told Shui. 'The surface finish possesses excellent reflective properties, and it is also very strong. Most importantly, it is soft and flexible under normal conditions but becomes rigid when a weak electric current is applied.'

Shui later learned that this 'nano mirror film' was one of Zhuang's own research achievements. After applying for a patent, he had invested everything he had into bringing products made from the new material to market. But no one had showed any interest in his products, even his portable solar cooker, and he lost all of his capital. Now he was so poor that he had to borrow money from Shui to make rent. But even though he had fallen so low, he remained relentlessly upbeat. Day in and day out, he scoured the city in pursuit of outlets for his new material. He told Shui that this was the thirteenth city he had visited in search of opportunities.

Besides the solar cooker, Zhuang also owned a smaller sheet of the mirror film. Normally, it rested on his bedside table, looking like a small silver handkerchief.

Every morning before he went out, Zhuang would hit a tiny power switch, and the silver handkerchief would immediately stiffen into a thin panel. Using it as a small mirror, he would groom and dress himself in front of it. One morning, as he brushed his hair in the mirror, he cast a sidelong glance at Shui, who had just rolled out of bed.

'You really ought to pay attention to your appearance,' he remarked. 'Wash your face regularly, tame your hair a bit. Not to mention your clothes. Can't you spare a little money for new ones?'

Shui reached for the mirror and held it to his face. Finally he laughed and shook his head. It was too much hassle for a shoeshiner.

'Modern society is full of opportunities,' Zhuang said, leaning toward Shui. 'The skies are thick with golden birds. Perhaps one day you will reach out and seize one, but only if you learn to take yourself seriously.'

Shui looked around, but he did not see a single golden bird. He shook his head and said, 'I never got an education.'

'That is certainly regrettable, but who knows? Maybe it will turn out to your advantage in the end. The greatness of this era lies in its unpredictability. Miracles can happen to anyone.'

'You,' Shui asked haltingly, 'went to university, right?'

'I have a doctorate in solid-state physics. Before I resigned, I was a professor.'

For a long time after Zhuang left, Shui sat with his mouth agape. Finally, he shook his head. If someone like Zhuang Yu could not catch a bird in thirteen different cities, he stood no chance. He felt like Zhuang was making fun of him, but in any case the guy was pitiable and ridiculous himself.

That night, while some of the men slept and others played a game of poker, Shui and Zhuang went to watch television in the small restaurant just a few doors down.

It was already midnight, and a news broadcast was on. The screen showed only the anchor, and there were no other graphics.

'In a press conference held this afternoon, a State Council spokesperson revealed that the remarkable China Sun Project has formally launched. The largest ecological engineering project since the Three-North Shelterbelt, its construction is expected to fundamentally transform our nation's soil...'

Shui had heard of the project before, and he knew it involved constructing another sun in the sky. The second sun would bring more rain to the arid Northwest.

It all sounded very farfetched to Shui. He wanted to ask Zhuang about it, as he usually did when he encountered such matters. When he turned his head, however, his friend was staring with wide eyes at the television, slack-jawed, as if the screen had snatched the soul from his body.

Shui waved his hand in front of the other man's face, but received no response. Zhuang did not recover his senses until long after the broadcast had ended. 'Really,' he mumbled to himself, 'how did I not think of the China Sun?'

Shui looked at him blankly. If even he knew about it, there was no way Zhuang was not aware of the China Sun. Who in China had not heard of it? Of course he knew about it – he just hadn't thought about it until now. But what new possibility had captured his attention? What could this project possibly have to do with Zhuang Yu, a down-and-out tramp living in a stuffy, ramshackle apartment?

'Do you remember what I said this morning?' Zhuang asked. 'Right now, a golden bird has swooped in front of me, and it is *huge*. It has been right overhead all this time, but I never fucking noticed!'

Shui continued to stare at him in total confusion.

'I am going to Beijing,' Zhuang announced, rising. 'I'll catch the 2:30 train. Come with me, brother!'

'To Beijing? To do what?'

'Beijing is so big, what can't be done?' he replied. 'Even if you just shine shoes, you'll still make much more money there than you do here!'

And so, that very night, Shui and Zhuang boarded a train so crowded that there was not a single seat available. All through the night, the train rolled across the vast open spaces of the West, racing toward the rising sun.

Life Goal #3:

Go to a bigger city, see more of the world, make even more money.

When Shui saw the capital for the first time, one thing became clear: some things had to be seen to be understood. The power of his imagination alone was inadequate. For instance, he had imagined nighttime in Beijing countless times. At first, he had simply doubled or trebled the lights in his village or at the mining district; after he moved to the provincial capital, he repeated the trick with the lights there. But when the bus he and Zhuang had boarded at Beijing West Railway Station turned onto Chang'an Avenue, he knew he could multiply the lights of the provincial capital a thousand times and never match the spectacle of Beijing at night. Of course, the lights of Beijing were not really a thousand times brighter than those of the provincial capital, but there was something about central Beijing that the cities out west could never hope to capture.

Shui and Zhuang stayed the night in a cheap basement motel and then went their separate ways in the morning. Before he took his leave, Zhuang wished Shui good luck and said that, if he ran into any trouble, he could always come find him. But when Shui asked him for a telephone number or address, he admitted he had neither.

'Then how will I find you?' asked Shui.

'Just wait a while. Soon, you'll know where I am by glancing at the television or the newspaper.'

As he watched Zhuang's receding figure, Shui shook his head in bewilderment. What a puzzling response! The man did not have a cent to his name. Today, he had not been able to afford the room at the motel, and Shui had bought their breakfast. Before they left for Beijing, he had even given his solar cooker to the landlord in place of rent. Now, he was no better than a beggar with a dream.

After he parted from Zhuang, Shui immediately went out in search of work, but the city shocked him so deeply he soon forgot his original objective. He spent the entire day strolling aimlessly through the city streets. It was as though he had walked into a fairyland, and he did not feel tired in the slightest. As dusk fell, he stood before one of the new symbols of the capital. Completed just last year, the Unity Tower stood five hundred meters tall. Shui craned his neck to look up at the glass precipice that rose above the clouds. On its surface, the fading glow of the sunset and the swiftly brightening sea of lights below staged a breathtaking performance of light and shadow. Shui watched until his neck grew sore. Just as he turned to leave, the lights of the tower itself came on. The potent spectacle took possession of Shui, and he stood transfixed, his gaze turned skyward.

'You've been staring for a long time. Are you interested in this sort of work?'

Shui turned to see who had addressed him. It was a young man. He was dressed like any other resident of the city, but he held a yellow hardhat in his hand.

'What work?' Shui asked, confused.

'What were you looking at just then?' the man asked in return, pointing upward with the hand that still held the helmet.

Shui lifted his head and looked in the direction the man was pointing. To his surprise, he spotted several people high up on the glass precipice. From the ground, they looked like little black dots.

'What are they doing so high up there?' Shui asked as he strained for a closer look. 'Cleaning the glass?'

The man nodded. 'I'm the human resources manager of the Blue Skies Window Cleaning Company. Our company primarily provides high-rise cleaning services. Are you willing to do that kind of job?'

Shui raised his head again. Looking at the antlike black dots high above him, he felt dizzy. 'It seems... scary.'

'If you are concerned about safety, you can rest assured. The job looks dangerous, and that does make recruitment quite difficult. We're short of hands right now. But I guarantee you that our safety precautions are very thorough. As long as you follow the operating procedures to the letter, there is absolutely no danger. And we pay higher wages than companies in similar industries. You could make fifteen hundred per month plus free lunch on work days, and the company would buy you personal insurance.'

Shui was taken aback by the sum. Astonished, he just stared at the manager. The other man misunderstood his silence. 'Fine, I'll cancel your probation period and throw in another three hundred. That's eighteen hundred per month. I can't go any higher than that. The base pay for this kind of work used to be four or five hundred yuan, plus additional piece work. Now we pay a fixed monthly salary, which is not bad in comparison.'

So Shui became a high-rise window cleaner, otherwise known as a 'spiderman'.

Life Goal #4:

Become a Beijinger.

Together with four other window cleaners, Shui cautiously descended from the top floor of the Aerospace Tower. It took them forty minutes to reach the eighty-third floor, where they had left off the previous day. One of the spidermen's biggest headaches was cleaning canted facades, those that formed angles smaller than ninety degrees with the ground. The architect of the Aerospace Tower, in a display of his own pathological creativity, had designed the entire building on a slant. The top of the tower was supported by a slender column driven into the ground. According to the celebrity architect, the slanted design was supposed to impart the sensation of rising upward. His statement seemed reasonable, and the skyscraper became famous throughout the world as a landmark of Beijing. But the architect and eight generations of his ancestors were routinely and inventively cursed by Beijing's spidermen. For them, cleaning the Aerospace Tower was a nightmare. The entirety of one side was at an incline, which stood four hundred meters tall and met the ground at a sixty-five-degree angle.

Once he reached his workstation, Shui looked up. Above him, the huge glass face looked like it was toppling down on him. With one hand, he removed the cap from his detergent container.

With his other hand, he clutched the handle of his suction cup. This kind of suction was specially made for cleaning surfaces beyond the vertical, but even so, it was difficult to use and often came unsealed. When this happened, the spiderman would swing away from the wall, dangling from his safety line. Such accidents were frequent while cleaning the Aerospace Tower, and each time, it would near frighten the soul out of the cleaner's body. Just yesterday, Shui's workmate lost suction and swung far out from the building. As he swung back in, he was caught by a gust of wind and sent crashing into the building, shattering a large sheet of glass. His forehead and arms were cut to ribbons, and the cost of replacing the expensive coated architectural glass set him back an entire year's wages.

Shui had joined the ranks of the spidermen more than two years ago, but the work had not grown easier with time. Category 2 winds on the Beaufort scale on the ground strengthened to Category 5 winds at one hundred meters. On buildings that exceeded four or five hundred meters, the winds were stronger still. That the job was hazardous went without saying. Plummeting to one's death in the streets below wasn't an unusual fate for spidermen. In winter, strong winds felt as sharp as knives, and the hydrofluoric acid solution commonly used to clean glass windows was so corrosive that it would cause their fingernails to turn black and fall off. To protect themselves from the detergent, the spidermen had to wear watertight jackets, pants, and boots, even in summer. When cleaning coated glass, the blazing sun would beat down on their backs, and the reflected glare in front of them was so blinding it was difficult to keep their eyes open. It made Shui feel like he had been placed into Zhuang's solar cooker.

But Shui loved his job. The past two years had been the happiest time of his life. It undoubtedly helped that the spidermen were highly paid relative to the other uncultured migrant laborers who flocked to Beijing. More importantly, however, he derived a wonderful sense of fulfillment from his work. He relished the jobs his fellow spidermen were unwilling to do: cleaning newly constructed super-skyscrapers. Each of these buildings stood at least two hundred meters tall, and the tallest topped five hundred meters. Hanging off the sides of these skyscrapers, Shui commanded a magnificent view of Beijing, stretched out below him. The so-called 'high-rises' built during the previous century looked squat from up there. A little farther away, they became small bunches of twigs stuck in the ground. In the heart of the city, the Forbidden City looked like it had been built with golden toy blocks. From this height, he could not hear the clamor of Beijing, and he could survey the city with a single glance. It breathed quietly below him, a super-organism surrounded by a spider's web of arterial roads. Sometimes, a skyscraper he was cleaning would push through the clouds. The world below his waist could be enveloped in a dark and dreary rainstorm even as the sun shined brightly overhead. Looking at the endless sea of clouds billowing beneath his feet, Shui always felt as though the howling winds above blew right through him.

The experience taught Shui a philosophical truth: some things only became clear when seen from above. Swallowed up in the capital, everything around him seemed hopelessly complicated. On the ground, the city was like an unending labyrinth. Up here, it was nothing more than an anthill with ten million inhabitants, and the world around it was so vast!

The first time he received his paycheck, Shui had gone for a stroll through a large shopping mall. Riding the elevator to the third floor, he was met by a peculiar scene. Unlike the bustling floors below, this hall was empty except for a few staggeringly large, low tables. The broad tabletops were covered with clusters of tiny buildings, each one no taller than a book. The space between the buildings was filled with bright green grass, dotted with white pavilions and winding corridors. The little structures were lovely, like they were carved from ivory or cheese. Together with the green lawn, they formed an exquisite miniature world. In Shui's eyes, it looked like a model of paradise. At first he guessed that these were some sort of toys, but he did not see any children in the hall. All of the adults at the tables wore attentive, serious expressions. Bewitched, he stood next to one of the tiny paradises and studied it for a long time. It was not until an attractive young woman came over to greet him that he realized this was a real estate office. He pointed to a building at random and asked how much the apartment on the top floor cost. The saleslady told him it was a three-bedroom, one-den apartment and that it cost thirty-five hundred yuan per square meter, which worked out to three hundred and eighty thousand yuan in total. Shui drew a sharp gasp when he heard the number, but the woman's next statement softened the brutal figure considerably: 'You can pay by monthly installments of fifteen hundred to two thousand yuan.'

'I–I'm not from Beijing. Could I still buy it?' he asked carefully.

The saleslady flashed him a winning smile. 'You are too funny. The household registration system was dismantled years ago. Is there such a thing as a "real" Beijinger anymore? If you settle down here, doesn't that make you a Beijinger?'

After Shui left the mall, he had wandered aimlessly through the streets for a long time. All around him, Beijing's brilliant mosaic of lights glittered in the night. In his hand he held the colorful fliers the saleslady had given him, and every so often he stopped to look at them. Just two years ago, in that rundown room in that distant western city, even owning an apartment in the provincial capital had seemed like a fairytale. Now, he was still a long way away from buying an apartment in Beijing, but it was a fairytale no longer. It was a dream, and like those delicate little models, it was right before his eyes. He could reach out and touch it.

Just then, someone rapped on the window Shui was cleaning, interrupting his daydream. This was a common nuisance. For white-collar workers, the appearance of high-rise window cleaners at their office windows was a source of indescribable irritation. It was like the cleaners really were large, aberrant

121

spiders, as their nickname suggested, and far more than a single pane of glass separated the workers without from those within.

While the spidermen worked, the people inside would complain that they were too noisy, or that they were blocking the sunlight, or about any of the million other ways in which the cleaners had ruined their day. The glass of the Aerospace Tower was semi-reflective, and Shui had to strain to see through it. When he finally made out the man inside, he was astonished to see Zhuang Yu.

After they parted ways, Shui had often worried about Zhuang. In his mind, the man had remained a dapper tramp, making his way through the big city step by arduous step. Then, one night in late autumn, as Shui sat in his dormitory silently fretting about Zhuang's winter wardrobe, he saw him on television. The China Sun Project had begun the selection process for the critical technology at the heart of the project: the material that would be used to build its reflector. In the end, Zhuang's nano mirror film was chosen from among a dozen other materials. Overnight, the scientifically inclined vagrant was transformed into one of the chief scientists of the China Sun Project, recognized the world over. Afterward, even though Zhuang made frequent media appearances, Shui gradually forgot about him. He believed they no longer had anything to do with each other.

When Shui arrived in that spacious office, he saw that Zhuang had not changed one bit over the past two years. He even wore the same suit. Shui now saw that the attire he had once considered so luxurious was, in truth, very shabby. He told Zhuang all about his life in Beijing. 'It looks like we've both done well here,' he concluded, grinning.

'Yes, yes, very well!' Zhuang agreed, nodding excitedly. 'To tell the truth, that morning when I told you about the opportunities of these times, I had lost faith in just about everything. I was mostly saying those things for my own benefit, but these days the world truly is brimming with opportunities!'

Shui nodded too. 'There are golden birds everywhere.'

Shui took stock of the large, modern-looking office around him. A few unusual decorations stood out from the rest of the room. A holographic image of the night sky was projected across the entire ceiling of the office; anyone who stood in the center of the room would feel as though they had been transported to a courtyard beneath the brilliant stars. A curved silver plate hung suspended against the background of stars. It was a mirror that looked very similar to Zhuang's solar cooker, but Shui knew that the real thing was likely twenty or thirty times larger than Beijing.

In one corner of the ceiling, there was a spherical lamp. Like the mirror, it floated in the air without any means of support, shining with a bright yellow light. The mirror reflected its rays onto a globe next to Zhuang's desk, creating a circle of light on its surface. As the lamp slowly floated across the ceiling, the mirror rotated to track it, throwing its light upon the globe without interruption. The starlit sky, the mirror, the lamp, its light, the globe and the illuminated spot composed an abstract and mysterious mural.

'This is the China Sun? Shui asked in awe, pointing to the mirror.

Zhuang nodded. 'It is a thirty-thousand-square-kilometer reflector. From geosynchronous orbit – at an altitude of thirty-six thousand kilometers – it will reflect sunlight onto Earth. Viewed from the surface, it will look like there is another sun in the sky.'

'There's something I don't understand. How does an extra sun in the sky bring more rain?'

'This artificial sun can employ many different methods to influence the weather. For instance, by disturbing the thermodynamic equilibrium of the atmosphere, it can influence atmospheric circulation, increase ocean evaporation or shift weather fronts,' Zhang answered. 'But that doesn't really explain it. In fact, the orbital reflector is just one part of the China Sun Project. The other part is a complex model of atmospheric motion, which will run on multiple supercomputers. It will be able to accurately simulate motion in any given region of the atmosphere and then identify a critical point. If heat from the artificial sun is brought to bear upon this point, the effect would be dramatic enough to completely transform the climate of a targeted area for a period of time.' He paused. 'The process is extremely complicated, and it is outside my area of expertise. I don't quite understand it myself.'

Shui decided to ask another question which Zhuang could certainly answer. He knew his question was foolish, but he steeled his nerve and asked anyway. 'How can something so big hang in the sky without falling down?'

Zhuang gazed silently at Shui for several long seconds. Finally, he glanced down at his watch and then clapped Shui on the shoulder. 'Let's go. I'm treating you to dinner. I'll explain why the China Sun will not fall while we eat.'

The explanation did not turn out to be as easy as Zhuang expected. He was forced to set aside his original topic and start with the basics. While Shui knew he lived on a round planet, the traditional Chinese model of a heavenly dome over a square Earth was still rooted deep in his mind. It required a great deal of effort from Zhuang to make Shui really understand that the world in which he lived was a small spherical rock floating through an endless void. Although Shui came no closer to understanding why the China Sun would not fall, the universe was greatly changed in his mind's eye that evening. He entered his own Ptolemaic Era. The second evening, Zhuang ate dinner with Shui at a roadside food stall and successfully dragged him into the Copernican Era. Over the next two evenings, Shui slogged through the Newtonian Era, acquiring an elementary understanding of universal gravitation. The evening after that, with the help of the globe in his office, Zhuang ushered Shui into the Space Age. On the next public holiday, in front of that globe, Shui finally grasped the meaning of a geosynchronous orbit. At last, he understood why the China Sun would not fall down.

That day, Zhuang took Shui on a tour of the China Sun

Command Center. At the center, a massive monitor displayed a panoramic view of the ongoing construction of the China Sun in geosynchronous orbit. Several thin silver sheets floated in the blackness of space, so large that the space shuttles hovering next to them seemed like tiny mosquitoes.

But what shook Shui the most was an image on another monitor. It showed Earth from an altitude of thirty-six thousand kilometers. The continents floated on the oceans like large scraps of brown packing paper. Mountain ranges became creases in the paper, and clouds looked like residual smudges of powdered sugar on its surface.

Zhuang showed Shui the location of his home village and Beijing. He gawked at the monitor for a long minute before he blurted, 'People must think differently up there.'

The main construction of the China Sun was finished three months later. As night fell on National Day, the reflector was turned towards the night-shrouded Earth, training its immense spotlight on Beijing and Tianjin. That night, standing amid a crowd of several hundred thousand people gathered in Tiananmen Square, Shui witnessed a magnificent sunrise. In the western sky, a star began to brighten dramatically, creating a little ring of blue around itself. As the China Sun approached peak luminosity, the halo expanded, filling half the sky. Around its edges, the clear blue bled into yellow and then orange-red and dark purple, forming a circular rainbow that became known as the 'Wreath of Dawn'.

By the time Shui returned to his dormitory, it was already four o'clock in the morning. As he lay on his narrow upper bunk, the light of the China Sun streamed through his window, illuminating the real estate fliers pasted to the wall above his pillow. He ripped the glossy pages down.

Under the divine radiance of the China Sun, the ideal that had once thrilled him now seemed dull and insignificant.

*

Two months later, the manager of the cleaning company came to find Shui. He told him that Director Zhuang of the China Sun Command Center wished to see him. Shui had not seen Zhuang since he had finished his work on the Aerospace Tower.

'Your sun is really something!' Shui exclaimed in heartfelt admiration when he met Zhuang in his office at the Aerospace Tower.

'It is our sun, and yours especially!' answered Zhuang. 'Right now you cannot see it from Beijing because it is bringing snow to your village!'

'My parents mentioned in their letter that they were getting more snow than usual this winter!'

'However, the China Sun has a big problem,' said Zhuang, pointing to a large monitor behind him. Two images of a single circular spot of light were displayed on the screen. 'These images of the China Sun were taken from the same location, two months apart. Can you see the difference?'

'The one on the left is brighter.'

'You see, the decrease in reflectivity can be seen with the naked eye after just two months.'

'How can that be? Has the mirror grown dusty?'

'There is no dust in space, but there is the solar wind, or the stream of particles ejected by the sun. With time, the wind will transform the China Sun's mirrored surface. As the reflector accumulates a fine film of particles, its reflectivity will decrease. One year from now, it will look like it is covered with water vapor. Then, the China Sun will have become the China Moon, and it will be useless,' explained Zhuang.

'You didn't think of this earlier?'

'Of course we thought of it!' Zhuang paused. 'Let's talk about you. How do you feel about switching jobs?'

'Switching jobs? What else could I do?'

'You would still be working as a high-altitude cleaner, but you would be working for us.'

Shui glanced around in confusion. 'Wasn't your tower just

cleaned? Why would you need to specially employ a high-rise window cleaner?'

'No, we don't want you to clean buildings. We want you to clean the China Sun.'

Life Goal #5:
Fly to space, clean the China Sun.

There was a meeting of the senior directors of the China Sun Project Operations Division to discuss the establishment of a reflector cleaning unit. Zhuang introduced Shui to the assembled parties and explained his profession to them. When someone inquired about his educational background, Shui honestly replied that he had only finished three years of primary school.

'But I can recognize characters and can read without problems,' he told the attendees.

The conference room dissolved into laughter.

'Director Zhuang, is this a joke?' someone shouted indignantly.

'I'm not joking,' Zhuang replied evenly. 'If we assembled a crew of thirty cleaners, it would take them six months to clean the entire China Sun if they worked around the clock. In reality, we would need at least sixty to ninety people working in shifts. If the new aerospace labor protection law goes into effect as scheduled, we may need even more, perhaps one hundred and twenty to one hundred and fifty cleaners. Can we really send one hundred and fifty astronauts with doctorates and three thousand flight hours in high-performance fighter jets up into space to do the job?'

'Surely we can find more qualified candidates? Higher

education is practically universal in the cities these days. How can we send an illiterate hick into space?'

'I am not illiterate!' Shui objected.

The man ignored him and continued speaking to Zhuang. 'You would debase this great project!'

The other participants nodded in agreement.

Zhuang nodded, too. 'I thought you might react like this. Ladies and gentlemen, except for this cleaner, you all hold doctorates. Well then, let us see the quality of your cleaning work! Please come with me.'

A dozen bewildered participants followed Zhuang out of the conference room and into the elevator. Three types of lifts had been installed in the tower: standard, fast, and express. They boarded the fastest elevator and shot up at breakneck speed to the top floor of the building.

'This is my first time in this elevator,' someone remarked. 'I feel like I am blasting off in a rocket!'

'After we enter geosynchronous orbit, everyone will experience what it is like to clean the China Sun,' said Zhuang, drawing strange glances from the people around him.

After they stepped out of the elevator, Zhuang led the group up a narrow flight of stairs. Finally, they emerged from a low metal door onto the open roof of the tower. They were immediately thrust into bright sunlight and powerful winds. The blue sky overhead seemed even clearer than usual, and the directors looked all around, admiring the panoramic view of Beijing. Another small group of people stood waiting for them. Shui was startled to see his company's manager and his fellow spidermen!

'Now, everyone will try their hand at Shui's profession!' Zhuang announced in a loud voice.

The spidermen stepped forward and strapped each director into a safety harness. They then led them to the edge of the roof and carefully helped them onto narrow suspended platforms that normally served as a workstation for a dozen or more spidermen. The boards were slowly lowered until they were suspended five or six meters beneath the edge of the rooftop, where they halted. Screams of unadulterated terror rose from where the directors dangled against the glass face of the tower.

'Ladies and gentlemen, let us continue the meeting where we left off!' Zhuang called down to his colleagues below, leaning over the edge of the roof.

'You bastard! Quick, pull us up!'

'Every one of you has to clean a pane of glass before I let you up!'

It was an impossible demand. The people below could only cling to their safety harnesses or the ropes supporting the platforms for dear life, not daring to move. They were utterly incapable of loosening one hand to pick up a squeegee or remove the lid from the detergent bucket. Every day, these aerospace officials dealt with altitudes as high as tens of thousands of kilometers in the form of blueprints and documents; but now, as they gained a first-hand feel for four hundred meters, they were scared witless.

Zhuang rose and walked to the spot above an air force colonel. Of the dozen people hanging off the side of the building, he was the only one who remained calm and collected. The colonel began to clean the glass, keeping his motions steady and controlled. What astonished Shui most, however, was that the man was working with both hands, and he had relinquished his grip on anything he might use to steady himself. Even so, his board remained motionless against the wall in the strong wind, a feat that only veteran spidermen could accomplish. When Shui recognized the man, the scene in front of him no longer seemed as strange; he was an astronaut who had flown on the Shenzhou 8 spacecraft more than a decade earlier.

'Colonel Zhang, in your candid opinion, is the task before you really easier than a spacewalk in orbit?' asked Zhuang.

'With respect to the physical ability and skill required, the difference is not great,' the former astronaut replied.

'Well said. According to studies conducted at the Aerospace Training Center, from an ergonomic standpoint, there are many similarities between cleaning skyscrapers and cleaning the reflector in space. Both tasks require workers to constantly maintain their balance in the face of danger, while performing repetitive, monotonous, physically demanding labor. Both tasks require constant vigilance, as the slightest carelessness can lead to an accident. For an astronaut, that might mean deviation from orbit, lost tools or materials, or a malfunction in his life support system. For a spiderman, that might mean shattered glass, dropped tools or detergent, or breakage or slippage of his safety harness. In terms of physical strength, technical skill, and psychological fortitude, the spidermen are fully qualified to work as reflector cleaners.'

The former astronaut lifted his head and nodded at Zhuang. 'I am reminded of that old parable about the oil peddler who could pour oil into a bottle through the square hole in a copper coin. He was every bit as skilled as a general who never missed a bull's-eye. The only difference between them was their social status.'

'Columbus discovered America and Cook discovered Australia, but these New Worlds were settled by ordinary people, pioneers who came from the lowest rungs of European society,' added Zhuang. 'The development of space is no different. In the next Five-Year Plan, we have designated near-Earth space as a second western frontier. The era of exploration has ended, and the aerospace industry will never again be the exclusive domain of an elite minority. Sending ordinary people into orbit is the first step toward the industrialization of space!'

'Okay! Fine! You have made your point! Now quickly, let us up!' his colleagues shouted hoarsely below.

In the elevator on the way down, the manager of the cleaning company leaned toward Zhuang and whispered in his ear, 'Director Zhuang, that was a moving and impassioned speech back there, but wasn't it a little much? But of course, it is difficult to discuss the key issue at hand in front of Shui and my boys.'

'Eh?' Zhuang shot him an inquiring look.

'Everyone knows that the China Sun Project is a quasi-commercial operation. Halfway to completion, a funding shortfall nearly led to the project's cancellation, and now you have next to no operations budget. In the commercial aerospace sector, the annual salary of a qualified astronaut is over one million yuan. My guys will save you tens of millions every year.'

Zhuang smiled enigmatically. 'You think such a paltry sum would be worth the risk? Today, I deliberately slashed the educational standards required of reflector cleaners to set a precedent. After this, I will be able to hire ordinary university graduates to fill the jobs in orbit needed to operate the China Sun. This way, we will save a lot more money than just a few tens of millions. As you said, it is the only course of action available. We really don't have any money left.'

'Growing up, going to space was such a romantic endeavor. I can clearly remember that, when Deng Xiaoping visited the Johnson Space Center, he called an American astronaut a god. Now,' said the manager with a bitter smile, shaking his head and slapping Zhuang on the back, 'I am no better or worse than you.'

Zhuang turned to look at the young spidermen and then told the manager in a raised voice, 'But, sir, the salary I am offering is eight to ten times better than what you pay them!'

The next day, Shui and sixty of his fellow spidermen arrived at the National Aerospace Training Center in Shijingshan. Each and every one of them was a farm boy who had come from some remote corner of China's vast countryside to Beijing, looking for work.

Mirror Farmers

At the Xichang Space Center, the nose cone of the space shuttle *Horizon* emerged from the billowing white clouds of exhaust produced by its engines. With a thunderous roar, it rose straight into the clear blue sky. Shui and fourteen other reflector cleaners sat strapped into their seats in the cabin. After three months of training on the ground, they had been chosen from the sixty candidates to be part of the first crew assigned to actual operations in space.

To Shui, the lift-off g-forces were not nearly as terrible as the tales said they would be. He even found a familiar comfort in them. It was the feeling of being held tightly in his mother's arms as a child. Outside the porthole to his upper right, the blue sky began to deepen. There was a faint pop of bolts blasting apart outside the cabin, and the booster rockets separated. As they left the rockets behind, the earsplitting roar of the engines became a mosquito-like drone. The sky faded to dark purple and then full black. The stars appeared, unblinking and intensely luminous.

The drone ceased abruptly, and silence fell over the cabin. The vibration of Shui's seat disappeared along with the pressure pinning his torso to the seatback. They had entered microgravity. Shui and the other spidermen had trained in a colossal swimming pool to prepare for weightlessness. It really did feel like he was floating in water.

But it was not yet safe to unfasten his seatbelt. The hum of the engine returned, and the shuttle's acceleration pressed the men back into their seats. The long maneuver into orbit had begun. The starry sky and the ocean appeared by turns in the tiny porthole. One moment the cabin flooded with the blue glow reflected by Earth, the next with the white light of the Sun. Each time Earth appeared in the porthole, the curvature of the horizon grew more conspicuous, and more of the planet's surface came into view. From start to finish, it took six hours to maneuver into geosynchronous orbit. The continuous alternation of sky and earth outside the porthole had a hypnotic effect on Shui, lulling him into an unexpected sleep. He was jarred awake by the commander's voice over the intercom. He informed them that the orbit insertion maneuver was complete.

One after another, his companions floated from their seats, pressing their faces to the viewing ports to peer outside. Shui unfastened his own seatbelt and, using swimming motions, floated clumsily through the air to the nearest porthole. For the first time, he saw Earth in its entirety with his own eyes. Most of the other men, however, had gathered in front of the viewing ports on the other side of the cabin. He pushed off against the bulkhead with his foot and shot across to join them. Unable to control his speed, he bumped his head on the opposite wall. As he gazed through a porthole, he realized the *Horizon* was already directly beneath the China Sun. The reflector took up most of the starry sky. Their space shuttle seemed like a small mosquito trapped under a silver dome. As the *Horizon* continued its approach, Shui gradually came to appreciate the sheer immensity of the reflector. Its mirrored surface occupied the entire view from the porthole, and its curvature was imperceptible, as if they were flying above a boundless silver plain. A reflection of the *Horizon* appeared on its surface as the distance continued to shrink. Shui could see long seams on the silver ground, which formed a grid like the latitude and longitude lines on a map. The grid was his sole reference point for judging the shuttle's relative velocity. After a time, the longitude lines no longer ran parallel. They began to converge in one direction, gradually at first and then more sharply, as if the *Horizon* was bound for a pole on this great map. Soon, the pole came into view. All of the longitudinal seams met at a small black dot. As the shuttle began its descent toward the dot, Shui realized with a start that it was actually a gigantic tower rising above the silver plain. He knew that this hermetically sealed cylinder was the China Sun Control Station. For the next three months, it would be their only home in the desolation of space.

*

And so the spidermen began their new lives in space. Every day – the China Sun orbited Earth once every twenty-four hours – they piloted small tractor-like machines onto the mirrored surface to polish it. They drove their tractors to and fro across the wide expanse of the reflector, as if they were tilling the silver earth. As a result, the Western media coined a more poetic name for the spidermen. They were now 'mirror farmers'.

The world in which these farmers lived was quite peculiar. A silver plain lay beneath their feet. Though the reflector's curved form caused the plain to rise slowly in the distance in every direction, it was so vast that it looked as flat and calm as still water. Overhead, both Earth and the Sun were visible. The latter appeared much smaller than Earth, as if it was the planet's radiant satellite. On the surface of the Earth, which occupied most of the sky, they could see a slowly moving circle of light. It was a particularly striking sight when it drifted onto the nighttime hemisphere. This was the region illuminated by the China Sun. The reflector could change the size of the light spot by adjusting its own shape. When the silver plain rose steeply in the distance, the spot grew smaller and brighter. When the slope was gentler, the spot grew larger and dimmer.

The work of the reflector cleaners was extremely difficult.

They soon realized that buffing the reflector was far more monotonous and draining than scrubbing skyscrapers on Earth. When they returned to the control station at the end of each day, they were often too exhausted to even take off their spacesuits. As more personnel arrived from Earth, the control station began to feel cramped, and they lived like crewmen aboard a submarine. Nonetheless, they considered themselves fortunate if they could return to the station at all. The most remote point on the reflector was nearly one hundred kilometers from the station. Cleaners working on the reflector's outer rim often could not make it back after a day on the job and had to spend the 'night' in the 'wilderness'. After suctioning a liquid dinner from their suit, they would fall asleep suspended in space.

The work was incredibly dangerous, to boot. Never before in the history of human spaceflight had so many people performed space walks. In the 'wilderness', the slightest malfunction in one's space suit could mean death. There were also micrometeorites, bits of space debris, and solar storms to worry about. The control station engineers carped bitterly about these living and working conditions, but the mirror farmers, who had been born into hardship, adapted to their new circumstances without complaint.

On his fifth day in space, Shui received a call from his family. He was working more than fifty kilometers away from the control station, and the China Sun had its beam trained on his home village.

He heard Pa's voice. 'Wah, are you on that sun? It's shining above our heads right now. The night is as bright as day!'

Shui replied, 'Yeah, Pa, I'm right above you.'

Then Ma spoke. 'Wah, is it hot up there?'

'You could say it's both hot and cold. Right now, everything outside of my shadow is hotter than ten summers in our village, but inside my shadow is colder than ten winters.'

'I can see our Wah,' Ma told Pa. 'That little black dot on the Sun right there!'

Shui knew this was impossible, but as tears rolled down his cheeks, he said, 'Pa, Ma, I can see you, too. There are two little black dots on the Asian continent where you are! Dress warmly tomorrow. I can see a cold front moving in from the north!'

*

Three months later, the second cleaning crew arrived to relieve the first of its duties, and Shui and his coworkers returned to Earth for three months' leave. After they landed, the first thing that every one of them did was buy a high-powered monocular telescope. When they returned to the China Sun three months later, they used their new purchases to observe the planet below during the breaks between work. They most often turned their lenses toward home, but at an altitude of nearly forty thousand kilometers it was impossible to see their villages. One of the men scrawled a simple, inelegant poem on the reflector with a felt-tip pen:

From this silver earth, I watch my distant home
On the edge of the village, my mother looks up at the
   China Sun
Its disc is the image of her son's eye
The yellow earth is clad in green under his gaze

The mirror farmers did an outstanding job. Over time, they began to take on responsibilities beyond the scope of their cleaning work. At first, they simply repaired damage done to the reflector by meteor strikes, but later they were tasked with more demanding work: monitoring and reinforcing sections at risk for overstress failure.

As the China Sun moved in orbit, it was constantly reorienting itself. These adjustments were made by three thousand engines distributed across the back face of the reflector. The actual mirrored surface of the reflector was very thin, and it was joined to the whole structure with a great number of slender beams. When the engines fired, parts of the reflector surface could become overstressed. If the engine outputs were not corrected in time, or the location was not reinforced, the unchecked overstress could tear the mirrored surface. Discovering and reinforcing stress points required both great technical skill and ample experience.

Apart from reorientation or reshaping periods, overstress was most likely to occur during an 'orbital haircut', or a 'Radiation Pressure and Solar Wind-Induced Drag Correction', as the operation was formally known. Together, solar wind and radiation exerted a significant force on the enormous surface of the reflector. Approximately two kilograms of pressure pushed against every square kilometer of the reflector, causing an outward drift in its orbit. The earthbound control center constantly monitored these changes, comparing the altered track to the intended orbit on a large screen. On screen, it looked as if long, wavy hairs were sprouting from the intended orbit, hence the curious nickname for the operation.

The reflector's acceleration was much greater during an orbital haircut than during reshaping or reorientation, and the work of the mirror farmers was critical during this period. Flying above the silver plain, they would scrutinize every anomaly on its surface and perform emergency reinforcements when necessary. They acquitted themselves splendidly and their salaries were raised accordingly. But the greatest beneficiary was Zhuang Yu, who rose to the highest office of the China Sun Project – without having to hire a single university graduate.

Nevertheless, it was clear to the mirror farmers that they would be the first and last group of workers in space to receive only a primary school education. Those who followed them would be university graduates at the very least. Still, they served the purpose envisioned by Zhuang. They had proven that skill, experience, and the ability to adapt to adverse circumstances were more important than knowledge and creativity in the blue-collar jobs created by space development. Ordinary people were fully up to the task.

However, space did alter the way the mirror farmers thought. No one else had the privilege of gazing down upon Earth from thirty-six thousand kilometers every day. With a glance, they could take in the whole planet. To them, the global village was no longer just a metaphor but a reality before their very eyes.

As the first laborers in space, the mirror farmers had been a global sensation, but the industrial development of near-Earth orbit was now in full swing. Mega-projects were commissioned, including vast solar power stations that beamed microwave energy down to the planet below, microgravity processing plants, and many others. Construction even began on an orbital city that could accommodate one hundred thousand residents. Industrial workers arrived in space in droves. They, too, were ordinary people, and so the world gradually forgot about the mirror farmers.

*

Several years passed. Shui bought a house in Beijing, married, and had a child. He spent half of every year at home, and the other half in space. He loved his job. His long patrols on that silver land more than thirty thousand kilometers above Earth filled his heart with detached peacefulness. He felt as though he had found his ideal life, and the future stretched before him as level and smooth as the silver plain underfoot. But then something happened that shattered his tranquility and thoroughly changed the course of his mental journey. Shui encountered Stephen Hawking.

No one had expected that Hawking would live to be one hundred. It was a medical miracle, but it was also a testament to his force of will. After the first low-gravity assisted living facility was constructed in near-Earth orbit, he became its first resident. However, the hypergravity of launch nearly claimed his life. Because he would have to endure the same forces during reentry, returning to Earth was out of the question, at least until the invention of a space elevator, antigravity cabin module or similar delivery vehicle. In fact, his doctors advised him to permanently settle in space, as the weightless environment perfectly suited his body.

At first, Hawking expressed little interest in the China Sun. Only a survey of anisotropy in the cosmic background radiation was sufficient to persuade him to subject himself to the g-forces generated by the trip from near-Earth orbit to geosynchronous orbit (though, of course, these forces were smaller than those he had experienced during launch). The observation station had been installed on the back face of the China Sun, as the reflector would block all interference from the Sun and Earth. But when the survey was complete, the observation station dismantled and the survey team withdrawn, Hawking did not want to leave. He said he liked it there and wished to stay a while longer. Something had drawn his attention to the China Sun. The press had a field day with speculations of all kinds, but only Shui knew the whole truth.

What Hawking enjoyed most about his life on the China Sun were his daily excursions across the surface of the reflector. To the consternation of many, he would simply drift along the underside of the reflector for several hours every day. Shui, who by now was the China Sun's most experienced spacewalker, was assigned to accompany the professor on his outings. At that time, Hawking's fame rivaled Einstein's – even Shui had heard of him. Nevertheless, Shui was shocked when they met for the first time in the control center. He had never imagined that someone with such a severe disability could achieve so much – not that he understood the great scientist's achievements in the slightest. On their excursions, however, Hawking betrayed no hint of his paralysis. Perhaps it was his experience controlling an electric wheelchair that allowed him to operate the micro-engines in his spacesuit as nimbly as any able-bodied person.

Hawking found it difficult to communicate with Shui. He did have an implant that allowed him to control a speech synthesizer with his brain waves, which made speaking less of a chore than it had been in the previous century. However, his words still had to be run through a device that provided real-time translation into Chinese so that Shui could understand him. Shui's superiors instructed him that he was never to initiate conversation with the professor in case he disturbed his thoughts. Hawking, however, was more than willing to talk to him.

He first asked Shui for an account of his life and then began to reminisce about his own early years. Hawking told Shui about his cold, sprawling childhood home in St Albans; in winter, the frigid, lofty parlor would ring with the music of Wagner. He told him about the Gypsy caravan his parents placed in a field at Osmington Mills, and how he and his younger sister Mary would ride it to the seashore. He talked about the times he and his father visited the Ivinghoe Beacon in the Chiltern Hills. Shui marveled at the centenarian's memory, but he was even more amazed that they shared a common vocabulary. The professor greatly enjoyed Shui's accounts of life in his home village. Floating on the outer rim of the reflector, he asked Shui to point out its location.

After a while, their conversations inevitably turned to science. Shui feared this would bring their discussions to an end, but it was not the case. For the professor, it was relaxing to discuss deep topics in physics and cosmology using language that even ordinary people could follow. He told Shui about the Big Bang, black holes, and quantum gravity. When Shui returned to the station, he began to wrestle with the thin little book Hawking had written in the previous century, consulting the station's engineers and scientists when he encountered something he did not understand. He grasped far more of its contents than anyone thought he would.

One day, the two men traveled to the outskirts of the reflector. 'Do you know why I like this place?' the professor asked Shui, facing a sliver of Earth visible beyond the rim of the reflector. 'This huge mirror separates us from Earth below. It lets me forget about the world and devote my entire focus to the cosmos.'

'The world below is complicated,' agreed Shui, 'but seen from so far away, the universe seems so simple, just stars scattered in space.'

'Yes, my boy, it does indeed,' said the professor.

Just like the reflector's front face, its back face was also mirrored. The only real difference was that it was dotted with the engines that adjusted the reflector's orientation and shape, which resembled small black towers. On their daily strolls, Shui and Hawking would leisurely float along, staying just above the ground. They often drifted all the way from the control station to the outer rim. When the Moon was not visible, the back face of the reflector was extremely dark, and its surface reflected the starlit sky. Compared to the front face, the horizon was closer here, and visibly curved. By the light of the stars, the black latitude and longitude lines formed by the support beams passed beneath their feet, as if they were skimming above the surface of a tiny, tranquil planet. Whenever the reflector was reoriented or reshaped, the engines on the back face would ignite. Illuminated by countless jets of flame, the surface of this tiny planet seemed even more beautiful and mysterious. And shining above, always, the Milky Way, bright and unwavering.

It was here that Shui first encountered the deepest secrets of the cosmos. He learned that the starry sky that filled his vision was but a speck of dust in the unimaginable vastness of the universe, and that this entire creation was nothing but the embers of a ten-billion-year-old explosion.

Many years ago, when he had taken his first step as a spiderman onto the roof of a skyscraper, Shui had seen all of Beijing. When he arrived on the China Sun, he had seen all of Earth. Now, Shui faced the third such glorious moment of his life. Standing on the roof of the cosmos, he could see things beyond his wildest dreams. Although he possessed only a superficial understanding of those distant worlds, they still held an irresistible attraction for him.

Once Shui expressed his confusion to an engineer in the

station. 'Humanity landed on the Moon in the sixties. And what next? Even now, we have not set foot on Mars. We don't even visit the Moon anymore.'

'Humans are practical creatures,' replied the engineer. 'What was driven by idealism and faith in the middle of the last century was not viable in the long term.'

'What's wrong with idealism and faith?'

'There's nothing wrong with them per se, but economic interests are better. If in the sixties humanity had spared no expense in the pursuit of spaceflight and racked up enormous losses, Earth might still be mired in poverty. Ordinary people like you and me would never have made it to space at all, even if we are no further than near-Earth orbit. Pal, don't let Hawking poison you. Normal folk shouldn't toy with the things he does.'

The conversation changed Shui. On the surface he appeared calm, working as hard as ever, but deep down he was contemplating new horizons.

*

Twenty years flew by. From an altitude of thirty-six thousand kilometers, Shui and his compatriots commanded a clear view of two decades of changes creeping across the globe. They watched as the Three-North Shelter Belt formed a verdant ribbon that traversed northwestern China, slowly turning the yellow desert green. Their home villages would never lack rain or snow again. The dry riverbeds on the outskirts of the villages flowed once more with clear, clean water.

The China Sun deserved the credit for all of this. It had played a major role in the great campaign to transform the climate of northwestern China. Not only that, it also performed a number of innovative extracurricular activities: once it melted the snows of Mount Kilimanjaro to ease a drought in Africa; on another occasion it turned an Olympic host city into a city that truly never slept.

But with the advent of newer technologies, the China Sun's methods of manipulating the weather began to seem clumsy and encumbered with too many side effects. The China Sun had accomplished its mission.

The Ministry of Space Industry held a grand ceremony to decorate the first group of industrial workers in orbit. They were honored not only for their twenty years of exceptional hard work, but more importantly, these sixty men were recognized for the singular accomplishment of entering space as youths with nothing but an elementary or middle-school education. In doing so, they had thrown the doors of space development wide open to everyone. Economists unanimously agreed that this had been the true beginning of the industrialization of space.

The ceremony attracted widespread attention from the press. In addition to the aforementioned reasons, the mirror farmers' story had acquired a legendary quality in the hearts of the public. It was also an excellent opportunity to indulge in nostalgia in an age where things were rapidly acquired and then forgotten.

Those simple and honest lads were already well into middle age, but they did not appear greatly changed. Audiences could still recognize them on their holographic television sets. Over the years most of the men had attained some form of higher education, and a few had even earned the title of space engineer. In their own eyes and the eyes of the public, however, they remained that same group of migrant laborers from the countryside.

Shui gave a speech on behalf of his companions. 'With the completion of the electromagnetic conveyor system, the cost of entering near-Earth orbit is only half the cost of a flight across the Pacific Ocean,' he said. 'Space travel has become an ordinary, unglamorous affair. New generations are hard-pressed to imagine what traveling to space meant to an ordinary person twenty years ago, how the opportunity would excite him, how it would make his blood boil. We were the lucky ones.

'We are ordinary men, and there is little to be said about us. Our extraordinary experience was entirely thanks to the China

Sun. Over the past twenty years, it has become our second home. In our hearts, it is like a miniature Earth. At first, we used the seams on the reflector's mirrored surface to represent the latitude and longitude lines of the northern hemisphere. When we marked our positions, we would specify our coordinates in degrees north and degrees east or west. Later, as we grew familiar with the reflector, we gradually blocked out the continents and oceans on it. We would say were in Beijing or Moscow. Each of our home villages had a corresponding position on the reflector's surface, and we cleaned those areas the hardest.'

Shui became momentarily lost in thought. 'We worked hard on that small, silver Earth, and we did our duty. All in all, five reflector cleaners gave their lives for the China Sun. Some had no time to take cover from solar magnetic storms, and others were hit by meteors or space debris. Soon, our silver world, where we lived and worked for two decades, will vanish. It is difficult to express our feelings in words.'

Shui fell silent. Zhuang, who had risen to the office of Minister for Space Industry, picked up the thread. 'I completely understand how you must feel, but I am pleased to be able to tell everyone that the China Sun will not disappear! As I expect you all know, such a massive object cannot be allowed to burn up in the atmosphere, as was common practice in the last century. But there is another, rather elegant, way to find the China Sun a final resting place. If we simply discontinue the orbital haircuts and make the appropriate adjustments to its orientation, solar wind and radiation pressure will accelerate it until it reaches the second cosmic velocity. In the end, it will escape Earth's orbit and become a satellite of the Sun. Perhaps, many years in the future, interplanetary spaceships will rediscover it. We could turn it into a museum and return to that silver plain and reminisce about these unforgettable years.'

Shui lit up with sudden excitement. 'Minister, do you really think that day will come?' he asked Zhuang in a loud voice. 'Do you really think there will be interplanetary spaceships?'

Zhuang stared at him, at a loss for words.

'In the middle of the last century,' Shui continued, 'when Armstrong left the very first footprint on the Moon, almost everyone believed that humanity would land on Mars within the next ten to twenty years. Now, many decades have passed. No one has returned to the Moon, let alone Mars. The reason is simple: it is a losing proposition.

'Since the end of the Cold War, economics has come to rule our day-by-day lives, and under its rule humanity has made great strides. Today, we have eliminated war and poverty and restored the environment. Truly, Earth is becoming a paradise. This has reinforced our belief in the efficiency of the economic principle. It has grown paramount, permeating our very DNA. There is no doubt human society has become an economic society. Never again will we undertake any endeavor that yields less than the investment it requires. The development of the Moon makes no economic sense, the large-scale manned exploration of the planets would qualify as an economic crime, and as for interstellar flight, that is downright lunacy! Now humanity knows only input, output and consumption.'

Zhuang nodded. 'In this century, human development of space has been confined to near-Earth space. That is a fact,' he said. 'There are many underlying reasons for it, but they are beyond the scope of today's topic.'

'No, they are well within it! We have been given an opportunity. If we just spend a little money, we can leave near-Earth space behind and embark on a great voyage into the cosmos. Just as solar radiation pressure can push the China Sun out of orbit around Earth, it can also push it to more distant places.'

Zhuang chuckled and shook his head. 'Oh, you mean to use the China Sun as a solar sail? That might work in the abstract. The body of the reflector is thin and light, and its surface area is large. After a long period of acceleration by radiation pressure, it would become the fastest spacecraft ever launched by humanity. However, I am only speaking in a theoretical sense.

In reality, a ship with only a sail cannot travel far. It needs a crew. An unmanned sailboat will only drift in circles on the ocean without ever sailing out of the harbor – I recall Stevenson's *Treasure Island* contained a particularly vivid description of such a ship. Returning from a long voyage by means of radiation pressure requires precise, complex control over the reflector's orientation. But the China Sun was designed to operate in orbit around Earth. Without human control, it will follow an aimless path as it drifts blindly through space, and it will not make it far.'

'Yes, but it will have a crew aboard. I will pilot it,' Shui replied calmly.

At that moment, the audience measurement system indicated that the channel's ratings had risen sharply. The eyes of the entire world were focused upon them.

'But you cannot control the China Sun by yourself. Its orientation controls require at least—'

'At least twelve people,' Shui interrupted. 'Taking other factors of interstellar travel into account, at least fifteen to twenty people. I believe we will have that many volunteers.'

Zhuang gave a helpless laugh. 'I truly did not expect that today's conversation would take this turn.'

'Minister Zhuang, over twenty years ago, you changed the course of my life on more than one occasion.'

'But I never, ever imagined you would travel so far, much further than I have.' Zhuang sighed deeply. 'Well, this is very interesting. Let us continue our discussion! Ah,' he said, frowning, 'I'm afraid your idea is not feasible. The most sensible target for the China Sun is Mars, but you have not considered that the China Sun cannot land. If you want to land, it will require a huge expenditure, and the plan will lose its economic viability. If you do not want to land, the whole endeavor is tantamount to launching an unmanned probe. What would be the point?'

'The China Sun is not bound for Mars.'

Zhuang looked at Shui, baffled. 'Then where? Jupiter?'

'Not Jupiter, either. Even farther afield.'

'Farther? To Neptune? Pluto?' Zhuang abruptly stopped. For a long while, he gazed at Shui in disbelief. 'My god, you don't mean to say—'

Shui nodded firmly. 'Yes, the China Sun will fly beyond the solar system and become the first interstellar spaceship!'

All around the world, people stared at their televisions with the same open-mouthed incredulity as Zhuang.

Zhuang stared straight ahead and nodded mechanically. 'Well, if you are not joking, let me make a quick estimate...' he said, his eyes half-closed as he began to do mental calculations. 'I have it figured out. Using solar radiation pressure, the China Sun would accelerate to one-tenth of the speed of light. Taking into account the time needed to accelerate, it would reach Proxima Centauri in forty-five years. The China Sun would then use the radiation pressure of Proxima Centauri to decelerate. After you complete a survey of the Alpha Centauri system, you would accelerate in the opposite direction, returning to the solar system after another few decades. It sounds like a marvelous plan, but in fact, it is a dream that cannot be realized.'

'Wrong again,' Shui replied. 'When we reach Proxima Centauri, the China Sun will not decelerate. We will skim by it at a speed of thirty-thousand kilometers per second, using its radiation pressure to accelerate even faster as we fly toward Sirius. If possible, we will continue to leapfrog through space, to a third star, a fourth...'

'What the hell is your game plan here?' Zhuang shouted, losing patience.

'All we ask of Earth is a highly reliable but small-scale ecological life support system—'

'And you would use this system to sustain the lives of twenty people for over a century?'

'Let me finish,' Shui replied. 'And a cryogenic hibernation system. We will spend most of the voyage in a dormant state, only powering up the life support system when we approach

Proxima Centauri. At the current level of technology, this should be enough to let us travel through the cosmos for over a thousand years. Of course, these two systems do not come cheap, but it will require just one-thousandth of the capital required to build a manned interstellar probe from scratch.'

'Even if you did not want a cent, the world cannot permit twenty people to commit suicide.'

'This is not suicide, it is exploration,' Shui countered. 'Maybe we will not even make it past the asteroid belt right in front of us, but maybe we will reach Sirius or beyond. If we do not try, how will we know?'

'But there is something that sets this expedition apart from exploration,' said Zhuang. 'There is no possibility of return.'

Shui nodded. 'Yes, we will not return. Some people are satisfied with a wife, children and a warm bed, never so much as glancing at the parts of the world that do not concern them. But some people will spend their whole lives trying to glimpse something humanity has never seen before. I have been both of these people, and I have the right to choose the life I want to lead,' he concluded. 'That includes living out my days on a mirror, drifting through space ten light-years away.'

'One final question,' Zhuang said. 'In one thousand years' time, as you race past stars at speeds of tens or hundreds of thousands of kilometers per second, it will take decades or even centuries for humanity to receive the weak radio signals you send out. Is it worth the sacrifice?'

With a smile, Shui announced to the whole world, 'As the China Sun flies beyond the solar system, humans will look away from all our creature comforts and up toward the starry sky again. We will recall our dream of space travel and rekindle our desire for interstellar exploration.'

Life Goal #6:

Fly to the stars, draw humanity's gaze back to the depths of the cosmos.

Zhuang stood on the roof of the Aerospace Tower and gazed at the China Sun as it moved swiftly through the sky. Its light caught the capital's high-rises and threw countless fast-moving shadows, as if Beijing was an upturned face following the China Sun.

This was the China Sun's last revolution around Earth. It had already reached escape velocity and would soon fly beyond the planet's gravitational field, entering into orbit around the Sun. There were twenty people aboard humanity's first manned interstellar spaceship. Besides Shui, the others had been selected from among more than one million volunteers. They included three other mirror farmers who had worked with Shui for many years. The China Sun had accomplished its goal before it ever began its journey. Humanity's enthusiasm for exploring beyond the solar system was reborn.

Zhuang's thoughts returned to that sultry summer night in that northwestern city twenty-three years ago, when he and a farm boy from the arid countryside had boarded the night train to Beijing.

In parting, the China Sun trained its spot of light on each major city in turn, giving humanity one last look at its radiance.

Finally, the spot of light came to rest on northwestern China. At its center lay the little village in which Shui had been born.

By the side of the road on the outskirts of town, Shui's parents stood together with their neighbors, watching the China Sun fly east.

Pa shouted into the phone, 'Wah, you are going somewhere far away?'

'Yeah, Pa,' Shui replied from space. 'I am afraid I will not come home.'

'Is it very far away?' Ma asked.

'Very far, Ma,' Shui answered.

'Farther than the Moon?' Pa asked.

Shui fell silent for a few seconds. Then, in a voice much lower than before, he said, 'Yeah, Pa, a little farther than the Moon.'

Shui's parents were not especially distraught. Their son was going to do great things at that place beyond the Moon! Besides, these were extraordinary times. Even from the remotest corners of the Earth, they could talk to him at any time, they could even see him on their little television. It was no different from speaking to him face-to-face. It did not occur to them that there would be an ever longer delay; that Shui's answers to their concerned questions would come slower and slower. At first, it would only be a few seconds, but the pauses would grow. In a year's time, every question would require hours for a response.

Finally, their son would vanish. They would be told that Shui had gone to sleep and that he would not wake for forty years.

After that, Shui's parents would continue to tend that plot of once-barren but now fertile land and live out the remainder of their once-backbreaking but now satisfying lives. Their last wish would be that, someday in the distant future, their son would return to see an even more beautiful homeland.

As the China Sun left Earth's orbit, it steadily dimmed in the eastern sky, its blue halo shrinking to a star-like point as it dissolved into the night. Then dawn arrived, and its light was completely swallowed by the glow of the morning Sun.

The morning Sun also shone down on the path that led out of the village. White poplars now lined the path, and a short distance away a small river ran parallel to it. On that day twenty-four years ago, in the small hours of the morning, under the same light of dawn, the son of northwestern peasants gradually disappeared into the distance on this very road, nursing vague hopes.

It was now broad daylight in Beijing, but Zhuang remained standing on the roof of the Aerospace Tower, gazing at the point where the China Sun had vanished. It had embarked on its endless voyage of no return. The China Sun would first pass Venus' orbit, getting as close as possible to the sun to boost radiation pressure and maximize the distance it had in which to accelerate. This would be realized through a complex series of orbital transfer maneuvers, much like the way ocean-going vessels of the Age of Navigation would tack and jibe upwind. After seventy days, it would pass Mars' orbit. After one hundred and sixty days, it would sweep by Jupiter. After two years, it would fly beyond Pluto's orbit and become an interstellar spaceship, and its crew would enter hibernation. After forty years, it would fly past Alpha Centauri, and its crew would briefly reawaken. One century after the China Sun began its journey, Earth would receive information obtained during their exploration of Alpha Centauri. By then, the China Sun would already be soaring toward Sirius. Thanks to the speed boost from Alpha Centauri's three suns, it would have reached fifteen percent of the speed of light. Another sixty years later, one hundred and sixty years after setting out from Earth, it would reach Sirius. After passing the binary star system formed by Sirius A and Sirius B, its speed would increase to twenty percent of the speed of light, and it would hurtle even deeper into the night sky. Given the limits of the onboard cryogenic hibernation system's lifespan, the China Sun might reach ε Eridani or – though the probability was quite small – even 79 Ceti. Both star systems were thought to harbor planets.

No one knew how far the China Sun would fly, or what strange worlds Shui and the others would behold. Perhaps one day they would send a message to Earth, but it would be over a thousand years before they received a reply.

No matter what happened, Shui would always remember a country called China on his mother planet. He would always remember a little village in that country's arid northwest. He would always remember the path that led out of that village, the path on which his journey began.

For the Benefit of Mankind

B usiness was business, nothing more, nothing less. This was the principle by which Smoothbore operated, but this partic-ular client had left him feeling bewildered.

First, the client had gone about the commission all wrong. He wanted to speak in person, which was extremely unusual in this line of business. Smoothbore remembered his instructor's repeated admonitions three decades prior: their relationship with clients should be like that of the forehead to the back of the skull; the two should never meet. This, of course, was in the best interest of both parties.

Smoothbore was even more surprised by the client's choice of meeting place. The opulent Presidential Hall in the most lux-urious five-star hotel in the city was a fucking spectacularly unsuitable venue for this sort of transaction. According to the other party, this contract would involve processing three units. This was no trouble – he did not mind a little extra work.

An attendant held open the gilded doors of the Presidential Hall. Before he entered, Smoothbore inconspicuously reached a hand into his jacket and gently undid the snaps on the hol-ster under his left armpit. In truth, it was unnecessary – no one would try to pull anything unexpected in a place like this.

The hall was resplendent in glittering greens and golds, a world apart from the reality outside. This world's sun was a massive crystal chandelier, shining down on an endless plain of scarlet carpet. At first glance the room seemed empty, but Smoothbore quickly spied its occupants clustered around two French windows in the corner of the hall, lifting the heavy curtains to look at the sky outside. He swept an eye over them and counted thirteen people. Smoothbore had anticipated a client, not clients. His instructor had also said that clients were like mistresses: you could have more than one, but you should never let them meet.

Smoothbore knew exactly what they were looking at: the Elder Brothers' spaceship. It had moved back over the southern hemisphere and was clearly visible in the sky. Three years had passed since the Creator civilization had left Earth. Their grand cosmic visit had drastically increased humanity's ability to mentally cope with alien civilizations. Moreover, the Creators' fleet of 20,000 spaceships had blotted out the sky, but only one ship from the Elder Brothers' world had arrived on Earth. It was not as bizarrely shaped as the spaceships of the Creators. Cylindrical with rounded ends, it looked like an intergalactic cold-relief capsule.

Seeing Smoothbore enter, the thirteen clients left the windows and returned to the large round table in the center of the hall. When Smoothbore recognized some of the faces around the room, the magnificent hall suddenly felt shabby. The most conspicuous among them was SinoSys Group's Zhu Hanyang, whose 'Orient-3000' operating system was replacing the outdated Windows OS worldwide. The others all ranked in the top fifty on a list of the world's wealthiest people. Their annual earnings were probably equivalent to the GDP of a middle-income country.

These people were nothing like Brother Teeth, thought Smoothbore. Brother Teeth had made his fortune overnight; these were dynastic heirs, the polished products of generations of wealth. They were the aristocrats of this age, utterly habituated to the wealth and power they wielded. It was just like the delicate diamond ring that sat on Zhu Hanyang's slender finger: it was barely visible but for the occasional glint of warm light, but it was easily worth a dozen times more than the shiny, walnut-sized golden baubles that adorned Brother Teeth's fingers.

But now, these thirteen financial princelings had assembled to hire a professional hitman to kill three people, and according to his contact this was only the first batch.

Smoothbore paid the diamond ring no attention. His eyes were fixed on the three photographs in Zhu's hand – clearly the units that required processing. Zhu leaned across the table and slid the photographs in front of him.

Glancing down, Smoothbore felt faint frustration creep in again. His instructor had said that in the area in which he did business, it was wise to familiarize himself with units who might conceivably be processed in the future. In this city, at least, Smoothbore had done just that. But Smoothbore was completely unable to identify the three faces in front of him. The photographs had been taken with a long-focus lens, and the disheveled and dirty subjects hardly seemed of the same species as the refined figures in front of him. Closer inspection revealed that one of the three faces belonged to a woman. She was still young, and her appearance was tidier than that of the others. Her hair, though coated with dust, was neatly combed. The look in her eyes was unusual. Smoothbore paid attention to people's expressions – people in this business always did. He usually saw one of two expressions: anxious desire or numbness. But her eyes were filled with rare serenity. Smoothbore's heart stirred faintly, but the feeling passed as quickly as it came, like a fine mist blown away on the wind.

'This is the task that the Council for Liquidation of Social Wealth entrusts to you. This is the standing committee of the Council, and I am its chairman,' said Zhu.

The Council for Liquidation of Social Wealth? It was a strange name. Apart from signifying an organization composed of the world's wealthiest individuals, Smoothbore could not ponder the implications of its name. Without further particulars, it was probably impossible to unravel its true purpose.

'Their locations are written on the back. They have no fixed addresses, so those are approximations. You will have to search for them, but they should not prove difficult to find. The money has already been wired to your account. Please verify the transfer,' instructed Zhu.

Looking up, Smoothbore found the expression on Zhu's face to be anything but noble. His eyes were dull and empty. Somewhat to Smoothbore's surprise, they held not even a trace of desire.

Smoothbore pulled out his cellphone and checked his account. After counting the long string of zeroes after the number, he said coolly: 'First, not so much. My original quote stands. Second, pay half up front, and half on completion.'

'Fine,' Zhu sniffed disapprovingly.

Smoothbore punched several keys. 'The excess funds have been returned. Please verify the transfer, sir. We, too, have professional standards.'

'Indeed. These days your line of work is oversubscribed. But we value your professionalism and sense of honor,' said Xu Xueping with a charming smile. She was the chief executive of Far Source Group, Asia's largest energy development entity born out of the full liberalization of the electric power market.

'This is the first order, so please handle it cleanly,' said the offshore oil baron Xue Tong.

'Fast cooling or delayed cooling?' asked Smoothbore, quickly adding, 'I can explain if necessary.'

'We understand, and it doesn't matter. Do as you see fit,' answered Zhu.

'Verification method? Video or physical specimen?'

'No need for either. Just complete the task – we have our own methods of checking.'

'Will that be all?'

'Yes, you may go.'

*

As he left the hotel, Smoothbore could see the Elder Brothers' spaceship passing slowly overhead in the narrow strips of sky between the towering buildings. The ship seemed larger than before, and its speed had increased. Evidently it had reduced the altitude of its orbit. The ship's smooth sides bloomed with slowly shifting iridescent patterns, producing a hypnotic effect on those who looked too long. In fact, the surface of the ship was a perfect mirror, and the patterns seen by observers on the ground were only the distorted reflections of Earth below. Smoothbore imagined the ship as purest silver, a thing of beauty in his eyes. He preferred silver to gold. Silver was quiet, cold.

Before their departure three years ago, the Creators told humanity that they had created six Earths in total; the four that now remained were within two hundred light-years of each other. They urged the people of Earth to devote their full efforts to technological development – we needed to eliminate our brother planets, lest we be destroyed ourselves.

But this warning came too late.

Locking their ship into orbit around Earth, emissaries from one of those three planets, the first Earth, arrived in the solar system not long after the departure of the Creators. The First Earth civilization was twice as old as mankind, and so the people of this Earth came to call them 'Elder Brothers'.

Smoothbore took out his cellphone and checked his account balance again. *Brother Teeth, I'm as rich as you now, but it still feels like I'm missing something. And you always thought you already had it all, and everything you did was only a desperate attempt to keep it.* He shook his head, as if to clear the dark cloud from his mind. It was an ill omen to think of Brother Teeth now.

*

Brother Teeth took his name from the saw that never left his side. The blade was thin and flexible, its serrations razor-sharp. The handle was carved from solid coral and decorated with beautiful *ukiyo-e* patterns. He kept the saw wrapped around his waist like a belt, and in idle moments he would unwind it and draw a violin bow across the back of the blade. By bending the blade and bowing across sections of different widths, he could produce haunting, melancholy music that hung in the air like the mournful cries of spirits. Of course, Smoothbore had heard tales of the saw's other application, but he had only seen Brother Teeth use it in action once. It was during a high-stakes game of dice in an old warehouse. Brother Teeth's second-in-command, a man named Half-Brick, had gambled big and lost everything, even his parents' house. With bloodshot eyes, he offered to put both his arms on the table in a double-or-nothing bet.

Brother Teeth rattled the dice and smiled at him. Half-Brick's arms, he said, were an unacceptable bet. After all, the future was long – and without hands, how could they play dice together?

'Bet your legs,' he said.

So Half-Brick had bet both his legs – and when he lost again, Brother Teeth unwound his saw and removed both of his legs where the calf met the knee.

Smoothbore distinctly remembered the sound of the sawblade as it carved through tendon and bone. Brother Teeth had placed a foot on Half-Brick's throat to muffle his hideous shrieks, and only the snarl of the blade on flesh echoed through the dark, cavernous warehouse. As the saw sang merrily across Half-Brick's knee caps, it produced a rich, resonant timbre. Fragments of snow-white bone lay scattered in a pool of bright red blood, forming a beautiful, even seductive, composition.

The strange beauty shook Smoothbore to his core. Every cell in his body was bewitched by the song of saw on flesh. *This* was fucking living! It had been his eighteenth birthday, and this was the best possible rite of passage.

When he was finished, Brother Teeth wiped the blood off his beloved saw and wrapped it around his waist once more. Half-Brick and his legs had already been carried away. Pointing at the trail of blood, he said, 'Tell Brick that I will provide for him from now on.'

Although Smoothbore was young, he had been a trusted member of Brother Teeth's entourage. Having followed the man in his rise to power from a very young age, he was no stranger to bloodshed. When Brother Teeth finally scraped together a fortune from the bloody gutters of society and sought to shift his business empire into more respectable channels, his most loyal retainers were dubbed Chairman of the Board, Vice President, and other such titles. Only Smoothbore was left to serve as Brother Teeth's bodyguard.

Those who knew Brother Teeth understood that the level of trust implied by this appointment was no small matter. The man was extraordinarily cautious, perhaps as a result of the fate that befell his godfather. Brother Teeth's godfather had also been extremely cautious; in Brother Teeth's words, the man would have wrapped himself in iron if given the opportunity. After many years without incident, he boarded a flight and took his assigned seat, flanked on either side by one of his most trusted bodyguards. When the plane landed in Zhuhai, the stewardess noticed the three men remained seated, as if lost in thought. A second look revealed that their blood had already trickled past more than ten rows. Long, micro-thin steel needles had been inserted through their seat backs, and the bodyguards had been impaled through the heart with three needles each. As for Brother Teeth's godfather, he had been pierced through with fourteen needles, like a butterfly carefully pinned and mounted in a specimen box. The number of needles was certainly some sort of message. Perhaps it hinted at fourteen million embezzled yuan, or the fourteen years his killer waited to take vengeance... Like his godfather before him, Brother Teeth's journey to the top had been eventful. Now, navigating society was like crossing a forest of hidden blades or a marsh cratered with pitfalls. He was truly placing his life into Smoothbore's hands.

But Smoothbore's new status soon came under threat with the arrival of Mr K. Mr K was Russian. At that time, it was the fashion among those who could afford it to employ ex-KGB officers as bodyguards. Having such a person in one's employ was something worth flaunting, like a movie star lover. Those who ran in Brother Teeth's circles struggled to pronounce his Russian name, and simply called the newcomer 'KGB'. Over time, they settled on Mr K. In reality, Mr K had no relation to the KGB. Most former KGB officers were cubicle-bound civil servants, and even those on the front lines of the secret conflict were untrained in the art of personal security. Instead, Mr K had worked in the Central Security Bureau of the Soviet Union, serving as bodyguard to Andrei Gromyko, the then Minister of Foreign Affairs known in the West as 'Mr Nyet'. He was every bit the genuine article, a true expert in keeping his clients breathing. Brother Teeth had hired him on a vice-chairman's salary not out of a desire to boast, but out of real concern for his own safety.

From the moment of Mr K's arrival, it was clear that he was utterly unlike other bodyguards. At the dinner table, other bodyguards would out-eat and out-drink their wealthy employers and felt perfectly comfortable interrupting their shop talk. When real danger reared its head, they would either charge in with all the art of a street thug or leave their client in the dust of their panicked retreat. In stark contrast, at banquets or negotiations, Mr K would stand quietly behind Brother Teeth, his hulking figure like an immovable wall, ready to intercept any potential threat. While Mr K never had the opportunity to protect his client in a crisis situation, his professionalism and dedication left no doubt that, should such a situation arise, he would fulfill his duties with consummate expertise. Smoothbore was more professional than the other bodyguards and did not share their obvious failings, but he was fully aware of the world of difference between himself and Mr K. For example, it was a long time before he realized that Mr K wore sunglasses at all hours of the day not to look cool, but to conceal his gaze.

Although Mr K picked up Chinese quickly, he kept aloof from the people in his employer's inner circles. He maintained this distance carefully, until one day he asked Smoothbore to step into his spartan room. After he poured two glasses of vodka, he told Smoothbore in stilted Chinese, 'I want to teach you to speak.'

'To speak?'

'A foreign language.'

So Smoothbore began to learn a foreign language from Mr K. He did not realize he was being taught English and not Russian until a few days later. Smoothbore was a quick learner, and when they could communicate in both English and Chinese Mr K told him, 'You are not like the others.'

'I know,' nodded Smoothbore.

'In my thirty years of experience, I have learned to accurately distinguish those people with potential from the rest. You are one such rare talent, and the first time I saw you it chilled me. It's easy to act in cold blood, but it's difficult to stay cold-blooded without ever thawing. You could become one of the best in this business, if you don't bury your talents.'

'What can I do?'

'First, study abroad.'

Brother Teeth agreed readily to Mr K's suggestion and promised to cover Smoothbore's expenses in full. He had hoped to rid himself of Smoothbore ever since Mr K's arrival, but there were no open positions in the company.

And so, one wintry night, this boy who had been orphaned at a young age and raised in the underbelly of society boarded a passenger jet bound for a strange and distant land.

*

Driving a rundown Santana, Smoothbore made his way across the city to inspect each of the locations written on the photographs. His first stop was Blossom Plaza. It did not take him long to find the man in the photo. He was rummaging through a garbage can when Smoothbore arrived, and after a few minutes he hauled his bulging trash bag to a nearby bench. His search had borne fruit in the form of a large and almost untouched takeout box, a pork sausage missing only a bite, several perfectly good slices of bread and half a bottle of cola. Smoothbore had expected him to eat with his hands, but he watched with surprise as the tramp pulled out a small aluminum spoon from the pocket of the dirty overcoat he wore despite the summer heat. He finished his dinner slowly and then threw what remained back into the garbage can. Looking around the plaza, Smoothbore saw the lights of the city begin to flicker on in all directions. He was very familiar with this area, but something felt off. In a flash, it occurred to him *why* the man had been able to leisurely eat his fill. The plaza was a common gathering place for the city's homeless population, but at that moment no one could be seen but his mark. Where had they gone? Had they all been processed?

Smoothbore drove on to the address on the second photograph. Under an overpass on the outskirts of the city, faint yellow light spilled out from a shack cobbled together from corrugated cardboard. Smoothbore cautiously pushed the busted door of the shack open just a crack. As he poked his head in, he suddenly found himself in a fantastical world of color. The walls of the shack were covered with oil paintings of all sizes, creating a separate wall of art. Smoothbore's eyes traced a wisp of smoke back to the itinerant artist, who lay splayed out beneath a broken easel like a bear in hibernation. His hair was long, and his paint-splattered T-shirt was so baggy it looked like a robe. He was smoking a cheap pack of jade butterfly cigarettes. His eyes roved over his artwork, and his gaze was filled with wonder and loss, as if he was seeing it for the first time. Smoothbore guessed most of his time was spent fawning over his own works. This particular breed of starving artist had been common in the nineties of the previous century, but nowadays they were few and far between.

'It's all right, come in,' said the artist, his eyes never leaving his paintings. His tone was more befitting of an imperial palace than a shack. As soon as Smoothbore stepped inside, he asked, 'Do you like my paintings?'

Smoothbore glanced around and saw that most of the paintings were just chaotic splotches of color – paint splashed directly onto a canvas would have seemed rational by comparison. But there were a few pictures in a very realistic style, and Smoothbore's eyes were quickly drawn to one of these: a canvas dominated by a cracked yellow earth. A few dead plants protruded from the fissures in the ground, looking as if they had withered away centuries ago, if indeed water had ever existed in this world at all. A skull lay on the parched earth. Though it was bleach-white and permeated with cracks, two green, living plants sprouted from its mouth and one eye-socket. In sharp contrast with the drought and death surrounding them, these plants were green and luxuriant, and a tiny, delicate flower crowned the tip of one sprout. The skull's other eye-socket contained a human eyeball. Its limpid pupil stared at the sky, and its gaze was filled with the same wonder and loss as that of its painter.

'I like this one,' Smoothbore said, pointing to the painting.

'It's called *Barren No. 2*. Will you buy it?'

'How much?'

'How much you got?'

Smoothbore pulled out his wallet and removed all the hundred-yuan notes it contained. He handed them to the artist, but the latter only took two bills.

'It's only worth this much. It's yours now.'

Smoothbore started the car and picked up the third photograph to study the last address. He cut the ignition a moment later, as his destination lay right alongside the overpass: the city's largest landfill. He took out his binoculars and peered through the windshield, searching for his mark amongst the scavengers clambering over the rubbish dump.

Three hundred thousand junkmen made a living off the garbage of the metropolis, forming their own class, complete with its own distinct castes. The highest-ranking junkmen could enter the city's ritzy villa districts. There, it was possible to pick a daily haul of shirts, socks and bed sheets, each used only once, from the delicately sculpted waste bins – in these neighborhoods, these were considered single-use goods. All kinds of things found their way into the garbage: lightly scuffed premium leather shoes and belts, half-smoked Havana cigars, expensive chocolate nibbled only at the corners... But picking garbage there necessitated hefty bribes to the residential security guards that only a few could afford, and those who could afford it became aristocrats among scavengers.

The middle ranks of junkmen gathered around the city's many waste transfer stations, the first collection stops for municipal waste. There, the most valuable refuse – waste electronics, scrap metal, intact paper products, discarded medical devices and expired pharmaceuticals – was quickly snapped up. These sites were not open to just anyone, however. Each station was the domain of a junk boss. Any scavenger who entered without their permission was harshly punished: perpetrators of minor offenses were violently beaten and driven off, while serious offenders could lose their lives.

Little of value remained in the waste that passed through the transfer stations to the rubbish dumps and landfills on the outskirts of the city, and yet it was this waste that supported the largest number of people. These were the lowliest of junkmen, the kind of people right in front of Smoothbore. Worthless, unrecyclable broken plastic and shredded paper was all that was left for the scavengers on the bottom rungs of junkman society. There were also scraps of rotten food, which could be gleaned from the rubbish and sold as pig feed to neighboring farms at ten yuan to the kilo. In the distance, the metropolis shone like a great brilliant jewel, its radiance casting a flickering halo over the fetid mountain of garbage. The junkmen experienced the luxury of the nearby city by sifting through its trash. Mingled in the rotten food, it was often possible to make out a roast suckling pig with only the legs eaten away, a barely-touched grouper, whole chickens... Recently, it had become common to find whole Silkie hens, owing to the popularity of a new dish called White Jade Chicken. The dish was prepared by slitting open the stomach of the chicken, filling it with tofu, and letting it simmer. The slices of tofu were the real delicacy; the chicken, while delicious, was merely casing. Like the reed leaves around rice dumplings, any diner foolish enough to eat the chicken itself would become the laughingstock of more discerning epicureans ...

The last garbage truck of the day pulled into the lot. As it tipped its load onto the ground, a group of junkmen scrambled to meet the avalanche of waste, quickly vanishing into the rising dust and debris. It was like they had passed into a new phase of evolution, unaffected by the stench of the garbage heap, the germs and the toxic filth. Of course, this was an illusion, maintained by people who only saw how they lived and not how they died. Like the corpses of insects and rats, the bodies of junkmen littered the landfill. They passed away quietly here, soon buried by new trash.

In the dim light emanating from the flood lamps at the edge of the lot, the junkmen appeared as dusty, indistinct shadows, but Smoothbore still swiftly located his mark among them. The speed with which he spotted her was due in part to his own keen vision, but there was also another reason: like the vagrants in Blossom Plaza, there were significantly fewer junkmen than usual on the landfill today. *What was going on?* Smoothbore observed his mark through his binoculars. At first glance, she seemed no different than any other scavenger. There was a rope tied around her waist, and she carried a large woven bag and a long-handled rake. She was perhaps a bit skinnier than the others. Unable to squeeze through the throng of junkmen, she could only scrounge along the periphery, sifting through the trash of the trash.

Smoothbore lowered the binoculars and thought for a moment, shaking his head slightly. Something truly fantastical was unfolding before him: a homeless man, an itinerant starving artist, and a girl who lived off garbage – three of the poorest, weakest people in the world – somehow posed a threat to the world's wealthiest and most powerful plutocrats. The threat was so great, in fact, that they felt compelled to hire a hitman to deal with the problem.

Barren No.2 lay on the back seat. In the dark, the skull's single eye bored into Smoothbore, like a thorn in his flesh.

There was a chorus of panicked cries from the landfill, and Smoothbore saw that the world outside his car was bathed in a blue light. The glow emanated from the east, where a blue sun was rapidly rising over the horizon. It was the Elder Brothers' spaceship, arriving in the Southern hemisphere. The spaceship did not typically emit light; at night, the sunlight reflecting off its sides made it shine like a small moon. But every so often it would suddenly illuminate the world in a bluish glow, thrusting humanity into nameless terror. This time, the spaceship's glow was brighter than ever before, perhaps because it was in a lower orbit than usual. The blue moon rose above the city, stretching the shadows of skyscrapers all the way to the landfill like the grasping arms of giants. As the spaceship continued its ascent, the shadows gradually shrank away.

The scavenger girl on the landfill was illuminated by the glow of the Elder Brothers' spaceship. Smoothbore raised his binoculars again and confirmed his earlier observations. She was indeed his mark. She knelt with her bag in her lap, the slightest trace of alarm in her upturned gaze, but she otherwise projected the same sort of serenity Smoothbore had seen in the photograph. Smoothbore's heart stirred again, but it was as fleeting as before. He knew it was a ripple of emotion from somewhere deep within his soul, and he regretted having lost it again.

The spaceship streaked across the sky and sank below the western horizon, leaving an eerie blue afterglow in the heavens.

The landfill settled back into darkness, and the lights of the city sparkled once more. Smoothbore's thoughts returned to the puzzle at hand: the thirteen wealthiest people on Earth desired to kill the three poorest people. It was beyond absurd, and any possible explanation escaped his imagination. But his mind had not strayed far before he slammed the brakes on his thoughts. He slapped the steering wheel in self-reproach as he suddenly realized he had violated the cardinal rule of his own profession. His tutor's words unfurled in his mind, laying out their profession's maxim: the gun does not care at whom it is aimed.

*

To this day, Smoothbore did not even know in which country he had studied abroad, much less the exact location of the academy. He knew only that the first leg of the trip was to Moscow. Upon arrival, he was met by several men who spoke English without a trace of a Russian accent. He was made to put on opaque sunglasses, and, disguised as a blind person, he passed the remainder of the journey in darkness. After another three-hour flight and a day's drive, he arrived at the academy, and Smoothbore could not say for certain that he was still in Russia at that point.

The academy was located deep in the mountains and bordered by high walls. Under no circumstances were students permitted to leave before graduation. After he was permitted to remove the sunglasses, Smoothbore discovered that the buildings of the academy were divided into two distinct styles: the first type of building was gray and devoid of any distinguishing features, and the second type was very peculiar in both shape and form. He later found out that the latter buildings were actually assembled from giant building blocks and could be reconfigured at will to simulate a myriad of combat environments. The entire institute was essentially one big state-of-the-art target range.

The convocation ceremony was the first and only time the student body would gather together, and their number just exceeded four hundred. The silver-haired principal, who had the commanding manner of a classical scholar, gave the following address:

'Students, over the next four years you will learn the theoretical knowledge and the practical skills required for our line of work – a line of work whose name we shall never speak aloud. It is one of humanity's most ancient professions, and it is a profession assured of a bright future. On a small scale, our work, and *only* our work, can resolve difficult problems for desperate clients; but on a large scale, our work can change history.

'In the past, various government organizations have offered us great sums of money to train guerilla fighters. We refused them all because we only train independent professionals. Yes, *independent*, from everything but money. After today, you must think of yourself as a gun. Your duty is to perform the function of a gun and to demonstrate its beauty in the process. A gun does not care at whom it is aimed. Person A raises his gun and shoots person B; B wrests the gun away and shoots A – the gun makes no distinction between the two and completes both assignments with the same level of excellence. This is the most basic principle of our profession.'

During the ceremony, Smoothbore also learned a few of the most common terms in his new profession: their fundamental business was called 'processing', their targets were 'units' or 'work', and death was 'cooling'.

The academy was divided into L, M and S disciplines, or long-, mid- and short-range. L discipline was the most mysterious and most expensive course of study. The few students who elected this specialty kept to themselves and rarely mixed with M and S students. Likewise, Smoothbore's instructors advised him and his classmates to keep their distance from L students: 'They are the nobility of this profession, as they are the most likely to change the course of history.'

The knowledge taught to L students was broad and profound, and the sniper rifles reserved for their use cost hundreds of thousands of dollars and were nearly two meters long when fully assembled. L specialists processed work at an average distance of one thousand meters, although it was said that some could hit their marks from three thousand meters away. Processing at distances over fifteen hundred meters was a complicated operation, and part of the preparatory work included placing a series of 'wind chimes' at set distances along the firing range. The ingeniously crafted micro-anemometers could wirelessly transmit data to goggles worn by the shooter, sharpening his (or her) understanding of wind speed and direction along the entire range of the shot.

M specialists processed work at a distance of ten to three hundred meters. It was the most traditional discipline and it boasted the largest number of students, who generally used standard-issue rifles. While there was rarely a shortage of work for M specialists, this discipline was considered pedestrian and rather lacking in mystique.

Smoothbore belonged to S discipline, learning to process work at a range of less than ten meters. This discipline lacked stringent weapons requirements, and S specialists typically used pistols or even blades and other melee weapons. Of the three specialties, S discipline was undoubtedly the most dangerous, but it was also the most romantic.

The principal was a master of this discipline, and he personally instructed S courses. But, to everyone's surprise, the first course he taught was English literature.

'You must first understand the value of S discipline,' the principal said gravely, gazing at the baffled students before him. 'In the L and M disciplines, the unit and the processor never meet, and the unit is processed and cooled without ever realizing its plight. A blessing for the unit, perhaps, but not necessarily for the client. Some clients need their targets to know who has marked them for processing and why, and it falls to us to inform them.

In that moment, we are not ourselves but an incarnation of the client. We must solemnly and perfectly communicate his or her final message to the unit, and thus inflict the maximum psychic shock and torment possible prior to cooling. This is the romance and beauty of S discipline – the look of terror and despair in the unit's eyes just before cooling. We can find no greater pleasure than this in our work; but to this end, we must cultivate our verbal dexterity and literary acumen.'

So, for one year, Smoothbore studied literature. He read Homer's epics, memorized Shakespeare and studied works by many other classical and contemporary authors. Smoothbore felt this was the most rewarding year of his overseas education. He was more or less familiar with the subjects that followed it, and if he did not master them at the institute he could learn them elsewhere. But this was his only chance to deeply engage with literature. Through literature, he rediscovered humanity, and he marveled at the subtleties of human nature. Before, killing had simply felt like smashing a crudely-made pot filled with red liquid; now, he was amazed to find that he had smashed exquisite jadeware, which only heightened the thrill of the act.

His next course of study was human anatomy. Compared to the other two disciplines, the other major advantage in S discipline was that it was possible to control the time needed to cool units during processing. The technical terms were 'fast cooling' and 'delayed cooling'. Many clients requested delayed cooling and a recording of the entire process – a treasured keepsake they could appreciate forever. Of course, this required precise technical skills and extensive experience, and knowledge of human anatomy was indispensable.

Then, his real courses began.

*

The junkmen on the landfill gradually dispersed until only his mark and a few others remained. Smoothbore decided then and there to process this unit by the end of the night. It went against standard practice to act during the initial observation period, but there were exceptions when a suitable opportunity for processing presented itself.

Smoothbore maneuvered his car out from under the overpass and jolted along the pot-holed road next to the landfill. He observed that any junkman leaving the landfill had to pass this way. The darkness revealed only the shadows of the wild grass swaying in the night breeze. It was an excellent location for processing, and he decided to wait there for the unit.

Smoothbore drew out his gun and placed it gently on the dashboard. It was an inelegant, 7.6 mm revolver that was chambered for large Black Star cartridges. He called it Snubnose because of its shape. He had purchased the privately-made, untraceable gun for three thousand yuan on the black market in Xishuangbanna. Although it looked crude, it was made well, and each component part had been machined with precision. Its biggest flaw was that the manufacturer had not bothered with rifling: the barrel walls were smooth metal. It was not as if Smoothbore was unable to procure better, name-brand firearms. Brother Teeth had equipped him with a thirty-two-round Uzi when he had started his body-guard career and had later gifted him a Type 77 as a birthday present. But Smoothbore had stuffed both guns in the bottom of his trunk, and he never carried them on his person. He simply preferred Snubnose. It glinted icily in the halo of the metropolis, drawing Smoothbore's thoughts back to his years at the academy.

On the first day of their real training, the principal made each student present his or her weapon. As he placed Snubnose in that line of finely-crafted pistols, Smoothbore had felt deeply embarrassed. The principal, however, picked up Snubnose, hefted it in his hand, and said with sincere admiration: 'This is a fine gun.'

'It doesn't have rifling, and you can't even attach a silencer,' sneered another student.

'Precision and range are of little importance to S specialists, and rifling even less so. And silencers? A small pillow will do the trick. Boy, do not allow yourself to be limited by stale convention. In the hands of a master, this gun can yield artistry that all your expensive toys cannot.'

The principal was right. Without rifling, bullets fired by Snubnose would turn somersaults in flight, emitting a shrill, terror-inducing whistle that ordinary bullets lacked. They would continue to spin even after striking their targets, like a rotary blade shredding everything in its path.

'From now on, we will call you Smoothbore!' said the headmaster, handing the gun back to its owner. 'Hold on to this, boy. It looks like you will have to study knife-throwing.'

Smoothbore immediately grasped the principal's meaning: an expert knife thrower held his knife by the blade as he threw it in order to build momentum through rotation, but this required that the knife arrive point-first as it reached its target. The principal hoped Smoothbore would learn to wield Snubnose as a knife thrower mastered his blades! Such artistry would give Smoothbore unprecedented control over the wounds Snubnose's tumbling bullets inflicted. After two years of bitter practice and nearly thirty thousand bullets, Smoothbore acquired a level of skill that was beyond even the academy's best firearms instructors.

During his studies abroad, Smoothbore became completely inseparable from Snubnose. In his fourth year, he became familiar with another student in his own discipline who went by the name of Fire, perhaps because of her mane of red hair. It was impossible to know her nationality, but Smoothbore guessed she came from Western Europe. There were few female students at the academy, and almost all of them were natural sharpshooters. Fire, however, had terrible aim, and her dagger skills were downright embarrassing. Smoothbore had no idea how she made a living before the academy. But in their first garroting class, she plucked a filament so fine it was nearly invisible from the delicate ring on her finger. She wrapped the razor wire around the neck of the goat being used as a teaching aid and, with a deftness that spoke of practice, neatly sliced its head off. Fire had called it a nanowire, a super-strong material that might be used to build space elevators in the future.

Fire felt no real affection for Smoothbore – that sort of thing was impossible at the academy. She also hung around Frost Wolf, a Nordic student from another discipline. She hopped back and forth between them like a fighting cricket, trying to instigate a bit of bloodshed to disrupt the monotony of student life. She soon succeeded, and the two men agreed to settle their feud with a game of Russian roulette. In the dead of night, their classmates reconfigured the enormous building blocks of the shooting range into the shape of the Coliseum. The duel was to commence in the center of the arena, and the weapon of choice was Snubnose.

Fire presided over the entire scene. With a graceful flourish, she inserted a single cartridge into Snubnose's empty cylinder. Then, holding the barrel, she rolled the cylinder across her pale, slender forearm a dozen times. After the two men politely declined their chance to go first, she smiled and handed the gun to Smoothbore. Smoothbore slowly raised the gun to his head. As the cool muzzle touched his temple, a wave of emptiness and isolation, stronger than anything he had ever felt, washed over him. He felt a formless, frigid wind sweep through the world, until his heart was the last speck of heat in a pitch-dark universe. He steeled his heart and pulled the trigger five times. The hammer fell five times. The cylinder turned five times. The gun did not fire.

Click click click click click – just like that, a crisp, metallic death knell sounded for Frost Wolf. A cheer rose from their classmates. Shedding tears of delight, Fire cried to Smoothbore that she was his. In the middle of all this, Frost Wolf stood with an easy smile on his face. He nodded towards Smoothbore and said with sincerity, 'You Oriental bastard, that was the most brilliant wager since the first Colt was made.' He turned to Fire, 'It's all right, my dear. Life was only ever a gamble anyway.'

He seized Snubnose and pointed it against his temple. With a muffled bang, blood and bone bloomed across the arena floor.

Smoothbore graduated not long after. Wearing the same dark glasses he wore when he arrived, he departed the nameless academy and returned to the place he grew up in. He never heard another word about the academy, and it was as if it had never really existed at all.

*

It was not until he returned to the outside world that Smoothbore heard the news: the Creators had arrived to claim the support of the human civilization they themselves had once fostered, but, unable to live comfortably on Earth, they left after only one year. Their fleet of twenty thousand ships had already vanished into the endless cosmos.

Smoothbore had barely stepped off the plane when he received his first processing order.

Brother Teeth warmly welcomed Smoothbore home with an extravagant banquet in his honor. Smoothbore asked to meet privately with him after dinner, saying he had many things he wanted to get off his chest. When everyone else had left, Smoothbore told Brother Teeth, 'I grew up at your side. In my heart, you have never been my brother, but rather my father. I ask you, should I practice the profession I have studied? Just say the word, and I will obey.'

Brother Teeth put his arm around Smoothbore's shoulder. 'If you like it, you should do it. I can tell you enjoy it. Don't worry about high roads and low roads – people with bright futures will do well whatever path they follow.'

'As you say.'

Smoothbore drew his pistol and fired into Brother Teeth's stomach. At just the right angle, the twisting bullets ripped a line across the man's abdomen and buried themselves into the floorboards. As the smoke cleared, Brother Teeth looked at Smoothbore. A flicker of shock registered in his eyes before it was replaced by the numbness that follows revelation. He laughed faintly and nodded.

'You've already made something of yourself, kid.' Brother Teeth spat blood as he spoke and sank gently to the ground.

Smoothbore's processing order had specified an hour of delayed cooling, but no recording. The client trusted him. He poured a glass of liquor and watched the blood pool around Brother Teeth with cold detachment. The dying man slowly rearranged his spilled intestines, as thoughtfully as if he were stacking mahjong tiles. As soon as he pushed them back into his abdomen, the slippery lengths slid right out again. Gingerly, Brother Teeth began to gather them up... As he repeated the process for the twelfth time, he gasped his last breath. Precisely one hour had passed since Snubnose had been fired.

Smoothbore had spoken truthfully when he said Brother Teeth was like a father to him. On a rainy day when he was five, Smoothbore's biological father, livid after a huge gambling loss, demanded that his mother relinquish every savings deposit book in the house. When she refused, he simply beat her to death. And when Smoothbore tried to block his father, the man broke his son's nose and arm and then vanished into the rain. Later, Smoothbore had searched far and wide for him without success. If he ever did find his father, the man had earned himself the pleasure of a slow cooling.

Smoothbore heard afterwards that Mr K had returned every penny of his salary to Brother Teeth's family and flown back to Russia. Before leaving, the Russian said that the day he sent Smoothbore to study abroad, he knew Brother Teeth would die by his hand. Brother Teeth had lived his life on a knife's edge, but he never understood what made a true killer.

*

One after another, the few remaining junkminers left the landfill until only Smoothbore's mark remained. She rooted through the garbage, buried in her work. She was too weak to claim a good spot when the trucks arrived, and she could only make up for it by working longer hours. Her persistence meant there was no need for Smoothbore to wait for her outside. Thrusting Snubnose into his jacket pocket, he left the car and headed straight for his mark on the garbage heap.

There was a sponginess and tepid warmth to the garbage underfoot, like he was walking on the body of some enormous beast. When he was within four or five meters of his target, Smoothbore drew his revolver from his pocket.

At that moment, a bolt of blue light shot up from the east. The Elder Brothers' spaceship had completed a full orbit around Earth and returned, still glowing, to the Southern hemisphere. The abrupt appearance of the blue sun drew the gaze of the two figures on the landfill. They studied the strange star for a moment and then glanced at each other. When their eyes met, Smoothbore did something no professional hitman should ever do: he nearly let his gun slip out of his hand. For an instant, the shock made him forget Snubnose even existed, and he almost cried out without thinking: Sweet Pea! – but Smoothbore knew it was not Sweet Pea. Fourteen years ago, he had watched Sweet Pea's agonizing death. But she had lived on in Smoothbore's heart, growing older and stronger. He often saw her in his dreams, and he imagined she would look just like the young woman in front of him now.

In his upstart years, Brother Teeth had dealt in an unspeakable trade: he purchased disabled children from the hands of human traffickers and put them to work in the city as beggars. In those years, the public had not yet exhausted its compassion, and the children proved quite profitable, playing no small part in Brother Teeth's accumulation of seed capital.

Once, Smoothbore accompanied Brother Teeth to receive a new group of children from a trafficker. When they arrived at the old warehouse, they found five children waiting there. Four of them suffered from congenital conditions, but one little girl was completely healthy. Sweet Pea was six years old and adorable. In stark contrast to the children around her, her big, wide eyes were still full of life. Smoothbore's heart broke as he recalled those eyes and the curiosity with which the little girl examined everything around her, totally unaware of the fate that awaited her.

'That's them,' said the trafficker, pointing at the four physically disabled children.

'I thought we agreed on five?' asked Brother Teeth.

'The carriage was packed. One of them didn't make it.'

'What about this one?' Brother Teeth pointed at Sweet Pea.

'She's not for sale.'

'I want her. Same price as the others.' The tone in his voice brooked no argument.

'But... she's perfectly fine. How will you make money with her?'

'You ass. A few finishing touches will do it.'

As Brother Teeth spoke, he unwound his saw from his waist and drew it across one of Sweet Pea's delicate calves, opening a gaping wound on the girl's leg. Blood gushed out and Sweet Pea shrieked and shrieked.

'Bind it up and stop the bleeding, but don't give her antibiotics. It needs to fester,' Brother Teeth instructed Smoothbore.

So Smoothbore bandaged the Sweet Pea's wound, but the blood continued to seep through the layers of gauze, and the little girl's face grew deathly pale. He snuck her a few doses of Erythromycin and Sulfamethoxazole behind Brother Teeth's back, but it was no use. Sweet Pea's wound grew infected.

Two days later, Brother Teeth sent Sweet Pea to beg on the streets. The effect produced by her pathetic expression and maimed leg immediately exceeded Brother Teeth's expectations. On the very first day she earned three thousand yuan, and over the week that followed she never brought in less than two thousand per day. On her last day on the street, a foreign couple took one glance at her and handed her four hundred US dollars.

Despite this, Sweet Pea was rewarded with only a single box of spoiled food per day. This was not just miserliness on the part of Brother Teeth; it was also a deliberate way to preserve the child's starved appearance. Smoothbore could only give her scraps under the cover of darkness.

One evening, as Smoothbore went to retrieve Sweet Pea from the curbside on which she begged, the little girl leaned close to his ear and whispered, 'Brother, my leg doesn't hurt anymore.' She looked cheerful about this.

Except for his mother's death, this was the only time Smoothbore could remember crying. Sweet Pea's leg did not trouble her because the nerves were dead. Her entire leg had turned black, and she had run a high fever for the past two days. Smoothbore could not bear to follow Brother Teeth's orders any longer, and he carried Sweet Pea to the hospital. The doctors informed him that it was already too late: the girl had blood poisoning. She passed away late the next night, consumed by fever.

From that moment on, Smoothbore's blood ran cold, and just as Mr K predicted, it never warmed again. Killing others became a pleasure for Smoothbore, more addictive than any drug. He lived to smash the delicate jade vessels called 'humans', to watch the red liquid contained within gush out and cool to room temperature. That alone was the truth – that any warmth in that liquid was only ever a charade.

Without conscious intent, Smoothbore had burned a pixel-perfect image of the gash on Sweet Pea's leg into his memory. Later, the image had manifested itself on Brother Teeth's torn abdomen, a precise copy of the original wound.

*

The junkminer stood, slung her oversized sack over her shoulder and slowly turned to leave. It was not Smoothbore's arrival that prompted her departure. She had not noticed what he held in his hand, and she could not imagine that this well-dressed man might have any connection to herself. It was simply time for her to go. As the Elder Brothers' ship sank below the western horizon, Smoothbore stood motionless on the landfill, watching her figure vanish into the fading blue twilight.

Smoothbore returned his gun to its holster. He drew out his cellphone and dialed Zhu Hanyang's number: 'I want to meet with you. There is something I need to ask.'

'Nine o'clock tomorrow, same place.' Zhu Hanyang's answer was unfazed and concise, as if he had expected Smoothbore's call.

*

As he entered the Presidential Hall, Smoothbore discovered that the entire thirteen-person standing committee of the Council for Liquidation of Social Wealth was already assembled there, their stern gazes focused upon his own person.

'Please ask what you came to ask,' said Zhu Hanyang.

'Why do you want to kill these three people?' asked Smoothbore.

'You have violated the ethics of your profession,' Zhu observed drily, slicing the cap off a cigar with an elegant cigar cutter.

'Yes, and it will cost me. But I need to know the reason, or I cannot do this job.'

Zhu lit the cigar with a long match and nodded slowly: 'I cannot help but think that you only accept work that targets the wealthy. If this is the case, then you are not a true professional hitman, just a thug with a penchant for petty class vengeance – a psychopath who has killed forty-one people in three years, who is being desperately pursued by the police at this very moment. Your reputation will come crashing down around you.'

'You could call the police right now,' Smoothbore replied calmly.

'Has this task touched upon a bit of personal history?' asked Xu Xueping.

Smoothbore could not help but admire her keen insight. His silence answered for him.

'Was it the woman?'

Smoothbore did not reply. The conversation had veered too far off course.

'Very well.' Zhu exhaled a lungful of white smoke. 'This task is important, and we cannot find anyone more suited to it on such short notice. We have no choice but to accept your terms and tell you the reason, but know that it will exceed your wildest dreams. We, the wealthiest few in this society, desire to kill its poorest and weakest members, and this has made us deranged, hateful creatures in your eyes. Before we explain our motivations, we must first correct this impression.'

'I'm not interested in issues of light and dark.'

'But the facts say otherwise. Come with us, please.' Tossing away his barely smoked cigar, Zhu stood and walked out of the room.

Smoothbore exited the hotel in the company of the full standing committee of the Council for Liquidation of Social Wealth. Something strange was occurring overhead, and pedestrians anxiously craned their heads towards the sky. The Elder Brothers' spaceship was sweeping past in low orbit. In the light of the rising sun, it seemed especially visible against the early morning skies. The ship scattered a trail of shining silver stars in its wake, which stretched behind it to the horizon. The ship's length had shortened significantly, and as it released star after star its bulk grew jagged, like a broken stick. Smoothbore had learned from the news that the Elder Brothers' enormous spaceship was actually assembled from thousands of smaller vessels. Now it seemed that the composite whole was splitting apart into an armada.

'Attention, everyone!' Zhu beckoned to the committee. 'You can see the situation has developed, and there may not be much time. We must accelerate our efforts. Each team should report immediately to their assigned liquidation area and continue yesterday's work.'

As he finished, he and Xu Xueping climbed into a truck and called for Smoothbore to join them.

Only then did Smoothbore notice that the vehicles waiting outside the hotel were not the billionaires' usual limousines but a line of Isuzu trucks.

'So we can transport more cargo,' explained Xu, reading the confusion on Smoothbore's face. Smoothbore looked into the bed of the truck and saw that it was neatly packed with small, identical black suitcases. The cases looked elegant and expensive, and he estimated there were over a hundred of them.

There was no hired driver, and Zhu himself pulled the vehicle out onto the main road. The truck soon turned onto a tree-lined avenue and reduced its speed. Smoothbore realized that Zhu was driving slowly alongside a pedestrian – a vagrant. Although in this day and age the homeless did not necessarily dress in rags, there was always something that gave them away. This man had tied a plastic bag around his waist, and its contents rattled with every step.

Smoothbore knew that the mystery behind the vanishing homeless and junkmen was about to unravel, but he did not believe Zhu and Xu would dare to kill the man right here. In all likelihood, they would first lure their target into the truck and dispose of him at another location. Given their status, it was wholly unnecessary for them to dirty their hands with this sort of work. Perhaps they were setting an example for him? Smoothbore had no inclination to interrupt them, but he certainly would not help them either. This was not in his contract.

The tramp was quite unconscious of the fact that the truck had slowed for him until Xu Xueping called out to him.

'Hello!' said Xu, rolling down the window. The man stopped and turned his head to look at her. His face had the anesthetized look common among his class. 'Do you have a place to live?' Xu asked, smiling.

'In the summer, I can live anywhere,' said the man.

'And in the winter?'

'Hot air vents. Some restrooms are heated, too.'

'How long have you lived like this?'

'Don't really remember. Came to the city after my land requisition payments ran out, lived like this ever since.'

'Would you like a three-bedroom house in the city? A home?'

The tramp stared blankly at the billionaire. There was not an inkling of comprehension on his face.

'Can you read?' asked Xu. After the man nodded, she pointed to a large billboard in front of the truck. 'Look over there.' The billboard displayed a grassy knoll dotted with cream-colored buildings, like an idyllic paradise. 'That's an advertisement for commercial housing.' The man turned his head to the billboard, and then looked back at Xu. He did not have the faintest clue what she meant. 'Okay, now take a case from the truck.'

He obediently walked to the rear of the truck, picked out a case and walked back to the passenger door. Pointing at the case, Xu told him, 'Inside is one million yuan. Use five hundred thousand to buy yourself a house like the ones on the billboard, and use the rest to live in comfort. Of course, if you can't spend all that money yourself, you can do what we're doing and give it to someone poorer.'

The tramp's eyes moved back and forth rapidly, but he remained expressionless and did not let go of the box. He knew there had to be a catch.

'Open it and see for yourself.'

He fumbled at the lid with one grimy hand. He opened the case just a crack and then snapped it shut again, the mask of apathy frozen on his face finally shattered. He looked like he had seen a ghost.

'Do you have an ID card?' Zhu Hanyang asked.

The man nodded mechanically, holding the case as far away from himself as possible, as if it were a bomb.

'Then make a deposit at the bank. It'll be more convenient.'

'What do you want me to do?' asked the tramp hesitantly.

'We just need you to do us one little favor: the aliens are coming. If they ask you, tell them you have this much money. That's all. Can you promise to do this?'

The man nodded.

Xu stepped down from the truck and bowed deeply to the tramp. 'Thank you.'

'Thank you,' added Zhu from the truck.

What shocked Smoothbore most was that their gratitude seemed *sincere*.

They drove on, losing sight of the newly-minted millionaire in the rearview windows. Not far down the road, the truck stopped at a corner. Smoothbore spotted three migrant day-laborers squatting on the curb, waiting for work. Each man had a small metal trowel, and a small cardboard sign on the ground read: 'Scrapers.' The three men ran over as soon as the truck pulled up and clamored for work: 'Got a job for us, boss?'

Zhu Hanyang shook his head. 'No. Has business been good lately?'

'No business to be had. Everybody uses that new thermal spray coating nowadays; no need for scrapers anymore.'

'Where are you from?'

'Henan.'

Zhu rattled off several questions: 'The same village? Is it poor? How many households?'

'It's up in the hills, there are maybe fifty families. Everyone's poor. It never rains. Boss, you wouldn't believe it – we have to irrigate our plants one by one with a watering can.'

'Don't bother with farming. Do you have bank accounts?'

All three shook their heads.

'You'll have to take cash, then. They're heavy, but I'll still trouble you to take a dozen cases from the back.'

'A dozen?' It was the scrapers' only question as they unloaded the cases from the bed of the truck and piled them on the side-walk. They did not pause to consider Zhu's instructions – work was work.

'It doesn't matter, take as many as you like.'

Fifteen cases soon lay on the ground. Pointing to the stack, Zhu told them, 'Each box contains one million yuan – fifteen million in total. Go home and share the money with your whole village.'

One of the men laughed at this, as if Zhu had cracked a joke. One of his companions crouched down and opened one of the cases. The men stared at its contents, the same flabbergasted expression as the tramp's creeping over their faces.

'The cases are heavy, so you should hire a car to return to Henan. Actually, if one of you can drive, buy a car. It will be more convenient,' said Xu Xueping.

The three scrapers gaped at the two people in front of them, unsure if they were angels or devils. Like clockwork, one of the men raised the same question as the tramp before him: 'What do you want with us?'

The answer was the same: 'We just need you to do us one little favor: the aliens are coming. If they ask you, tell them you have this much money. That's all. Can you promise to do this?'

The three men nodded in assent.

'Thank you.'

'Thank you.' The two plutocrats bowed in sincere appreciation and drove off, leaving the three baffled scrapers standing next to the stack of cases.

'You must be wondering if they will keep the money for themselves,' Zhu said to Smoothbore, his eyes still on the steering wheel. 'Perhaps in the beginning, but they will soon share their wealth with the less fortunate, just as we have done.'

Smoothbore kept silent. Confronted with such absurdity, he felt it was best to say nothing at all. His intuition told him that the world as he knew it was about to undergo a fundamental change.

'Stop the car!' cried Xu. She called to a small, filthy child who was rummaging through a trash can for tin cans and cola bottles: 'Kid, come here!' The urchin dashed over, dragging his half-filled sack of cans and bottles behind him as if afraid of losing it. 'Take a case from the truck bed.' The boy obliged. 'Look inside.' He opened the case and peered inside. He was surprised, but not as shocked as the four adults had been. 'What is it?' prompted Xu.

'Money,' replied the boy, lifting his head to gaze at her.

'One million yuan. Take it home and give it to your parents.'

'So it's true?' The boy blinked, turning his head to look at the boxes still stacked high in the truck bed.

'What do you mean?'

'I heard people were giving away money all over the city.'

Like throwing away scrap paper, thought Smoothbore. Xu continued: 'You have to promise something before you can keep it. The aliens are coming. If they ask you, you must tell them you have this much money – exactly this much money, okay? That's all we want. Will you do it?'

'Yes!'

'Then take your money and go home, boy. No one will ever be poor again,' said Zhu as he started the truck.

'No one will ever be rich again, either,' said Xu, a dark look on her face.

'Pull yourself together. It's a bad situation, but we have a responsibility to stop it from getting worse,' said Zhu.

'You really think there is a point to this little game of ours?'

Zhu slammed the brakes and brought the truck to a lurching halt. Gesticulating wildly over the steering wheel, he shouted, 'Yes, *of course* it has a point! Or do you *want* to live the rest of your life like these people? Starving and homeless?'

'I don't even want to go on living anymore.'

'Your sense of duty will sustain you. In these dark days, it's the only thing that keeps me going. Our wealth demands that we devote ourselves to this mission.'

'Our wealth *what*?' shrieked Xu. 'We never stole, we never coerced, every yuan we earned was *clean*. Our wealth pushed society forward. Society should thank us!'

'Try telling that to the Elder Brothers,' said Zhu, stepping down from the truck. He tilted his face to the sky and heaved a long sigh.

'Now do you see that we're not psycho killers with a grudge against the poor?' The question was addressed to Smoothbore, who had followed him outside. 'No, on the contrary, we've been spreading our wealth amongst the very poorest, like you just witnessed. In this city and many others, in our nation's most impoverished areas, the employees of our companies are doing the same thing. They are utilizing every resource available to our conglomerate – billions of checks, credit cards, savings accounts, truckload upon truckload of cash – to eliminate poverty.'

Just then, Smoothbore noticed the curious spectacle in the sky: the line of silver stars now stretched from one horizon to the other. The Elder Brothers' mothership had completely disintegrated, and thousands of smaller ships had formed a gleaming halo around Earth.

'Earth is surrounded,' said Zhu. 'Each of those ships is the size of an aircraft carrier, and the weapons of just one of them could destroy the whole planet.'

'Last night, they destroyed Australia,' interjected Xu.

'Destroyed? What do you mean destroyed?' asked Smoothbore, his head craning towards the sky.

'They swept a laser over the Australian continent from space. It pierced right through buildings and bunkers, and every human and large mammal was dead within the hour. Insects and plants were left unscathed, though, and porcelain in shop windows wasn't so much as scratched.'

Smoothbore glanced momentarily at Xu and then turned his gaze back to the sky. He was better equipped to deal with this sort of terror than most.

'It was a show of force. They chose Australia because it was the first country to explicitly reject the 'reservation' plan,' added Zhu.

'What plan is that?' Smoothbore asked.

'Let me start from the beginning,' began Zhu. 'The Elder Brothers have come to our solar system as refugees, unable to survive on First Earth. 'We have lost our homeland'— those were the words they used. They have not elaborated on the causes. They want to occupy our Earth, Fourth Earth, and use it as a new habitat. As for this Earth's inhabitants, they will be relocated to a human 'reservation', located in what used to be Australia. Every other territory will belong to the Elder Brothers... An anouncement will be made in tonight's news.'

'*Australia?* It's a big chunk of rock in the middle of the ocean.' Smoothbore considered it for a moment. 'Actually, it *is* pretty suitable. The Australian outback is one big desert – if they squeeze five billion people on the island, starvation will set in before the week is out.'

'Things aren't that bleak. Human agriculture and industry will not exist on the reservation. There will be no need to engage in production to survive.'

'How will they live?'

'The Elder Brothers will support us – they will provide for humanity. In the future, everything humans need to live will be provided by the Elder Brothers and distributed evenly among us. Every person will receive the same amount. In the future, wealth inequality will cease to exist in human society.'

'But how will they determine how much to allocate each person?'

'You've grasped the key issue at hand,' replied Zhu. 'According to the reservation plan, the Elder Brothers will conduct a comprehensive census of humanity, the goal of which is to determine the absolute minimum standard of living that humans can tolerate. The Elder Brothers will then allocate resources according to the results.'

Smoothbore lowered his head and thought for a moment, and then suddenly chuckled, 'I think I get it. At least, I think I see the big picture now.'

'You understand the plight that humanity currently faces?'

'Actually, the Elder Brothers' plan is very fair to humanity.'

'What? You think it's fair?! You—' Xu sputtered.

'He's right, it is fair,' Zhu calmly interrupted. 'If there is no gap between poor and rich, no difference between the lowest and highest standards of living, then the reservation will be paradise on Earth.'

'But now...'

'Now, what we must do is simple: before the Elder Brothers conduct their census, we must rapidly level the sharp divide between rich and poor.'

'So this is 'social wealth liquidation'?' asked Smoothbore.

'Precisely. At present, society's wealth has solidified. It has its ups and downs, like the high-rises on this street or a mountain towering over a plain. But once it has been liquefied, it will become like the smooth surface of the ocean.'

'But what you are doing now will only create chaos.'

'True,' nodded Zhu. 'We are merely making a gesture of goodwill on behalf of people of means. The real liquidation of wealth will soon commence under the unified leadership of national governments and the United Nations. A sweeping campaign to eliminate poverty is about to begin. Rich countries will pour capital into the developing world, rich people will shower the poor with money – and it will be carried out with perfect sincerity.'

Smoothbore gave a cynical laugh. 'Things may not be that simple.'

'What do you mean, you bastard?' Xu snarled through clenched teeth. She jabbed a finger at Smoothbore's nose, but Zhu instantly stopped her.

'He's a smart fellow. He figured it out,' said Zhu, tilting his head in Smoothbore's direction.

'Yes, I have figured it out. There are poor people who don't want your money.'

Xu glowered at Smoothbore, then she lowered her head and fell silent. Zhu nodded. 'Right. There are those who do not want money. Can you imagine? Scrounging in the garbage for scraps of food, but refusing an offer of one million yuan? Yes, you hit the nail on the head.'

'But those people must surely be a tiny minority,' said Smoothbore.

'Of course, but even if they account for just one in every

hundred thousand poor people, they will be counted as a separate social class. According to the Elder Brothers' advanced survey methods, their standard of living will be identified as humanity's minimum standard of living, which in turn will be adopted as the criterion for the Elder Brothers' resource allocation to the reservation! Do you get it? Just one thousandth of one percent!'

'What percentage of the population do they account for at present?'

'About one in every thousand.'

'Perverted, despicable traitors!' Xu cursed loudly at the sky.

'So you contracted me to kill them.' At the moment, Smoothbore did not feel like using professional jargon.

Zhu nodded.

Smoothbore stared at Zhu with a queer expression, and then threw his head back and burst into laughter. 'I'm killing for the benefit of humankind!'

'You are benefiting humanity. You are rescuing human civilization.'

'Actually,' mused Smoothbore, 'death threats would do the trick.'

'That's no guarantee!' Xu leaned towards Smoothbore and whispered in a low voice. 'We are dealing with lunatics, twisted with class hatred. Even if they did take the money, they would still swear to the Elder Brothers that they were penniless. We have to wipe them off the planet as soon as possible.'

'I understand,' nodded Smoothbore.

'So what's your plan now? We have explained our reasoning just as you asked us. Of course, money will soon be meaningless, and you certainly don't care about helping humanity.'

'Money was never of great concern to me, and I've never considered the latter... But I will fulfill the contract – by midnight tonight. Please prepare whatever you need to verify its completion.' As he finished speaking, Smoothbore stepped down from the truck and began to leave.

'I have one question,' Zhu called after Smoothbore's retreating back. 'Perhaps it's impolite, so you don't have to answer. If you were poor, would you refuse our money?'

'I am not poor,' Smoothbore answered, without looking back. He took a few more steps, and then paused and turned. He fixed the pair with a hawkish gaze. 'If were... then yes, I would not take it.' Then he strode away.

*

'Why did you refuse their money?' Smoothbore asked his first mark. He had last seen the homeless man in Blossom Plaza; now, they stood in a grove of trees in a nearby park. Two types of light filtered through the canopy. The first was the eerie blue glow that emanated from the ring of the Elder Brothers' ships, casting dappled shadows across the ground. The second was the shifting, kaleidoscopic brilliance of the metropolis itself, wavering wildly as it slanted through the trees, as if terrified of the blue glow.

The tramp snickered. 'They were begging me. All those rich people were begging *me!* One woman even cried! If I took their money, they wouldn't care about me, and it felt so refreshing to *be* begged for a change.'

'Yes, very refreshing,' said Smoothbore, as he pulled Snubnose's trigger.

The tramp was an enterprising thief. He had seen at a glance that the man who had called him into the grove was holding something wrapped beneath his coat, and he was curious to discover what it was. He saw a sudden flash from beneath the man's coat, like the wink of some strange creature within, and he was plunged into endless darkness.

The job was processed and cooled almost instantly. The rapidly spinning bullet severed most of the unit's head above the brow. The gunshot was muffled under layers of clothing. No one noticed.

*

Returning to the landfill, Smoothbore discovered that only his next mark remained – the other junkmen had evidently claimed their new fortunes and left.

Under the blue light of the ring of starships, Smoothbore picked his way across the warm, springy waste heap with purposeful strides, heading straight for his target. He had reminded himself a hundred times beforehand that this was not Sweet Pea, and there was no need to repeat the warning again. His blood ran cold, and it would not be warmed by a handful of youthful memories. The scavenger girl had not even noticed his arrival when Smoothbore fired his gun. There was no need to silence his weapon on the landfill. Freed from his coat, the shot rang clear, and the flash lit up the garbage around him like a small bolt of lightning. The range gave the bullet time to sing as it tumbled through the air, its whine like the wailing of spirits.

This job was also processed and cooled expeditiously. In an instant, the bullet shredded the unit's heart like the whirling blade of a buzzsaw. She was dead before she hit the ground. Her body was quickly swallowed into the landfill, and the blood that might have testified to her existence was quickly sopped up by the garbage.

Without warning, Smoothbore became aware of a presence behind him. He spun on his heel to face the itinerant artist. The man's long hair fluttered in the evening breeze like blue flames in the light of the ring of stars.

'They had you kill her?' asked the artist.

'Merely honoring a contract. Did you know her?'

'Yes. She often came to look at my art. She couldn't read much, but she understood the paintings. She liked them, just like you.'

'I've been contracted to kill you, too.'

The artist dipped his head in calm acknowledgment. He did not betray a hint of fear. 'I thought so.'

'Out of curiosity, why did you refuse the money?'

'My paintings describe poverty and death. If I became a millionaire overnight, my art would die.'

Smoothbore nodded. 'Your art will live on. I truly do like your painting.' He raised his gun.

'Wait a moment. You said you were fulfilling a contract. Can I sign one with you?'

Smoothbore nodded again. 'Of course.'

'My death doesn't matter, but I want you to avenge her.' The artist pointed to where the scavenger lay amid the garbage.

'Let me rephrase your request in the language of my profession: you want to contract me to process an order of work, the same units that contracted me to process you and this other unit.'

The artist responded with a nod. 'Just like that.'

Smoothbore gravely assented, 'Not a problem.'

'I have no money.'

Smoothbore laughed, 'You sold me that painting far too cheaply. It has already paid for this job.'

'Then, thank you.'

'You're welcome. I am merely honoring a contract.'

Snubnose's muzzle spat deadly fire once more. The bullet twisted, careening through the air, and struck the artist in the heart. Blood sprayed from his chest and his back as he fell, and the droplets showered the ground like a hot, red rain.

'There was no need for that.'

The voice came from behind Smoothbore. He whirled around again and saw a person standing in the center of the landfill, a man. He wore a leather jacket almost identical to Smoothbore's own, and he looked young but otherwise unremarkable. The blue light from the ring of stars glinted in his eyes.

Smoothbore lowered his gun and trained it away from the newcomer, but he lightly squeezed the trigger. Snubnose's hammer rose unhurriedly to the fully-cocked position, ready to fire at the slightest touch.

'Are you police?' Smoothbore asked casually.

The stranger shook his head.

'Then go call them.'

The man stood still.

'I will not shoot you in the back. I only process work specified in my contract.'

'Currently, we are not to intervene in human affairs,' the man replied evenly.

His words struck Smoothbore like a bolt of lightning. His grip slackened, and the hammer of his revolver fell back into place. He peered closely at the stranger. In the glow of the starships, he was, by all appearances, an ordinary man.

'You've... already landed, then?' Smoothbore asked, an uncommon waver in his voice.

'We landed quite some time ago.'

Standing atop a landfill somewhere on Fourth Earth, a long silence settled over the two individuals from different worlds. The thick, warm air suddenly felt stifling. Smoothbore wanted to say something, anything, and the events of the past few days prompted a question: 'Are there poor people and rich people where you come from?'

The First Earthling smiled and said, 'Of course. I am poor.' He gestured towards the ring of stars above them. 'As are they.'

'How many people are up there?'

'If you mean those of us in the ships you can see now, about five hundred thousand. But we are just the vanguard. Ten thousand more ships will arrive in a few years from now, carrying one billion.'

'A billion?' wondered Smoothbore. 'They... can't all be poor, can they?'

'Every last one,' confirmed the alien.

'How many people are there on First Earth?'

'Two billion.'

'How can so many people on one world be poor?'

'How can so many people on one world *not* be poor?' countered the alien.

'I would think,' Smoothbore said, 'that too many poor people would destabilize a world, which would make things difficult for the middle and upper classes as well.'

'At this stage of Fourth Earth's development, that is true.'

'But it won't always be true?'

The First Earthling bowed his head and considered this, and then replied, 'Why don't I tell you the story of the rich and poor of First Earth?'

'I'd like to hear it.' Smoothbore tucked Snubnose back into his underarm holster.

'Our two human civilizations are remarkably similar,' began the alien. 'The paths you follow now, we travelled before you, and we, too, lived through an era similar to your present. Although the distribution of wealth was uneven, our society struck a certain balance. The population, rich and poor alike, was a manageable size, and it was commonly believed that wealth inequality would disappear as society progressed. Most people looked forward to an age of perfect prosperity and great harmony. But we soon discovered that things were far more complicated than we had imagined, and the balance we had achieved would soon be destroyed.'

'Destroyed by what?'

'Education. You know that in the present age of Fourth Earth, education is the sole means of social ascendancy. If society is an ocean, stratified by differences in temperature and salinity, then education is a pipe that connects the ocean floor to the surface and prevents the complete isolation of each layer.'

'So you're saying that fewer and fewer poor people could afford to attend university?'

'Yes. The cost of higher education grew increasingly expensive, until it became a privilege reserved for the sons and daughters of the social elite. However, the price of traditional education did have limits, even if they were only crude market considerations, so while the pipe grew gossamer-thin, it did not vanish completely. But one day, the appearance of a dramatic new technology fundamentally changed education.'

Smoothbore hazarded a guess. 'Do you mean the ability to transmit knowledge directly to the brain?'

'Yes, but the direct infusion of knowledge was only part of it. A human brain could be implanted within a supercomputer with a capacity that far exceeded that of the brain itself; the inventoried knowledge of the computer could then be recalled by the implantee as distinct memories.' The alien continued, 'But this was only one of the computer's secondary functions. It was an amplifier of intelligence, an amplifier of understanding, and it could raise human thought to a whole new level. Suddenly, knowledge, intelligence, depth of thought – even perfection of mind, character, and aesthetic judgment – were commodities that could be purchased.'

'Must have been expensive,' observed Smoothbore.

'Incredibly so. Expressed in your current monetary terms, the cost of this premium education for a single person was equivalent to buying two or three one hundred fifty square meter apartments in one of Shanghai or Beijing's prime neighborhoods.'

'Even if it cost that much, there would still be a few who could afford it.'

'Yes,' the First Earthling admitted, 'but they were a tiny segment of the upper class. The pipeline from the bottom of society to the top was completely severed. Those who received this premium education were vastly more intelligent than those who did not. The cognitive differences between these educated elites and ordinary humans were as large as those between humans and dogs, and these differences manifested themselves in every aspect of human life – even artistic sensibility, for example. This super-intelligentsia formed a new culture – a culture as incomprehensible to the rest of humanity as a symphony is incomprehensible to a dog. They could master hundreds of languages, and on any given occasion they would use the particular language that etiquette demanded. From the perspective of these super-intellects, conversing with ordinary people seemed as condescending as cooing to puppies. And so, quite naturally, something happened. You're smart, you should be able to guess.'

Smoothbore hesitated. 'Rich people and poor people were no longer the same... the same...'

'The rich and the poor were no longer the same species. The rich were as different to the poor as the poor were to dogs. The poor were no longer people.'

Smoothbore gasped. 'That must have changed everything.'

'It changed many things. First, the factors you mentioned that maintained a balance of wealth and limited the poor population ceased to exist. Even if dogs outnumbered humans, they would be unable to destabilize the foundations of human society. At worst, the disruption would be a nuisance but unthreatening.' The alien frowned. 'Though the willful killing of a dog might be a punishable offense, it is not like killing a person. When human health and safety is threatened by rabies, it is judged acceptable to put all dogs down. Sympathy for poor people hinged on one shared characteristic – personhood. When the poor ceased to be people, and all commonalities between rich and poor vanished, sympathy followed suit. This was humanity's second evolution. When we first split from apes, it was due to natural selection. When we split from the poor, it was due to an equally sacred law: the inviolability of private property.'

'Property is sacred in our world, too.'

'On First Earth, it was upheld by something called the Social Machine,' explained the alien. 'The Social Machine was a powerful enforcement system, and its Enforcers could be found in every corner of the planet. Some of these units were no bigger than mosquitoes, but they were capable of killing hundreds in a single strike. They were not governed by the Three Laws proposed by your Asimov, but by the fundamental principle of the First Earth Constitution: that private property shall be inviolable. But it would be inaccurate to say they brought about autocracy. They enforced the law with absolute impartiality and showed no favor to the wealthy. If the pitiful property of some poor fellow came under threat, they would protect it in strict accordance with the constitution.

'Under the powerful protection of the Social Machine, the wealth of First Earth flowed relentlessly towards the pockets of an elite minority. To make matters worse, technological development eliminated the reliance of the propertied classes on the propertyless. On your world, the rich still need the poor, because factories still need workers. On First Earth, machines no longer needed human operators, and high-efficiency robots could perform any required task. The poor could not even sell their labor, and they sank into absolute destitution as a result. This transformed the economic reality of First Earth, vastly accelerating the concentration of wealth in just a few people's hands.

'I would not be able to explain the highly complex process of wealth concentration to you,' the alien said, 'but in essence it resembles the movements of capital on your world. During my great-grandfather's lifetime, sixty percent of the wealth on First Earth was controlled by ten million people. During my grandfather's lifetime, eighty percent of our world's wealth was controlled by ten thousand people. During my father's lifetime, ninety percent of the wealth belonged to just forty two people. When I was born, capitalism had reached its apex on First Earth and had worked an unbelievable miracle: ninety-nine percent of the planet's wealth was held by a single person! This person became known as the Last Capitalist.

'While disparities in standards of living still existed among the other two billion, they controlled just one percent of the world's wealth in total. That is to say, First Earth had become a world with one rich person and two billion impoverished people. All the while, the constitutional inviolability of private property remained in effect, and the Social Machine faithfully carried out its duty to protect the property of a sole individual.'

'Do you want to know what the Last Capitalist owned?' The alien raised his voice. 'He owned First Earth! Every continent and ocean on the planet became his parlor rooms and private gardens. Even the atmosphere of First Earth was among his personal property.

'The remaining two billion individuals inhabited fully enclosed dwellings – miniature, self-contained life-support units. They lived sealed away in their own tiny worlds, sustained by their own paltry supplies of water, air, soil and other resources. The one resource that did not belong to the Last Capitalist, and the only thing they could lawfully take from the outside world, was sunlight.

'My home sat next to a small river, edged by green grass. The meadows stretched down to the riverbed and beyond, sweeping all the way to the emerald foothills in the distance. From inside, we could hear the sounds of birds twittering and fish leaping from the water, and we could see unhurried herds of deer grazing by the riverbanks, but it was the sight of the grass rippling in the breeze that I found particularly bewitching.

'But none of this belonged to us. My family was strictly cut off from the outside world, and we could only watch through airtight portholes that could never be opened. To go outside, it was necessary to pass through an airlock, as if we were exiting a spaceship into outer space. In truth, our home was very much like a spaceship – the difference was that the hostile environment was on the inside! We could only breathe the foul air supplied by our life-support system, could only drink the water that had been re-filtered a million times over, could only choke down food produced using our own raw excrement. And all the while, only a single wall separated us from the vast, bountiful world of nature. When we stepped outside, we dressed like astronauts and brought our own food and water. We even brought our own oxygen tanks, because the air, after all, belonged not to us, but to the Last Capitalist.

'Of course, we could afford the occasional splurge. For weddings or holidays, we would leave our closed little home and luxuriate in the great outdoors. That first breath of natural air was positively intoxicating. It was faintly sweet – sweet enough to make you cry. It wasn't free, though. We had to swallow pill-sized air meters before we went out, which measured exactly how much air we breathed. Every time we inhaled, a fee was deducted from our bank account. This was a luxury for most of the poor, something they could afford once or twice a year. We never dared to exert ourselves while outdoors. We mostly just sat and controlled our breathing. Before we returned home, we had to carefully scrape the soles of our shoes, because the soil outside was not ours to keep.'

The First Earthling paused for a moment. 'I will tell you how my mother died,' he said slowly. 'In order to cut down on expenditures, she refrained from leaving the house for three years. She could not bear to go out even on holidays. On the night it happened, she managed to slip past the airlock doors in her sleep. She must have been dreaming about nature. When she was discovered by an Enforcer, she had already wandered quite far. It saw that she had not swallowed an air meter, so it dragged her back home, cuffing her about the neck with a metal claw. It never intended to strangle her. By preventing her breathing, it only meant to protect another citizen's inviolable private property – the air. She was dead by the time she arrived home. The Enforcer dropped her corpse and informed us that she had committed larceny. We were fined, but we could not pay, so my mother's body was confiscated instead. You should know that a corpse is a precious thing for a poor family – seventy percent of its weight is water, plus a few other resources. The value of my mother's corpse, however, could not cover the fine, and the Social Machine siphoned off an amount of air that corresponded to the remainder of the debt.

'The air supply in our family's life-support system was already critically low, as we lacked the funds to replenish it. The removal of more air put our very survival at risk. In order to replace the lost oxygen, the life-support system was forced to separate some of its water resources through electrolysis. Unfortunately, this operation caused the entire system to deteriorate sharply. The main control computer issued an alarm: if we did not add fifteen liters of water to the system, it would crash in exactly thirty hours. The crimson glow of the warning lights filled every room.

'We considered stealing water from the river outside but soon abandoned the plan. We would not make it back home with the water without being shot dead by the omnipresent Enforcers. My father thought for a while, and then he told me not to worry and to go to bed. Though I was terrified, oxygen deprivation crept in, and I slept. I do not know how much time had passed when a robot nudged me awake. It had entered via the resource conversion vehicle that was docked to my home. It pointed to a bucket of crystal-clear water and told me: 'This is your father.'

'Resource conversion vehicles were mobile installations that converted human bodies into resources that could be utilized by household life-support systems. My father had utilized the service to extract every last drop of water from his own body, while not one hundred meters from our house, that pretty little river burbled in the moonlight. The resource conversion truck also extracted a few other useful things from his body for our life-support system: a container of grease, a bottle of calcium tablets, even a piece of iron as large as a coin.'

The alien paused again to collect himself. 'The water from my father rescued our life-support system, and I lived on. I grew up day by day, and soon five years had passed. One fall evening, as I looked through the porthole at the world outside, I suddenly noticed someone jogging along the riverbank. I was astonished: who was so extravagant that they would dare breathe like that outside?! Upon a closer look, I realized it was the Last Capitalist himself!

'He slowed his pace to a stroll, and then he sat down on a rock by the river's edge, dipping one bare foot into the water. He looked like a trim middle-aged man, but in reality he was over two thousand years old. Genetic engineering guaranteed that he would live for at least another two millennia, perhaps even forever. But he seemed perfectly ordinary to me.

'Two years later, my home's life support system functions deteriorated once more. Small-scale ecosystems like that were bound to have limited lifespans. Eventually, the whole system broke down. As the oxygen content in the air supply dwindled, I swallowed an air meter and walked out the door before I fell into an anoxic coma. Like every other person whose life-support system had failed, I stoically accepted my fate: I would breathe away the last of the pitiful savings in my account, and then I would be suffocated or shot by an Enforcer.

'I found there were many other people outside. The mass failures of household life-support systems had begun. A gargantuan Enforcer hovered above us and broadcast a final warning: "Citizens, you have intruded into someone else's home. You have committed an act of trespassing. Please leave immediately! Otherwise..."'

'Leave? Where could we go? There was no air left to breathe in our homes. Together with the others, I bounded through the green grass along the river, letting the fresh, sweet spring breeze rush over my pallid face, looking to go out in a blaze of glory...

'I don't know how long we ran before we realized we had long since breathed up the last of our savings, and yet the Enforcers had not taken action. Just then, the Last Capitalist's voice boomed forth from the massive Enforcer floating in the air.

Hello, everyone. Welcome to my humble home!

I am pleased to have so many guests, and I hope you have enjoyed yourselves in my garden. You will have to forgive me, however, but there are just too many of you. As of this moment, almost one billion people worldwide have left their own homes, as their life-support systems failed, and walked into mine. Another billion may be close behind. You have trespassed on my private property and violated the habitation and privacy rights of your fellow citizen. The Social Machine is lawfully empowered to take action to end your lives, and if I had not dissuaded it from doing just that, you would all have been vaporized by the Enforcers' lasers long ago. In any case, I did dissuade it. I am a gentleman who has received the best education available, and I treat guests in my home – even unlawful intruders – with courtesy and respect. But you must imagine things from my perspective. Two billion guests is a few too many for even the most thoughtful host, and I am someone who enjoys quiet solitude. Therefore, I must ask you all to leave. I recognize, of course, that there is nowhere on Earth for you to go, but I have taken it upon myself to prepare a fleet of twenty thousand spaceships for you.

Each ship is the size of a medium city and can travel at one percent of the speed of light. While the ships are not equipped with complete life-support systems, there are enough cryogenic chambers onboard to hold all two billion of you for fifty thousand years. This is the only planet in our solar system, so you will have to search for a new homeland among the stars, but I am certain you will find such a place. In the vastness of the cosmos, is it really necessary to crowd this little cottage of mine? You have no cause to resent me. I obtained my home through perfectly reasonable and legitimate means. I got my start as the manager of a small feminine hygiene products company, and to this day, I have relied only on my own business savvy. I am a law-abiding citizen, so the Social Machine has protected and will continue to protect me and my legal property. It will not tolerate your wrongdoing, however, so I advise everyone to get going as soon as possible.

Out of respect for our common evolutionary origin, I will remember you, and I hope you will remember me. Take care.

'And that is how we came to Fourth Earth,' concluded the First Earthling. 'Our voyage lasted for thirty thousand years. We lost nearly half our fleet while wandering endlessly through the stars. Some disappeared amidst interstellar dust; some were swallowed by black holes... But ten thousand ships survived, and one billion of us reached this world. And that is the story of First Earth, the story of two billion poor people and one rich man.'

'If you did not intervene, would our world repeat this tale?' Smoothbore asked after the First Earthling finished his narration.

'I do not know. Perhaps, but perhaps not. The course of a civilization is like the fate of an individual – fickle and impossible to predict.' The alien paused. 'I should go now. I am only an ordinary census taker, and I must work for my living.'

'I have things to attend to as well,' replied Smoothbore.

'Farewell, little brother.'

'Farewell, elder brother.'

Under the light of the ring of stars, two men from two different worlds parted in two different directions.

*

As Smoothbore entered the Presidential Hall, the thirteen members of the standing committee of the Council for Liquidation of Social Wealth turned to face him. Zhu Hanyang spoke first: 'We have verified your work, and you have done well. The second half of your payment has been transferred into your account, although it will not be of use for much longer.' He paused. 'There is something else you must already know: the Elder Brothers' census takers have landed on Earth. Our work is meaningless now, and we have no further tasks to give you.'

'Actually, I've taken another commission.'

As he spoke, Smoothbore drew his pistol with one hand and stretched his opposite hand forward, fist clenched.

Bang, bang, bang, bang, bang, bang, bang – seven glinting bullets fell to the table in front of him. Together with the six shots in Snubnose, that made thirteen in all.

Thirteen faces, shaped by the weight of their immense wealth, twisted in unison as shock and horror flashed across their refined features. Then, a calm settled. Maybe they felt relief.

Outside, a shower of massive meteors split the sky. Their brilliant light pierced through the heavy curtains and eclipsed the crystal chandelier, and the ground shook violently. The ships of First Earth had entered the atmosphere.

'Have you had dinner?' Xu Xueping asked Smoothbore. She pointed towards a heap of instant noodles on the table. 'Let's eat first.'

They stacked a large silver punch basin atop three crystal ashtrays and added water to the basin. Then, they lit a fire beneath it with one hundred yuan notes. Everyone took turns feeding bills into the fire, gazing absently at the yellow and green flames that leapt like a small joyful creature.

After the fire consumed 1.35 million yuan, the water began to boil.

Curse 5.0

Curse 1.0 was born on 8 December 2009.

It was the second year of the financial crisis. The crisis was supposed to end quickly; no one expected it was only just beginning. Society was mired in anxiety. Everyone needed to let off steam, and they poured their energies into creating new ways to do so. Perhaps the Curse was a product of this prevailing mood.

The author of the Curse was a young woman aged between eighteen and twenty-eight. That was all the information that later IT archaeologists could uncover about her.

The target of the Curse was a young man of twenty years old. His personal details were well-documented. His name was Sa Bi,[1] and he was a fourth-year student at Taiyuan University of Technology. Nothing extraordinary had occurred between him and the young woman, just the usual garden-variety drama that afflicts young men and women. Later there were thousands of versions of the story, and perhaps one of them was true, but no one had any way of knowing what had actually transpired between this couple. In any case, after things ended between them the young woman felt only bitter hatred toward the young man, and so she wrote Curse 1.0.

---

1 The young man was unfortunately named. 'Sa Bi' sounds very similar to the Chinese word for 'stupid asshole'.

The young woman was an expert programmer, although it is not known where and how she learned her craft. In that day and age, despite the ballooning ranks of IT practitioners, the number of people who had truly mastered low-level systems programming had not increased. There were *too* many tools available; programming was *too* convenient. It was unnecessary to struggle through line after line of code like a coolie when most of it could be generated directly with existing tools. This was even true for viruses like the one the young woman was about to write. Many hacker tools made creating a virus as easy as assembling a few ready-made modules or, simpler still, slightly modifying a single module. The last big virus before the Curse, the so-called 'Panda Burning Incense' worm, was created in this way. The young woman, however, elected to start from scratch, without the assistance of any tools whatsoever. She wrote her code line by line, like a hardworking peasant weaving cotton threads into cloth on a rudimentary loom. Imagining her hunched in front of a monitor, grinding her teeth and hammering away at the keyboard, brings to mind lines from Heinrich Heine's 'The Silesian Weavers': *Old Germany, we weave your funeral shroud; And into it we weave a three-fold curse – we weave; we weave.*

Curse 1.0 was the most widely disseminated computer virus in history. Its success can be attributed to two principal factors. First, the Curse did not inflict any damage on infected host computers. In fact, most viruses lacked destructive intent; the damage they caused was largely the result of shoddy propagation and execution mechanisms. The Curse was perfectly designed to avoid such side effects. Its behavior was quite restrained, and most infected host computers exhibited no symptoms whatsoever. It was only a certain combination of system conditions – present in approximately one out of every ten infected computers – that triggered the virus, and then it only ever manifested on a given computer once. The virus displayed a notification on the screen of an infected computer that read:

>Go die, Sa Bi!!!!!!!!!

If the user clicked the notification window, the virus would display further information about Sa Bi, informing them that the accursed was a student at Taiyuan University of Technology in Taiyuan, Shanxi Province, China. He was enrolled in the xx Department, was majoring in xx, belonged in Class xx, and lived in Dormitory xx, Room xx. The virus was recorded on the computer's firmware, so even if the user reinstalled the operating system the result was the same.

The second factor underlying the success of Curse 1.0 was its ability to mimic operating systems. This feature was not the young woman's own invention, but she made expert use of it. System mimicry involved editing many parts of the virus' own code to match that of the host system and then adopting behaviors that were similar to normal system processes. When anti-malware programs attempted to eliminate the virus, they risked damaging the system itself. In the end, they simply gave up, like a housewife unwilling to throw a slipper at a mouse sitting next to the good china.

In fact, Rising, Norton and other anti-malware developers had put Curse 1.0 in their sights, but they quickly discovered that pursuing it was getting them into trouble, with even worse consequences than in 2007 when Norton AntiVirus mistakenly deleted Windows XP operating system files. This, coupled with the fact that Curse 1.0 caused no real harm and placed a negligible strain on system resources, led one developer after another to delete it from their virus signature databases.

On the day the Curse was born, science fiction author Cixin Liu visited Taiyuan on business for the 264th time. Although it was the city he hated most in the world, he always paid a visit to a small shop in the red-light district to buy a bottle of lighter fluid for his archaic Zippo lighter. It was one of the very few things he could not buy on Taobao or eBay. Snow had fallen two days prior, and, like always, it was quickly packed down into a blackened crust of ice. Cixin slipped and fell painfully on his backside. When he arrived at the train station, the pain in his ass caused him to forget to move the little bottle of lighter fluid from his travelling bag to his pocket. As a result, it was discovered during the security check, and after it was confiscated he was fined 200 yuan.

He *loathed* this city.

*

Curse 1.0 lived on. Five years passed, ten years passed, and still it quietly multiplied in an ever-expanding virtual world.

Meanwhile, the financial crisis passed and prosperity returned.

As the world's petroleum reserves gradually dried up, coal's share of the world energy balance rapidly increased. All that buried black gold brought the money rolling into Shanxi, transforming the formerly impoverished province into the Arabia of East Asia. Taiyuan, the provincial capital, naturally became a new Dubai. The city had the character of a coal boss who was terrified of being poor again. In those promising days at the beginning of the century, its denizens wore designer suit jackets over tattered pants. Even as unemployed laborers jammed the city streets day in and day out, the construction of China's most luxurious concert hall and bathhouse continued apace.

Taiyuan had now joined the ranks of the *nouveau riche*, and the city howled with hysterical laughter at its own wanton extravagance. The skyline of Shanghai's Pudong district paled in comparison to the colossal high-rises that lined Yingze Avenue, and the thoroughfare – second only to Chang'an Avenue[2] in terms of width – became a deep, sunless canyon. Rich and poor alike flocked to the city with their dreams and desires, only to

---

2 The thoroughfare that runs east-to-west through Beijing just north of Tiananmen Gate.

instantly forget who they were and what they wanted as they tumbled into a vortex of affluence and commotion that churned 365 days a year.

That day, on his 397th trip to Taiyuan, Cixin Liu had gone to the red-light district to buy yet another bottle of lighter fluid. Walking along the city's streets, he suddenly saw an elegant and handsome young man with a distinctive white streak in his long, dark hair. The man was Pan Dajiao, who had started out writing science fiction, switched to fantasy and then finally settled somewhere in between. Attracted by the city's newfound prosperity, Pan Dajiao had abandoned Shanghai and moved to Taiyuan. At the time, Cixin and Pan stood on opposite sides of the soft–hard divide in science fiction. This chance meeting was a delightful coincidence.

Tucked away in a *tounao*³ restaurant and flushed with liquor, Cixin chattered excitedly about his next grand endeavor. He planned to write a ten-volume, three-million-character sci-fi epic describing the two thousand deaths of two hundred civilizations in a universe repeatedly wiped clean by vacuum collapses. The tale would conclude with the entire known universe falling into a black hole, like water draining from a toilet bowl. Pan was captivated, and he raised the possibility of collaboration: working from the same concept, Cixin would write the hardest possible science fiction edition for male readers, while Pan would write the softest possible fantasy edition for female readers.

Cixin and Pan got on like a house on fire and immediately abandoned all worldly affairs in favor of feverish creation.

*

As Curse 1.0 turned ten years old, its final day drew near.

After Vista, Microsoft was hard-pressed to justify frequent upgrades to its operating system, which prolonged the life of

---

3 A traditional local lamb soup.

Curse 1.0 for a time. But operating systems were like the wives of new-made billionaires: upgrades were inevitable. The Curse's code grew less and less compatible, and it began to sink toward the bottom of the Internet. But just as it lay poised to disappear, a new field of study was born: IT archaeology. Although common sense suggested that the Internet, with less than a half-century of history, lacked any artifacts ancient enough to study, there were quite a few nostalgic individuals who devoted themselves to the field. IT archaeology was largely concerned with uncovering various relics that still lived in the nooks and crannies of cyberspace, like a ten-year-old webpage that had never felt the click of a mouse, or a Bulletin Board System that had not seen a visitor in twenty years but still permitted new posts. Of these virtual artifacts, the viruses of 'antiquity' were the most highly sought-after by IT archaeologists. Finding a living specimen of a virus written over a decade ago was like discovering a dinosaur at Lake Tianchi.

It was in this way that Curse 1.0 was discovered. Its finder upgraded the entire code of the virus to a new operating system, thus ensuring its continued survival.

The upgraded version was Curse 2.0. The woman who had created Curse 1.0 was dubbed the Primogenitor, and the IT archaeologist who rescued it became known as the Upgrader.

*

The moment at which Curse 2.0 appeared online found Cixin and Pan next to a trash can in the vicinity of the Taiyuan train station. They were fighting over half a pack of ramen that had been fished from the garbage only moments before. They had slept on floorboards and tasted gall for six years, until at last they had produced one three-million-character, ten-volume work of science fiction and one three-million-character, ten-volume work of fantasy. They had titled their works *The Three-Thousand-Body Problem* and *Novantamililands*, respectively. The two men had full confidence in their masterpieces but were unable to find a publisher. So, together, they sold off every last possession – including their houses – borrowed against their pensions and self-published. In the end, *The Three-Thousand-Body Problem* and *Novantamililands* sold fifteen and twenty-seven copies, respectively. This made forty-two copies in total, which sci-fi fans knew was a lucky number. After a grand signing session in Taiyuan – also at personal expense – the two men began their careers as drifters.

There was no city friendlier to vagrants than Taiyuan. The trash cans of the profligate metropolis were an inexhaustible source of food. At worst, it was always possible to find a few discarded nine-to-five pills. Finding a place to live was not much of a problem, either. Taiyuan modeled itself after Dubai, and each of its bus stops was equipped with heating and air conditioning. If they grew tired of the streets, it was simple enough to spend a few days in a shelter. There they would receive more than just food and lodging; Taiyuan's thriving sex industry had answered the government's call and designated every Sunday as a Day for Sexual Aid to Vulnerable Groups. The shelters were popular locations at which volunteers from the red-light district conducted their charitable activities. In the city's official Social Happiness Index, migrant beggars ranked first. Cixin and Pan rather regretted that they had not adopted this lifestyle earlier.

The weekly invitations from the *King of Science Fiction* editorial department were by far the most pleasant occasions in their new lives. They usually went somewhere fancy, like Tang Dou Restaurant. *King of Science Fiction* had grasped the essence of what it meant to be a sci-fi magazine. The soul of this literary vehicle was wonder and alienation, but high-tech fantasies had lost the ability to evoke those feelings. Technological miracles were trite: they happened every day. It was low-tech fantasies that awed and unsettled modern readers. So the editors developed a subgenre known as 'counter-wave science fiction' that imagined an unsophisticated future era. Its enormous success ushered in a second golden age of science fiction. In an effort to embrace the spirit of counter-wave science fiction, the *King of Science Fiction* editorial department rejected computers and the Internet wholesale. They accepted only handwritten manuscripts and adopted letterpress printing. They bought dozens of Mongolian steeds at the price of one BMW per horse and built a luxurious stable next to the editorial office. The magazine's staff only rode steeds that had never surfed the web. The clip-clop of horseshoes around the city signaled the imminent approach of an SFK company man.

The editors often invited Cixin and Pan to dinner. In addition to being a sign of respect for the stories they had written in the past, this gesture was also in acknowledgement of the fact that, while the science fiction they wrote now could hardly be called science fiction, their adherence to counter-wave science fiction principles was *very* science fiction. They lived completely offline; low-tech indeed.

Neither Cixin, nor Pan, nor the SFK staff could ever have guessed that this mutual quirk would save their lives.

Curse 2.0 thrived for another seven years. Then, one day, the woman who became known as the Weaponizer found it. She carefully studied the code of Curse 2.0. She could sense the hatred and bile the Primogenitor had woven into its code even seventeen years old and in its upgraded form. She and the Primogenitor had had the same experience, and she, too, hated a man so much it made her teeth ache. But she thought the other young woman was pathetic and laughable: what was the point? Had it touched a hair on the head of that jerk Sa Bi? The Primogenitor was like the scorned maidens of the last century, sticking pins into little cloth effigies. Silly little games could solve nothing and would only make her sink deeper into depression. But Big Sister was here to help. (In fact, the Primogenitor was almost certainly still alive, but given their age difference the Weaponizer should have called her Auntie.)

*

Seventeen years had passed since the birth of the Curse, and a new era had arrived – the entire world was caught in the web. Once, only computers had been connected to the Internet, but the Internet of the present was like a spectacular Christmas tree, festooned and blinking with almost every object on Earth. In the home, for example, every electric appliance was connected to and controlled by the web. Even nail clippers and bottle openers were no exception. The former could detect calcium deficiencies in nail trimmings and send an alert via text or email. The latter could determine whether the alcohol about to be consumed was legally produced or send notifications to sweepstakes winners. The bottle openers could also prevent users from drinking to excess by refusing to open a bottle until enough time had passed since opening the previous one. Under these circumstances, it became possible for the Curse to directly manipulate hardware.

The Weaponizer added a new function to Curse 2.0:

>If Sa Bi rides in a cab, kill him in a car crash!

In fact, this was hardly a difficult task for the AI programmers of this age. All modern vehicles were already driverless, piloted by the web. When a passenger swiped his credit card to hire a cab, the Curse could identify him via the name on the card. Once Sa Bi was identified as the passenger in a taxi, the ways in which he could be killed were innumerable. The simplest method was to crash the cab into a building or drive it off a bridge. But the Weaponizer decided a simple collision would not do. Instead, she chose a far more romantic death for Sa Bi, one more fitting for the man who had wronged Little Sister seventeen years prior. (In truth, the Weaponizer knew no better than anyone else what Sa Bi had done to the Primogenitor, and it was possible the fault did not lie with him.)

Once the upgraded Curse learned its target was in the cab, it would ignore his selected destination and burn up the road from Taiyuan to Zhangjiakou, which had become a vast wasteland.

The cab would park itself deep in the desert and cut off all communication with the outside world. (By then the Curse would have taken up residence in the onboard computer and would not need the Internet.) The risk of detection was very small. Even if people or other vehicles occasionally drew near, the cab would just hide in another corner of the desert, no matter how much time had passed. The car doors would remain sealed from the inside. That way, in winter Sa Bi would freeze to death; in summer he would bake to death; in the spring or fall he would die of thirst or starvation.

Thus, Curse 3.0 was born, and it was a true curse.

The Weaponizer was a member of a new breed of AI artists. They manipulated networks to produce performance art of no practical significance but of great beauty. (Naturally, the aesthetics of the present era were markedly different from the aesthetics of just a decade before.) They might, for instance, strike up a tune by causing every vehicle in the city to honk simultaneously or arrange brightly-lit hotel windows to form an image on the building's exterior. Curse 3.0 was one such creation. Whether or not it could truly realize its function, it was a remarkable work of art in and of itself. As a result, it received high critical praise at Shanghai Biennale 2026. Even though the police declared it illegal due to its intent to cause bodily harm, it continued to percolate through the web. A multitude of other AI artists joined in the collective creation. Curse 3.0 evolved rapidly as more and more functions were added to its code:

>If Sa Bi is at home, suffocate him with gas fumes!

This was relatively easy, as the kitchen in every household was controlled via the web, which allowed homeowners to prepare meals remotely. Naturally, this included the ability to turn on the gas, and Curse 3.0 could disable the hazardous gas detectors in the room.

>If Sa Bi is at home, kill him with fire!

This, too, was straightforward. In addition to the gas, there were many things in every household that could be set alight. For example, even mousse and hairspray were connected to the web (which allowed a professional stylist to do one's hair without leaving their own home). Fire alarms and extinguishers could, of course, be made to fail.

>If Sa Bi takes a shower, kill him with scalding water!

Like the other methods above, this was a piece of cake.

>If Sa Bi goes to the hospital, kill him with a toxic prescription!

This was slightly more complicated. It was simple enough to prescribe a specific medicine to a target; pharmacies in modern hospitals dispensed prescriptions automatically, and their systems were connected to the web. The key issue was the packaging of the medication. Sa Bi, despite his name, was no fool, and the plan fell apart if he was unwilling to take the medicine. To achieve its end, Curse 3.0 had to trace medicine back to the factory where it was produced and packaged and then follow it down the sales chain. Ensuring that the fatal drug was sold to the target was complicated, but feasible. And for the AI artists, the more complicated it was the more beautiful the finished product would be.

>If Sa Bi gets on plane, kill him!

This was not easy. It was significantly more difficult than taking control of a cab, because only Sa Bi had been cursed and Curse 3.0 could not kill others. Since it was unlikely Sa Bi had a personal jet, crashing a plane carrying him was not an option. But there was an alternative solution: any plane that Sa Bi boarded would suffer a sudden loss of cabin pressure (by opening a cabin door or some other method). Then, when all of the passengers put on their oxygen masks, only Sa Bi's mask would fail.

>If Sa Bi eats, choke him to death!

This sounded absurd but was actually quite simple to implement. The superfast pace of modern society had given rise to superfast food: a small pill known as a 'nine-to-five' pill. Nine-to-five pills were incredibly dense and felt weighty like a bullet in the hand. Once ingested, the pills would expand in the stomach, like hardtack. The key was to tamper with the manufacturing process to produce a rapidly-expanding pill; then the Curse could control the sales process to ensure Sa Bi was the one who bought it. As soon as he popped the pill on his lunch break and washed it down with water, the pill would balloon in his throat.

But Curse 3.0 never found its target and never killed anyone. After the birth of Curse 1.0, Sa Bi had been harassed by strangers and hounded by reporters. He had no choice but to change his given name and even his surname. There were few people surnamed Sa to begin with, and thanks to the name's indecent homophone, there were exactly zero other people in the city named Sa Bi. At the same time, it was not as if Sa Bi had updated his address and place of employment since the Curse. The virus still thought he attended Taiyuan University of Technology, which made it impossible to locate him. The Curse had been outfitted with the function to search for records of its target's name change in the Public Security Department, but its search was fruitless. So in the four years that followed, Curse 3.0 remained nothing but a piece of AI art.

Then, the wildcards appeared: Cixin and Pan.

A wildcard character was an ancient concept, originating from the Age of Mentors (the ancient era of DOS computing). The two most commonly used wildcard characters were '*' and '?'. These two characters could represent one or more characters in a string: '?' referred to a single character, while '*' referred to any number of characters and was the most frequently used wildcard.

For instance, 'Liu*' referred to every person with the surname Liu and 'Shanxi*' referred to every string of characters starting with 'Shanxi'. A single '*' referred to any and all possible strings of characters. Therefore, in the Age of Mentors, 'del*.*' was a most wicked command because 'del' was a delete command and all file names consisted of a name and an extension separated by a dot. As operating systems evolved, wildcards survived, but as graphical user interfaces began to replace command-line interfaces in popular usage, they gradually faded from the memories of most computer users. In some software programs, however, including Curse 3.0, they could still be used.

The Mid-Autumn Festival had arrived. Next to the glittering lights of Taiyuan, the full moon looked like a greasy sesame seed cake. Cixin and Pan were sitting on a bench in Wuyi Square. They had laid out the goodies they'd scavenged that afternoon: five half-empty bottles of liquor, two half-full bags of Pingyao beef strips, one almost-untouched bag of Jinci donkey meat, and three nine-to-five pills. It was a good haul, and the two were ready to celebrate. Just after nightfall, Cixin had fished a broken laptop computer from a trashcan. He swore he would fix it up, or else a lifetime of working with computers would have been for naught. He squatted next to the bench and set to fiddling with the computer's innards. Meanwhile, Pan continued to air his thoughts about the sexual aid they had received at the shelter that afternoon. Cixin enthusiastically invited Pan to help himself to the three nine-to-five pills in the hopes of scoring a large share of the liquor and meat for himself. But Pan was not fooled, and he skipped the pills altogether.

The computer was soon running again, and its screen emitted a faint blue glow as it booted up. When Pan saw that the laptop had a functioning wireless internet connection, he snatched it from Cixin's hands. He checked QQ first, but his account had long since been deactivated. Next, he checked the *Novoland* website, the Castle in the Sky MMORPG, Douban, the NewSMTH Tsinghua BBS, Jiangdong – but those links were now broken. He threw the laptop aside and sighed: 'Long ago, a man flew away on the back of a yellow crane.'

Cixin, who had been consolidating the bottles of liquor, glanced at the screen and responded with the next line in the thirteen-hundred-year-old poem: 'And all that is left is the Yellow Crane Tower.' He picked up the laptop and began to carefully examine its contents. He discovered many hacker tools and virus specimens installed on it. Perhaps the laptop had belonged to a hacker and had been ditched in a trashcan as its owner fled from the AI police.

Cixin opened a file on the desktop and found a decompiled C-language program. He recognized it: it was Curse 3.0. Casually skimming through the code, he recalled his own days as a digital poet. As the liquor set to work upon his brain, he browsed the target identification section of the code. At his side, Pan was prattling on about the towering science fiction of bygone years, and Cixin was soon infected with nostalgia. He pushed the laptop away and joined Pan in reminiscing. Those were the days! His omniscient, virile epics of destruction had struck chords with so many young men, had made their hearts overflow with martial and dogmatic fervor! But now, fifteen copies… he had sold only fifteen copies! Fuck! He took a big swig from his bottle. The flavor was no longer recognizable but its alcohol content was unmistakable. Cixin was overcome with a hatred for male readers, and then all men. He fixed a loathsome stare on the target parameters of Curse 3.0. 'Nowerdays there snotta single deshent man alive,' he slurred, as he changed the target name from 'Sa Bi' to '*'. Then, he changed the occupation and address parameters from 'Taiyuan University of Technology, enrolled in xx Department, majoring in xx, living in Dormitory xx Room xx' to '*, *, *, *, *'. Only the gender parameter remained unchanged: 'male'.

By now, Pan was sniveling alongside him. He thought of the

colorful, profound works of his early years, like poems, like dreams. It was not so long ago that his prose had bewitched hordes of teenage girls. He had been their idol. But now, those young women passed him by without a single glance! What an indignity! Hurling away an empty bottle, Pan muttered, 'If men are all rotten, then whad are wimmen?' He changed the gender parameter from 'male' to 'female'.

Cixin would not have it. He had nothing against women; his vulgar novels never stood a chance with female readers anyway. He changed the gender parameter back to 'male', but Pan immediately changed it to 'female' again. The two men began to argue over how to punish their ungrateful, treacherous readers, and Taiyuan's future vacillated between widowhood and bachelorhood. Cixin and Pan began to take wild swings at each other with empty bottles until a patrolman intervened. Rubbing the bumps on their heads, the two men came to a compromise: they changed the gender parameter to '*', thereby completing the wildcarding of Curse 3.0. Perhaps it was the officer's intervention, or perhaps it was their utter inebriation, but three parameters escaped their alterations: 'Taiyuan, Shanxi Province, China.'

Thus, Curse 4.0 was born.

Taiyuan had been cursed.

*

At the instant of its creation, the new version of the Curse fully understood the grand mission with which it had been entrusted. Because of the immensity of the task before it, Curse 4.0 did not immediately spring to action. Instead, it gave itself time to penetrate and propagate. Once it was thoroughly entrenched throughout the web, it considered its plan of attack: it would start by eliminating soft targets, then transition to hard targets and escalate things from there.

Ten hours later, as the first rays of dawn appeared on the horizon, Curse 4.0 went live.

The Curse's soft targets were the sensitive, the neurotic and the impulsive – in particular, those men and women who suffered from depression or bipolar disorder. In an era of rampant mental illness and ubiquitous psychological counseling, it was easy for Curse 4.0 to find this sort of target. In the first round of operations, thirty thousand individuals who had just undergone hospital examinations were notified that they had been diagnosed with a liver, gastric, lung, brain, colon or thyroid cancer, or leukemia. The most common diagnosis was esophageal cancer (which had the highest incidence rate in the region). Another twenty thousand individuals who had recently drawn blood were informed that they had tested positive for HIV. This was not a matter of simply falsifying diagnostic results. Instead, Curse 4.0 took direct control of ultrasounds, CT scans, MRIs, and blood testing instruments to produce 'genuine' results. Even if patients sought a second opinion at a different hospital, the results would remain the same. Of the initial fifty thousand, most elected to begin treatment. But about four hundred individuals, already weary of life, immediately ended it all. In the days that followed, a steady trickle of people made the same choice.

Soon afterward, fifty thousand sensitive, depressed or bipolar men and women received phone calls from their spouses or significant others. The men heard their wives and girlfriends say: 'Look at you, shit brick. Are you even a man? Well, I'm with [*] now and we are very happy together, so you can go to hell.' For their part, the women heard their husbands and boyfriends say: 'You're really looking your age and, to be honest, you were fugly from the get-go. I have no idea what I ever saw in you. Well, I'm with [*] now, and we are very happy together, so you can go to hell.'

By and large, these fabricated rivals were people the targets already loathed. Of these fifty thousand, most of them sought out their loved one and directly resolved the misunderstanding. But about one per cent elected to kill their partner or themselves, and some did both. The Curse picked out a few other soft targets.

For instance, it provoked bloody fights between irreconcilably opposed gangs, and it changed the sentences of criminals serving long terms or life in prison and slated them for immediate execution. But overall, the efficacy of these operations was low, and they eliminated only a few thousand targets in total. Curse 4.0 had the right attitude, though. It knew that great things came from small beginnings. It would shy away from no evil, no matter how small, and it would leave no method untried.

In the initial phase of its plan, Curse 4.0 eliminated its own creator. In the years after she created the Curse, the Primogenitor had maintained a rigorous mistrust of men. She had become a surveillance expert, using the most up-to-date methods to monitor her (unwaveringly faithful) husband for twenty years. So when she received one of *those* phone calls, she suffered a heart attack. Once admitted to the hospital, she was given drugs that further exacerbated her myocardial infarction, and she died at the hand of her own Curse.

The Weaponizer also died in this phase. She received an HIV-positive test result and originally had no intention of killing herself, but she overdosed on anti-anxiety medication. In a drug-induced hallucination, she mistook a window for a gate to a charming garden and tumbled fifteen stories to her death.

*

Five days later, hard target operations commenced. The abnormally high suicide and homicide rates caused by the preceding soft operations had thrown the city into a panic. But Curse 4.0 was still flying beneath the government's radar, so the first few hard operations were conducted with great secrecy. First, the number of patients receiving the wrong drugs skyrocketed. The medicines were packaged normally, but ingesting a single dose now proved fatal. At the same time, there was a surge in the number of people choking to death at the dinner table. The compression density of nine-to-five pills began to vastly exceed industry standards. Diners, weighing the heavy pills in their hands, thought they were getting great value for their money.

The first large-scale elimination attempt targeted the water supply. Even in a city completely controlled by artificial intelligence, it was impossible to add cyanide or mustard gas directly to the tap water. Curse 4.0 chose to introduce two species of genetically modified bacteria. While harmless on their own, they would produce a deadly toxin when combined. The Curse did not add the two cultures simultaneously; instead, it added one species first, and when most of that culture had cleared from the system the second culture was added. The actual mixing of the two species of bacteria took place inside the human body. As the bacteria met in the stomach or the blood, they would produce the deadly toxin. If the toxin did not prove fatal, when the target was admitted to hospital they would receive medicine that would react with the two bacterial cultures, striking the final blow.

By now, the Public Security Department and the Ministry of Artificial Intelligence Safety had pinpointed the source of the disaster and were frantically developing specialized tools to combat Curse 4.0. In response, the Curse rapidly accelerated and escalated its operations. Its covert machinations became an earth-shaking nightmare.

One day, during the early morning rush hour, a series of muffled explosions echoed beneath the city. It was the sound of trains colliding. Taiyuan had only recently built its subway; the design process had coincided with the city's explosive growth, so it was a highly advanced system. The maglev trains that zipped through vacuum tunnels became known for their incredible speeds. They were nicknamed 'Punctual Portals' – almost as soon as they stepped into the carriage, passengers arrived at their terminal destinations. The trains' speed made for exceptionally violent collisions. The ground swelled and bulged with the force of the explosions, heaving smoke-belching hummocks skyward like angry pustules erupting on the face of the city.

Almost all of the vehicles in the city were now under the control of the Curse. (In this day and age, all vehicles could be piloted by AI.) These were the most powerful tools in the virus' arsenal. All at once, like particles set in Brownian motion, millions of vehicles began to zigzag recklessly all over the city. Though the whole scene looked chaotic, the collisions actually conformed to rigorously optimized patterns and sequences. Each vehicle was instructed to first run down as many pedestrians as possible. With precise coordination, cars herded people through the city streets and closed together in enormous rings in plazas and other open spaces. The largest such formation was in Wuyi Square. Several thousand cars surrounded the square and then rushed towards the center in unison, swiftly eliminating tens of thousands of targets.

When most of the pedestrians had been eliminated or had taken shelter, the cars began to slam themselves against the nearest buildings, killing all passengers still trapped inside. These collisions, too, were precisely organized. Cars would assemble in groups and concentrate their attacks against high-occupancy buildings. Those in the rear would barrel across the pulverized remains of their compatriots, stacking themselves one by one. At the foot of the tallest building in the city, the three-hundred-story Coal Exchange Tower, the cars formed a pile-up that reached ten stories high. The twisted wrecks blazed fiercely, like an immense funeral pyre. The night before the Great Crash, Taiyuan's citizens beheld a peculiar spectacle: the city's taxis had all gathered in long lines to refuel. The virus had guaranteed that their tanks would be full when the moment of disaster came. Now they smashed into buildings like an endless rain of firebombs, fanning the flames ever higher.

The government issued an emergency bulletin declaring a state of emergency and instructing all citizens to remain in their homes. At first, this seemed like the correct response. Compared to the skyscrapers, the Great Crash's assault on residential buildings was minor. The streets of the residential districts were much narrower than the city's main thoroughfares, and soon after the Great Crash began they were completely grid-locked. Instead, Curse 4.0 set about turning each house into a deathtrap. It opened up gas valves, and when the air-to-gas ratio reached an explosive threshold it lit a spark. Row upon row of apartment buildings were engulfed in flames. Entire buildings were blown sky-high.

The government's next step was to cut all power to the city. But it was too late; Curse 4.0 may have been knocked out of action, but it had accomplished its mission. The whole city was in flames. As the inferno strengthened, its ferocity replicated the effect of the firebombing of Dresden during World War II: as the oxygen was sucked from the air, even those who escaped the fire could not escape death.

*

At this point, the Upgrader was consumed by the flames – the third key figure in the virus' history to fall victim to their own creation.

Because of their minimal contact with the web, Cixin and Pan, together with their vagrant brothers, had managed to escape the early operations of the Curse. As the later operations began, they relied on the skills they had honed from years of roving the city streets to keep themselves alive. With agility that belied their ages, they dodged every car that hurtled towards them. Armed with a deep familiarity with every avenue and alley, they managed to survive the Great Crash. But circumstances soon grew more perilous. As the entire city became a sea of fire, they stood at the center of the four-way intersection near Dayingpan. Suffocating waves of heat billowed down upon them, and flames lashed out from the surrounding skyscrapers like the tongues of giant lizards.

Cixin, who had described the destruction of fictional universes on innumerable occasions, was scared witless. On the other hand, Pan, whose works brimmed with humanist warmth, was calm and collected.

Stroking his beard, Pan looked at the inferno all around them. In drawn-out tones, he mused: 'Who knew... that destruction... could be so spectacular... Why did I never... write about it?'

Cixin's legs buckled beneath him. 'If I had known that destruction was so terrifying, I would not have written so much of it,' he moaned. 'Damn me and my big mouth. This is just perfect.'

Eventually, they came to a consensus: the most gripping destruction was one's own destruction.

Just then, they heard a silvery voice, like the touch of an ice crystal in the sea of flames: 'Cixin, Pan, come quick!' Following the voice, they saw a pair of stallions emerge from the flames like spirits. Two beautiful young women from the SFK editorial department rode atop the horses, their long hair trailing behind them. The riders pulled Cixin and Pan up onto the backs of the horses. Then, like lightning, they took off through the gaps in the blistering sea, vaulting the burning wreckage of cars.

A moment later, the smoke cleared from their vision. The horses had galloped onto the bridge that spanned the Fen River. Cixin and Pan took deep breaths of the clean, cool air. Holding the slender waists of the young women and enjoying the tickle of hair against their faces, the men lamented that their flight had not been longer.

The riders crossed the bridge into safety. They were shortly reunited with the rest of the SFK editorial department, all mounted on powerful steeds. The magnificent cavalry set off in the direction of Jinci Temple, drawing surprised and jealous looks from the survivors fleeing on foot as they passed. Cixin, Pan and the SFK staff spotted a single cyclist among the ranks of the survivors. His presence was noteworthy for a single reason: in this day and age bicycles were connected to and controlled by the web, and the Curse had locked their wheels as soon as it began its assault.

The cyclist was an old man, the man once known as Sa Bi.

Thanks to the Curse's early campaign of harassment, Sa Bi

had developed an instinctive fear and abhorrence of the web. He had minimized his exposure to it in his daily life – by riding a twenty-year-old antique bicycle, for instance. He lived on the bank of the Fen River, near the outskirts of the city. When the Great Crash began, he made a break for safety on his absolutely offline bicycle. In fact, Sa Bi was one of the few people at that time who was truly content. He had found satisfaction in a series of romantic affairs, and he was prepared to face death with no complaints or regrets.

Sa Bi and the cavalry crested a mountain on the edge of the city. Standing on the summit, they gazed down at the burning city below. A fierce gale howled through the hills, sweeping in from every direction and down into the Taiyuan basin, replenishing the air lost to the rising heat.

Not far from them, the prominent officials from the provincial and municipal governments were disembarking from the helicopter that had plucked them from the inferno. A draft of a speech still lay tucked inside the mayor's pocket. He had prepared it in advance of the city's anniversary celebrations. Founded in 497 BCE as the capital of the state of Jin, the city had survived the turbulence of the Spring and Autumn period and the Warring States period. During the Tang Dynasty, Taiyuan waxed in importance as a strategic military stronghold in Northern China. The city was razed by Song troops in 979 CE, but it rose again, flourishing throughout the Song, Jin, Yuan, Ming and Qing dynasties. It was not just a city of great military significance but also a renowned hub of culture and trade. The suggested slogan for the city's anniversary festivities was 'Celebrating 2,500 years of Taiyuan!' But now, the city that had survived twenty-five centuries had been reduced to ashes by a sea of flames.

A military radio communications link was briefly established with the central government. The officials were informed that aid was rushing toward Taiyuan from every corner of the country. But communications were soon lost again, and they heard only static. One hour later, they received a report that the rescuers had halted their advance and the rescue planes had turned back to base.

Back at the Shanxi Bureau of Artificial Intelligence Safety, a senior director opened his laptop computer. The screen displayed the most recently compiled version of the virus; Curse 5.0. The target parameters for 'Taiyuan, Shanxi Province, China' now read '*, *, *'.

The Micro-Era

Chapter 1

Return

The Forerunner now knew that he was the only person left in the universe. He'd realized when he crossed the orbit of Pluto. From here, the Sun was but a dim star, no different from when he had left the solar system thirty years ago.

The divergence analysis the computer had just performed, however, told him that Pluto's orbit had significantly shifted outward. Using this data, he could calculate that the Sun had lost 4.74 per cent of its mass since he had left. And that led to only one conclusion, one that sent shivers straight through his heart, chilling his soul.

It had already happened.

In fact, humanity had known about this long before he had embarked on his journey. They had learned this after thousands upon thousands of probes had been shot into the Sun. The probes' findings had allowed astrophysicists to determine that a short-lived energy flash would erupt from the star, reducing its mass by about five per cent.

If the Sun could think and could remember, it would have almost certainly been untroubled. In the billions of years of its life, it had already undergone much greater upheavals than this. When it was born from the turbulence of a spiraling stellar nebula, greater changes had been measured in milliseconds. In those brilliant and glorious moments, the Sun's gravitational collapse had ignited the fires of nuclear fusion, illuminating the grim, dark chaos of stellar dust.

It knew that its life was a process and, even though it was currently in the most stable phase of this progression, occasional minor, yet sudden, changes were inevitable. The Sun was like the calm surface of water: perfectly still for the most part, but every so often broken by the bursting of a rising bubble. The loss of energy and mass meant very little to it. The Sun would remain the Sun, a medium-sized star with an apparent visual magnitude of -26.8.

The flash would not even have a significant effect on the rest of the solar system. Mercury would probably dissolve, while the dense atmosphere of Venus would likely be stripped to nothing. The effect on the more distant planets would be even less severe. It could be expected that the surface of Mars would melt, likely scorching its color from red to black. As for Earth, its surface would only be heated to seven thousand degrees, probably for no longer than a hundred hours or so. The planet's oceans would certainly evaporate. On dry land, strata of continental rock would liquefy, but that would be all.

The Sun would then quickly revert to its previous state, albeit with reduced mass. This reduction would cause the orbits of all the planets to shift outward, but that would hardly be consequential. Earth, for example, would only experience a slight drop in temperature, falling to about -80 degrees on average. In fact, the cold would advance the re-solidification of the melted surface, and it would ensure that some of Earth's water and atmosphere would be preserved.

There was a joke that became popular in those days. It was a conversation with God, and it went like this:

'Oh, God, for you thousands of years are just a brief moment!'

God answered, 'Indeed, they are just a second to me.'

'Oh, God, for you vast riches are just small change!'

God answered, 'Just a nickel.'

'Oh, God, please spare me a nickel!'

To which God then answered, 'Certainly. Just give me a second.'

Now it was the Sun that was asking humanity for 'just a second'. It had been calculated that the energy flash would not happen for another eighteen thousand years.

For the Sun this was certainly no more than a second, but in humanity – faced with an entire 'second' of waiting – it engendered an attitude of apathy. 'Apathism' was even elevated to a kind of philosophy. All this did not occur without repercussions; with every passing day, humanity grew more cynical.

Then again, there were at least four or five hundred generations in which humankind could find a way out.

After two centuries, humanity took the first step: a spaceship was launched into interstellar space, tasked with finding a habitable planet within one hundred light-years to which humanity could migrate. This spaceship was called the *UNS Ark*, and its crew became known as the Forerunners.

The *Ark* swept past sixty stars, thus past sixty infernos. Only one was accompanied by a satellite. This satellite was a five-thousand-mile-wide droplet of incandescent molten metal, its liquid form in constant flux as it orbited.

This was the *Ark*'s only achievement, further proof of humanity's loneliness.

The *UNS Ark* sailed for twenty-three years. However, as she traveled close to light speed, this 'Ark Time' equated to twenty-five thousand years on Earth. Had it followed its mission plan, the *UNS Ark* should have returned to Earth long ago.

Flying close to the speed of light made communication with Earth impossible. Only by reducing its velocity to less than half the speed of light could the *Ark* be contacted by Earth. This maneuver, however, cost significant amounts of time and energy, and therefore the *Ark* would usually only do this once a month in order to receive a dispatch from Earth. When it slowed down, the *Ark* would pick up Earth's most recent message, sent more than a hundred years after the previous one. The relative time between the *Ark* and Earth made communication much like targeting a high-powered scope; if the scope was off by even the slightest degree, it would miss the target by a vast distance.

The *UNS Ark* had received its last message from Earth thirteen 'Ark Years' after its departure. On Earth, seventeen thousand years had passed since it had left. One month after that message, the *Ark* had again slowed, but it only received silence. The predictions made many millennia ago could certainly have been off. One month on the *Ark* was more than a hundred years on Earth. That was when it must have happened.

The *UNS Ark* had truly become an ark – one with a lone Noah. Of the other seven Forerunners, four had been killed by radiation when a star exploded in a nova four light-years from the *Ark*; two others had succumbed to illness and one man had, in the silence of that fateful slow-down, shot himself.

The last Forerunner had kept the *Ark* at communication speed for a long stretch. Finally, he had accelerated the *Ark* back to near-light-speed, but a tiny flame of hope burning within him had soon tempted him to reduce the ship's speed once more. Again he had listened anxiously, but all he heard was silence. And so it went on; his frequent cycles of acceleration and deceleration prolonged the return journey countless times.

And through it all, the silence remained.

The *Ark* returned to the solar system twenty-five thousand years after its departure from Earth, nine thousand years later than originally planned.

Chapter 2

The Monument

Passing the orbit of Pluto, the *Ark* continued its flight deep into the solar system. For an interstellar vessel such as the *UNS Ark*, traveling in the solar system was like sailing in the calm of a harbor. Soon the Sun grew brighter. As the sunlight began to bathe the *Ark*, the Forerunner caught his first glimpse of Jupiter. Through his telescope he could see that the huge planet had changed almost beyond recognition. Its red spot was nowhere to be seen, and its tempestuous bands appeared more chaotic than ever. He paid no heed to the other planets and continued the tranquil last leg of his journey, straight on to Earth.

The Forerunner's hand trembled as he pushed the button. The massive metal shield covering the porthole slowly opened.

'Oh, my blue sphere, blue eye of the universe, my blue angel,' the Forerunner prayed, his eyelids firmly closed.

After a long while, he finally forced his eyes open.

The planet he saw was black and white.

The black was rock, melted and re-hardened, tombstone-black. The white was seawater, vaporized and refrozen, corpse- shroud white.

As the *Ark* entered low-Earth orbit, slowly passing over the black land and white oceans, the Forerunner spotted no vestiges of humanity; everything had been melted to nothing. Civilization was gone, lost in a wisp of smoke.

But surely there should have been a monument, some memorial capable of withstanding the seven thousand degrees that had destroyed all else.

Just as these thoughts crossed the Forerunner's mind, the monument appeared. It was a video signal, originating from the surface and transmitted to his spaceship. The computer streamed the signal's millennia-old contents onto his screen. Obviously shot by extremely heat-resistant cameras, it revealed the catastrophe that had befallen Earth. The moment when the energy flash hit was very different from what he had so often imagined. The Sun did not suddenly grow brighter; most of the cataclysmic radiation it blasted forth remained well outside the visible spectrum. He could see, however, the final moments of the blue sky. It suddenly turned inferno-red, only to change again to a nightmarish purple.

He saw the cities of that era, the so-familiar forms of skyscrapers, oozing with thick black smoke as the temperature surged by thousands of degrees. Soon they began to glow like the dim red of kindled charcoal but they could not last, finally melting like countless wax candles.

Scorching red magma streamed from the mountaintops, forming cascading waterfalls of molten rock. These incandescent rapids converged to form a massive crimson river of lava that buried the Earth under its pyroclastic floods. And from where there had been ocean waters now rose giant mushroom clouds of steam. The bellies of these ferociously billowing mountains shone with the red glow of the molten world beneath. Their crests were permeated with the sky's cruel purple. The endless ranges of steam clouds expanded with relentless speed and abandon. Soon they swallowed all of the Earth...

Years passed before this haze finally dispersed, revealing that there was still a planet beneath. The burned and melted world below had begun to cool, leaving all of it covered in rippling black rock. In some parts, magma still flowed, forming intricate webs of fire that spanned the Earth. All traces of humanity had disappeared. Civilization had vanished, forgotten like a dream from which the Earth had awoken.

A few years later, the Earth's water, having been dissociated to oxyhydrogen under the incredible heat, began to recombine. It fell in great torrents, once again covering the burning world in steam. It was as if the Earth had been trapped in a gigantic steamer: dark, moist and stiflingly hot. The deluge lasted for dozens of years as the Earth continued to cool. Slowly, the oceans began to fill again.

Centuries passed. The dark clouds of evaporated seawater had finally dispersed, and the sky turned blue once more. In the heavens, the Sun reappeared. Earth's new, more distant orbit forced a sharp decline in temperatures, freezing the oceans. Now the sky was without clouds, and the long-dead world below froze in complete silence.

The picture changed again, this time revealing a city. First, a forest of tall, slender buildings came into view. As the camera slowly descended from some unseen peak, a plaza came into view. Its spacious dimensions were filled with a sea of people. The camera descended further, allowing the Forerunner to discern that all of the faces in the forum were turned upward, appearing to look right at him. The camera finally stopped, hovering above a platform in the middle of the plaza.

A beautiful girl, probably in her teens, stood on this platform. Through the screen, she waved right at the Forerunner, and as she waved, she shouted, 'Hey, we can see you! You came to us like a shooting star!' Her voice was delicate and fair. 'Are you the *UNS Ark One?*'

In the final years of his voyage the Forerunner had spent most of his time playing a virtual reality game. To run this game, the computer directly interfaced with the player's brain signals, using his thoughts to generate three-dimensional images. The people and objects in these images were obviously restricted in many ways, bound by the limits of the player's imagination. In his loneliness, the Forerunner had created one virtual world after another, ranging from single households to entire realms.

Having spent so much time in unreal realities, he quickly recognized the city on his screen for what it was: just another virtual world – and one of inferior quality, at that – most likely the product of a distracted mind. Virtual projections such as this one, born from the imagination, were always prone to errors. The pictures he saw now, however, seemed to have more wrong with them than right.

First and worst, when the camera passed the skyscrapers the Forerunner had watched as numerous people exited the buildings through windows on the top floors. These people had jumped straight out, leaping hundreds of feet down to the ground below. After falling from such dizzying heights, they landed without a scratch, apparently completely unharmed. He also saw people leap off the ground only to rise, as if being pulled by invisible wires. These strange jumps carried them several stories up a skyscraper's side. They ascended even higher, pushing off from foot-holds that ran up the side of each of the buildings, as though they had been put there specifically for just that purpose. In this manner they could reach the top of any building or enter it through any of its countless windows. These skyscrapers seemed to have neither elevators nor doors. At least, the Forerunner never saw them use anything except a window to enter or leave a building.

When the virtual camera moved above that plaza, the Forerunner could see another error: amongst the sea of people hung crystal balls suspended by strings. These balls were about three feet in diameter each. Occasionally people would reach into these balls and pull out a segment of the crystal substance with great ease. As they removed the piece, the ball would immediately recover its spherical shape. The extracted segment would do the same; but even as the small piece became round, the person who had extracted it would put it into his mouth and swallow it...

In addition to these obvious mistakes, the confusion and irrationality of the image's creator was most evident in the bizarre objects that were floating through the city's sky. Some were large, ranging from five to ten feet long, while others were smaller, only a foot or so long. Some resembled pieces of broken sponge, while others brought to mind the crooked branches of some giant tree; all slowly floated through the air.

The Forerunner saw one large branch drifting toward the girl on the platform. She simply gave it a light push, sending it spiraling into the distance. The Forerunner suddenly understood: in a world on the brink of destruction, it must have been impossible to remain of sound mind and thought.

The image was most likely being sent out by an automated installation, which had probably been buried deep beneath the surface before the catastrophe struck. Shielded from the radiation and heat, it must have lain hidden and waited, automatically rising to the surface once it was safe. This installation, then, probably kept an unending vigil, monitoring space, projecting these images to any of the scattered remnants of humanity returning to Earth. Chances were that these comical and jumbled images had been created with good will, intended to comfort the survivors.

'Did you say that other *Ark* ships were launched?' the Forerunner asked, hoping to get something from this bizarre display.

'Of course. There were twelve others!' the girl answered enthusiastically. The absurdity of the other elements of the image notwithstanding, this girl was not half bad at all. Her beautiful face combined the best features typical of Eastern and Western cultures, and she beamed with pure innocence. To her, the entire cosmos was a great big playground. Her large, round eyes seemed to sing with every flutter of her eyelids, while her long hair floated and fanned in the air, appearing completely weightless. She reminded the Forerunner of a mermaid swimming in an unseen ocean.

'So, is anyone still alive?' the Forerunner asked, his final hope blazing like wildfire.

'Aren't you?' the girl innocently asked in return.

'Of course. I'm a real human. Not like you, a computer-generated virtual person,' the Forerunner replied, slightly exasperated.

'The last *Ark* arrived seven hundred and thirty years ago. You are the last *Ark* to return, but please tell us: do you have any women aboard?' the girl enquired with great interest.

'There is only me,' the Forerunner replied, his head heavy with the memories.

'So, you say that there are no women with you?' the girl asked again, her eyes widening in genuine shock.

'As I said, I am the only one. Are there no other spaceships out there that have yet to return?' the Forerunner enquired in return, desperate to keep the spark of hope alive.

The girl wrung her delicate, elfin hands. 'There are none! It's so sad, so very terribly sad! You are the last of them, if… oh…' She could barely contain her sobs. 'If not by cloning…' The girl was now crying uncontrollably. 'Oh,' she finished, her beautiful face now covered with tears. Around her, the people in the plaza were crying a sea of tears.

While he did not cry, the Forerunner, too, felt his breaking heart sink to new depths. Humanity's destruction had become a fact beyond denial.

'Why do you not ask me who I am?' the girl asked, raising her face again. She had reclaimed her innocent demeanor, her recent sorrow – merely seconds past – apparently forgotten.

'I couldn't care less,' the Forerunner answered flatly.

With tears in her eyes again, the girl shouted, 'But I am Earth's leader!'

'Yes! She is the High Counsellor of Earth's Unity Government!' the people in the plaza shouted in unison. Their rapid shift from sorrow to excitement reflected marked deficiencies in their programming.

The Forerunner felt himself growing tired of this senseless game, and he rose to turn away.

'How can you not care? All the capital has gathered here to welcome you, forefather! Do not ignore us!' the girl cried, emitting a tearful wail.

Remembering his original and still-unresolved question, the Forerunner turned and enquired, 'What has humanity left behind?'

'Follow our landing beacon, then you can learn for yourself!' came the happy reply.

Chapter 3

The Capital

The Forerunner climbed into his landing module. Leaving the *UNS Ark* to orbit, he began his descent to Earth, following the landing beacon's directions. He wore a pair of video specs, their lenses displaying the images being broadcast from the planet below.

'Forefather, you must immediately come to Earth's capital. Even though it is not the planet's biggest city, it is certainly the most beautiful,' the girl calling herself Earth's leader prattled on. 'You will like it! Note, though, that the landing coordinates we have given you will lead you to a spot a good distance from the city, as we wish to avoid possible damage...'

The Forerunner changed the focus of his specs to show the area directly below his lander. Now, at only thirty thousand feet in the air, he could still see nothing but black wasteland below.

As he descended, the virtual image grew even more confusing. Perhaps its creator, thousands of years before, had been in the grip of an unimaginable depression; or perhaps the computer projecting it, left to its own devices for thousands upon thousands of years, was showing signs of its age. In any case, for some unfathomable reason the virtual girl had begun to sing:

Oh, you dear angel! From the macro-era you return!
Oh, glorious macro-era
Magnificent macro-era
Oh, beautiful macro-era
Oh, vanished vision! In the fires the dream did burn.

As this beautiful singer began her hymn, she leapt into the air. She lifted off the platform, jumping thirty feet into the air. After falling back to the platform, she sprang back up, this time clearing the plaza in a single bound. She landed on top of a building, and from there she jumped again, this time across the entire width of the plaza. Landing at its other side, she looked like a charming little flea.

She leapt once more, and in mid-air she caught one of the strange objects that was floating past her. Several feet long, the object looked like the trunk of a strange tree, and it carried her spiraling through the air, above the sea of people. Even as she rose, her svelte body continued to writhe rhythmically.

The sea of people below began to buzz with raw excitement, that soon boiled over into song: 'Oh, macro-era! Oh, macro-era!' As the song continued, they all began to jump. The crowd now looked like sand on a drum, rising in waves with every invisible beat.

The Forerunner simply refused to take any more of this, and he shut off both the image and the sound. He was certain now that the situation was even worse than he had first thought. Before the catastrophe had struck, the people of Earth must have felt venomous envy toward the survivors who had slipped through time and space, thus eluding their appointed destruction. Fuelled by such emotions, they had created this gross perversion to torment those who returned.

As his descent continued the annoyance the images had caused slowly began to ebb, and by the time he felt the shock of the landing that annoyance had almost completely left him. For a moment he succumbed to fantasy: maybe he had truly landed near a city that simply wasn't visible from up high.

All illusion dissolved as he stepped out of the lander. He was surrounded by boundless, black desolation. Despair chilled his entire body.

The Forerunner carefully slid open his visor. Immediately, he felt a surge of cold air against his face. The air was very thin, but it was thick enough for him to breathe. The temperature was somewhere around forty degrees below freezing. The sky was a dark blue, as it had been at dawn and dusk in the age before the catastrophe. It was neither time now, as the Sun hanging overhead clearly confirmed.

The Forerunner removed his gloves, but he could not feel the Sun's warmth. In the thin air, the sunlight was scattered and weak. He could see stars twinkling brightly in the sky above.

The ground beneath his feet had solidified about two thousand years before. All around, he could see the ripples of hardened magma. Even though the first signs of weathering were visible, the surface remained hard and jagged. No matter how closely he looked, he could only make out the barest traces of soil. Before him the undulating land stretched to the horizon, punctuated only by small hills. Behind him lay the frozen ocean, gleaming white against the skyline.

Scanning his surroundings, the Forerunner searched for the source of the transmission. He finally spotted a transparent shield dome embedded in the rocky ground. This shell was about three feet in diameter, and it covered what appeared to be an array of highly complex structures.

The Forerunner was soon able to make out several similar domes scattered in the distance. They were roughly fifty to one hundred feet apart. From where he stood, they looked a little like bubbles, frozen as they burst through the Earth's surface and now glinting under the Sun.

Reactivating the left lens of his video specs, the Forerunner opened a virtual window into the strange imaginary world created for him. It's shameless 'leader' was still floating through the air, riding her bizarre branch, singing and writhing deliriously.

As she flew, she blew kisses toward the camera. The masses below, down to the last man, cheered:

Oh, great macro-era!
Oh, romantic macro-era!
Oh, melancholic macro-era!
Oh, frail macro-era...

Numbed, the Forerunner stopped cold. Standing beneath the deep blue sky in the light of the shining Sun under the sparkling stars, he felt the entire universe revolving around him. Him. The last human.

He was overcome by an avalanche of dark loneliness. Covering his face, he sank to his knees and began to sob.

As he descended into despair, the singing ceased. Everyone in the virtual image stared straight toward him, their myriad eyes filled with deep concern. The girl, still riding her branch through mid-air, beamed a sweet smile right up at him.

'Do you have so little faith in humanity?' she asked, her eyes twinkling.

She continued speaking, and, as she did, something that the Forerunner could not place sent a shiver through his body, heightening all his senses. Disturbed, he slowly began to rise back to his feet. As he stood, he suddenly saw it: a shadow was falling over the city in his left lens. It was as if a dark cloud had appeared out of the blue, blackening the entire sky in an instant. He took a step to the side. Light was immediately restored to the city.

He slowly approached the dome, intrigued. Standing before it, he bent forward, carefully studying it. Inside he could indistinctly make out a dense array of tiny, yet incredibly detailed, structures. He immediately noticed that something magnificently strange had completely dominated the sky in his video specs.

That something was his face.

'We can see you! Can you see us? Use a magnifier!' the girl

shouted as loudly as she could. The sea of people below over-flowed with exhilaration once more.

Now the Forerunner finally understood it all: he recalled the people jumping out of tall buildings, which made sense because gravity could cause them no harm in their microscopic environment. This also explained their leaps. In such an environment, people would easily be able to leap up a building a thousand feet high – or should that be a thousand microns? The large crystal balls must, in fact, be drops of water; in this tiny environment, their shape would be completely at the mercy of the water's surface tension. And when these microscopic people wanted a drink, they could simply pull out a tiny droplet. Finally, the strange, elongated things that floated through the urban landscape – and that the girl was riding – these, too, made sense. They were nothing other than tiny particles of dust.

This city was not virtual at all. It was a city just as real as any city twenty-five thousand years ago had been, only it was covered by a three-foot, transparent dome.

Humanity still existed. Civilization still existed.

In this microscopic city floated a girl on a branch of dust – the High Counsellor of Earth's Unity Government – confidently stretching her open hand toward the man who, at the moment, filled almost her entire cosmos: the Forerunner.

'Forefather, the micro-era welcomes you!'

Chapter 4

Micro-Humanity

'In the seventeen thousand years before the catastrophe,' the girl told the Forerunner, 'humanity left no stone unturned in its search for some way out. The easiest way out would have been migrating to another star. But no *Ark*, including yours, was able to locate even a single star with a habitable planet. And it did not really matter; a mere century before the catastrophe, our spaceship technology was still not developed enough to migrate even one-thousandth of humanity.

'Another plan,' she continued, 'was to have humanity migrate deep underground, well-hidden from the Sun's energy flash, ready to emerge once its effects subsided. That plan, however, would have done little other than prolong everyone's inevitable deaths. After the catastrophe, Earth's ecosystem was completely destroyed. Humanity could not have survived.

'There was a time when humanity fell into total despair. It was in that darkest night that an idea came to life in the mind of a certain genetic engineer: what if humanity's size could be reduced by nine orders of magnitude?' A pensive look crossed her face. 'Everything about human society could also be scaled to that size, creating a microscopic ecosystem, and such an eco-system would only consume microscopic amounts of natural

253

resources. It did not take long before all of humanity came to agree that this plan was the only way in which our species could be saved.'

The Forerunner listened intently, thoroughly considering the implications of this plan.

She continued. 'The plan relied on two types of technology. The first was genetic engineering: by modifying the human genome, humans would be reduced to the height of about ten microns, no larger than a single body cell. Human anatomy, however, would remain completely unchanged. This was a completely plausible goal. In essence, there is very little difference between the genome of a bacterium and that of a human. The other piece of the puzzle was nanotechnology. This technology had been developed as far back as the twentieth century, and even in those days people were able to assemble simple generators the size of bacteria. Based on these humble beginnings, humanity soon learned to build everything from nano-rockets to nano-microwave ovens; but the nano-engineers of ages past could have never imagined where their technologies would ultimately be put to use.

'Fostering the first batch of micro-humans was very similar to cloning: the complete genome was extracted from a human cell and then cultivated to form a micro-human that resembled the original in all ways except size. Later generations were born just like macro-humans. That, by the way,' she added, 'is what we call you. And you may have already guessed that we call your era the "macro-era".

'The first group of micro-humans took to the world stage in a rather dramatic fashion,' she told him. 'One day, about 12,500 years after the departure of your *Ark*, a classroom was shown on all of Earth's TV screens. Thirty students sat in this classroom. Everything seemed perfectly normal. The children were normal children, and the classroom was a normal classroom. There was nothing at all that would have seemed out of the ordinary. But then the camera panned out and humanity could see that this classroom in fact stood on the stage of a micro-scope.' The High Counsellor would have continued her account had she not been interrupted by the Forerunner's curiosity.

'I would like to ask,' he interjected, 'if micro-humans, with their microscopic brains, can achieve the intelligence levels of macro-humans?'

The girl shook her head, more bemused than angry. 'Do you take me for some kind of fool? Whales are no smarter than you are! Intelligence is not a matter of brain size. In regard to the number of atoms and quantum states in our brains, well, let us just say that our ability to process information easily matches that of a macro-human brain.' She paused, then continued with great curiosity in her voice. 'Could you please show us to your spacecraft?'

'Of course, very gladly.' It was the Forerunner's turn to pause. 'How exactly will you go?'

'Please wait just a moment!' the girl shouted exuberantly.

After saying this, the High Counsellor leapt into the air and onto a truly bizarre flying machine. The machine resembled a large, propeller-powered feather. Soon everyone on the plaza below was leaping into the air, competing for a spot on this 'feather'. It was apparent that this society had no concept or system of rank or status. The people indiscriminately jumping onto this strange vehicle were perfectly ordinary citizens, both young and old. Regardless of their age, they all wore the childish demeanor that seemed so inappropriate on the High Counsellor; the result was a noisy, excited, chaotic ruckus.

The feather was almost instantly jam-packed with people, but a continuous stream of new feathers was already coming into view. No sooner did one appear before it was covered with excited micro-humans. In the end, the city's sky was filled with several hundred feathers, each stuffed to capacity, or beyond, with people. They were all led by the High Counsellor's feather flier. The girl led this formidable flying armada through the city.

The Forerunner bent over the dome again, carefully observing the microscopic city within. This time he was able to make out the skyscrapers. To him, they looked like a dense forest of matchsticks. He strained his eyes and was finally able to spot the feather-like vehicles. They looked like tiny white grains of powder floating on water. If it had not been for the sheer number of them, they would have been impossible to see with the naked eye.

The picture in the left lens of the Forerunner's video specs remained as clear as ever. The micro-camera-person and their unimaginably small camera had evidently also boarded a feather, and from there they continued to stream a live feed. Through this feed, the Forerunner was able to catch a glimpse of traffic in the micro-city.

He was in for an immediate shock: it appeared that collisions were near-constant occurrences. The fast-flying feathers were continually knocking into each other and into the dust particles floating through the air. They even frequently hit the sides of the towering skyscrapers! But the flying machines and their passengers were no worse for wear, and no one seemed to pay any heed to these collisions.

This was actually a phenomenon that any junior high physics student could have explained: the smaller the scale of an object, the stronger its structural integrity. There is a vast difference between two bicycles colliding and two ten-thousand-ton ships ramming into each other. And if two dust particles collide, they will suffer no harm whatsoever. Because of this, the people of the micro-world seemed to have bodies of steel and could live lives free from the fear of injury.

As the feathers flew, people would occasionally jump out of the skyscraper windows, trying to board one of the machines in mid-air. They were not always successful, however, and some would fall from what seemed like hundreds of yards. The sheer height left the watching Forerunner with a feeling of vertigo. The falling micro-humans, on the other hand, plummeted with perfect grace and composure, even taking the time to greet acquaintances through skyscraper windows as they rushed toward the ground.

'Oh, your eyes are as black as the ocean, so very, very deep,' the High Counsellor said to the Forerunner. 'So deep with melancholy! Your melancholy shrouds our city. You should make them a museum! Oh, oh, oh...' She began to cry, clearly distressed.

The others, too, began to cry, and their feather fliers started bouncing between the skyscrapers, smashing into buildings left, right and center.

The Forerunner could see his own huge eyes in the image on his left video spec. Their melancholy, magnified a million times over, shocked even him. 'Why a museum?' he asked, perplexed.

'Because melancholy is only for museums. The micro-era is an age without worries!' Earth's leader loudly proclaimed. Even though tears still lingered on her tender face, there was no longer any trace of sorrow to be found behind them.

'We live in an age without worries!' the others joined in excitedly, shouting in unison.

It seemed to the Forerunner that moods in the micro-era shifted hundreds of times faster than they had ever done in the macro-era. These shifts seemed particularly pronounced when it came to negative emotions such as sadness and melancholy. Micro-humans could bounce back from such feelings in the blink of an eye.

However, there was another aspect of this discovery that was even harder for the Forerunner to truly fathom. All negative emotions were incredibly rare in this era; so rare, in fact, that they were like fascinating artefacts to the people of the micro-era. When they encountered them, they grasped the opportunity to experience them.

'Don't be depressed like a child! You will quickly see that there is nothing to worry about in the micro-era!' the High Counsellor shouted, now full of joy.

Hearing her words, the Forerunner could not help but do a double-take. He had previously observed that the general mental state of the micro-humans seemed much like that of macro-era children, but he had just assumed that their children would be even more, well, childish. 'Are you saying,' he asked in astonishment, 'that in this era, as people age, they grow...?' He almost couldn't believe what he was asking. 'Grow more childish?'

'We grow happier with age!' The High Counsellor giggled.

'Yes! In the micro-era we grow happier with age!' the crowd echoed loudly.

'But melancholy can be very beautiful,' the girl continued. 'Like the moon's reflection on a lake; it reflects the romanticism of the macro-era. Oh, oh, oh...' The Earth's leader emitted plaintive cries at the thought.

'Yes! What a beautiful age it was!' the others chimed in, their eyes brimming with tears.

The Forerunner could not help but laugh. 'You little people really don't understand melancholy. Real melancholy sheds no tears.'

'You can show us!' the High Counsellor shouted, returning to her exuberant state.

'I hope not,' the Forerunner said, sighing gently.

'Look, this is our monument to the macro-era!' the High Counsellor announced as the feathers flew over another square in the city.

The Forerunner saw the monument. It was a massive black pillar, vaguely reminding him of a giant broadcast tower. Its rough exterior was covered with countless tiles, each about the size of a wheel. It called to mind the pattern of fish scales.

Staring at the towering structure, it took the Forerunner a long while to understand: it was a strand of macro-human hair.

Chapter 5

The Banquet

Flying upwards, the feather fliers emerged from the transparent dome, passing through some unseen hole. As they left their city's cover behind, the High Counsellor turned to the Forerunner through the video screen in his specs.

'We are now a hundred miles or so from your spacecraft. If we can land on your fingers, you can carry us. It would greatly speed up our journey.'

The Forerunner turned his head to his lander, which was right behind him. Her reference could only mean that units of measurement had also shrunk in the micro-era. He stretched out his hand, and the feather-fliers landed. They looked like a fine white powder drifting onto his fingers.

In the video lens he could now see his fingerprints. They looked like massive, semi-translucent ranges of mountains that seemed to swallow these feathers as they floated into their great canyons. The High Counsellor was the first to leap from a feather. Immediately she fell, sprawling prone on the Forerunner's finger.

'Your oily skin is far too slippery!' she complained loudly, taking off her shoes. In frustration, she tossed them into the distance. Now barefoot, she turned, looking around curiously as the others also leapt onto his skin. A sea of people soon gathered between the semi-opaque cliffs of his fingers. By the Forerunner's best guess, there were now more than ten thousand micro-humans gathered on his hand.

The Forerunner raised himself and very, very carefully walked toward his lander, keeping his hand stretched out and steady before him.

He had not even fully entered the lander when the crowd of micro-humans began to shout. 'Wow! Just look, a metal sky! An artificial Sun!'

'Don't be so dramatic; you're being silly! This is just a small shuttle. The ship above is much larger!' the High Counsellor chastened her people. But she, too, was staring in wonder, looking in all directions. As she did this, the crowd again began singing its strange song:

> *Oh, glorious macro-era*
> *Magnificent macro-era*
> *Melancholic macro-era*
> *Oh, vanished vision! In the fires the dream did burn.*

As the lander took off, setting out on its flight to the *UNS Ark*, the High Counsellor finally continued her account of the history of the micro-era.

'For a time, micro- and macro societies co-existed. During this period, the early micro-humans came to fully absorb the knowledge of the macro-world, and so we inherited macro-human culture,' she told the Forerunner. 'At the same time, micro-humanity began developing its own extremely technologically advanced society. It was a society based on nanotechnology. This transitional era between the macro-era and micro-era lasted for about... hmm...' The High Counsellor's tiny mouth twitched ever so slightly as she recalled. 'About twenty generations or so.

'Then, as the catastrophe approached, the macro-humans ceased bearing children, and their numbers dwindled day by day. At the same time, the micro-human population skyrocketed, and the scope of our society expanded along with it. Soon it exceeded that of macro-human society. At this point the micro-humans requested that they be handed the reins of global governance. This demand shook macro-society to its core and led to a powerful backlash. Some diehards refused to surrender political power; they claimed it would have been like a batch of bacteria ruling mankind. It ended with a global war between macro- and micro-humanity!'

'How horrible for your people!' The Forerunner gasped in sympathy.

'Horrible for the macro-humans, since they were quickly defeated,' the High Counsellor replied.

'How did that happen? A single macro-human with a sledge-hammer could obliterate a micro-city of millions,' the perplexed Forerunner objected.

'But micro-humanity did not fight them in its cities, and macro-humanity's arsenal was utterly unsuitable for fighting an unseen enemy,' she told him. 'The only real weapon at their disposal was disinfectant. Throughout the history of their civilization they had used it to battle micro-organisms, yet it had never achieved a decisive victory. Now that they were seeking to vanquish micro-humans, an enemy equal to them in intelligence, their chances of victory were even slimmer. They could not track the movements of the micro-armies, and so we could corrupt their computer chips right under their noses. And what could they do without their computers? Power does not come from size,' the High Counsellor explained.

The Forerunner nodded in agreement. 'Now that I think about it...'

The High Counsellor continued, a fierce fire now burning brightly in her eyes. 'Those war criminals met their just fate. Several thousand micro-human special forces armed with laser drills parachuted onto their retinas...' She let the Forerunner's imagination do the rest before continuing more calmly. 'After the war, the micro-humans had claimed control of Earth. As the macro-era ended, the micro-era began.'

'Very interesting!' the Forerunner exclaimed.

The lander docked with the *Ark* in low-Earth orbit. The micro-humans immediately boarded their feather-fliers again and began exploring their new surroundings. The enormous size of the spacecraft left them dumbstruck. The Forerunner initially thought their utterances reflected admiration, but the High Counsellor soon explained her feelings about the ship.

'Now we understand. Even without the Sun's energy flash, the macro-era could not have endured,' she said. 'You consume billions of times more resources than we do!'

'But consider that this spaceship is capable of traveling at near-light speed. It can reach stars hundreds of light-years away. This is something, small people, which could only be produced in the great macro-era,' the Forerunner countered.

'At the moment, we certainly cannot create its equal. Our spaceships at present can only reach one-tenth of the speed of light,' the High Counsellor conceded.

'You are capable of space travel?' the Forerunner stammered. The sheer surprise was enough to drain the color from his face.

'Certainly not as capable as you were. The spaceships of the micro-era can reach no further than Venus. In fact, we have just heard back from them, and they tell us that as things stand, it seems far more habitable than Earth,' the High Counsellor answered, paying no heed to his shock.

'How big are your ships?' the Forerunner asked, as he regained his composure.

'The big ones are the size of your age's... hmm...' She paused, searching for the right analogy. 'Soccer ball,' she finally said. 'They can carry hundreds of thousands of passengers. The small ones, on the other hand, are only the size of a golf ball – a macro-era golf-ball, of course.'

These words shattered the Forerunner's sense of superiority.

'Forefather, would you please offer us something to eat? We are starving!' the High Counsellor asked, speaking for her people as the feather fliers gathered on the *Ark*'s control console.

The Forerunner could see ten thousand micro-humans on his command console, looking at him eagerly.

'I never thought I would be asked to invite so many to lunch,' he answered with a smile.

'We would certainly not want to ask too much of you!' the girl said, bristling with anger.

The Forerunner retrieved a tin of canned meat from storage. He opened it then used a small knife to carefully scoop out a tiny piece. He then cautiously placed it to one side of the crowd standing on the command console. The Forerunner could make out the crowd's location with his naked eye. It was a tiny, circular area on the console, about the size of a coin. This area was less smooth than the surrounding area, like someone's breath on a cold surface.

'Why did you take so much? That is very wasteful!' the Earth's leader scolded.

Now using a large monitor, the Forerunner could see her; and behind her stood a towering mountain of meat toward which her people were swarming. As they reached the pink pillar, they extracted small pieces and ate them.

Looking back to the console before him, the Forerunner could not make out even the slightest change in the size of that small piece of meat. On the screen, he could see that the crowd had quickly dispersed, some discarding half-eaten pieces of meat on the way. The High Counsellor picked a piece for herself and took a bite.

As she chewed, she began shaking her head. 'This is not very nice at all,' she commented as she finally finished.

'Of course not; it was synthesized in the eco-cycler. It was impossible to make it taste any better – the machine has limited capacity for taste production,' the Forerunner acknowledged apologetically.

'Give us some alcohol to wash it down!' The Earth's leader issued another request almost immediately. This demand caused a cheer to erupt among the gathered micro-humans. The Forerunner raised an eyebrow; after all, he knew that alcohol could kill micro-organisms!

'You drink beer?' he asked cautiously.

'No, we drink Scotch or vodka!' the Earth's leader replied with gusto.

'Mao-tai would also do!' someone shouted.

In fact, the Forerunner still had a bottle of Mao-tai, a bottle he had kept on the *Ark* ever since its departure from Earth. He had intended it for the day they found a colonizable world. He fetched it.

Wistfully holding the white porcelain bottle, he removed its cap. He then carefully poured some of the spirits into the cap, setting it down next to the crowd.

On the screen, he could see that the micro-humans had begun to scale the unassailable cliff face that was the cap. On the micro-scale, the seemingly smooth surface of the cap offered many hand-holds. Using the climbing skills they had honed on their city's skyscrapers, the micro-humans were quickly able to ascend to the cap's rim.

'Wow, what a beautiful lake!' the chorus of micro-humans shouted in admiration.

On the screen, the Forerunner could see the surface of that vast lake of alcohol bulge upward in a giant arc formed by the forces of its surface tension. The micro-human camera operator followed the High Counsellor as she first tried to scoop out some of the liquid with her hand. This attempt failed, however, as her tiny arms could not reach. Instead, she then sat herself down on the edge of the cap. From there, she let a slender foot brush the surface of the alcohol. Her delicate foot was immediately encased in a clear bead of liquid. Lifting her leg, she used her hands to extract a small drop of alcohol from the bead. She let the drop fall into her mouth.

'Wow!' she exclaimed, nodding in satisfaction. 'Macro-era alcohol really is a lot better than our micro-era spirits.'

'I am very glad to hear that we still have something that is better. But using your feet to drink like that – that's very unhygienic,' the Forerunner noted.

'I don't understand,' she replied, looking up at him in confusion.

'You walked around on your bare feet for quite a while; they must be covered in germs,' the Forerunner explained.

'Oh, now I see!' the Earth's leader called out. She was handed a box that one of her attendants had been carrying. She opened the box, and immediately a strange animal emerged. It was a round football-sized organism with tiny, chaotically twitching legs. The High Counsellor lifted the creature by one of its small legs and explained. 'Look, this is one of our city's gifts to you! A lacto-chicken!'

The Forerunner strained his mind trying to recall his microbiology education. 'Are you saying that that is a...' He paused in disbelief. 'A lactobacillus?'

'That is what it was called in the macro-era. It is a creature that gives yogurt its taste. A very useful animal indeed!' the High Counsellor replied.

'A very useful bacterium,' the Forerunner corrected. 'But I now understand that bacteria cannot harm you at all. Our concept of hygiene has become meaningless in the micro-era.'

Earth's leader shook her head. 'Not necessarily. Some animals—Ah,' she caught herself, 'some bacteria can seriously hurt us. For example, there are the coli-wolves. Overpowering one of them is a great feat. But most animals, like the yeast pigs, are quite lovable.' As she spoke, she took another drop from her foot and placed it into her mouth. When she shook off the remains of the alcohol bead from her foot and stood up, the High Counsellor was already quite tipsy, and her speech had begun to slur.

'I never would have expected for alcohol to still be around!' the Forerunner frowned, genuinely astonished.

'We,' the Earth's leader said, her speech faltering, 'we have inherited all that was beautiful about civilization, even though those Macros thought that we had no right to.' She stumbled. 'The right to become the carriers of human civilization,' she slurred. Looking slightly dizzy, she plopped herself back down.

'We inherited all of humanity's philosophy – Western, Eastern, Greek and Chinese!' the crowd shouted with one voice.

Now seated, the Earth's leader stretched her hands toward heaven and intoned, 'No man ever steps in the same river twice. The Tao gave birth to One. The One gave birth to Two. The Two gave birth to Three. The Three gave birth...' Her words trailed off, but she quickly slurred on: 'Gave birth to all of creation! We appreciate the paintings of van Gogh. We listen to Beethoven's music. We perform Shakespeare's plays. To be or not to be; that is...' Again she paused. 'That is the question.' She rose again, stumbling tipsily as she gave her best Hamlet performance.

'In our era, we never would have imagined a girl like you becoming the world's leader,' the Forerunner noted.

'The macro-era was a melancholic age with melancholic politics. The micro-era is a carefree age. We need happy leaders,' the High Counsellor replied, already looking a good deal more sober.

'We have not finished our discussion.' She paused, gathering herself. 'Our discussion of history. We had just talked about...' She paused again, thinking. 'Ah, yes, war. After the war between macro- and micro-humanity, a world war broke out amongst micro-humanity.'

The Forerunner interrupted in shock. 'What? Certainly not for territory?'

'Of course not,' the High Counsellor answered. 'If there is one thing that is truly inexhaustible in the micro-era, it is territory. It was because of some,' here she again paused, this time for reasons only known to her before continuing, 'some reasons that a macro-human could not understand. But know that in one of our largest campaigns, the battlefields were so large they covered...' She paused once more. 'Oh, in your units, more than three hundred feet. Imagine an area that vast!'

'You inherited much more from the macro-era than I could have ever imagined,' the Forerunner stated soberly.

'Later, the micro-era focused all of its energies on preparing for the impending catastrophe. Over five centuries, we built thousands of super-cities, deep within the Earth's crust. These cities would have looked to you like six-foot-wide, stainless-steel balls, and each one could house tens of millions. These cities were built fifty thousand miles underground...'

'Wait just a second; the Earth's radius is just under four thousand miles,' the Forerunner interjected.

'Oh, I again used our units,' the Earth's leader apologized. 'In your units, it would be about...' She did the calculation in her head. 'Yes, half a mile! When the first signs of the Sun's energy flash were observed, the entire micro-world migrated beneath the Earth's surface. Then, then the catastrophe struck.

'Four hundred years after the catastrophe, the first group of micro-humans made its way up through a massive tunnel roughly the size of a macro-era water pipe. Boring their way through the solidified magma with a laser drill, they made it to the surface,' she explained. 'It would, however, be another five centuries before micro-humanity could establish a new world for itself on the surface. When we finally did, we built a world with tens of thousands of cities, a world of eighteen billion inhabitants.

'We were full of optimism about humanity's future then. It was an all-pervading, boundless optimism that would have been unimaginable in the macro-era. We were optimistic precisely because of our micro-society's tiny scale. It meant that humanity's ability to survive in this universe had been increased many millions of times over. For example,' she said, 'the contents of that can you just opened could feed our entire city for two years. And the can itself could supply our city with all the metal it needed for those two years.'

'As a macro-human, I now have a much better understanding of the enormous advantages of the micro-era. It's all so mythical, so very epic!' the Forerunner exclaimed in admiration.

The High Counsellor smiled and continued. 'Evolution trends toward the small. Size does not equal greatness. Microscopic life has a much easier time coexisting with nature in harmony. When the giant dinosaurs died out, their contemporaries, the ants, persisted. Now, should another great disaster approach, a spaceship the size of your lander could evacuate all of humanity. Micro-humanity could rebuild its civilization on a smallish asteroid and live comfortably.'

A long silence followed.

Finally, the Forerunner, firmly focusing on that coin-sized sea of humanity before him, solemnly stated, 'When I saw the Earth again, when I thought myself the last human in the universe, I was heartbroken, and I felt all hope die. No one had ever faced such heartrending agony. But, now! Now I am the happiest person alive; at least, I am the happiest macro-human there ever was. I see that humanity's civilization has persisted. In fact, civilization has achieved much more than just survival; yours is the true apex of civilization! We are all human, originating from the same source. So now, I entreat micro-humanity to accept me as a citizen of your society.'

'We accepted you when we first detected the *Ark*. You can come live on Earth. It will be no problem for the micro-era to support one macro-human,' the Earth's leader replied in equally solemn tones.

'I will live on Earth, but all I need can come from the *Ark*. The ship's life eco-cycler will be able to sustain me for the rest of my natural life. There is no reason for a macro-human to ever again consume Earth's resources,' the Forerunner said, his face glowing with deep, silent joy.

'But our situation is improving. Not only has Venus's climate become far more hospitable to human life, Earth's temperature is also warming again. Maybe next year, we will even have rainfall in many parts of the world. Then plants will be able to grow again,' the Earth's leader stated.

'Speaking of plants, have you ever seen any?' the Forerunner asked.

The High Counsellor answered. 'We grow lichen on the inside of our protective dome. They are huge plants, every filament as tall as a ten-story building! Then there's also the chlorella in the water...'

The Forerunner interjected. 'But have you ever heard of grass? Or trees?'

'Are you talking about the macro-era plants that grew as tall as mountains? My, they are legends of ancient times,' she replied.

The Forerunner smiled slightly and said, 'I just want to do one thing. When I return, I will show you the gifts I bring the micro-era. I think you will greatly enjoy them!'

Chapter 6

Rebirth

Alone again, the Forerunner made his way to the *Ark*'s cold storage, which was filled with tall, neatly arranged racks. Thousands upon thousands of sealed tubes filled these racks. It was a seed bank, storing the seeds of millions of Earth's plant species. The *Ark* had been meant to carry these seeds to the distant world that humanity would eventually adopt.

There were also a few rows that constituted the embryo storage. Here the embryonic cells of millions of Earth's animal species were banked.

When the temperatures warmed the following year, the Forerunner would plant grass on the Earth below. Amongst these millions of kinds of seeds, there were strains of grass hardy enough to grow in ice and snow. They would certainly be able to grow on the present-day Earth.

If only a tenth of the planet's ecosphere could be restored to what it had been in the macro-era, the micro-era would become a heaven on Earth. In fact, much more could probably be restored. The Forerunner indulged in the warm bliss of imagination: he could picture the micro-humans' wild joy when they would first see a colossal green blade of grass rising to the heavens. And what about a small meadow? What would a meadow mean to micro-humanity?

An entire grassland! What would a grassland mean? A green cosmos for micro-humanity! And a small brook in the grassland? What a majestic wonder the sight of the brook's clear waters snaking through the grassland would be in the eyes of micro-humans. Earth's leader had said there could be rain soon. If rain fell, there could be a grassland and that brook could spring to life! Then there could certainly be trees! My God, trees!

The Forerunner envisioned a group of micro-human explorers setting out from the roots of a tree, beginning their epic and wondrous journey upward. Every leaf would be a green plain, stretching to the horizon.

There could be butterflies then. Their wings would be like bright clouds, covering the heavens. And birds, their every call angelic trumpets blaring from the heavens.

Indeed, one-trillionth of the Earth's ecological resources could easily support a micro-human population of a trillion! Now the Forerunner finally understood the point that the micro-humans had so repeatedly emphasized.

The micro-era was an age without worries.

There was nothing that could threaten this new world, nothing but...

A terrible thought darkened the Forerunner's mind and soul as he realized what he must do; and it had to be done immediately. There was no time to delay. He went over to one of the racks and retrieved one hundred sealed tubes.

They contained the embryonic cells of his contemporaries – the embryonic cells of macro-humans.

The Forerunner took these tubes and dropped them into the laser waste incinerator. He then went back to cold storage, walking up and down the rows several times, carefully checking every nook and cranny. Only when he was absolutely certain that no macro-human tubes had been left behind did he return to the laser incinerator. He felt a sense of deep tranquility as he pushed the button.

The laser beam burned at tens of thousands of degrees. In its blazing light, the tubes and the embryos they contained were vaporized in the blink of an eye.

Devourer

Chapter 1

The Crystal from Eridanus

It was right in front of him, but the Captain could still barely make out its translucent crystalline structure. Floating through the black void of space, it was hidden by the darkness, like a piece of glass sunken in the murky depths. Only the slight distortion of starlight provoked by its passage allowed the Captain to make out its position. Soon it was lost again, disappearing in the space between the stars.

Suddenly the Sun distorted, its distant, eternal light twisting and twinkling before his eyes. It gave the Captain a start, but he maintained his proverbial 'Asian cool'. Unlike the dozen soldiers floating beside him, he managed not to gasp in shock. The Captain immediately understood; the crystal, a mere thirty feet away, had moved in front of the Sun, shining sixty million miles in the distance. In the three centuries to come, this strange vista would frequently play across his mind and he would wonder if this had been an omen of humanity's fate.

As the highest ranking officer of the United Nations' Earth Protection Force in space, the Captain commanded the force's interplanetary assets. It was a tiny unit, but it was equipped with the most powerful nuclear weapons humanity had ever devised.

Its enemies were lifeless rocks hurtling through space: asteroids and meteorites that the early warning system had determined to be a threat to Earth. The mission of the Earth Protection Force was to redirect or to destroy these objects.

They had been on space patrol for more than two decades, yet they had never had a chance to deploy their bombs. All rocks large enough to warrant their use seemed to avoid Earth, wilfully denying them their chance for glory.

Now, however, a sweep had discovered this crystal at a distance of two astronomical units. The crystal's trajectory was as precipitous as it was utterly unnatural, propelling it straight toward Earth.

The Captain and his unit cautiously approached, their spacesuits' boosters spinning a web of trails around the strange object. Just as they closed to thirty feet, a misty light flashed to life inside the crystal, clearly revealing a prismatic outline about ten feet long. As the space patrol drew nearer, they could make out the intricate, crystalline pipes of its propulsion system. The Captain was now floating directly in front of it. Stretching his gloved right hand toward the crystal, he initiated humanity's first contact with extra-terrestrial intelligence.

As he reached out, the crystal became transparent once more. A brilliantly colored image now sprang to life inside it. It was a manga girl, with huge, rolling eyes and long hair that cascaded down to her feet. She was wearing a beautiful, flowing skirt and she seemed to drift dreamily in invisible waters.

'Warning! Alert! Warning! The Devourer approaches!' she shouted immediately, stricken with obvious panic. Her large eyes stared at the Captain, a lithe arm pointing away from the Sun in unmistakable alarm. There could be little doubt the unseen pursuer was hot on her dainty heels.

'Where do you come from?' the Captain enquired, by all appearances unperturbed.

'Epsilon Eridani, as you apparently call it, and by your reckoning of time I have traveled for sixty thousand years,' she replied, before again raising her cry. 'The Devourer approaches! The Devourer approaches!'

The Captain continued his enquiry. 'Are you alive?'

'Of course not. I am merely a message,' came the response. But it was only a short reprieve. 'The Devourer approaches! The Devourer approaches!'

'How is it that you can speak English?' the Captain continued.

The girl again replied without hesitation. 'I learned in transit,' she said, only to carry on: 'The Devourer approaches! The Devourer approaches!'

'And that you look as you do...?' The Captain let his question trail off.

'I saw it in transit,' she said, before continuing to shout with ever greater urgency. 'The Devourer approaches! The Devourer approaches! Oh, surely the Devourer must terrify you.'

'What is the Devourer?' the Captain finally asked.

'In appearance, it resembles a gigantic tire. Hm, yes, that would be an analogy that works for you,' the girl from Eridanus began her explanation.

'You are very well acquainted with how things work on our world,' the Captain interrupted, raising an eyebrow behind his visor.

'I became acquainted in transit,' the girl replied, before again crying out: 'The Devourer approaches!' With that last cry, she flashed to one end of the crystal. Where she had been a second ago an image of the 'tire' appeared, and it indeed closely resembled a tire, even though its surface glowed with phosphorescent light.

'How large is it?' one of the other officers queried.

'Thirty-one thousand miles in total diameter. The "tire"'s body is six thousand miles wide, and the hole in the middle has a diameter of nineteen thousand miles.'

There was a long pause before someone asked the question now on everyone's mind. 'Are the miles you are talking about *our* miles?'

The girl answered immediately and calmly. 'Of course. It is so large that it can encircle an entire planet, just as one of your tires might fit around a soccer ball. Once it has encased a world, it begins plundering the planet's natural resources, only to spit out the remains like a cherry pit when it is done!'

There was another pause before the officer spoke again, his voice quivering with trepidation. 'But we still do not understand what the Devourer really is.'

The girl in the crystal offered more information without hesitation. 'It is a generation ship, although we do not know where it came from or where it is going. In fact, even the giant lizards that pilot the Devourer surely do not know. Having wandered the Milky Way for tens of millions of years, they have certainly forgotten both their origin and their original purpose. But this much is certain: in the distant past, when the Devourer was built, it was much smaller. It eats planets in order to grow, and it devoured our world!'

As she fell silent, the image of the Devourer in the crystal grew, eventually dominating the screen's entire surface. It soon became apparent that it was slowly descending upon the unseen camera operator's world. Seen through the eyes of the planet's inhabitants, their world had become nothing more than the bottom of a slowly spinning, cosmic well. Complex structures were clearly visible, covering the walls of this titanic well. At first, they reminded the Captain of infinitely magnified microprocessor circuitry. Then he realized that they were an endless string of cities stretching the entire inner ring of the Devourer. Looking up, the image in the crystal revealed a circle of blue radiance emanating from the well's mouth. In the sky above, it formed a gigantic halo of fire, encircling the stars.

The girl from Eridanus told them that they were seeing the jets of the Devourer's aft ring engine. As she spoke, her entire body erupted into flowing tendrils, with even her cascading hair waving like countless twisting arms. Every last part of her expressed boundless terror.

'What you are seeing is the devouring of the third planet of Epsilon Eridani,' she told them. 'The first thing you would have noticed, had you been on our world then, was your body becoming lighter. You see, the Devourer's gravitational pull was powerful enough to counteract our planet's gravity. The destruction this wrought was devastating. First, our oceans surged to meet the Devourer as it passed over our planet's pole. Then, as the Devourer moved to fully encircle our world, the waters followed it to the equator. As the oceans swept the globe, the waves towered high enough to engulf the clouds.

'The incredible gravitational forces tore at our continents, ripping them apart as if they were nothing but tissue paper. Our sea floor and dry land were pockmarked by countless volcanic eruptions.' The girl paused in her narrative, only to pick it up with a flutter of her eyelids. 'Once it had encircled our equator, the Devourer stopped, perfectly matching our planet in its orbit around our Sun. Our world was right in its maw.

'When the plunder of a world commences, countless cables thousands of miles long are lowered from the Devourer's inner wall to the planet's surface below. An entire world is trapped, like a fly in the web of a cosmic spider. Giant transport modules are then sent back and forth between the planet and the Devourer, taking with them the planet's oceans and atmosphere. As they shuttle to and fro, other huge machines begin to drill deep into the planet's crust, frenziedly extracting minerals to satisfy the Devourer's hunger.' The girl paused again, her eyes staring intensely into the distance. She resumed as abruptly as she had stopped. 'Devourer and planet cancel out each other's gravity, creating a low-gravity zone between this tire-like entity and the planet. This zone makes it that much easier to bring the planet's resources to the Devourer. The epic plunder is extremely efficient.

'Expressed in Earth time, the Devourer only needs to chew on a world for a century or so. After it is done, all of the planet's water and its atmosphere will have been reduced to nothing.

As the Devourer ravages, its gravity will also eventually deform the planet, slowly stretching it along its equator. In the end, the planet will become...' the girl paused a third time, this time struggling for words rather than for effect, 'how would you call it? Yes, disc-shaped. The Devourer, having sucked the planet completely dry, will move on, spitting the planet out. When it leaves, the planet will return to its spherical shape. As it reforms, the entire world will suffer a final global catastrophe, its surface resembling the molten sea of magma that heralded its birth many billions of years ago. Much like then, no trace of life will survive this inferno.'

'How far is the Devourer from our solar system?' the Captain asked as soon as she finished.

'It is just behind me!' she warned urgently. 'In your reckoning, it will arrive in a mere century! Alert! The Devourer approaches! The Devourer approaches!'

Chapter 2

Emissary Fangs

Just as the debate over the crystal's credibility began to rage in earnest, the first small Devourer ship entered the solar system. It was heading straight toward Earth.

The first contact was again initiated by the space patrol led by the Captain. The mood of this contact could not have been more different than the last, and the mood was, by far, not the only contrast. The exquisitely wrought structure of the Eridanus Crystal bore all the hallmarks of the ethereal technology of a refined civilization. The Devourer's ship was the polar opposite. Its exterior appeared exceedingly crude and ungainly, somewhat like a frying pan that had spent the better part of a century forgotten in the wilderness. It immediately reminded onlookers of a giant steampunk machine.

The envoy of the Devourer Empire matched his vehicle in appearance: a massive, awkward lizard covered in huge slabs of scales. Erect, he stood nearly thirty feet tall. He introduced himself as 'Faingsh', but his appearance and later behavior quickly led to him being called 'Fangs' instead.

When Fangs landed at the feet of the United Nations Building, his craft's engines blasted a large crater, the splattering concrete leaving the surrounding buildings scarred and battered. Since the alien emissary's massive size prevented him from entering the Assembly Hall, the delegates gathered on the United Nations Plaza in front of the building to meet him. Some among them now covered their faces with bloody handkerchiefs, staunching foreheads gashed open by flying glass and concrete.

The ground shook with every step Fangs took toward them, and when the alien spoke, he roared. It was a sound like the screaming horns of a dozen train engines, and it made the hair of all who heard it stand on end. Although he had learned English in transit, Fangs spoke through an unwieldy translator hanging around his neck, the device repeating his words back in English. The rough male voice the translator produced, despite being much quieter than Fangs' real voice, nonetheless made his listeners' flesh crawl.

'Ha! Ha! You white and tender worms, you fascinating little worms,' Fangs began jovially.

All around, people covered their ears until the thunderous roar had ended, only removing their hands slightly to hear the translation.

'You and I will live together for a century, and I believe we shall come to like each other,' Fangs continued.

'Your honor, you must know that we are very concerned as to the purpose of your great mothership's arrival in our solar system!' the Secretary-General stated, raising his head to address Fangs. Even though he was shouting at the top of his lungs, he still managed to sound no louder than a mosquito's buzz.

Fangs adopted a human-like posture, raising himself on his hind legs. As he shifted his weight, the ground trembled. 'The great Devourer Empire will consume the Earth so that it may continue its epic journey!' he proclaimed. 'This is inevitable!'

'What, then, of humanity?' the Secretary-General asked, his voice quivering ever so slightly.

'That is something I will determine today,' Fangs replied.

In the pause that followed, the heads of state exchanged meaningful glances. The Secretary-General finally nodded and said, 'It is necessary that we discuss this fully amongst ourselves.'

Fangs shook his massive head, interrupting before they could speak further. 'It is a very simple matter: I must merely have a taste...'

And with that, his giant claw reached into the gathered crowd and snatched up a European head of state. He gracefully tossed the man, a throw of twenty-odd feet, straight into his mouth. Then he carefully began to chew. From the first crunch to the last, his victim remained completely mute; it was impossible to tell whether it was dignity or terror that stayed his screams.

In the terrible moments that followed, the only sound was that of the man's skeleton snapping and cracking between Fangs' giant, dagger-like teeth. After about half a minute, Fangs spat out the man's suit and shoes, much as a human might spit out watermelon seeds. Even though the clothes were covered in oozing blood, they remained horrifyingly intact.

All the world seemed to have fallen completely silent, until a human voice broke the deathly quiet.

'How, sir, could you just pick him up and eat him?' the Captain asked as he stood amongst the crowd.

Fangs walked toward him with colossal, thundering steps. The crowd scattered in his wake. He stood before the Captain and lowered his gaze of pitch black, basketball-sized eyes until he was staring right at him. He asked, 'I shouldn't have?'

'Sir, how could you have known that you can eat him?' the Captain asked flatly. 'From a biochemical perspective, it is almost impossible that a being from such a distant world should be edible.'

Fangs nodded, his large maw almost seeming to grin. 'I have had my eye on you. You watched me with cool detachment, lost in thought. What is it that you were contemplating?'

The Captain returned his smile and replied, 'Sir, you breathe our air and speak using sound waves. You have two eyes, a nose and a mouth. You have four limbs arranged along a bilateral symmetry…' He let his thought drift off into silence.

'And you don't understand it?' Fangs asked, snaking his giant head right in front of the Captain's face. With a hiss, he exhaled a nauseating breath reeking of blood and gore.

'That is correct. I do understand the principles of the matter well enough to find it incomprehensible that we should be so similar,' the Captain answered, showing no signs of revulsion or fear.

'There is something I do not understand. Why are you so calm? Are you a soldier?' Fangs asked in response.

'I am warrior who defends of Earth,' the Captain answered.

'Hm, but does pushing around small stones really make you a warrior?' Fangs countered with more than a hint of mockery.

'I am ready for greater tests,' the Captain stated solemnly, lifting his chin.

'You fascinating little worm.' Fangs laughed, nodding. Raising his body to its full height, he turned back to the heads of state. 'But let us return to the real topic at hand: humanity's fate. You are tasty. There is a smooth and mild quality about you that reminds me of certain blue berries we found on a planet in Eridanus. I therefore congratulate you. Your species will continue. We will raise you as livestock in the Devourer Empire. We will allow you to live a good sixty years before we bring you to market.'

'Sir, do you not think that our meat will be too gamey at that age?' the Captain asked with a cold chuckle.

Fangs roared with laughter, his voice like an erupting volcano. 'Ha, ha, ha, ha! The Devourers like chewy snacks!'

Chapter 3

Ants

The United Nations engaged Fangs in several further meetings. Even though no one else was eaten, the verdict on humanity's fate remained unchanged.

A meeting was scheduled to take place at a meticulously prepared archaeological excavation site in Africa.

Fangs' ship landed right on schedule, about fifty feet away from the dig site. The deafening explosion and storm of debris that accompanied the craft's arrival had, by this point, become all too familiar.

The girl from Eridanus had advised them that the vessel's engine was powered by a miniature fusion reactor. The concept, like most of the information she had provided on the Devourers, was easy enough for the human scientists to understand; the things she told them about the technology of Eridanians, on the other hand, never failed to baffle the people of Earth. Her crystal, for example, began to melt in Earth's atmosphere. In the end, the entire section containing its propulsion system dissolved, leaving nothing but a thin slice of crystal floating gracefully through the air.

As Fangs arrived at the excavation site, two UN staffers presented him with a large album, a full square yard in

285

size. It had been meticulously designed to accommodate the Devourer's huge stature. The album's hundreds of beautifully constructed pages revealed all aspects of human culture in brilliantly colored detail. In some ways, it resembled an opulent primer for children.

Inside the large pit of the excavation site itself, an archaeologist vividly described the glorious history of Earth's civilizations. He threw all his passion into his desperate attempt to make this alien understand, to comprehend that there was so much on this blue planet worth cherishing. As he spoke, his fervor moved him to tears. It was a pitiable spectacle.

Finally, he pointed to the excavation and intoned: 'Honorable emissary, what you see here are the newly discovered remains of a town. This fifty-thousand-year-old site is the oldest human settlement discovered to date. Could the hearts of your people truly be hard enough to destroy this magnificent civilization of ours? A civilization that has developed, step by slow step, over fifty thousand years?'

While all this was going on, Fangs was leafing through the album with obvious, playful amusement. As the archaeologist finished, Fangs raised his head and glanced at the excavation pit. 'Hey, archaeologist worm, I care neither for your hole nor your old city in the hole. I would, however, very much want to see the earth you removed from the pit,' he said, pointing at a large pile of dirt.

The archaeologist went from baffled to completely stunned as the artificial voice of the translator finished relaying Fangs' request. 'The earth?' he asked, fumbling for words. 'But there's nothing in that pile of dirt.'

'That is your opinion,' Fangs said, approaching the mound of dirt. Bending his gigantic body toward the ground, he reached into the pile with two of his huge claws and began digging. A circle of onlookers quickly formed, many gasping at the deceptive deftness of Fangs' seemingly unwieldy claws. Prodding the soft earth, he repeatedly retrieved tiny specks from the soil, only to place them on the album. Fangs seemed completely engrossed in this strange labor for a good ten minutes. Having finished whatever he had been up to, he carefully lifted the album with both claws and straightened his body. Walking toward the gathered humans, he gave them a chance to see what it was that he had placed on the album.

Only by looking very carefully could those gathered make out that it was hundreds of ants. They were gathered in a tight bunch: some alive, others curled up in death.

'I want to tell you a story,' Fangs said as the humans studied the ants. 'It is the story of a kingdom. This kingdom was descended from a great empire, and it could trace its ancestry all the way back to the ends of Earth's Cretaceous period, during which its founders built a magnificent city in the shadow of the towering bones of a dinosaur.' Fangs paused, deep in thought, before continuing. 'But that is long-lost, ancient history, and when winter suddenly fell only the last in a long line of queens remembered those glory days. It was a very long winter indeed, and the land was covered by glaciers. Tens of millions of years of vigorous life were lost as existence became ever more precarious.

'After waking from her last hibernation, the queen could not rouse even one out of every hundred of her subjects. The others had been entombed by the cold, some being frozen to nothing but transparent, empty shells. Feeling the walls of her city, the queen realized that they were as cold as ice and hard as steel. She understood that the Earth remained frozen. In this age of terrible cold, even summer brought no thaw. The queen decided it was time to leave the homeland of her ancestors and to seek out unfrozen earth to establish a new kingdom.

'And so the queen led her surviving subjects to the surface to begin their long and arduous journey in the shadow of looming glaciers,' Fang said. 'Most of her remaining subjects perished during their protracted wanderings, consumed by the deadly cold. But the queen and a few straggling survivors finally found a patch of earth that remained untouched by frost. Overflowing geothermal energy warmed this sliver of land. The queen, of course, knew nothing of this. She did not understand why there should be moist and soft soil anywhere in this frozen world, but she was in no way surprised that she had found it: a race that persevered through sixty million long years could never suffer extinction!

'In the face of a glacier-covered Earth and a dim Sun, the queen proclaimed that it was here that they would found a new mighty kingdom – a kingdom that would endure for all eternity. Standing under the summit of a tall, white mountain, she declared that this new kingdom would be known as the "Realm of the White Mountain",' he said grandly.

'In fact, the eponymous summit was the skull of a mammoth,' he continued. 'It was the zenith of the Late Pleistocene of the Quaternary Glaciation. In those days, you human worms were still dumb animals, shivering in your scattered caves. It would still be ninety thousand years before the first flicker of your civilization would appear a continent away on the plains of Mesopotamia.

'Living off the frozen remains of mammoths in the vicinity of the Realm of the White Mountain, the new settlement survived ten thousand hard years. Then, as the ice age ended, spring returned to Earth and the land was again draped in green. In this great explosion of life, the Realm of the White Mountain quickly entered a golden age of prosperity. Its subjects were beyond number, and they ruled a vast domain. Over the next ten thousand years the kingdom was ruled by countless dynasties, and countless epics told its stories.'

As he continued, Fangs pointed at the large pile of earth in front of them. 'That is the final resting place of the Realm of the White Mountain. As you archaeologist worms were preoccupied by your excavations of a lost and dead fifty-thousand-year-old city, you completely failed to realize that the soil above those ruins was teeming with a city that was very much alive. In scale it was easily comparable to New York, and the latter is a city on merely two dimensions. The city here was a grand three-dimensional metropolis with numerous layers. Every layer was densely packed with labyrinthine streets, spacious forums and magnificent palaces. The design of the city's drainage and fire prevention systems handily outshone those of New York.

'The city was home to a complex social structure and a strict division of labor,' he told his captive audience. 'Its entire society ran with machine-like precision and harmonious efficiency. The vices of drug use and crime did not exist here, and hence there was neither depravity nor confusion. But its inhabitants were by no means devoid of emotion, showing their abiding sorrow whenever a subject of the Realm passed away. They even had a cemetery on the surface at the edge of the city, and there they would bury their dead an inch under the ground.

'However, the greatest acclaim must be reserved for the grand library nestled in the lowest layer of this city. In this library, one could find a multitude of ovoid containers. Each container was a book filled with pheromones. The exceedingly complex chemistry of these pheromones stored the city's knowledge. Here the epics detailing the enduring history of the Realm of the White Mountain were recorded. Here you could have learned that in a great forest fire all the subjects of the kingdom embraced each other to form countless balls, and that, with heroic effort, they were able to escape a sea of fire by floating down a stream. You could have learned the history of the hundred-year war against the White Termite Empire or of the first time that an expedition from the kingdom saw the great ocean...' Fangs let his translator's voice trail off.

Then his booming voice rang out again. 'But it was all destroyed in three short hours. Destroyed when, with an earth-shattering roar, the excavators came, blackening the sky. Then their giant steel claws came cutting down, grabbing the soil of the city, utterly destroying it and crushing all within. They even destroyed the layer where all the city's children and the tens of thousands of snow-white eggs, yet to become children, rested.'

All of the world again seemed to have fallen deathly quiet. This silence outlasted the quiet that had followed Fangs' horrible feast. Standing before the alien emissary, humanity was, for the first time, at a loss of words.

Finally Fangs said, 'We still have a very long time to get along and very many things to talk about, but let us not speak of morals. In the universe, such considerations are meaningless.'

Chapter 4

Acceleration

Fangs left the people at the dig site in a state of deep shock and despair. The Captain was again the first to break the silence. He turned to the surrounding dignitaries of all nations and said, 'I know that I am a mere nobody and that the only reason I am fortunate enough to attend these occasions is because I was the first to come into contact with the two alien intelligences. Nonetheless, I want to say a couple of things: first, Fangs is right; second, humanity's only way out is to fight.'

'Fight? Oh, Captain, fight…' The Secretary-General shook his head with a bitter simile.

'Right! Fight! Fight! Fight!' the girl from Eridanus shouted from her crystal pane as she flitted several feet above the heads of those assembled. In her sun-drenched crystal, the long-haired girl's entire body began writhing and flowing.

'You people from Eridanus fought them. How did that end?' someone called out. 'Humanity must think of its survival as a species, not of satisfying your twisted desire for vengeance.'

'No, sir,' the Captain said, turning to face the assembled crowd. 'The Eridanians engaged an enemy they knew nothing about in a war of self-defense. Furthermore, they were a society that had historically not known war. Given the circumstances, it is hardly surprising that they were defeated. Nonetheless, in a century of bitter warfare they meticulously acquired a deep understanding of the Devourer. We now have been handed that vast reservoir of knowledge by this spaceship. It will be our advantage.

'Careful preliminary studies of the material have shown that the Devourer is by no means as terrible as we had first feared,' he told them. 'Foremost, beyond the fact that it is inconceivably large, there is little about the Devourer that exceeds our understanding. Its life forms, the ten-billion-plus Devourers themselves, are carbon-based, just like us. They even resemble us on a molecular level, and because we share a biological basis with the enemy nothing about them will remain beyond our grasp. We should count our blessings; consider that we could just as well have been faced with invaders made of energy fields and the stuff of neutron stars.

'But there is even more cause for hope,' he said. 'The Devourer possesses very little, shall we say, "super-technology". The Devourer's technology is certainly very advanced when compared to humanity's, but that is primarily a question of scale, not of theoretical complexity. The main energy source of the Devourer's propulsion system is nuclear fusion. In fact, the primary use for water plundered from planets – beyond providing basic life support – is fuel for this system. The Devourer's propulsion technology is based on the principle of recoil and the conservation of momentum; it is not some sort of strange, space-time bending nonsense.' The Captain paused, studying the faces before him. 'All of this may dismay our scientists; after all, the Devourer, with its tens of millions of years of continuous development, clearly shows us the limits of science and technology, but it also clearly shows us that our enemy is no invincible god.'

The Secretary-General mulled over the Captain's words and then asked, 'But is that enough to ensure humanity's victory?'

'Of course, we have more specific information. Information that should allow us to formulate a strategy that will give a good shot at victory. For example—'

'Acceleration! Acceleration!' the girl from Eridanus shouted over their heads, interrupting the Captain.

The Captain explained her outburst to the baffled faces around him. 'We have learned from the Eridanian data that the Devourer ship's ability to accelerate is limited. The Eridanians observed it for two long centuries, and they never once saw it exceed this specific limit. To confirm this, we used the data we received from the Eridanian spaceship to establish a mathematical model that accounts for the Devourer's architecture and the material strength of its structural components. Calculations using this model verify the Eridanians' observations. There is a firm limit to the speed at which the Devourer can accelerate, and this limit is determined by its structural integrity. Should it ever exceed this mark, the colossus will be torn to pieces.'

'So what?' the head of a great nation asked, underwhelmed.

'We should remain level-headed and carefully consider it,' the Captain answered with a laugh.

Chapter 5

The Lunar Refuge

Humanity's negotiations with the alien emissary finally showed some small signs of progress: Fangs yielded to the demand for a lunar refuge.

'Humans are nostalgic creatures,' the Secretary-General had explained in one of their meetings, tears in his eyes.

'So are the Devourers, even though we no longer have a home,' Fangs had sympathetically answered, nodding his head.

'So, will you allow a few of us to stay behind? If you permit, they will wait for the great Devourer Empire to spit out the Earth after it has finished consuming the planet. After waiting for the planet's transformed geology to settle, they will return to rebuild our civilization.'

Fangs shook his gargantuan head. 'When the Devourer Empire consumes, it consumes completely. When we are done, the Earth will be as desolate as Mars. Your worm-technology will not be enough to rebuild a civilization.'

The Secretary-General would not be dissuaded. 'But we must try. It will soothe our souls, and it will be especially important for those of us in the Devourer Empire being raised as livestock. It will surely fatten them if they can think back on their distant home in this solar system, even if that home no longer necessarily exists.'

Fangs now nodded. 'But where will those people go while the Earth is being devoured? Besides Earth, we will also consume Venus. Jupiter and Neptune are too large for us to consume, but we will devour their satellites. The Devourer Empire is in need of their hydrocarbons and water. We will also take a bite out of the barren worlds of Mars and Mercury, as we are interested in their carbon dioxide and metals. The surfaces of all these worlds will become seas of fire.'

The Secretary-General had an answer ready. 'We can take refuge on the Moon. We understand that the Devourer Empire plans to push the Moon out of orbit before consuming the Earth.'

Fangs nodded. 'That is correct. The combined gravitational forces of the Devourer and the Earth will be very powerful. They could crash the Moon into our ship. Such a collision would be enough to destroy our Empire.'

The Secretary-General smiled ever so slightly as he replied. 'All right then, let a few of us live up there. It will be no great loss to you.'

'How many do you plan to leave behind?' Fangs queried.

'The minimum to preserve our civilization: one hundred thousand,' the Secretary-General answered flatly.

'Well then, you should get to work,' Fangs concluded.

'Get to work? What work?' the Secretary-General asked, perplexed.

'Pushing the Moon out of its orbit. For us, that is always a great inconvenience,' Fangs answered dismissively.

'But,' said the Secretary-General, grasping his hair in despair. 'Sir, that would be no different than denying humanity our meagre and pitiable request. Sir, you know that we do not possess such technological prowess!'

'Ha, worm, why should I care? And besides, don't you still have an entire century?' Fangs concluded with a chuckle.

Chapter 6

Planting the Bombs

On the gleaming white plains of the Moon, a spacesuit-clad contingent stood next to a tall drilling tower. The emissary of the Devourer Empire stood somewhat apart, his giant frame another towering silhouette against the horizon. All eyes were firmly focused on a metal cylinder being slowly lowered from the top of the drilling tower down into the drill well below. Soon the cable was speeding into the well. On Earth, 240,000 miles away, an entire world was glued to the unfolding events. Then came the signal: the payload had reached the bottom of the well. All observers, including Fangs, broke into applause as they celebrated the arrival of this historic moment.

The last nuclear bomb that would propel the Moon out of orbit had been put in place. A century had passed since the Eridanus Crystal and the emissary of the Devourer Empire had arrived on Earth. For humanity, it had been a century of despair, a hundred years of bitter struggle.

In the first half of the century, the entire Earth had zealously thrown itself at the task of constructing an engine that could propel the Moon. The technology needed to build such an engine, however, utterly failed to materialize. All that was accomplished was that the Moon's surface had gained a few scrap metal mountains, the remains of failed prototypes. Then there were also the lakes of metal, formed where experimental engines had melted under the heat of nuclear fusion.

Humanity had asked Fangs for technological assistance; after all, the lunar engines would not even have to be a tenth of the scale of the countless super-engines the Devourer possessed.

Fangs, however, refused and instead quipped, 'Don't assume that you can build a planetary engine just because you understand nuclear fusion. It's a long way from a firecracker to a rocket. Truth be told, there is no reason at all for you to work so hard at it. In the Milky Way, it is perfectly commonplace for a weaker civilization to become the livestock of a stronger civilization. You will discover that being raised for food is a splendid life indeed. You will have no wants and will live happily to the end. Some civilizations have sought to become livestock, only to be turned down. That you should feel uncomfortable with the idea is entirely the fault of a most banal anthropocentrism.'

Humanity then placed all its hopes in the Eridanus Crystal, but again they were disappointed. The technology of the Eridanian civilization had developed along completely different lines from Earth's or those of the Devourer. Their technology was wholly based on their planet's organisms. The crystal, for example, was a symbiont to a kind of plankton that floated in their world's oceans. The Eridanians merely synthesized and utilized the unusual abilities of their planet's life forms without ever truly understanding their secrets. And so, without Eridanian life forms, their technology remained completely unworkable.

After over fifty valuable years were wasted, in desperation humanity suddenly produced an exceedingly eccentric scheme to propel the Moon. It was the Captain who first came up with this plan. At the time, he had a leading role in the Moon propulsion program and had advanced to the rank of marshal. Even though his plan was unapologetically illogical, its technological demands were modest and humanity's available technology was fully capable of making it work; so much so, in fact, that many were surprised that no one had come up with it earlier.

The new plan to propel the Moon was very simple: a large array of nuclear bombs would be installed on one side of the Moon. These bombs would, for the most part, be buried roughly two miles under the lunar surface. Their spacing would ensure that no bomb was destroyed by the blast of another. According to this plan, five million nuclear bombs were to be installed on the Moon's 'propulsion side'. Compared to these bombs, humanity's most powerful Cold War-era nuclear bombs were mere toy weapons.

When the time came to detonate these super-powerful nuclear bombs under the lunar surface, the force of their explosions would be wholly incomparable to the nuclear tests of earlier ages, suffocated deep underground. These denotations would blow off a complete stratum of lunar matter. In the Moon's low gravity, the exploded strata's rocks and dust would reach escape velocity. As they launched into space, they would exert an enormous propulsive force on the Moon itself.

If a certain number of bombs were detonated in rapid succession, this momentum could become a continual propelling force, just as if the Moon had been fitted with a powerful engine. By detonating nuclear bombs in different places it would be possible to control the Moon's flight path.

The plan would even go one step further, calling for not one but two layers of nuclear bombs within the lunar surface. The second layer would be installed at a depth of about four miles. After the top layer had been completely used up, two miles of lunar matter would be stripped from the propulsion side of the Moon. The unceasing denotations would then smoothly transition to the second layer. This would double the duration for which the 'engine' could propel the Moon.

When the girl from Eridanus heard of this plan, she came to the conclusion that humanity was truly insane. 'Now I understand.

If you had technology to match the Devourers, you might be even more brutal than they are!' she exclaimed.

Fangs, on the other hand, was full of praise. 'Ha, ha! What a wonderful idea you worms managed to dream up. I love it. I love your vulgarity. Vulgarity is the highest form of beauty!' he exclaimed.

'Absurd! How can vulgarity be beautiful?' the girl from Eridanus retorted.

'The vulgar is naturally beautiful, and nothing is more vulgar than the universe! Stars burn manically in the pitch-black cold abyss of space. Isn't that vulgar? Do you understand that the universe is masculine? Feminine civilizations, like yours, are fragile, fine and delicate, a sickly abnormality in a tiny corner of the universe. And that is that!' Fangs replied.

A hundred years had passed, and Fangs' huge frame still brimmed with vitality. The girl from Eridanus was still vivid and bright, but the Captain felt the weight of years. He was 130 years old, an old man.

At the time, the Devourer had just passed the orbit of Pluto. It was awakening after its long, sixty-thousand-mile journey from Epsilon Eridani. In the dark of space, its huge ring was lit up brilliantly, and its immense society set to work, preparing to plunder the solar system.

After the Devourer had plundered the peripheral planets it flung itself onto a precipitous trajectory toward Earth.

Chapter 7

Humanity's First and Last Space War

The acceleration of the Moon away from Earth had begun. The Moon was hanging in the sky of Earth's day side when the first bombs were detonated. The flare from each explosion briefly lit up the Moon in the blue sky, giving it the appearance of a giant silver eye frantically blinking in the heavens. When night fell on Earth, the one-sided flashes of the Moon still shone the light of human handiwork to the surface twenty-five thousand miles below. A pale silver trail following the Moon's dark side was now visible. It was composed of the rocks blasted into space from the Moon's surface. Cameras installed on the propulsion side of the Moon showed strata of rock being blasted into space like billowing floodwaters. The waves of rock quickly faded into the distance, becoming thin strands trailing the Moon. Turning toward the Earth's other side, the Moon circumscribed an accelerating orbit.

Humanity's attention, however, was now squarely focused on the great and terrible ring that had appeared in the sky: the Devourer loomed over the Earth. The enormous tides that its gravity caused had already destroyed Earth's coastal cities.

The Devourer's aft engines flashed in a circle of blue light as it engaged in final orbital adjustments on its approach. It eventually perfectly matched the Earth's orbit around the Sun, while at the same time it aligned its axis of rotation with Earth's. Having completed these adjustments, it ever so slowly began to move toward the Earth, ready to surround the planet with its huge ring body.

The Moon's acceleration continued for two months. During this time, a bomb had exploded within its surface every two or three seconds, resulting in an almost incomprehensible total of 2.5 million nuclear explosions. As it entered into its second orbit around the Earth, the Moon's acceleration had forced its once circular orbit into a distinctly elliptical shape. As the Moon moved to the far end of this ellipse, Fangs and the Captain arrived on its forward-facing side, away from the exploding bombs. The Captain had expressly invited the alien emissary for this occasion.

As they stood on the lunar plain surrounded by craters, they felt the tremors from the other side shake deep beneath their feet. It almost seemed as if they could sense the powerful heartbeat of Earth's satellite. In the pitch-black sky beyond, the Devourer's giant ring dazzled with its brilliant light, its huge shape consuming half the sky.

'Excellent, Captain-worm, most excellent indeed!' Fangs applauded, his voice full of sincere praise. 'But,' he continued, 'you should hurry. You only have one more orbit to accelerate. The Devourer Empire is not accustomed to waiting for others. And I have another question: the cities you built below the surface a decade ago are still empty. When will their inhabitants arrive? How can your spaceships transport one hundred thousand humans here from Earth in only one month?'

'We will bring no one here,' the Captain calmly replied. 'We will be the last humans to stand on the Moon.'

Hearing this, Fangs twisted his body in surprise. The Captain had said 'we', meaning the five thousand officers and soldiers of Earth's space force. They formed a perfect phalanx on the crater-covered lunar plain. At the front of the phalanx a soldier brandished a blue flag.

'Look! This is our planet's banner. We declare war upon the Devourer Empire!' the Captain announced defiantly.

Fangs stood dumbfounded, more confused than surprised. Immediately, his body began to reel as he was thrown onto his back by the Moon's sudden gravitational surge. Fangs was knocked prone to lunar ground, stunned beyond any thought of movement. All around him lunar dust kicked up by his massive fall slowly began to drift to the ground.

But the dust was quickly thrown up again, stirred by massive shock waves reverberating from the other side of the Moon. These shocks soon left the entire plain covered in a layer of white dust.

Fangs realized the frequency of nuclear explosions on the other side of the Moon had abruptly increased several times over. Judging by the sharp increase of gravity, he could infer that the Moon's acceleration must have increased several times as well. Rolling over, he retrieved a large handheld computer from a pocket in the front of his spacesuit. He brought up the Moon's current orbital trajectory on it. Immediately, he realized that this tremendous increase of acceleration would take the Moon out of orbit. The Moon would break free of Earth's gravity and shoot off into space. A flashing red line of dots showed its predicted course.

It was on a collision course with the Devourer.

Discarding his computer without a second thought, Fangs slowly rose to his feet. Straining his neck against the explosive increase in gravity, he peered through the billowing clouds of lunar dust. Standing in front of him was Earth's army, still upright, stalwart like standing stones.

'A century of conspiracy and deceit,' Fangs mumbled under his breath.

The Captain just nodded in agreement. 'You now realize that it is too late,' he pointed out gravely.

Fangs spoke after a long sigh. 'I should have realized that the humans of Earth were a completely different breed from the Eridanians. Life on their world had evolved symbiotically, free of natural selection and the struggle for survival. They did not even know what war was.' He halted, digesting what had happened. 'We let that guide our assessment of Earth's people. You have ceaselessly butchered one another from the day that you climbed down from the trees. How could you be easily conquered? I...' Again he paused. 'It was an unforgivable dereliction of duty!'

When the Captain spoke, his steady, level tone explained further what Fangs was realizing. 'The Eridanians brought us vast quantities of vital information. The information included the limits of the Devourer's ability to accelerate. It is this information that formed the basis of our battle plan. As we detonate the bombs that change the Moon's trajectory, its maneuvering acceleration will come to exceed the Devourer's acceleration limit three-fold. In other words,' he said, 'it will be thrice as agile as the Devourer. There is no way you can avoid the coming collision.'

'Actually, we were not completely off guard,' Fangs said. 'When the Earth began producing large quantities of nuclear bombs, we began to monitor their whereabouts. We made sure that they were installed deep within the Moon, but we did not think...' Fangs trailed off.

Behind his visor, the Captain smiled faintly. 'We aren't so stupid as to directly attack the Devourer with nuclear bombs,' he said. 'We know that the Devourer Empire has been steeled by hundreds of battles. Earth's simple and crude missiles would certainly have been intercepted and destroyed, one and all. But you cannot intercept something as large as the Moon. Perhaps the Devourer, with its immense power, could have eventually broken or diverted the Moon, but it is far too close for that now. You are out of time.'

Fangs snarled. 'Crafty worms. Treacherous worms, vicious worms!' He shook his head, bristling. 'The Devourer Empire is an honest civilization. We put all things out in the open, yet we have been cheated by the deceitful treachery of the Earth worms.'

He gnashed his huge teeth as he finished speaking, his fury almost goading him to lock his giant claws around the Captain. The soldiers, with their rifles aimed right at him, however, stayed his talons. Fangs had not forgotten that his body, too, was but flesh and blood. One burst of bullets would end him.

With his eyes firmly fixed on Fangs, the Captain stated, 'We will leave, and you, too, should make your way off the Moon, otherwise you will surely be killed by the Devourer Empire's nuclear weapons.'

The Captain was quite correct. Just as Fangs and the human space forces left the Moon's surface, the interceptor missiles of the Devourer struck. Both sides of the Moon now flashed with brilliant light. The forward-facing side of the Moon exploded as huge waves of rocks were blasted into space. All around the Moon, lunar matter was violently scattered in every imaginable direction. Seen from the Earth, the Moon, on its collision course with the Devourer, looked like a warrior, wild hair ablaze with rage. There was no force that could have stopped it now! Wherever on Earth this spectacle was visible, seas of people erupted into feverish cheers.

The Devourer's interception action was short-lived and soon ceased. It realized that it's attack had been completely futile. In the moments it would take for the Moon to close the short distance between them, there was no way to divert its course or to destroy it.

The nuclear explosions that the Moon's pulled propulsion had also ceased. It had reached a suitable velocity, and Earth's defenders wanted to preserve enough nuclear bombs to carry out any last-minute maneuvers. All was silent.

In the cold tranquility of space, the Devourer and the Earth's satellite floated toward each other in complete silence. The distance between the two rapidly decreased. As it dwindled to thirty thousand miles, the control ship of Earth's Supreme Command could already see the Moon overlapping the giant ring of the Devourer. From there, it looked like a ball bearing in a track.

Up to this point, the Devourer had not made any changes to its trajectory. It was easy to understand why: the Moon could have easily matched any premature orbital maneuver. Any meaning- ful evasive action would have to be taken in the final moments before the Moon's impact. The two cosmic giants were almost like ancient knights in a joust. They were charging toward one another, galloping across the distance separating them, but the victor would only be decided in the blink of an eye before they made contact.

Two great civilizations of the Milky Way held their breath in rapt anticipation, awaiting that decisive moment.

At twenty thousand miles, both sides began their maneuvers. The Devourer's engines were the first to flare, shooting blue flames more than five thousand miles out into space. It began its evasion. On the Moon, nuclear bombs were once again ignited, ferociously detonating with unprecedented intensity and frequency. It carried out its adjustments, matching its course to ensure a collision. Its arcing tail of debris clearly described its change of direction. The blue light of the Devourer's five- thousand-mile flames merged with the silver flashes of the Moon's nuclear blasts; it was the most magnificent vista ever to grace the solar system.

Both sides maneuvered like this for three hours. The dis- tance between them had already shrunk to three thousand miles when the computer displays showed what no one in the control ship ever would have believed to be possible: the Devourer was changing course with an acceleration speed four times greater than the limit the Eridanians had claimed possible!

All this time they had unreservedly believed in this limit. They had made it the foundation of Earth's victory. Now, the nuclear bombs remaining on the Moon no longer had the capacity to make the necessary adjustments to give chase. Cal- culations showed that in three short hours, even if they did all they could, the Moon would brush pass the Devourer, falling short by 250 miles.

One last burst of dizzying flashes washed over the control ship, exhausting all of the Earth's nuclear bombs. At almost exactly the same moment, the Devourer's engines fell silent. In a deathly quiet, the laws of inertia told the final verses of this magnificent epic: the Moon scraped past the Devourer's side, barely missing. Its velocity was so high that the Devourer's gravity could not catch it, only twisting its trajectory a little as it zoomed past. After the Moon had passed the Devourer, it silently sped away from the Sun.

On the control ship, the Supreme Command fell into a complete silence. Minutes passed.

'The Eridanians betrayed us,' a commander finally whispered in shock.

'The crystal was probably just a trap set by the Devourer Empire!' a staff officer shouted.

In an instant, the Supreme Command descended into utter chaos. Most people began to scream and shout: some to vent their utter despair, others to conceal it. All were on the verge of hysteria. A few of the non-military personnel wept; others tore the hair from their heads. Spirits stood teetering on the verge of the abyss, ready to fall forever.

Only the Captain remained serene, standing quietly in front of a large screen. He slowly turned and with one simple question calmed the chaos. 'I would ask all of you to pay attention to one detail: why did the Devourer cut its engine?'

Pandemonium was immediately replaced by deep thought. Indeed, after the Moon had used its last nuclear bomb, the enemy had no reason to shut down its engine. They had no way of knowing whether or not there were any bombs left on the Moon. Furthermore, there was the danger of the Devourer's gravity catching the Moon. Had the Devourer continued to accelerate, it could have easily extended the distance to the Moon's trajectory. It could have – should have – made it farther than those tiny, barely adequate 250 miles.

'Give me a close up of the Devourer's outer hull,' the Captain commanded.

A holographic image was displayed on the screen. It was a picture being transmitted by a miniature, high-speed reconnaissance probe flying three hundred miles above the Devourer's surface. The splendidly illuminated surface of the Devourer came into clear view. In awe, they beheld the massive steel peaks and valleys of its giant ring body slowly turn past their view. A long black seam caught the Captain's attention. In the past century, he had become very familiar with every detail of the Devourer's surface, but he was absolutely certain that *that* gap had not existed before. Others quickly noticed it as well.

'What is that? Is it... a crack?' someone asked.

'It is. A crack. A three-thousand-mile-long crack,' the Captain said, nodding. 'The Eridanians did not betray us. The data in the crystal was accurate. The acceleration limit is real, but as the Moon approached the despairing Devourer decided to risk the consequences and to exceed the limit by four-fold, desperate to avoid the collision. This, however, had a cost: the Devourer has cracked.'

Then they found more cracks.

'Look, what's going on now?' someone shouted as its rotation brought another part of Devourer's surface into view. A dazzling bright light began glowing on the edge of its metal surface, as if dawn were creeping over its vast horizon.

'It's the rotational engine!' an officer called out.

'Indeed. It is the rarely used equatorial rotational engine,' the Captain explained. 'It is firing at full power, trying to stop the Devourer's rotation!'

'Captain, you were spot on, and this proves it!'

'We must act now and use all available means to gather detailed data so that we can run a simulation!' the Captain commanded. Even as he spoke, the entire Supreme Command was already executing the task.

Over the past century, a mathematical model had been developed that precisely described the Devourer's physical structure. The required data was gathered and processed very efficiently, and so the results were quickly produced: it would take nearly forty hours for the rotational engine to reduce the Devourer's rotation to a speed at which it could avoid destruction. Yet in only eighteen hours the centrifugal forces would completely break the Devourer into pieces.

A cheer rose among the Supreme Command. The big screen shone with the holographic image of the Devourer's impending demise: the fragmentation process would be very slow, almost dreamlike. Against the pitch blackness of space, this giant world would disperse like milk sinking into coffee, its edges gradually breaking off, only to be swallowed by the darkness beyond. The Devourer would look like it was melting into space. Only the occasional flash of an explosion now revealed its disintegrating form.

The Captain did not join the others as they watched this soul-soothing display of destruction. He stood apart from the group, focused on another screen, carefully observing the real Devourer. His face betrayed no trace of triumph. As calm returned to the bridge, the others began to take notice of him. One after another they joined him at the screen, where they discovered that the blue light at the Devourer's aft had reappeared.

The Devourer had restarted its engine.

Given the critical state that the ring structure was already in, this seemed like an utterly baffling decision. Any acceleration, no matter how minute, could cause a catastrophic collapse. But it was the Devourer's trajectory that truly baffled the onlookers: it was ever so slowly retracing its steps, returning to the position it had held before its evasive maneuvers. It was carefully re-establishing its synchronous orbit and re-aligning its axis of rotation with Earth's.

'What? Does it still want to devour the Earth?' an officer exclaimed, both shocked and confused.

His question provoked a few scattered laughs. All laughter, however, soon fell silent as the others became aware of the look on the Captain's face. He was no longer looking at the screen. His eyes were closed. His face was blank and drained of all color.

In the past hundred years, the officers and personnel who had made fending off the Devourer their life's work had become very familiar with the Captain's countenance. They had never seen him like this. A calm fell over the gathered Supreme Command as they turned back to the screen. Finally, they understood the gravity of the situation.

The Devourer still had a way out.

The Devourer's flight toward the Earth had begun. It had already matched the Earth in both orbital speed and rotation as it approached the planet's South Pole.

If it took too long, the Devourer's own centrifugal forces would tear it apart; if it went too fast, the power of its propulsion would rip it to pieces. The Devourer's survival was hanging a thin thread. It had to hold a perfect balance between timing and speed.

Before the Earth's South Pole was enveloped by the Devourer's giant ring, the Supreme Command could see the shape of the frozen continent change rapidly. Antarctica was shrinking, like butter in a hot frying pan. The world's oceans were being pulled toward the South Pole by the immense gravity of the Devourer, and now the Earth's white tip was being swallowed by their billowing waters.

As this happened, the Devourer, too, was changing. Countless new cracks began to cover its body, and all of them were growing longer and wider. The first few tears were now no longer black seams but gaping chasms glowing with crimson light. They could easily have been mistaken for the portals to hell, thousands of miles in length.

In the midst of all this destruction, a few fine white strands rose from the ring's massive body. Then, more and more of these filaments emerged, flowing from every part of the ship. It almost looked like the huge ship had sprouted a sparse head of white hair. In fact, they were the engine trails of ships being launched from the great ring. The Devourers were fleeing their doomed world.

Half of the Earth had already been encircled by the Devourer when things took a turn for the worse: the Earth's gravity was acting like the invisible spokes of a cosmic wheel, holding the disintegrating Devourer. No new cracks were appearing on its surface and the already open rips had ceased growing. Forty hours later, the Earth was completely engulfed by the Devourer. The effect of the planet's gravity was stronger at this point, and the cracks on the Devourer's surface were beginning to close. Another five hours later, they had completely closed.

In the control ship, all the screens of the Supreme Command had gone black, and even the lights were now dark. The only remaining source of illumination was the deathly pale rays of the Sun piercing through the portholes. In order to generate artificial gravity, the mid-section of the ship was still slowly rotating. As it did, the Sun rose and fell, porthole to porthole. Light and shadow wandered, as if it were replaying humanity's bygone days and nights.

'Thank you for a century of dutiful service,' the Captain said. 'Thank you all.' He saluted the Supreme Command. Under the gaze of the officers and personnel, he calmly folded up his uniform. The others followed his example.

Humanity had been defeated. The defenders of Earth had done their utmost to discharge their duties and, as soldiers, they had done their duty gloriously. In spirit, they all accepted their unseen medals with clear consciences. They were entitled to enjoy this moment.

Chapter 8

Epilogue: The Return

'There really is water!' a young lieutenant shouted with joyous surprise. It was true; a vast surface of water stretched out before them. Sparkling waves shimmered under the dusky heavens.

The Captain removed the gloves of his spacesuit. With both hands, he scooped up some water. Opening his visor, he ventured a taste. As he quickly closed his visor again, he called, 'It's not too salty.' When he saw that the lieutenant was about to open his own visor, he stopped him. 'You'll suffer decompression sickness. The composition of the atmosphere is actually not the problem; the poisonous sulphuric components in the air have already thinned out. However, the atmospheric pressure is too low. Without a visor, it is like what being at thirty thousand feet was before the war.'

A general dug in the sand at his feet. 'Maybe there's some grass seeds,' he said, smiling as he raised his head to look at the Captain.

The Captain shook his head. 'Before the war, this was the bottom of the ocean.'

'We can go have a look at New Land Eleven. It's not far from here. Maybe we can find some there,' the lieutenant suggested.

'Any will have been burnt long ago,' someone commented with a sigh.

Each of them scanned the horizon in all directions. They were surrounded by an unbroken chain of mountains only recently born by the orogenic movements of the Earth. They were dark blue massifs made of bare rock. Rivers of magma spilling from their peaks glowed crimson, like blood oozing from the body of a slain stone titan.

The magma rivers of the Earth below had burned out.

This was Earth, 230 years after the war.

After the war had ended, the more than one hundred people aboard the control ship had entered the hibernation chambers. There they waited for the Devourer to spit out the Earth; then they would return home. During their wait, their ship had become a satellite, circling the new joint planet of Devourer and Earth in a wide orbit. In all that time, the Devourer Empire had done nothing to harass them.

One hundred and twenty-five years after the war, the command ship's sensors picked up that the Devourer was in the process of leaving the Earth. In response, it roused some of those in hibernation. By the time they woke, the Devourer had already left the Earth and flown on to Venus. The Earth had been transformed into a wholly alien world, a strange planet, perhaps best described as a lump of charcoal freshly out of the oven. The oceans had all disappeared, and the land was covered in a web of magma rivers.

The personnel of the control ship could only continue their hibernation. They reset their sensors and waited for the Earth to cool. This wait lasted another century.

*

When they again woke from hibernation, they found a cooled planet, its violent geology having subsided; but now the Earth was a desolate, yellow wasteland. Even though all life had disappeared, there was still a sparse atmosphere. They even discovered remnants of the oceans of old.

So they landed at the shore of such a remnant, barely the size of a pre-war continental lake.

A blast of thunder, deafening in this thin atmosphere, roared above them as the familiar, crude form of a Devourer Empire ship landed not far from their own vessel. Its gigantic doors opened, and Fangs took his first tottering steps out, leaning heavily on a walking stick the size of a power pole.

'Ah, you are still alive, sir!' the Captain greeted him. 'You must be around five hundred now?'

'How could I live that long? I, too, went into hibernation, thirty years after the war. I hibernated just so I could see you again,' Fangs retorted.

'Where is the Devourer now?' the Captain asked.

Fangs pointed into the sky above as he answered. 'You can still see it at night; it is but a dim star now, just having passed Jupiter's orbit.'

'It is leaving the solar system?' the Captain queried.

Fangs nodded. 'I will set out today to follow it.'

The Captain paused before speaking. 'We are both old now.'

Fangs sadly nodded his giant head. 'Old...' he said, his walking stick trembling in his hand. 'The world, now...' He continued pointing from heaven to Earth.

'A small amount of water and atmosphere remains. Should we consider this an act of mercy from the Devourer Empire?' the Captain asked quietly.

Fangs shook his head. 'It has nothing to do with mercy; it is your doing.'

The Earth's soldiers looked at Fangs in puzzlement.

'Oh, in this war the Devourer Empire suffered an unprecedented wound. We lost hundreds of millions in those tears,' Fangs admitted. 'Our ecosystem, too, suffered critical damage. After the war, it took us fifty Earth years just to complete preliminary repairs, and only once that was done could we begin to chew the Earth. But we knew that our time in the solar system was limited. If we did not leave in time, a cloud of interstellar dust would float right into our flight path. And if we took the long way round, we would lose seventeen thousand years on our way to the next star. In that time, the star's state would have already changed, burning the planets that we wished to consume. Because of this we had to chew the planets of the Sun in great haste and could not pick them clean,' Fangs explained.

'That fills us with great comfort and honor,' the Captain said, looking at the soldiers surrounding him.

'You are most worthy of it. It truly was a great interstellar war. In the lengthy annals of the Devourer's wars, ours was one of the most remarkable battles! To this day, all throughout our world, minstrels sing of the epic achievements of the Earth's soldiers,' Fangs stated.

'We would sooner hope that humanity would remember the war. So, how is humanity?' the Captain asked.

'After the war, approximately two billion humans were migrated to the Devourer Empire, about half of all of humanity,' Fangs answered, activating the large screen of his portable computer where pictures of life on the Devourer appeared. The screen revealed a beautiful grassland under blue skies. On the grass, a group of happy humans was singing and dancing. At first it was difficult to distinguish the gender of these humans. Their skin was a soft, subtle white, and they were all dressed in fine, gauzy clothes with beautiful wreaths of flowers on their heads. In the distance, one could make out a magnificent castle, clearly modelled on something from an Earth fairytale. Its vibrant colors made it look as if it were made of cream and chocolate.

The camera's lens drew closer, giving the Captain a chance to study these people's countenances in detail. He was soon completely convinced that they were truly happy. It was an utterly carefree happiness, pure as crystal. It reminded him of the few short years of innocent childhood joy that pre-war humans had experienced.

'We must ensure their absolute happiness,' Fangs said. 'It is the minimum requirement for raising them. If we do not, we cannot guarantee the quality of their meat. And it must be said that Earth people are seen as food of the highest quality; only the upper class of the Devourer Empire society can afford to enjoy them. We do not take such delicacies for granted.' Fangs paused for a moment. 'Oh, Captain. We found your great-grandson, sir. We recorded something from him to you. Do you care to see it?'

The Captain gazed at Fangs in surprise then nodded his head.

A fair-skinned, beautiful boy appeared on the screen. Judging by his face he was only ten years old, but his stature was already that of a grown man. He held a flower wreath in his effeminate hands, having obviously just been called from a dance.

Blinking his large, shimmering eyes, he said, 'I hear that my great-grandfather still lives. I ask only one thing of you, sir. Never, ever come see me. I am nauseated! When we think of humanity's life before the war, we are all nauseated. What a barbaric life that was, the life of cockroaches! You and your soldiers of Earth wanted to preserve that life. You almost stopped humanity from entering this beautiful heaven. How perverse! Do you know how much shame, how much embarrassment you have caused me? Bah! Do not come looking for me! Bah! Go and die!' After he had finished, he skipped off to join the dancing on the grassland.

Fangs was first to break the awkward silence that followed. 'He will live past the age of sixty. He will have a long life and will not be slaughtered.'

'If it is because of me, then I am truly grateful,' the Captain said, smiling miserably.

'It is not. After learning about his ancestry, he became very depressed and filled with feelings of hatred toward you. Such emotions prevented his meat from meeting our standards,' Fangs explained.

As Fangs looked at these last few humans before him, genuine emotions played across his massive eyes. Their spacesuits were extremely old and shabby, and the many years that have since past were etched into their faces. In the pale yellow of the Sun, they looked like a group of rust-stained statues. Fangs closed his computer and, full of regret, said, 'At first, I did not want you to see this, but you are all true warriors, more than capable of dealing with the truth, ready to recognize,' he paused for a long moment before continuing 'that human civilization has come to an end.'

'You certainly destroyed Earth's civilization,' the Captain said, staring into the distance. 'You have committed a monstrous crime!'

'We finally have started to talk about morals again,' Fangs said with a laugh and a grin.

'After invading our home and brutally devouring everything in it, I would think that you had forfeited all right to talk about morals,' the Captain said coldly.

The others had already stopped paying attention; the extreme, cold brutality of the Devourer civilization was just beyond human understanding. Nothing could have been less interesting to the others than a discussion with them about morals.

'No, we have the right. I now truly wish to talk about morals with humanity,' Fangs said before again pausing. '"How, sir, could you just pick him up and eat him?"' he continued, quoting the Captain. Those last words left nobody unshaken. They did not emanate from the translator, but came directly from Fangs' mouth. Even though his voice was deafening, Fangs somehow managed to imitate those three-hundred-year-old words with perfection.

Fangs continued, resuming his use of the translator. 'Captain, three hundred years ago your intuition did not mislead you: When two civilizations – separated by interstellar space – meet, any similarities should be far more shocking than their differences. It certainly shouldn't be as it is with our species.'

As all present focused their gaze on Fangs' frame, they were overcome with a sense of premonition that a world-shaking mystery was about to be revealed.

Fangs straightened himself on his walking-stick and, looking into the distance, said, 'Friends, we are both children of the Sun; and while the Earth is both our species' fraternal home, my people have the greater claim to her! Our claim is 140 million years older than yours. All those millennia ago, we were the first to live on this beautiful planet, and this is where we established our magnificent civilization.'

The Earth's soldiers stared blankly at Fangs. The waters of the remnant ocean rippled in the pale yellow sunlight. Red magma flowed from the distant new mountains. Sixty million years down the rivers of time, two species, each the ruler of this Earth in their own time, met in desolation on their plundered home world.

'Dino... saur!' someone exclaimed in a shocked whisper.

Fangs nodded. 'The Dinosaur Civilization arose one hundred million years ago on Earth, during what you call the Cretaceous period of the Mesozoic. At the end of the Cretaceous, our civilization reached its zenith, but we are a large species, and our biological needs were equally great. In the wake of our population increase, the ecosystem was stretched to its limit, and the Earth was pushed to its brink as it struggled to support our society. To survive, we completely consumed Mars' elementary ecosystem.

'The Dinosaur Civilization lasted twenty thousand years on Earth,' he continued, 'but its true expansion was a matter of a few thousand years. From a geological perspective its effects are indistinguishable from those of an explosive catastrophe; what you call the Cretaceous–Tertiary extinction event.

'Finally, one day all the dinosaurs boarded ten giant generation ships and, with these ships, sailed into the vast sea of stars.

In the end, all ten of these ships were joined together. Then, whenever this newly united ship reached another star's planet, it expanded. Sixty million years later, it has become the Devourer Empire you now know.'

'Why would you eat your own home world? Are dinosaurs bereft of all sentiment?' someone asked.

Fangs answered, lost in thought. 'It is a long story. Interstellar space is indeed vast and boundless, but it is also different than you would imagine. The places that truly suit us, as advanced carbon-based life forms, are few and far between. A dust cloud blocks the way to the center of the Milky Way just two thousand light-years from here. There is no way for us to pass through it and no way for us to survive in it. And after that it becomes an area of powerful radiation and a large group of wandering black holes.' Fangs paused, before continuing, still speaking more to himself than to the humans before him. 'If we should travel in the opposite direction, we would just come to the end of the Milky Way's spiral arm and then, not far beyond, there is nothing but a limitless, desolate void. The Devourer Empire has already completely consumed almost all the planets that could be found in the habitable areas that exist between these two barriers. Now the only way out is to fly to another arm of the Milky Way. We have no idea what awaits us there, but if we stay here we will certainly be doomed. It will be a journey of fifteen million years, taking us right through the void. To survive it, we must build large stocks of all possible expendables.

'Right now, the Devourer Empire is just like a fish in a drying stream. It must make a desperate leap before its water completely evaporates. It realizes that the most likely end is reaching dry land and succumbing to death under the scorching Sun but there is the slight chance that it may fall into a neighboring water hole and thereby survive.' Fangs lowered his gaze toward the humans, bending down to almost eye level. 'As far as sentiment is concerned, we have lived through tens of millions of arduous years and fought stellar wars beyond number. The hearts of the dinosaur race have long since hardened. Now the Devourer Empire must consume as much as it possibly can in preparation for our million-year journey.' Fangs again paused, deep in thought. 'What is civilization? Civilization is devouring, ceaselessly eating, endlessly expanding; everything else comes second.'

The Captain, too, was deep in thought. Looking at Fangs, he asked, 'Can the struggle for existence be the universe's only law of biological and cultural evolution? Can we not establish a self-sufficient, introspective civilization where all life exists in symbiosis? A civilization like that of the Eridanians?'

Fangs answered without hesitation or pause. 'I am no philosopher; perhaps it can be done. The crux is, who will take the first step? If one's survival is based on the subjugation and consumption of others and if that should be the universe's iron law of life and civilization, then whoever first rejects it in favor of introspection will certainly perish.'

With that Fangs returned to his spaceship, but he soon reemerged carrying a thin, flat box in both talons. The box was about ten feet square, and it would have easily taken four men to carry it. Fangs placed the box on the ground and opened its top. To the humans' surprise, the box was filled with dirt, and grass was growing on it. On this lifeless world, its green left no heart untouched.

As Fangs opened the box, he turned to the humans. 'This is pre-war soil. After the war, I put all of our planet's plants and all of its insects into suspended animation. Now, after more than two centuries, they have awoken. Originally, I wanted to take this soil with me as a memento. Alas, I have thought more about it, and I have changed my mind. I have decided to return it to where it truly belongs. We have taken more than enough from our home world.'

As they gazed upon this tiny piece of Earth, so full of life, the humans' eyes began to moisten. They now knew the dinosaurs' hearts had not turned to stone. Behind those scales, colder and crueler than steel and rock, beat hearts that longed for home.

Fangs rattled his claws, almost as if he wanted to cast off the emotions that had gripped him. Slightly shaken, he said, 'All right then, my friends, we will go together, back to the Devourer Empire.' Seeing the expression on the humans' faces, he raised a claw before continuing. 'You will, of course, not be food there. You are great warriors and you will be made citizens of the Empire. And there is still work that needs your attention. A museum to the human civilization needs to be built.'

The eyes of every single Earth soldier turned to the Captain. He stood deep in thought, then slowly nodded.

One after the other, the Earth's soldiers boarded Fangs' spaceship. Because its ladder was intended for dinosaurs, they had to pull the full length of their bodies up each rung to climb inside. The Captain was the last human to board the ship. Grasping the lowest rung of the ship's ladder, he pulled his body off the ground. Just at that moment, something in the ground beneath his feet caught his eye. He stopped in mid-pull, looking down. For a long time he hung there, motionless.

He had seen... an ant.

The ant had climbed out of that box of soil. Never losing sight of the tiny insect, the Captain let go of the ladder and squatted down. Lowering his hand, he let the ant clamber onto his glove. Raising it to his face, he carefully studied the small creature, its obsidian body glinting in the sunlight. Holding it, the Captain walked over to the box, where he cautiously returned the ant to the tiny blades of grass. As he lowered his hand, he noticed more ants climbing about the soil beneath the grass.

Raising himself, he turned to Fangs who was standing right by his side. 'When we leave, this grass and these ants will be the dominant species on Earth.'

Fangs was at a loss for words.

'Earth's civilized life seems to be getting smaller and smaller. Dinosaurs, humans and now probably ants,' the Marshal said, squatting back down. He looked on, his eyes deep with love and admiration as he watched these small beings live their lives in the grass. 'It is their turn.'

As he spoke, the Earth's soldiers re-emerged from the spaceship. Climbing down to Earth, they returned to the box of living soil. Standing around it they, too, were filled with deep love.

Fangs shook his head. 'The grass cannot survive. It might eventually rain here at the seaside, but it won't be enough for the ants.'

'Is the atmosphere too thin? They seem to be doing just fine at the moment,' someone noted.

'No, the air is not the problem. They are not like humans and can live well in this atmosphere. The real crux of the matter is that they will have nothing to eat,' Fangs replied.

'Can't they eat the grass?' another voice joined in.

'And then? How will they live on? In this thin air, the grass will grow very slowly. Once the ants have eaten all the blades, they will starve. In many ways, their situation mirrors the destiny of the Devourer civilization,' Fangs mused.

'Can you leave behind some food from your spaceship for them?' another soldier asked, almost pleadingly.

Fangs shook his massive head again. 'There is nothing on my spaceship besides water and the hibernation system. On that note, we will hibernate until we catch up with the Devourer. But what about your spaceship – do you have any food on board?'

Now it was the Captain's turn to shake his head. 'Nothing but a few injections of nourishment solution. Useless.'

Pointing to the spaceship, Fangs interrupted the discussion. 'We must hurry. The Empire is accelerating quickly. If we tarry, we will not catch up.'

Silence.

'Captain, we will stay behind.' It was the young lieutenant who broke the silence.

The Captain nodded forcefully.

'Stay behind? What are you up to?' Fangs asked in astonishment, turning from one to the other. 'The hibernation equipment on your spaceship is almost completely depleted and you have no food. Do you plan to stay and wait for death?'

'Staying will be the first step,' the Captain answered calmly.

'What?' Fangs asked, ever more perplexed.

'You just mentioned the first step toward a new civilization,' the Captain explained.

'You,' Fangs could hardly believe his own words, 'want to be the ants' food?'

Earth's soldiers all nodded. Without a word, Fangs gazed at them for what seemed like forever, before turning and slowly hobbling back to his spaceship, leaning heavily on his walking stick.

'Farewell, friend,' the Captain called after Fangs.

Fangs replied with a long, drawn-out sigh. 'An interminable darkness lies before me and my descendants: the darkness of endless war and a vast universe. Oh, where in it could there be a home for us?'

As he spoke, the humans saw that the ground beneath his feet had grown damp, but they could not tell if he had, or even could, shed tears.

With a thunderous roar, the dinosaur's spaceship lifted off and quickly disappeared into the sky. Where it had vanished, the Sun was now setting.

The last warriors of Earth seated themselves around the living soil in silence. Then, beginning with the Captain, they all, one by one, opened their visors and stretched out on the sandy earth.

As time passed, the Sun set. Its afterglow bathed the plundered Earth in a beautiful red. As it faded, a few stars began to twinkle in the sky. To his surprise, the Captain saw that the dusky sky was a beautiful blue. Just as the thin atmosphere began to render him unconsciousness, the Captain felt the tiny movements of an ant on his temple, filling him with a deep sense of contentment. As the ant climbed up to his forehead, he was transported back to his distant childhood. He was at the beach, lying in a small hammock that hung between two palm trees. Looking up to the splendid sea of stars above, he felt his mother's hand gently stroke his forehead...

Darkness fell. The remnant ocean lay flat as a mirror, pristinely reflecting the Milky Way above. It was the most tranquil night in the planet's history.

In this tranquility, the Earth was reborn.

Taking Care of God

Chapter 1

O nce again, God had upset Qiusheng's family.

This had begun as a very good morning. A thin layer of white fog floated at the height of a man over the fields around Xicen village like a sheet of rice paper that had just become blank: the quiet countryside being the painting that had fallen off of the paper. The first rays of morning fell on the scene, and the year's earliest dewdrops entered the most glorious period of their brief life... but God had ruined this beautiful morning.

God had gotten up extra early and gone into the kitchen to warm some milk for himself. Ever since the start of the Era of Support, the milk market had prospered. Qiusheng's family had bought a milk cow for just over ten thousand yuan, and then, imitating others, mixed the milk with water to sell. The unadulterated milk had also become one of the staples for the family.

After the milk was warm, God took the bowl into the living room to watch TV without turning off the liquefied petroleum gas stove.

When Qiusheng's wife, Yulian, returned from cleaning the cowshed and the pigsty, she could smell gas all over the house. Covering her nose with a towel, she rushed into the kitchen to turn off the stove, opened the window and turned on the fan.

'You old fool! You're going to get the whole family killed!' Yulian shouted into the living room. The family had switched to using liquefied petroleum gas for cooking only after they began supporting God. Qiusheng's father had always been opposed to it, saying that gas was not as good as honeycomb coal briquettes. Now he had even more ammunition for his argument.

As was his wont, God stood with his head lowered contritely, his broom-like white beard hanging past his knees, smiling like a kid who knew he had done something wrong. 'I... I took down the pot for heating the milk. Why didn't it turn off by itself?'

'You think you're still on your spaceship?' Qiusheng said, coming down the stairs. 'Everything here is dumb. We aren't like you, being waited on hand and foot by smart machines. We have to work hard with dumb tools. That's how we put rice in our bowls!'

'We also worked hard. Otherwise how did you come to be?' God said carefully.

'Enough with the "how did you come to be?" Enough! I'm sick of hearing it. If you're so powerful, go and make other obedient children to support you!' Yulian threw her towel on the ground.

'Forget it. Just forget it,' Qiusheng said. He was always the one who made peace. 'Let's eat.'

Bingbing got up. As he came down the stairs, he yawned. 'Ma, Pa, God was coughing all night. I couldn't sleep.'

'You don't know how good you have it,' Yulian said. 'Your dad and I were in the room next to his. You don't hear us complaining, do you?'

As though triggered, God began to cough again. He coughed like he was playing his favorite sport with great concentration.

Yulian stared at God for a few seconds before sighing, 'I must have the worst luck in eight generations.'

Still angry, she left for the kitchen to cook breakfast.

God sat silently through breakfast with the rest of the family. He ate one bowl of porridge with pickled vegetables and half a *mantou* bun. During the entire time he had to endure Yulian's disdainful looks – maybe she was still mad about the liquefied petroleum gas, or maybe she thought he ate too much.

After breakfast, as usual, God got up quickly to clean the table and wash the dishes in the kitchen. Standing just outside the kitchen, Yulian shouted, 'Don't use detergent if there's no grease on the bowl! Everything costs money. The pittance they pay for your support? Ha!'

God grunted nonstop to show that he understood.

Qiusheng and Yulian left for the fields. Bingbing left for school. Only now did Qiusheng's father get up. Still not fully awake, he came downstairs, ate two bowls of porridge and filled his pipe with tobacco. At last he remembered God's existence.

'Hey, old geezer, stop the washing. Come out and play a game with me!' he shouted into the kitchen.

God came out of the kitchen, wiping his hands on his apron. He nodded ingratiatingly at Qiusheng's father. Playing Chinese Chess with the old man was a tough chore for God; winning and losing both had unpleasant consequences. If God won, Qiusheng's father would get mad: *You fucking old idiot! You trying to show me up? Shit! You're God! Beating me is no great accomplishment at all. Why can't you learn some manners? You've lived under this roof long enough!* But if God lost, Qiusheng's father would still get mad: *You fucking old idiot! I'm the best chess player for fifty kilometers. Beating you is easier than squishing a bedbug. You think I need you to let me win? You... to put it politely, you are insulting me!*

In any case, the final result was the same: the old man flipped the board and the pieces flew everywhere. Qiusheng's father was infamous for his bad temper, and now he'd finally found a punching bag in God.

But the old man didn't hold a grudge. Every time God picked up the board and put the pieces back quietly, he sat down and played with God again – and the whole process was repeated. After a few cycles of this both of them were tired and it was almost noon.

God then got up to wash the vegetables. Yulian didn't allow him to cook because she said God was a terrible cook. But he still had to wash the vegetables. Later, when Qiusheng and Yulian returned from the fields, if the vegetables hadn't been washed she would be on him again with another round of bitter, sarcastic scolding.

While God washed the vegetables, Qiusheng's father left to visit the neighbors. This was the most peaceful part of God's day. The noon sun filled every crack in the brick-lined yard and illuminated the deep crevasses in his memory. During such periods God often forgot his work and stood quietly, lost in thought. Only when the noise of the villagers returning from the fields filled the air would he be startled awake and hurry to finish his washing.

He sighed. *How could life have turned out like this?*

This wasn't only God's sigh. It was also the sigh of Qiusheng, Yulian and Qiusheng's father. It was the sigh of more than five billion people and two billion Gods on Earth.

Chapter 2

I t all began one fall evening three years ago.

'Come quickly! There are toys in the sky!' Bingbing shouted in the yard. Qiusheng and Yulian raced out of the house, looked up and saw that the sky really was filled with toys, or at least objects whose shapes could only be those of toys.

The objects spread out evenly across the dome of the sky. In the dusk, each reflected the light of the setting sun – already below the horizon – and each shone as brightly as the full Moon. The light turned Earth's surface as bright as it is at noon. But the light came from every direction and left no shadow, as though the whole world was illuminated by a giant surgical lamp.

At first, everyone thought the objects were within our atmosphere because they were so clear. But eventually, humans learned that these objects were just enormous. They were hovering about thirty thousand kilometers away in geostationary orbits.

There were a total of 21,530 spaceships. Spread out evenly across the sky, they formed a thin shell around Earth. This was the result of a complex set of maneuvers that brought all the ships to their final locations simultaneously. In this manner, the alien ships avoided causing life-threatening tides in the oceans due to their imbalanced masses. The gesture reassured humans somewhat, as it was at least some evidence that the aliens did not bear ill will toward Earth.

During the next few days, all attempts at communicating with the aliens failed. The aliens maintained absolute silence in the face of repeated queries. At the same time, Earth became a nightless planet. Tens of thousands of spaceships reflected so much sunlight onto the night side of Earth that it was as bright as day, while on the day side the ships cast giant shadows onto the ground. The horrible sight pushed the psychological endurance of the human race to the limit so that most ignored yet another strange occurrence on the surface of the planet and did not connect it with the fleet of spaceships in the sky.

Across the great cities of the world, wandering old people had begun to appear. All of them had the same features: extreme old age, long white hair and beards, long white robes. At first, before their white robes, white beards, and white hair got dirty, they looked like a bunch of snowmen. The wanderers did not appear to belong to any particular race, as though all ethnicities were mixed in them. They had no documents to prove their citizenship or identity and could not explain their own histories.

All they could do was to gently repeat, in heavily accented versions of various local languages, the same words to all passersby:

'We are God. Please, considering that we created this world, would you give us a bit of food?'

If only one or two old wanderers had said this, then they would have been sent to a shelter or nursing home, like the homeless with dementia. But millions of old men and women all saying the same thing – that was an entirely different matter.

Within a fortnight, the number of old wanderers had increased to more than thirty million. All over the streets of New York, Beijing, London, Moscow... these old people could be seen everywhere, shuffling around in traffic-stopping crowds. Sometimes it seemed as if there were more of *them* than the original inhabitants of the cities.

The most horrible part of their presence was that they all repeated the same thing: 'We are God. Please, considering that we created this world, would you give us a bit of food?'

Only now did humans turn their attention from the spaceships to the uninvited guests. Recently, large-scale meteor showers had been occurring over every continent. After every impressive display of streaking meteors, the number of old wanderers in the corresponding region greatly increased. After careful observation, the following incredible fact was discovered: the old wanderers came out of the sky, from those alien spaceships.

One by one, they leaped into the atmosphere as though diving into a swimming pool, each wearing a suit made from a special film. As the friction from the atmosphere burned away the surface of the suits, the film kept the heat away from the wearer and slowed their descent. Careful design ensured that the deceleration never exceeded 4g, well within the physical tolerance of the bodies of the old wanderers. Finally, at the moment of their arrival at the surface their velocity was close to zero, as though they had just jumped down from a bench. Even so, many of them still managed to sprain their ankles. Simultaneously, the film around them had been completely burned away, leaving no trace.

The meteor showers continued without stopping. More wanderers fell to Earth, and their number rose to almost one hundred million.

The governments of every country attempted to find one or more representatives among the wanderers. But the wanderers claimed that the 'Gods' were absolutely equal and that any one of them could represent all of them. Thus, at the emergency session of the United Nations General Assembly, one random old wanderer, who was found in Times Square and who now spoke passable English, entered the General Assembly Hall.

He was clearly among the earliest to land: his robe was dirty and full of holes, and his white beard was covered with dirt like a mop. There was no halo over his head, but a few loyal flies did hover there. With the help of a ratty bamboo walking stick, he shuffled his way to the round meeting table and lowered himself under the gaze of the leaders. He looked up at the Secretary-General, and his face displayed the childlike smile common to all the old wanderers.

'I... ha—... I haven't had breakfast yet.'

So breakfast was brought. All across the world, people stared as he ate like a starved man, choking a few times. Toast, sausages and a salad were quickly ingested, followed by a large glass of milk. Then he showed his innocent smile to the Secretary-General again.

'Haha... uh... is there any wine? Just a tiny cup will do.'

So a glass of wine was brought. He sipped at it, nodding with satisfaction. 'Last night, a bunch of new arrivals took over my favorite subway grille, one that blew out warm air. I had to find a new place to sleep in the Square. But now, with a bit of wine, my joints are coming back to life... You, can you massage my back a little? Just a little.'

The Secretary-General began to massage his back. The old wanderer shook his head, sighed and said, 'Sorry to be so much trouble to you.'

'Where are you from?' asked the delegate from of the United States.

The old wanderer shook his head. 'A civilization only has a fixed location in her infancy. Planets and stars are unstable and change. Civilizations must then move. By the time she becomes a young woman, she has already moved multiple times. Then the civilizations will make this discovery: no planetary environment is as stable as a sealed spaceship. So they'll make spaceships their home, and planets will just be places where they sojourn. Thus, any civilization that has reached adulthood will be a starfaring civilization, permanently wandering through the cosmos. The spaceship is her home. Where are we from? We come from the ships.' He pointed up with a finger caked in dirt.

'How many of you are there?'

'Two billion.'

'Who are you really?' The Secretary-General had cause to ask this. The old wanderers looked just like humans.

'We've told you many times.' The old wanderer waved his hand impatiently. 'We are God.'

'Could you explain?'

'Our civilization – let's just call her the God Civilization – had existed long before Earth was born. When the God Civilization entered her senescence we seeded the newly formed Earth with the beginnings of life. Then the God Civilization skipped across time by traveling close to the speed of light. When life on Earth had evolved to the appropriate stage, we came back, introduced a new species based on our ancestral genes, eliminated its enemies and carefully guided its evolution until Earth was home to a new civilized species just like us.'

'How do you expect us to believe you?'

'That's easy.'

Thus began the half-year-long effort to verify these claims. Humans watched in astonishment as spaceships sent the original plans for life on Earth and images of the primitive Earth. Following the old wanderer's direction, humans dug up incredible machines from deep below Earth's crust – equipment that had through the long eons monitored and manipulated the biosphere on this planet.

Humans finally had to believe. At least with respect to life on Earth, the Gods really were God.

Chapter 3

At the emergency session of the United Nations General Assembly, the Secretary-General, on behalf of the human race, finally asked God the key question: why did they come to Earth?

'Before I answer this question, you must have a proper understanding of the concept of "civilization".' God stroked his long beard. This was the same God who had been at the first emergency session half a year before. 'How do you think civilizations evolve over time?'

'Civilization on Earth is currently in a stage of rapid development. If we're not hit by natural disasters beyond our ability to withstand, I think we will continue our development indefinitely,' said the Secretary-General.

'Wrong. Think about it: every person experiences childhood, youth, middle age and old age, finally arriving at death. The stars are the same way. Indeed, everything in the universe goes through the same process. Even the universe itself will have to terminate one day. Why would civilization be an exception? No, a civilization will also grow old and die.'

'How exactly does that happen?'

'Different civilizations grow old and die in different ways, just like different people die of different diseases or of just plain old age. For the God Civilization, the first sign of her senescence was

336

the extreme lengthening of each individual member's life span. By then, each individual in the God Civilization could expect a life as long as four thousand Earth years. By age two thousand, their thoughts had completely ossified, losing all creativity. Because individuals like these held the reins of power, new life had a hard time emerging and growing. That was when our civilization became old.'

'And then?'

'The second sign of the civilization's senescence was the Age of the Machine Cradle.'

'What?'

'By then our machines no longer relied on their creators. They operated independently, maintained themselves and developed on their own. The smart machines gave us everything we needed: not just material needs but also psychological ones. We didn't need to put any effort into survival. Taken care of by machines, we lived as though we were lying in comfortable cradles.

'Think about it: if the jungles of primitive Earth had been filled with inexhaustible supplies of fruits and tame creatures that desired to become food, how could apes evolve into humans? The Machine Cradle was just such a comfort-filled jungle. Gradually we forgot about our technology and science. Our civilization became lazy and empty, devoid of creativity and ambition, and that only sped up the aging process. What you see now is the God Civilization in her final dying gasps.'

'Then... can you now tell us the goal for the God Civilization in coming to Earth?'

'We have no home now.'

'But...' The Secretary-General pointed upward.

'The spaceships are old. It's true that the artificial environment on the ships is more stable than any natural environment, including Earth's. But the ships are so old, old beyond your imagination. Old components have broken down. Accumulated quantum effects over the eons have led to more and more software errors. The system's self-repair and self-maintenance functions have encountered more and more insurmountable obstacles. The living environment on the ships is deteriorating. The number of life necessities that can be distributed to individuals is decreasing by the day. We can just about survive. In the twenty thousand cities on the various ships, the air is filled with pollution and despair.'

'Are there no solutions? Perhaps new components for the ships? A software upgrade?'

God shook his head. 'The God Civilization is in her final years. We are two billion dying men and women, each more than three thousand years old. But before us, hundreds of generations had already lived in the comfort of the Machine Cradle. Long ago, we forgot all our technology. Now we have no way to repair these ships that have been operating for tens of millions of years on their own. Indeed, in terms of the ability to study and understand technology, we are even worse than you. We can't even connect a circuit for a lightbulb or solve a quadratic equation…

'One day, the ships told us that they were close to complete breakdown. The propulsion systems could no longer push the ships near the speed of light. The God Civilization could only drift along at a speed not even one-tenth the speed of light, and the ecological support systems were nearing collapse. The machines could no longer keep two billion of us alive. We had to find another way out.'

'Did you ever think that this would happen?'

'Of course. Two thousand years ago, the ships already warned us. That was when we began the process of seeding life on Earth so that in our old age we would have support.'

'Two thousand years ago?'

'Yes. Of course I'm talking about time on the ships. From your frame of reference, that was 3.5 billion years ago, when Earth first cooled down.'

'We have a question: you say that you've lost your technology. But doesn't seeding life require technology?'

'Oh. To start the process of evolving life on a planet is a minor operation. Just scatter some seeds, and life will multiply and evolve on its own. We had this kind of software even before the Age of the Machine Cradle. Just start the program, and the machines can finish everything. To create a planet full of life, capable of developing civilization, the most basic requirement is time – a few billion years of time.

'By traveling close to the speed of light, we possess almost limitless time. But now, the God Civilization's ships can no longer approach the speed of light. Otherwise we'd still have the chance to create new civilizations and more life, and we would have more choices. We're trapped by slowness. Those dreams cannot be realized.'

'So you want to spend your golden years on Earth.'

'Yes, yes. We hope that you will feel a sense of filial duty toward your creators and take us in.' God leaned on his walking stick and trembled as he tried to bow to the leaders of all the nations. As he did so, he almost fell on his face.

'But how do you plan to live here?'

'If we just gathered in one place by ourselves, then we might as well stay in space and die there. We'd like to be absorbed into your societies, your families. When the God Civilization was still in her childhood, we also had families. You know that childhood is the most precious time. Since your civilization is still in her childhood, if we can return to this era and spend the rest of our lives in the warmth of families then that would be our greatest happiness.'

'There are two billion of you. That means every family on Earth would have to take in one or two of you.' After the Secretary-General spoke, the meeting hall sank into silence.

'Yes, yes, sorry to give you so much trouble...' God continued to bow while stealing glances at the Secretary-General and the leaders of all the nations. 'Of course, we're willing to compensate you.'

He waved his cane and two more white-bearded Gods walked into the meeting hall, struggling under the weight of a silvery, metallic trunk they carried between them. 'Look: these are high-density information storage devices. They systematically store the knowledge that the God Civilization has acquired in every field of science and technology. With this, your civilization will advance by leaps and bounds. I think you will like this.'

The Secretary-General, along with the leaders of all the nations, looked at the metal trunk and tried to hide his elation. 'Taking care of God is the responsibility of humankind. Of course this will require some consultation between the various nations, but I think in principle...'

'Sorry to be so much trouble. Sorry to be so much trouble...' God's eyes filled with tears, and he continued to bow.

After the Secretary-General and the leaders of all the nations left the meeting hall, they saw that tens of thousands of Gods had gathered outside the United Nations building. A white sea of bobbing heads filled the air with murmuring words. The Secretary-General listened carefully and realized that they were all speaking, in the various tongues of Earth, the same sentence:

'Sorry to be so much trouble. Sorry to be so much trouble...'

Chapter 4

Two billion Gods arrived on Earth. Enclosed in suits made of their special film, they fell through the atmosphere. During that time, one could see the bright, colorful streaks in the sky even during the day. After the Gods landed, they spread out into 1.5 billion families.

Having received the Gods' knowledge about science and technology, everyone was filled with hopes and dreams for the future, as though humankind was about to step into paradise overnight. Under the influence of such joy, every family welcomed the coming of God.

*

That morning, Qiusheng and his family and all the other villagers stood at the village entrance to receive the Gods allocated to Xicen.

'What a beautiful day,' Yulian said.

Her comment wasn't motivated solely by her feelings. The spaceships had disappeared overnight, restoring the sky's wide open and limitless appearance. Humans had never been allowed to step onto any of the ships. The Gods did not really object to that particular request from the humans, but the ships themselves refused to grant permission. They did not acknowledge the various primitive probes that humans sent, and they sealed their doors tightly. After the final group of Gods leaped into the atmosphere, all the spaceships, numbering more than twenty thousand, departed their orbit simultaneously. But they didn't go far, only drifting in the Asteroid belt.

Although these ships were ancient, the old routines continued to function. Their only mission was to serve the Gods. Thus, they would not move too far away. When the Gods needed them again, they would come.

Two buses arrived from the county seat, bringing the 106 Gods allocated to Xicen. Qiusheng and Yulian met the God assigned to their family. The couple stood on each side of God, affectionately supported him by the arms and walked home in the bright afternoon sun. Bingbing and Qiusheng's father followed behind, smiling.

'Gramps... um... Gramps God?' Yulian leaned her face against God's shoulder, her smile as bright as the sun. 'I hear that the technology you gave us will soon allow us to experience true Communism! When that happens, we'll all have things according to our needs. Things won't cost any money. You just go to the store and pick them up.'

God smiled and nodded at her, his white hair bobbing. He spoke in heavily accented Chinese. 'Yes. Actually, "to each according to their needs" fulfills only the most basic needs of a civilization. The technology we gave you will bring you a life of prosperity and comfort surpassing your imagination.'

Yulian laughed so much her face opened up like a flower. 'No, no! "To each according to their needs" is more than enough for me!'

'Uh-huh,' Qiusheng's father agreed emphatically.

'Can we live forever without aging like you?' Qiusheng asked.

'We can't live forever without aging. It's just that we can live longer than you. Look at how old I am! In my view, if a man lives longer than three thousand years, he might as well be dead. For a civilization, extreme longevity for the individual can be fatal.'

'Oh, I don't need three thousand years. Just three hundred.' Qiusheng's father was now laughing as much as Yulian. 'In that case, I'd still be considered a young man right now. Maybe I can... hahahaha.'

*

The village treated the day like it was Chinese New Year. Every family held a big banquet to welcome its God, and Qiusheng's family was no exception.

Qiusheng's father quickly became slightly drunk on cups of vintage *huangjiu*. He gave God a thumbs-up. 'You're really something! To be able to create so many living things – you're truly supernatural.'

God drank a lot, too, but his head was still clear. He waved his hand. 'No, not supernatural. It was just science. When biology has developed to a certain level, creating life is akin to building machines.'

'You say that. But in our eyes, you're no different from immortals who have deigned to live among us.'

God shook his head. 'Supernatural beings would never make mistakes. But for us, we made mistake after mistake during your creation.'

'You made mistakes when you created us?' Yulian's eyes were wide open. In her imagination, creating all those lives was a process similar to her giving birth to Bingbing eight years before. No mistake was possible.

'There were many. I'll give a relatively recent example. The world-creation software made errors in the analysis of the environment on Earth, which resulted in the appearance of creatures like dinosaurs: huge bodies and low adaptability. Eventually, in order to facilitate your evolution, they had to be eliminated.

'In terms of events that are even more recent, after the disappearance of the ancient Aegean civilizations the world-creation software believed that civilization on Earth was successfully established. It ceased to perform further monitoring and micro-adjustments, like leaving a wound-up clock to run on its own. This resulted in further errors. For example, it should have allowed the civilization of ancient Greece to develop on her own and stopped the Macedonian conquest and the subsequent Roman conquest. Although both of these ended up as the inheritors of Greek civilization, the direction of Greek development was altered...'

No one in Qiusheng's family could understand this lecture, but all listened respectfully.

'And then two great powers appeared on Earth: Han China and the Roman Empire. In contrast to the earlier situation with ancient Greece, the two shouldn't have been kept apart and left to develop in isolation. They ought to have been allowed to come into full contact—'

'This "Han China" you're talking about? Is that the Han Dynasty of Liu Bang and Xiang Yu?' Finally Qiusheng's father heard something he knew. 'And what is this "Roman Empire"?'

'I think that was a foreigners' country at the time,' Qiusheng said, trying to explain. 'It was pretty big.'

Qiusheng's father was confused. 'Why? When the foreigners finally showed up during the Qing Dynasty, look how badly they beat us up. You want them to show up even earlier? During the Han Dynasty?'

God laughed at this. 'No, no. Back then, Han China was just as powerful as the Roman Empire.'

'That's still bad. If those two great powers had met, it would have been a great war. Blood would have flowed like a river.'

God nodded. He reached out with his chopsticks for a piece of beef braised in soy sauce. 'Could have been. But if those two great civilizations, the Occident and the Orient, had met, the encounter would have generated glorious sparks and greatly advanced human progress... Eh, if those errors could have been avoided, Earth would now probably be colonizing Mars and your interstellar probes would have flown past Sirius.'

Qiusheng's father raised his bowl of *huangjiu* and spoke admiringly. 'Everyone says that the Gods have forgotten science in their cradle, but you are still so learned.'

'To be comfortable in the cradle it's important to know a bit about philosophy, art, history and so on – just some common facts, not real learning. Many scholars on Earth right now have much deeper thoughts than our own.'

*

For the Gods, the first few months after they entered human society were a golden age in which they lived very harmoniously with human families. It was as though they had returned to the childhood of the God Civilization, fully immersed in the long-forgotten warmth of family life. This seemed the best way to spend the final years of their extremely long lives.

Qiusheng's family's God enjoyed the peaceful life in this beautiful southern Chinese village. Every day he went to the pond surrounded by bamboo groves to fish, chat with other old folks from the village, play chess and generally enjoy himself. But his greatest hobby was attending folk operas. Whenever a theatre troupe came to the village or the town he made sure to go to every performance.

His favorite opera was *The Butterfly Lovers*. One performance was not enough. He followed one troupe around for more than fifty kilometers and attended several shows in a row. Finally Qiusheng went to town and bought him a VCD of the opera. God played it over and over until he could hum a few lines of the *Huangmei* opera and sounded pretty good.

One day Yulian discovered a secret. She whispered to Qiusheng and her father-in-law, 'Did you know that every time Gramps God finishes his opera he always takes a little card out from his pocket? And while looking at the card, he hums lines from the opera. Just now I stole a glance. The card is a photo. There's a really pretty young woman on it.'

That evening, God played *The Butterfly Lovers* again. He took out the photograph of the pretty young woman and started to hum. Qiusheng's father quietly moved in. 'Gramps God, is that your... girlfriend from a long time ago?'

God was startled. He hid the photograph quickly and smiled like a kid at Qiusheng's father. 'Haha. Yeah, yeah. I loved her two thousand years ago.'

Yulian, who was eavesdropping, grimaced. *Two thousand years ago!* Considering his advanced age, this was a bit gag-inducing.

Qiusheng's father wanted to look at the photograph. But God was so protective of it that it would have been embarrassing to ask. So Qiusheng's father settled for listening to God reminisce.

'Back then we were all so young. She was one of the very few who wasn't completely absorbed by life in the Machine Cradle. She initiated a great voyage of exploration to sail to the end of the universe. Oh, you don't need to think too hard about that. It's very difficult to understand. Anyway, she hoped to use this voyage as an opportunity to awaken the God Civilization, sleeping so soundly in the Machine Cradle. Of course, that was nothing more than a beautiful dream. She wanted me to go with her, but I didn't have the courage. The endless desert of the universe frightened me. It would have been a journey of more than twenty billion light-years. So she went by herself. But in the two thousand years after that, I never stopped longing for her.'

'Twenty billion light-years? So like you explained to me before, that's the distance that light would travel in twenty billion years? Oh my! That's way too far. That's basically good-bye for life. Gramps God, you have to forget about her. You'll never see her again.'

God nodded and sighed.

'Well, isn't she now about your age, too?'

God was startled out of his reverie. He shook his head. 'Oh, no. For such a long voyage, her explorer ship would have to fly at close to the speed of light. That means she would still be very young. The only one that has grown old is me. You don't understand how large the universe is. What you think of as "eternity" is nothing but a grain of sand in space-time.

'Well, the fact that you can't understand and feel this is sometimes a blessing.'

Chapter 5

The honeymoon phase between the Gods and humans quickly ended.

People were initially ecstatic over the scientific material received from the Gods, thinking that it would allow mankind to realize its dreams overnight. Thanks to the interface equipment provided by the Gods, an enormous quantity of information was retrieved successfully from the storage devices. The information was translated into English, and in order to avoid disputes a copy was distributed to every nation in the world.

But people soon discovered that utilizing these God-given technologies was impossible, at least within the current century. Consider the futility of a time traveler providing information on modern technology to the ancient Egyptians, and you will have some understanding of the hopeless situation these humans faced.

As the exhaustion of petroleum supplies loomed, energy technology was at the forefront of everyone's minds. But scientists and engineers discovered that the God Civilization's energy technology was useless for humans at this time. The Gods' energy source was built upon the basis of matter–antimatter annihilation. Even if people could understand the materials and finally create an annihilation engine and generator – a near-impossible task within this generation – it would still have been for naught.

This was because the fuel for these engines, antimatter, had to be mined from deep space. According to the material provided by the Gods, the closest antimatter ore source was between the Milky Way and the Andromeda Galaxy, about 550,000 light-years away.

The technology for interstellar travel at near light-speed also involved every field of scientific knowledge, and the greater part of the theories and techniques revealed by the Gods were beyond human comprehension. Just grasping a basic understanding of the foundations would require human scholars to work for perhaps half a century. Scientists, initially full of hope, had tried to search the material from the Gods for technical information concerning controlled nuclear fission, but there was nothing. This was easy to understand: our current literature on energy science contained no information on how to make fire from sticks.

In other scientific fields, such as information science and life sciences (including the secret of human longevity), the problem was the same. Even the most advanced scholars could make no sense of the Gods' knowledge. Between the Gods' science and human science there was a great abyss of understanding that could not be bridged.

The Gods who arrived on Earth could not help the scientists in any way. Like the God at the United Nations had said, among the Gods now there were few who could even solve quadratic equations. The spaceships adrift among the asteroids also ignored all hails from the humans. The human race was like a group of new elementary school students who were suddenly required to master PhD material with no instructor.

At the same time, Earth's population had suddenly grown by two billion. These were all extremely aged individuals who could not be productive. Most of them were plagued by various diseases and put unprecedented pressure on human society. As a result, every government had to pay each family living with a God a considerable support stipend. Health care and other public services were strained beyond the breaking point. The world economy was pushed to the edge of collapse.

The harmonious relationship between God and Qiusheng's family was gone. Gradually the family began to see him as a burden that fell from the sky. They began to despise him, but each had a different reason.

Yulian's reason was the most practical and closest to the underlying problem: God made her family poor. Among all the members of the family God also worried the most about her; she had a tongue as sharp as a knife, and she scared him more than black holes and supernovas. After the death of her dream of true Communism, she unceasingly nagged God: *Before you came, our family had lived so prosperously and comfortably. Back then everything was good. Now everything is bad. All because of you. Being saddled with an old fool like you was such a great misfortune.* Every day, whenever she had the chance, she would prattle on like this in front of God.

God also suffered from chronic bronchitis. This was not a very expensive disease to treat, but it did require ongoing care and a constant outlay of money. Finally one day Yulian forbade Qiusheng from taking God to the town hospital to see doctors and stopped buying medicine for him. When the secretary of the village branch of the Communist Party found out, he came to Qiusheng's house.

'You have to pay for the care of your family God,' the secretary said to Yulian. 'The doctor at the town hospital already told me that if left untreated his chronic bronchitis might develop into pulmonary emphysema.'

'If you want him treated, then the village or the government can pay for it,' Yulian shouted at the secretary. 'We're not made of money!'

'Yulian, according to the God Support Law the family has to bear these kinds of minor medical expenses. The government's support fee already includes this component.'

'That minuscule support fee is useless!'

'You can't talk like that. After you began getting the support fee, you bought a milk cow, switched to liquefied petroleum gas

and bought a big, new color TV! You're telling me now that you
don't have money for God to see a doctor? Everyone knows that
in your family your word is law. I'm going to make it clear to
you: right now I'm helping you save face, but don't push your
luck. Next time, it won't be me standing here trying to persuade
you. It will be the County God Support Committee. You'll be in
real trouble then.'

Yulian had no choice but to resume paying for God's medical
care. But after that she became even meaner to him.

One time, God said to Yulian, 'Don't be so anxious. Humans
are very smart and learn fast. In only another century or so the
easiest aspects of the Gods' knowledge will become applicable to
human society. Then your life will become better.'

'Damn. A *whole century.* And you say "only". Are you even
listening to yourself?' Yulian was washing the dishes and didn't
even bother looking back at God.

'That's a very short period of time.'

'For you! You think we can live as long as you? In another
century you won't even be able to find my bones! But I want
to ask you a question: how much longer do you think *you'll*
be living?'

'Oh, I'm like a candle in the wind. If I can live another three
or four hundred years, I'll be very satisfied.'

Yulian dropped a whole stack of bowls on the ground. 'This
is not how "support" is supposed to work! Ah, so you think not
only should I spend my entire life taking care of you, but you
have to have my son, my grandson, my family for ten generations and more!? Why won't you die?'

*

As for Qiusheng's father, he thought God was a fraud, and in
fact, this view was pretty common. Since scientists couldn't
understand the Gods' scientific papers, there was no way to
prove their authenticity. Maybe the Gods were playing a giant

trick on the human race. For Qiusheng's father, there was ample evidence to support this view.

'You old swindler, you're way too outrageous,' he said to God one day. 'I'm too lazy to expose you. Your tricks are not worth my trouble. Heck, they're not even worth my grandson's trouble.'

God asked him what he had discovered.

'I'll start with the simplest thing: our scientists know that humans evolved from monkeys, right?'

God nodded. 'More accurately, you evolved from primitive apes.'

'Then how can you say that you created us? If you were interested in creating humans, why not directly make us in our current form? Why bother first creating primitive apes and then go through the trouble of evolving? It makes no sense.'

'A human begins as a baby, and then grows into an adult. A civilization also has to grow from a less evolved state. The long path of experience cannot be avoided. Actually, humans began with the introduction of a much more primitive species. Even apes were already very evolved.'

'I don't believe these made-up reasons. All right, here's something more obvious. This was actually first noticed by my grandson. Our scientists say that there was life on Earth even three billion years ago. Do you admit this?'

God nodded. 'That estimate is basically right.'

'So you're three billion years old?'

'In terms of your frame of reference, yes. But according to the frame of reference of our ships, I'm only 3,500 years old. The ships flew close to the speed of light, and time passed much more slowly for us than for you. Of course, once in a while a few ships dropped down and decelerated enough to come to Earth so that further adjustments could be made to the evolution of life on Earth. But this didn't require much time. Those ships would then return to cruise at close to the speed of light and continue skipping over the passage of time here.'

'Bullshit,' Qiusheng's father said contemptuously.

'Dad, this is the Theory of Relativity,' Qiusheng interrupted. 'Our scientists already proved it.'

'Relativity, my ass! You're bullshitting me, too. That's impossible! How can time be like sesame oil, flowing at different speeds? I'm not so old that I've lost my mind. But you – reading all those books has made you stupid!'

'I can prove to you that time does indeed flow at different rates,' God said, his face full of mystery. He took out that photograph of his beloved from two thousand years ago and handed it to Qiusheng. 'Look at her carefully and memorize every detail.'

The second Qiusheng looked at the photograph, he knew that he would be able to remember every detail. It would be impossible to forget. Like the other Gods, the woman in the picture had a blend of the features of all ethnicities. Her skin was like warm ivory, her two eyes were so alive that they seemed to sing and she immediately captivated Qiusheng's soul. She was a woman among Gods, the God of women. The beauty of the Gods was like a second sun. Humans had never seen it and could not bear it.

'Look at you! You're practically drooling!' Yulian grabbed the photograph from the frozen Qiusheng. But before she could look at it, her father-in-law took it away from her.

'Let me see,' Qiusheng's father said. He brought the photograph as close as possible to his ancient eyes. For a long time he did not move, as though the photograph provided sustenance.

'Why are you looking so closely?' Yulian said, her tone contemptuous.

'Shut it. I don't have my glasses,' Qiusheng's father said, his face still pressed against the photograph.

Yulian looked at her father-in-law disdainfully for a few seconds, curled her lips and left for the kitchen.

God took the photograph out of the hands of Qiusheng's father, whose hands lingered on the photo for a long while, unwilling to let go. God said, 'Remember all the details. I'll let you look at it again this time tomorrow.'

The next day, father and son said little to each other. Both were thinking about the young woman, leaving them nothing to say. Yulian's temper was far worse than usual.

Finally the time came. God had seemingly forgotten about it and had to be reminded by Qiusheng's father. He took out the photograph that the two men had been thinking about all day and handed it first to Qiusheng. 'Look carefully. Do you see any change in her?'

'Nothing really,' Qiusheng said, looking intently. After a while, he finally noticed something. 'Aha! The opening between her lips seems slightly narrower. Not much, just a little bit. Look at the corner of the mouth here...'

'Have you no shame? To look at some other woman that closely?' Yulian grabbed the photo again, and again her father-in-law took it away from her.

'Let me see...' Qiusheng's father put on his glasses and carefully examined the picture. 'Yes, indeed, the opening is narrower. But there's a much more obvious change that you didn't notice. Look at this wisp of hair. Compared to yesterday, it has drifted farther to the right.'

God took the picture from Qiusheng's father. 'This is not a photograph but a television receiver.'

'A... TV?'

'Yes. Right now it's receiving a live feed from that explorer spaceship heading for the end of the universe.'

'Live? Like live broadcasts of football matches?'

'Yes.'

'So... the woman in the picture, she's alive!' Qiusheng was so shocked that his mouth hung open. Even Yulian's eyes were now as big as walnuts.

'Yes, she's alive. But unlike a live broadcast on Earth, this feed is subject to a delay. The explorer spaceship is now about eighty million light-years away, so the delay is about eighty million years. What we see now is how she was eighty million years ago.'

'This tiny thing can receive a signal from that far away?'

'This kind of super-long-distance communication across space requires the use of neutrinos or gravitational waves. Our space-ships can receive the signal, magnify it and then re-broadcast to this TV.'

'Treasure, a real treasure!' Qiusheng's father praised sincerely. But it was unclear whether he was talking about the tiny TV or the young woman on the TV. Either way, after hearing that she was still 'alive', Qiusheng and his father both felt a deeper attachment to her. Qiusheng tried to take the tiny TV again, but God refused.

'Why does she move so slowly in the picture?'

'That's the result of time flowing at different speeds. From our frame of reference, time flows extremely slowly on a spaceship flying close to the speed of light.'

'Then... can she still talk to you?' Yulian asked.

God nodded. He flipped a switch behind the TV. Immediately a sound came out of it. It was a woman's voice, but the sound was unchanging, like a singer holding a note steadily at the end of a song. God stared at the screen, his eyes full of love.

'She's talking right now. She's finishing three words: 'I love you.' Each word took more than a year. It's now been three and a half years, and right now she's just finishing 'you'. To completely finish the sentence will take another three months.' God lifted his eyes from the TV to the domed sky above the yard. 'She still has more to say. I'll spend the rest of my life listening to her.'

*

Bingbing actually managed to maintain a decent relationship with God for a while. The Gods all had some childishness to them, and they enjoyed talking and playing with children. But one day, Bingbing wanted God to give him the large watch he wore and God steadfastly refused. He explained that the watch was a tool for communicating with the God Civilization. Without it, he would no longer be able to connect with his own people.

'Hmm, look at this. You're still thinking about your own civilization and race. You've never thought of us as your real family!' Yulian said angrily.

After that, Bingbing was no longer nice to God. Instead, he often played practical tricks on him.

*

The only one in the family who still had respect and feelings of filial piety toward God was Qiusheng. Qiusheng had graduated from high school and liked to read. Other than a few people who passed the college-entrance examination and went away for college, he was the most learned person in the village. But at home, Qiusheng had no power. On practically everything he listened to the direction of his wife and followed the commands of his father. If his wife and father had ever conflicting instructions, then all he could do was sit in a corner and cry. Given that he was such a softy, he had no way to protect God at home.

Chapter 6

The relationship between the Gods and humans had finally deteriorated beyond repair.

The complete breakdown between God and Qiusheng's family occurred after the incident involving instant noodles. One day, before lunch, Yulian came out of the kitchen with a paper box and asked why half the box of instant noodles she had bought yesterday had already disappeared.

'I took them,' God said in a small voice. 'I gave them to those living by the river. They've almost run out of things to eat.'

He was talking about the place where the Gods who had left their families were gathering. Recently there had been frequent incidents of abuse of the Gods in the village. One particularly cruel couple had been beating and cursing out their God, and they even withheld food from him. Eventually that God tried to commit suicide in the river that ran in front of the village, but luckily others were able to stop him.

This incident received a great deal of publicity. It went beyond the county, and the city's police eventually came, along with a bunch of reporters from CCTV and the provincial TV station, and took the couple away in handcuffs. According to the God Support Law, they had committed God abuse and would be sentenced to at least ten years in jail. This was the only law that was universal among all the nations of the world, with uniform prison terms.

After that, the families in the village became more careful and stopped treating the Gods too poorly in front of other people. But at the same time, the incident worsened the relationship between the Gods and the villagers. Eventually, some of the Gods left their families, and other Gods followed. By now almost one-third of the Gods in Xicen had already left their assigned families. These wandering Gods set up camp in the field across the river and lived a spartan, difficult life.

In other parts of the country and across the world, the situation was the same. Once again, the streets of big cities were filled with crowds of wandering, homeless Gods. The number quickly increased, a seeming repeat of the nightmare three years prior. The world, full of Gods and people, faced a gigantic crisis.

'Ha, you're very generous, you old fool! How dare you eat our food while giving it away?' Yulian began to curse loudly.

Qiusheng's father slammed the table and got up. 'You idiot! Get out of here! You like those Gods by the river? Why don't you go and join them?'

God sat silently for a while, thinking. Then he stood up, went to his tiny room and packed up his few belongings. Leaning on his bamboo cane, he slowly made his way out the door, heading in the direction of the river.

Qiusheng didn't eat with the rest of his family. He squatted in a corner with his head lowered and not speaking.

'Hey, dummy! Come here and eat. We have to go into town to buy feed this afternoon,' Yulian shouted at him. Since he refused to budge, she went over to yank his ear.

'Let go,' Qiusheng said. His voice was not loud, but Yulian let him go as though she had been shocked. She had never seen her husband with such a gloomy expression on his face.

'Forget about him,' Qiusheng's father said carelessly. 'If he doesn't want to eat, then he's a fool.'

'Ha, you miss your God? Why don't you go join him and his friends in that field by the river, too?' Yulian poked a finger at Qiusheng's head.

Qiusheng stood up and went upstairs to his bedroom. Like God, he packed a few things into a bundle and put it in a duffel bag he had once used when he had gone to the city to work. With the bag on his back, he headed outside.

'Where are you going?' Yulian yelled. But Qiusheng ignored her. She yelled again, but now there was fear in her voice. 'How long are you going to be out?'

'I'm not coming back,' Qiusheng said without looking back.

'What? Come back here! Is your head filled with shit?' Qiusheng's father followed him out of the house. 'What's the matter with you? Even if you don't want your wife and kid, how dare you leave your father?'

Qiusheng stopped but still did not turn around. 'Why should I care about you?'

'How can you talk like that? I'm your father! I raised you! Your mother died early. You think it was easy to raise you and your sister? Have you lost your mind?'

Qiusheng finally turned back to look at his father. 'If you can kick the people who created our ancestors' ancestors' ancestors out of our house, then I don't think it's much of a sin for me not to support you in your old age.'

He left, and Yulian and his father stood there, dumbfounded.

*

Qiusheng went over the ancient arched stone bridge and walked toward the tents of the Gods. He saw that a few of the Gods had set up a pot to cook something in the grassy clearing strewn with golden leaves. Their white beards and the white steam coming out of the pot reflected the noon sunlight like a scene out of an ancient myth.

Qiusheng found his God and said resolutely, 'Gramps God, let's go.'

'I'm not going back to that house.'

'I'm not, either. Let's go together into town and stay with my

359

sister for a while. Then I'll go into the city and find a job, and we'll rent a place together. I'll support you for the rest of my life.'

'You're a good kid,' God said, patting his shoulder lightly. 'But it's time for us to go.' He pointed to the watch on his wrist. Qiusheng now noticed that all the watches of all the Gods were blinking with red lights.

'Go? Where to?'

'Back to the ships,' God said, pointing at the sky. Qiusheng lifted his head and saw that two spaceships were already hovering in the sky, standing out starkly against the blue. One of them was closer, and its shape and outline loomed large. Behind it, another was much farther away and appeared smaller. But the most surprising sight was that the first spaceship had lowered a thread as thin as spider silk, extending from space down to Earth. As the spider silk slowly drifted, the bright sun glinted on different sections like lightning in the bright blue sky.

'A space elevator,' God explained. 'Already more than a hundred of these have been set up on every continent. We'll ride them back to the ships.' Later Qiusheng would learn that when a spaceship dropped down a space elevator from a geostationary orbit it needed a large mass on its other side, deep in space, to act as a counterweight. That was the purpose of the other ship he saw.

When Qiusheng's eyes adjusted to the brightness of the sky, he saw that there were many more silvery stars deep in the distance. Those stars were spread out very evenly, forming a huge matrix. Qiusheng understood that the twenty thousand ships of the God Civilization were coming back to Earth from the Asteroid belt.

Chapter 7

Twenty thousand spaceships once again filled the sky above Earth. In the two months that followed, space capsules ascended and descended the various space elevators, taking away the two billion Gods who had briefly lived on Earth. The space capsules were silver spheres. From a distance, they looked like dewdrops hanging on spider threads.

The day that Xicen's Gods left, all the villagers showed up for the farewell. Everyone was affectionate toward the Gods, and it reminded everyone of the day a year earlier when the Gods first came to Xicen. It was as though all the abuse and disdain the Gods had received had nothing to do with the villagers.

Two big buses were parked at the entrance to the village, the same two buses that had brought the Gods there a year ago. More than a hundred Gods would now be taken to the nearest space elevator and ride up in space capsules. The silver thread that could be seen in the distance was in reality hundreds of kilometers away.

Qiusheng's whole family went to send off their God. No one said anything along the way. As they neared the village entrance, God stopped, leaned against his cane and bowed to the family. 'Please stop here. Thank you for taking care of me this year. Really, thank you. No matter where I will be in this universe, I will always remember your family.' Then he took off the large watch from his wrist and handed it to Bingbing. 'A gift.'

'But... how will you communicate with the other Gods in the future?' Bingbing asked.

'We'll all be on the spaceships. I have no more need for this,' God said, laughing.

'Gramps God,' Qiusheng's father said, his face sorrowful, 'your ships are all ancient. They won't last much longer. Where can you go then?'

God stroked his beard and said calmly, 'It doesn't matter. Space is limitless. Dying anywhere is the same.'

Yulian suddenly began to cry. 'Gramps God, I... I'm not a very nice person. I shouldn't have made you the target of all my complaints that I'd saved up my whole life. It's just as Qiusheng said: I've behaved as if I don't have a conscience...' She pushed a bamboo basket into God's hands. 'I boiled some eggs this morning. Please take them for your trip.'

God picked up the basket. 'Thank you.' Then he took out an egg, peeled it and began to eat, savoring the taste. Yellow flakes of egg yolk soon covered his white beard. He continued to talk as he ate. 'Actually, we came to Earth not only because we wanted to survive. Having already lived for two or three thousand years, what did we have to fear from death? We just wanted to be with you. We like and cherish your passion for life, your creativity, your imagination. These things have long disappeared from the God Civilization. We saw in you the childhood of our civilization. But we didn't realize we'd bring you so much trouble. We're really sorry.'

'Please stay, Gramps,' Bingbing said, crying. 'I'll be better in the future.'

God shook his head slowly. 'We're not leaving because of how you treated us. The fact that you took us in and allowed us to stay was enough. But one thing made us unable to stay any longer: in your eyes, the Gods are pathetic. You pity us. Oh, you *pity* us.'

God threw away the pieces of eggshell. He lifted his face, trailing a full head of white hair, and stared at the sky, as though through the blue he could see the bright sea of stars. 'How can the God Civilization be pitied by man? You have no idea what a great civilization she was. You do not know what majestic epics she created, or how many imposing deeds she accomplished.

'It was 1857, during the Milky Way Era, when astronomers discovered that a large number of stars was accelerating toward the center of the Milky Way. Once this flood of stars was consumed by the supermassive black hole found there, the resulting radiation would kill all life found in the galaxy.

'In response, our great ancestors built a nebula shield around the center of the galaxy with a diameter of ten thousand light-years so that life and civilization in the galaxy would continue. What a magnificent engineering project that was! It took us more than 1,400 years to complete...

'Immediately afterward, the Andromeda Galaxy and the Large Magellanic Cloud united in an invasion of our galaxy. The interstellar fleet of the God Civilization leaped across hundreds of thousands of light-years and intercepted the invaders at the gravitational balance point between Andromeda and the Milky Way. When the battle entered into its climax, large numbers of ships from both sides mixed together, forming a spiraling nebula the size of the solar system.

'During the final stages of the battle, the God Civilization made the bold decision to send all remaining warships and even the civilian fleet into the spiraling nebula. The great increase in mass caused gravity to exceed the centrifugal force, and this nebula, made of ships and people, collapsed under gravity and formed a star! Because the proportion of heavy elements in this star was so high, immediately after its birth the star went supernova and illuminated the deep darkness between Andromeda and the Milky Way! Our ancestors thus destroyed the invaders with their courage and self-sacrifice and left the Milky Way as a place where life could develop peacefully...

'Yes, now our civilization is old. But it is not our fault. No matter how hard one strives, a civilization must grow old one day. Everyone grows old, even you.

'We really do not need your pity.'

'Compared to you,' Qiusheng said, full of awe, 'the human race is really nothing.'

'Don't talk like that,' God said. 'Earth's civilization is still an infant. We hope you will grow up fast. We hope you will inherit and continue the glory of your creators.' God threw down his cane. He put his hands on the shoulders of Bingbing and Qiusheng. 'I have some final words for you.'

'We may not understand everything you have to say,' Qiusheng said, 'but please speak. We will listen.'

'First, you must get off this rock!' God spread out his arms toward space. His white robe danced in the fall wind like a sail.

'Where will we go?' Qiusheng's father asked in confusion.

'Begin by flying to the other planets in the solar system, then fly to other stars. Don't ask why, but use all your energy toward the goal of flying away, the farther the better. In that process, you will spend a lot of money, and many people will die, but you must get away from here. Any civilization that stays on her birth world is committing suicide! You must go into the universe and find new worlds and new homes, and spread your descendants across the galaxy like drops of spring rain.'

'We'll remember,' Qiusheng said, and he nodded, even though neither he nor the rest of his family really understood God's words.

'Good,' God sighed, satisfied. 'Next I will tell you a secret, a great secret.' He stared at everyone in the family with his blue eyes. His stare was like a cold wind and caused everyone's hearts to shudder. 'You have brothers.'

Qiusheng's family looked at God, utterly confused. But Qiusheng finally figured out what God meant. 'You're saying that you created other Earths?'

God nodded slowly. 'Yes, other Earths, other human civilizations. Other than you, there were three others. All are close to you, within two hundred light-years. You are Earth Number Four, the youngest.'

'Have you been to the other Earths?' Bingbing asked.

God nodded again. 'Before we came to you, we went first to the other three Earths and asked them to take us in. Earth Number One was the best among the bunch. After they obtained our scientific materials, they simply chased us away.

'Earth Number Two, on the other hand, kept one million of us as hostages and forced us to give them spaceships as ransom. After we gave them one thousand ships, they realized that they could not operate the ships. They then forced the hostages to teach them how, but the hostages didn't know how either, since the ships were autonomous. So they killed all the hostages.

'Earth Number Three took three million of us as hostages and demanded that we ram Earth Number One and Earth Number Two with several spaceships each because they were in a prolonged state of war with them. Of course, even a single hit from one of our antimatter-powered ships would destroy all life on a planet. We refused, and so they killed all the hostages.'

'Unfilial children!' Qiusheng's father shouted in anger. 'You should punish them!'

God shook his head. 'We will never attack civilizations we created. You are the best of the four brothers. That's why I'm telling you all this. Your three brothers are drawn to invasion. They do not know what love is or what morality is. Their capacity for cruelty and bloodlust are impossible for you to imagine.

'Indeed, in the beginning we created six Earths. The other two were in the same solar systems as Earth Number One and Earth Number Three, respectively. Both were destroyed by their brothers. The fact that the other three Earths haven't yet destroyed one another is only due to the great distances separating their solar systems. By now, all three know of the existence of Earth Number Four and possess your precise coordinates. Thus, you must go and destroy them first before they destroy you.'

'This is too frightening!' Yulian said.

'For now, it's not yet too frightening. Your three brothers are indeed more advanced than you, but they still cannot travel faster than one-tenth the speed of light and cannot cruise more than thirty light-years from home. This is a race of life and death to see which one among you can achieve near-light-speed space travel first. It is the only way to break through the prison of time and space. Whoever can achieve this technology first will survive. Anyone slower will meet certain death. This is the struggle for survival in the universe. Children, you don't have much time. Work hard!'

'Do the most learned and most powerful people in our world know these things?' Qiusheng's father asked, trembling.

'Yes. But don't rely on them. A civilization's survival depends on the effort of every individual. Even the common people like you have a role to play.'

'You hear that, Bingbing?' Qiusheng said to his son. 'You must study hard.'

'When you fly into the universe at close to the speed of light to resolve the threat of your siblings, you must perform another urgent task: find a few planets suitable for life and seed them with some simple, primitive life from here, like bacteria and algae. Let them evolve on their own.'

Qiusheng wanted to ask more questions, but God picked up his cane and began to walk. The family accompanied him toward the bus. The other Gods were already aboard.

'Oh, Qiusheng.' God stopped, remembering. 'I took a few of your books with me. I hope you don't mind.' He opened his bundle to show Qiusheng. 'These are your high school textbooks on math, physics and chemistry.'

'No problem. Take them. But why do you want these?'

God tied up the bundle again. 'To study. I'll start with quadratic equations. In the long years ahead, I'll need some way to occupy myself. Who knows? Maybe one day, I'll try to repair our ships' antimatter engines and allow us to fly close to the speed of light again!'

'Right,' Qiusheng said, excited. 'That way, you'll be able to skip across time again. You can find another planet, create another civilization to support you in your old age!'

God shook his head. 'No, no, no. We're no longer interested in being supported in our old age. If it's time for us to die, we die. I want to study because I have a final wish.' He took out the small TV from his pocket. On the screen, his beloved from two thousand years ago was still slowly speaking the final word of that three-word sentence. 'I want to see her again.'

'It's a good wish, but it's only a fantasy,' Qiusheng's father said. 'Think about it. She left two thousand years ago at the speed of light. Who knows where she is now? Even if you repair your ship, how will you ever catch her? You told us that nothing can go faster than light.'

God pointed at the sky with his cane. 'In this universe, as long as you're patient you can make any wish come true. Even though the possibility is minuscule, it still exists. I told you once that the universe was born out of a great explosion. Now gravity has gradually slowed down its expansion. Eventually the expansion will stop and turn into contraction. If our spaceship can really fly again at close to the speed of light, then we will endlessly accelerate and endlessly approach the speed of light. This way, we will skip over endless time until we near the final moments of the universe.

'By then, the universe will have shrunk to a very small size, smaller even than Bingbing's toy ball, as small as a point. Then everything in the entire universe will come together, and she and I will also be together.'

A tear fell from God's eye and rolled onto his beard, glistening brightly in the morning sun. 'The universe will then be the tomb at the end of *The Butterfly Lovers*. She and I will be the two butterflies emerging from the tomb...'

Chapter 8

A week later, the last spaceship left Earth. God left.
Xicen village resumed its quiet life.

On this evening, Qiusheng's family sat in the yard looking at a sky full of stars. It was mid-fall, and insects had stopped making noises in the fields. A light breeze stirred the fallen leaves at their feet. The air was slightly chilly.

'They're flying so high. The wind must be so severe, so cold...' Yulian murmured to herself.

'There isn't any wind up there,' Qiusheng said. 'They're in space, where there isn't even air. But it is really cold. So cold that in the books they call it "absolute zero". It's so dark out there, with no end in sight. It's a place that you can't even dream of in your nightmares.'

Yulian began to cry again. But she tried to hide it with words. 'Remember those last two things God told us? I understand the part about our three siblings. But then he told us that we had to spread bacteria onto other planets and so on. I still can't make sense of that.'

'I figured it out,' Qiusheng's father said. Under the brilliant starry sky, his head, full of a lifetime of foolishness, finally opened up to insight. He looked up at the stars. He had lived with them above his head all his life, but only today did he discover what they really looked like. A new sensation spread over him, making him feel as if he had been touched by something greater. Even though it did not become a part of him, the feeling shook him to his core. He sighed at the sea of stars and said:

'The human race needs to start thinking about who is going to support us in our old age.'

With Her Eyes

Prologue

Two months of nonstop work had left me exhausted. I asked my director for a two-day leave of absence so that I could go on a short trip and clear my mind. He agreed, but only on the condition that I take a pair of eyes along with me. I accepted, and he took me to pick them up from the Control Center.

The eyes were stored in a small room at the end of a corridor. I counted about a dozen pairs. The director gestured to the large screen in front of us as he handed me a pair and introduced me to the eyes' owner, a young woman who appeared to be fresh out of university. She was staring blankly at me. The woman's puffy spacesuit made her appear even more petite than she probably was. She looked miserable, to be honest. No doubt she had dreamt of the romance of space from the safety of her university library; now she faced the hellish reality of the infinite void.

'I'm really sorry for the inconvenience,' she said, bowing apologetically. Never in my life had I heard such a gentle voice. Her soft words seemed to float down from space like a gentle breeze, turning those crude and massive orbiting steel structures into silk.

'Not at all. I'm happy to have some company,' I replied sincerely. 'Where do you want to go?'

'Really? You still haven't decided where you're going?' She looked pleased. But as she spoke, my attention was drawn to two peculiarities.

Firstly, any transmission from space reaches its destination with some degree of delay. Even transmissions from the Moon have a lag of two seconds. The lag time is even longer with communications from the Asteroid belt. Yet somehow her answers seemed to arrive without any perceptible delay. This meant that she had to be in LEO: low-Earth orbit. With no need for a transfer mid-journey, returning to the surface from there would be cheap and quick. So why would she want me to carry her eyes on a vacation?

Her spacesuit was the other thing that seemed odd. I work as an astro-engineer specializing in personal equipment, and her suit struck me as odd for a couple of reasons. For one thing, it lacked any visible anti-radiation system, and the helmet hanging by her side appeared to lack an anti-glare shield on its visor. Her suit's thermal and cooling insulation also looked incredibly advanced.

'What station is she on?' I asked, looking over at my director.

'Don't ask.' His expression was glum.

'Leave it, please,' echoed the young woman on the screen, abjectly enough to tug at my heartstrings.

'You aren't in lockup, are you?' I joked.

The room displayed on the monitor looked exceedingly cramped. It was clearly some sort of cockpit. An array of complex navigation systems pulsed and blinked around her, yet I could see no windows, not even an observation monitor. The pencil spinning near her head was the only visible evidence that she was currently in space.

Both she and the director seemed to stiffen at my words. 'OK,' I continued hurriedly. 'I won't ask about things that aren't my concern. So where are we going? It's your choice.'

Coming to a decision appeared to be a genuine struggle for her. Gloved hands gripped in front of her chest, she shut her eyes. It was as though she were deciding between life and death, or as if she thought the planet would explode after our brief vacation. I couldn't help but chuckle.

'Oh, this isn't easy for me. Have you read the book by Helen Keller *Three Days to See*? If you have, you'll understand what I'm talking about!'

'We don't have three days, though. Just two. When it comes to time, modern-day folk are dirt-poor. Then again, we're lucky compared to Helen Keller: in three hours, I can take your eyes anywhere on Earth.'

'Then let's go to the last place I visited before leaving!'

She told me the name of the place. I set off, her eyes in my hand.

Chapter 1

Grassland

Tall mountains, plains, meadows and forest all converged at this one spot. I was more than two thousand kilometers from the space center where I worked; the journey by ionospheric jet had taken all of fifteen minutes. The Taklamakan lay before me. Generations of hard graft had transformed the former desert into grassland. Now, after decades of vigorous population control, it was once again devoid of human habitation.

The grassland stretched all the way to the horizon. Behind me, dark green forests covered the Tian Shan mountain range. The highest peaks were capped with silvery snow. I took out her eyes and put them on.

These 'eyes' were, in reality, a pair of multi-sensory glasses. When worn, every image seen by the wearer is transmitted via an ultra-high-frequency radio signal. This transmission can be received by another person wearing an identical set of multi-sensory glasses, letting them view everything that the first individual sees. It's as if the transmitter is wearing the recipient's eyes.

Millions of people worked year-round on the Moon and the Asteroid Belt. The cost of a vacation back on Earth was astronomical – pardon the pun – which is why the space bureau, in all their stinginess, designed this little gadget. Every astronaut living in space had a corresponding pair of glasses planet-side. Those on Earth lucky enough to go on a real-life vacation would wear these glasses, allowing a homesick space-worker to share the joy of their trip.

People had originally scoffed at these devices. But as those willing to wear them received significant subsidies for their travels they actually became quite popular. These artificial eyes grew increasingly refined through the constant use of the most cutting-edge technology. The current models even transmitted their wearers' senses of touch and smell by monitoring their brainwaves. Taking a pair of eyes on vacation became an act of public service among terrestrial workers in the space industry. Not everyone was willing take an extra pair of eyes with them on vacation, citing reasons such as invasion of privacy. As for me, I had no problem with them.

I sighed deeply at the vista before my eyes. From her eyes, however, came the gentle sound of sobs.

'I have dreamed of this place ever since my last trip. Now I'm back in my dreams.' came her soft voice, drifting out from her eyes. 'I feel like I am rising from the depths of the ocean, like I'm taking my first breath of air. I can't stand being closed in.'

I could actually hear her taking long, deep breaths.

'But you aren't closed in at all. Compared to the vastness of space around you, this grassland might as well be a closet.'

She fell silent. Even her breathing seemed to have stopped.

I continued, if only to break the silence.

'Of course, people in space are still closed in. It's like when Chuck Yeager described the *Mercury* astronauts as being—

'Spam in a can.' She finished the thought for me.

We both laughed. Suddenly she called out in surprise.

'Oh! Flowers! I see flowers! They weren't here last time!' Indeed, the broad grassland was adorned with countless small blooms. 'Can you look at the flowers next to you?'

I crouched and looked down.

'Oh, how beautiful! Can you smell her? No, don't pick her!'

Left with little choice, I had to lie almost flat on my belly to pick up the flower's light fragrance

'Ah, I can smell it too! It's like she's sending us a delicate sonata.'

I shook my head, laughing. In this age of ever-changing fads and wild pursuits, most young women were restless and impulsive. Girls as dainty as this particular specimen, who was practically moved to tears at the sight of a flower, were few and far between.

'Let's give this little flower a name, shall we? Hmm… We'll call her Dreamy. How about that one? What should we call him? Umm, Raindrop sounds good. Now go to that one over there. Thanks. Her petals are light blue – her name should be Moonbeam.'

We went from flower to flower in this way, first looking, then smelling and finally naming them. Utterly entranced, she kept at it with no end in sight, all else forgotten. I, however, soon grew bored to death of this silly game, but by the time I insisted that we stop, we had already named over a hundred flowers.

Looking up, I realized we had wandered a good distance, so I went back to retrieve my backpack. As I bent down to pick it up, I heard a startled shout in my ear.

'Oh no! You crushed Snowflake!'

I gingerly propped the pale little wildflower back up. The whole scene suddenly felt comical. Covering a flower with both hands, I asked her, 'What are their names? What do they look like?'

'That one on the left is Crystal. She's white, too, and has three leaves on her stem. To the right we have Flame. He's pink, with four leaves. The top two leaves are separate, and the bottom two are joined.'

She got them all right. Actually, I felt somewhat moved.

'See? We all know each other. I'll think of them over and over again during the long days to come. It'll be like retelling a beautiful fairy tale. This world of yours is absolutely wonderful!'

'This world of mine? It's your world too! And if you keep acting like a temperamental child, those anal-retentive space psychologists will make sure you're grounded on it for the rest of your life.'

I began to roam aimlessly about the plains. It wasn't long before I came across a small brook concealed in the thick grass. I decided to forge ahead, but her voice called me back.

'I want to reach into that stream so much.'

Crouching, I put my hands into the water. A cool wave of refreshment flowed through my body. I knew she would feel it too, as the ultra-high-frequency waves carried the sensation into the far reaches of space. Again I heard her sigh.

'Is it hot where you are?' I was thinking of that cramped cockpit and her spacesuit's oddly advanced insulation system.

'Hot,' she replied. 'As hot as hell.' Her tone changed. 'Hey, what's that? The prairie wind?' I had taken my hands from the water, and the gentle wind was cool against my damp skin. 'No, don't move. This wind is heavenly!' I raised both hands to the breeze and held them there until they were dry. At her request, I dipped my hands back into the brook and then lifted them into the wind. Again it felt divine, and again we shared the experience. We idled away a long while like this.

I set out again, silently wandering for a while. I heard her murmur, 'This world of yours is truly magnificent.'

'I really wouldn't know. The grayness of my life has dulled it all.'

'How could you say that? This world has so many experiences and feelings to offer! Trying to describe them all would be like trying to count the drops of rain in a thunderstorm. Look at those clouds on the horizon, all silvery-white. Right now they look solid to me, like towering mountains of gleaming jade. The meadow below, on the other hand, looks wispy, as if all the grass decided to fly away from the earth and become a green sea of clouds. Look! Look at the clouds floating past the sun! Watch how majestically the light and shadows shift and twist over the grass! Do you honestly feel nothing when you see this?'

Wearing her eyes, I roamed the grassland for an entire day. I could hear the yearning in her voice as she looked at each and every flower, at every blade of grass, at every beam of sunlight leaping through the prairie and as she listened to all the different voices of the grassy plains. The sudden appearance of a stream, and of the tiny fish swimming within it, would send her into fits of excitement. An unexpected breeze, carrying with it the sweet fragrance of fresh grass, would bring her to tears... Her feelings for this world were so rich that I wondered whether something was wrong with her state of mind.

Before sunset, I made my way to a lonely white cabin standing forlornly on the grassland. It had been set up as an inn for travellers, although I seemed to be its first guest in quite some time. Besides myself, the cabin's only other resident was the glitchy, obsolete android that looked after the entire inn. I was as hungry as I was tired, but before I had a chance to finish my dinner, my companion suggested that we go outside right away to watch the sun set.

'Watching the evening sky gradually lose its glow as night falls over the forest – it's like listening to the most beautiful symphony in the universe.'

Her voice swelled with rapture. I dragged my leaden feet outside, silently cursing my misfortune.

*

'You really do cherish these common things,' I told her on our way back to the cabin. Night had already fallen, and stars shone in the sky.

'Why don't you?' she asked. 'That's what it means to truly be alive.'

'I can't really find any satisfaction in those things. Nor can most other people. It's too easy to get what you want these days. I'm not just talking about material things. You can surround yourself with blue skies and crystal-clear waters just like that.

If you want the peace and tranquility of the countryside or a remote island, you barely even need to snap your fingers. Even love. Think of how elusive that was for previous generations and how desperately they chased it, and now it can be experienced through virtual reality, at least for a few moments at a time.

'People don't cherish anything now. They see a platter of fruit an arm's length away, only to take a bite out of each piece before throwing the rest away.'

'But not everyone has such fruits within reach,' she said quietly.

I felt my words had caused her pain, but I wasn't sure why. The rest of the way back, we said nothing more.

I saw her in my dreams that night. She was in her spacesuit, confined to that tiny cockpit. There were tears in her eyes. She reached out to me, calling out, 'Take me outside! I don't want to be closed in!' I awoke with a start and realized that she really was calling me. I was looking up at the ceiling, still wearing her eyes.

'Please, will you take me outside? Let's go see the Moon. It should be up by now!'

My head seemed to be filled with sand as I reluctantly pulled myself out of bed. Once outside, I discovered the Moon had indeed just risen; the night mist lent it a reddish tinge. The vast wilderness below was sound asleep. Pinprick glows from countless fireflies floated through the hazy ocean of grass, as though Taklamakan's dreams were bleeding into reality.

Stretching, I spoke to the night sky. 'Hey, can you see where the Moon is shining from your position in orbit? What's your ship's position? Tell me, and I might even be able to see you. I'm positive your ship's in LEO.'

Instead of answering me, she began humming a song. She stopped after a few bars and said, 'That was Debussy's "Clair de Lune".'

She continued humming, seemingly forgetting that I was still listening on the other end – or that I even existed. From orbit, melody and moonlight descended upon the prairie in unison. I pictured that delicate girl in outer space: the silvery Moon shining from above, the blue Earth below. She flew between the two, smaller than a pinpoint, her song dissolving into moonlight...

When I returned to bed an hour later, she was still humming. I had no idea if it was still Debussy, but it made no difference. That delicate music fluttered through my dreams.

Some time later – I'm not sure how long – her humming turned into shouting. Her cries stirred me from sleep. She wanted to go outside again.

'Weren't you just looking at the Moon?' I was angry.

'But it's different now. Remember the clouds in the west? They might have floated over by now. The Moon will be darting in and out of the clouds; I want to see the light and shadows dance on the plains outside. How beautiful that must look. It's a different kind of music. Please, take my eyes outside!'

My head throbbed with anger, but I went out. The clouds had floated on, and the Moon was shining through them. Its light filtered hazily over the grassland. It was as though the Earth were pondering deep and ancient memories.

'You're like a sentimental eighteenth-century poet. Tragically unfit for these times. Even more so for an astronaut,' I said, peering into the night sky. I took off her eyes and hung them from a branch of a nearby salt cedar. 'If you want to look at the Moon, you can do it by yourself. I really need to sleep. Tomorrow I have to get back to the space center and continue my woefully prosaic life.'

That soft voice whispered from her eyes, but I could no longer hear what she was saying. I went back to the cabin without another word.

It was daytime when I awoke. Dark clouds covered the sky, shrouding the Taklamakan in a light drizzle. The eyes were still hanging from the tree, mist covering the lenses. I carefully wiped them clean and put them on. I assumed that after watching the Moon for an entire night she would be fast asleep by now. However, I heard her sobbing quietly. A wave of pity over-whelmed me.

'I'm really sorry. I was just too tired last night.'

'No, it isn't you,' she said between sobs. 'The sky grew over-cast at half past three. And after five o'clock, it started to rain…'

'You didn't sleep at all?' I nearly shouted.

'It started raining, and I… I couldn't see the sun when it rose,' she choked out. 'I really wanted to see the sun rise over the plains. I wanted to see it more than anything…'

Something had melted my heart. Her tears flowed through my thoughts, and I pictured her small nose twitching as she sniveled. My eyes actually felt moist. I had to admit: she had taught me something over the past twenty-four hours, though I couldn't put my finger on exactly what. It was hazy, like the light and shadows moving over the grasslands. My eyes now saw a differ-ent world because of it.

'There'll always be another sunrise. I'll definitely take your eyes out again to see it. Or maybe I'll see it with you in person. How does that sound?'

Her sobbing stopped. Suddenly she whispered to me.

'Listen…'

I didn't hear anything, but I tensed.

'It's the first bird of the morning. There are birds out, even in the rain.' Her voice was solemn, as though she were listening to the peal of bells marking the end of an era.

Chapter 2

Sunset 6

My memories of this experience quickly faded once I had returned to my drab existence and busy job. When I remembered to wash the clothes I had worn during my trip – which was some time afterwards – I discovered a few grass seeds in the cuffs of my trousers. At the same time, a tiny seed also remained buried within the depths of my subconscious. In the lonely desert of my soul, that seed had already sprouted, though its shoots were so tiny they were barely perceptible. This may have happened unconsciously, but at the end of each grueling work day I could feel the natural poetry of the evening breeze stir against my face. Birdsong could catch my attention. I would even stand on the overpass at twilight and watch as night enveloped the city... The world was still dreary to my eyes, but it was now sprinkled with specks of verdant green – specks that grew steadily in number. Once I began to perceive this change, I thought of her again.

She began to drift into my idle mind and even into my dreams. Over and over again, I would see that cramped cockpit, that strangely insulated spacesuit... Later on, these things retreated from my consciousness. Only one thing protruded from the void: that pencil, drifting in zero gravity around her head. For some reason, I would see that pencil floating in front of me whenever I shut my eyes.

One day I was walking into the vast lobby of the space center when a giant mural, one that I had passed countless times before, suddenly caught my eye. The mural depicted Earth viewed from space; a gem of deepest blue. That pencil again floated before my mind's eye, but now it was superimposed over the mural. I heard her voice again.

I don't want to be closed in.

Realization flashed through my brain like lightning. Space wasn't the only place with zero gravity!

I ran upstairs like a madman and banged on the Director's door. He wasn't in. Guided by what felt like a premonition, I flew down to the small room where the eyes were stored. The director was there, gazing at the girl on the large monitor. She was still inside that sealed-off cockpit, still wearing that 'space-suit'. The image was frozen; almost certainly a recording.

'You're here for her, I suppose,' he said, still looking at the monitor.

'Where is she?' My voice boomed inside the small room.

'You may have already guessed the truth. She's the navigator of *Sunset 6*.'

The strength drained from my muscles and I collapsed onto the carpet. It all made sense now.

The Sunset Project had originally planned to launch ten ships, from *Sunset 1* to *Sunset 10*. After the *Sunset 6* disaster, however, the project had been abandoned.

The project was an exploratory flight mission like many before it. It followed the same basic procedures as each of the space center's other flight missions. There was just one difference – the Sunset vessels were not headed to outer space. These ships were built to dive into the depths of the Earth.

One-and-a-half centuries after the first space flight, humanity began to probe in the opposite direction. The Sunset-series ter-racraft were its first attempt at this form of exploration.

Four years ago, I had watched the *Sunset 1* launch on television. It was late at night. A blinding fireball lit up the heart of the Turpan Depression so bright it caused the clouds in Xinjiang's night sky to glow with the gorgeous colors of dawn. By the time the fireball faded, *Sunset 1* was already underground. At the center of this circle of red-hot, scorched earth now churned a lake of molten magma. White-hot lava seethed and boiled, hurling bright molten columns into the air... The tremors could be felt as far away as Urumqi as the terracraft burrowed through the planet's inner layers.

Each of the Sunset Project's first five missions successfully completed their subterranean voyages and returned safely to the Earth's surface. *Sunset 5* set a record for the furthest any human had traveled beneath the planet's surface: 3,100 kilometers. It was a record that *Sunset 6* did not intend to break, and with good reason. Modern geophysics had concluded that the boundary between the Earth's mantle and core lay between 3,400 and 3,500 kilometers underground; this convergence is referred to academically as the 'Gutenberg Discontinuity'. Breaching this boundary meant entering the planet's iron-nickel core. Upon entering the core, the density of the surrounding matter would abruptly and exponentially increase to levels that went beyond the *Sunset 6*'s design specifications to navigate.

Sunset 6's voyage began smoothly. It took the terracraft all of two hours to pass through the boundary between the Earth's surface and mantle, also known as the 'Moho'. After resting upon the sliding surface of the Eurasian plate for five hours, the ship began its slow three-thousand-plus kilometer journey through the mantle.

Space travel may be lonely, but at least astronauts can gaze at the infinity of the universe and the majesty of the stars. The terranauts voyaging through the planet, however, had nothing but the sensation of endlessly increasing density to guide them. All they could glean from peering into the terracraft's holographic rearview monitors was the blinding glare of the seething magma following in their ship's wake. As the craft plunged deeper, the magma would merge behind the aft section, instantly sealing the path that the ship had just forged.

A terranaut once described the experience. Whenever she and her fellow crew members shut their eyes, they would see the onrushing magma gather behind them, pressing down and sealing them in all over again. The image followed them like a phantom, and it made the voyagers aware of the massive and ever-increasing immensity of matter pressing against their ship. This sense of claustrophobia was difficult for those on the surface to comprehend, but it tortured each and every terranaut.

Sunset 6 completed each of its research tasks with flying colors. The craft traveled at approximately fifteen kilometers per hour; at this rate, it would require twenty hours to reach its target depth. Fifteen hours and forty minutes into their voyage, however, the crew received an alert. Subsurface radar had picked up a sudden increase of density in their vicinity, leaping from 6.3 grams per cubic centimeter to 9.5 grams. The surrounding matter was no longer silicate-based but primarily an iron-nickel alloy; it was also no longer solid but liquid. Despite having only achieved a depth of 2,500 kilometers, all signs currently indicated that *Sunset 6* and its crew had entered the planet's core.

The crew would later learn that they had chanced upon a fissure in the Earth's mantle – one that led directly to its core. The fissure was filled with a high-pressure liquid alloy of iron and nickel from the Earth's core. Thanks to this crack, the Gutenberg discontinuity had reached up one thousand kilometers closer to the *Sunset 6*'s flight path. The ship immediately took emergency measures to change course. It was during this attempt to escape that disaster truly struck.

The ship's neutron-laced hull was strong enough to withstand the massive and sudden pressure increase to 1,600 tons per cubic centimeter, but the terracraft itself was comprised of three parts:

a fusion engine at the bow, a central cabin, and a rear-mounted drive engine. When it attempted to change direction, the section linking the fusion engine to the main cabin fractured due to the density and pressure of liquid iron-nickel alloy that far exceeded the ship's operating parameters. The images broadcast from *Sunset 6*'s neutrino communicator showed the forward engine splitting from the hull only to be instantly engulfed by the crimson glow of the liquid metal. A Sunset ship's fusion engine fired a super-heated jet that cut through the material in front of the vessel. Without it, the drive engine could barely push the *Sunset 6* an inch through the planet's solid inner layers.

The density of the Earth's core is startling, but the neutrons in the ship's hull were even denser. As the buoyancy created by the liquid iron-nickel alloy did not exceed the ship's deadweight, *Sunset 6* began to sink towards the Earth's core.

One-and-a-half centuries after landing on the Moon, humanity was finally capable of venturing to Mercury. It had been anticipated that we would travel from mantle to core in a similar time frame. Now a terracraft had accidentally entered the core, and, just like an Apollo-era vessel spinning off course and into the depths of space, the chance of a successful rescue was simply nonexistent.

Fortunately, the hull of the ship's main cabin was sturdy, and *Sunset 6*'s neutrino communications system maintained a solid connection with the control center on the surface. In the year that followed, the crew of the Sunset 6 persisted in their work, sending streams of valuable data gleaned from the core to the surface.

Encased as they were in thousands of kilometers of rock, air and survival were the least of their worries – what they lacked more than anything else was space. They were pummeled by temperatures of over five thousand degrees Celsius and surrounded by pressures that could crush carbon into diamonds within seconds. Only neutrinos could escape the incredible density of the material in which the *Sunset 6* was entombed. The ship was completely trapped in a giant furnace of molten metal. To the ship's crew, Dante's *Inferno* would depict a paradise. What could life mean in a world like this? Is there any word beyond 'fragile' that can describe it?

Immense psychological pressure shredded the nerves of the *Sunset 6*'s crew. One day, the ship's geological engineer woke, leapt from his cot and threw open the heat-insulation door protecting his cabin. Even though this was only the first of four such doors, the wave of incandescent heat that washed in through the remaining three layers instantly reduced him to charcoal. To prevent the ship's imminent destruction, the commander rushed to seal the open door. Although he was successful, he suffered severe burns in the process. The man died after making one last entry into the ship's log.

With one crew member remaining, *Sunset 6* continued its voyage through the planet's darkest depths.

By now, the interior of the vessel was entirely weightless. The ship had sunk to a depth of 6,800 kilometers – the planet's deepest point. The last remaining terranaut aboard the *Sunset 6* had become the first person to reach the Earth's core.

Her entire world had shrunk to the size of a cramped, stuffy cockpit. She had less than ten square meters to move around in. The ship's onboard pair of neutrino glasses allowed her a small measure of sensory contact with the planet's surface. However, this lifeline was doomed to be short-lived, as the craft's neutrino communications system was nearly out of power. By now, the power levels were already too low to support the super-high-speed data relay that these sensory glasses relied on. In fact, the system had lost contact three months ago, just as I was taking the plane back from my vacation in the plains. By that time, her eyes were already stored inside my travel bag.

That misty, sunless morning on the plains had been her final glimpse of the surface world.

From then on, *Sunset 6* could only maintain audio and data links with the surface. But late one night this connection had also ceased, sealing her permanently into the planet's lonely core.

Sunset 6's neutron shell was strong enough to withstand the core's massive pressure, and the craft's cyclical life support systems were fully capable of an additional fifty to eighty years of operation. So she would remain alive, at the center of the Earth, in a room so small she could traverse its area in less than a minute.

I hardly dared imagine her final farewell to the surface world. However, when the Director played the recording, I was shocked.

The neutrino beam to the surface was already weak when the message was sent, and her voice occasionally cut out, but she sounded calm.

'...have received your final advisement. I'll do all I can to follow the entire research plan in the days to come. Someday, maybe generations from now, another ship might find the *Sunset 6* and dock with it. If someone does enter here, I can only hope that the data I leave behind will be of use. Please rest assured; I have made a life for myself down here and adapted to these surroundings; I don't feel constrained or closed-in anymore. The entire world surrounds me. When I close my eyes, I see the great plains up there on the surface. I can still see every one of the flowers that I named.

'Goodbye.'

Epilogue

A Transparent World

M any years have passed, and I have visited many places. Everywhere I go, I stretch out upon the Earth.

I have lain on the beaches of Hainan Island, on Alaskan snow, among Russia's white birches and on the scalding sands of the Sahara. And every time the world became transparent to my mind's eye. I saw the terracraft, anchored more than six thousand kilometers below me at the center of that translucent sphere, whose hull once bore the name *Sunset 6*; I felt her heartbeat echo up to me through thousands of kilometers. As I imagined the golden light of the sun and the silvery glow of the Moon shining down to the planet's core, I could hear her humming 'Clair de Lune', and her soft voice:

> *'...How beautiful that must look. It's a different kind of music...'*

One thought comforted me: even if I traveled to the most distant corner of the Earth, I would never be any farther from her.

Cannonball

Prologue

Since mankind had depleted the Earth's natural resources, the world turned its gaze towards the last pristine continent: Antarctica. This shifted the Earth's political center of gravity and led to the Antarctic Treaty being discarded. Due to their proximity to Antarctica, two South American countries suddenly emerged as global powers, attaining a geopolitical status that rivaled their status on the soccer field. Mankind had also entered into the final phase of the complete eradication of nuclear weapons. This victory of enlighted reason over barbarism made humanity's struggle for Antarctica devoid of the fearful shadow of a thermonuclear apocalypse.

Chapter 1

New Solid State

In the immense cavern, Shen Huabei felt as if he were walking on a dark plain under a starless sky. Beneath his feet, rock that had melted in the heat of a nuclear blast had already cooled and solidified, though a powerful warmth still penetrated the thermal insulation of his boots, causing the soles of his feet to sweat. Farther inside, a section of cavern wall had not yet cooled. It glowed faintly red in the darkness, like a murky dawn sky.

Shen Huabei's wife, Zhao Wenjia, walked to his left, and their eight-year-old son, Shen Yuan, was in front of them. Shen Yuan skipped ahead, seemingly unconstrained by his heavy radiation suit. They were joined by members of the UN Nuclear Inspection Team whose headlamps sent long beams of light into the darkness.

Two methods were employed to destroy nuclear weapons: disassembly and underground detonation. This was one of China's subterranean detonation sites.

Professor Kavinsky, leader of the inspection team, caught up to Shen Huabei. His headlamp shined on the three people ahead of him and threw their long, swaying shadows across the cavern floor.

'Doctor Shen, why did you bring your family? This is no place for a picnic.'

Shen Huabei halted to allow the Russian physicist to catch up. 'My wife is a geological engineer working for the central command of the Eradication Operation. As for my son, I think he likes it here.'

'Our son has always been fascinated by the strange and the extreme,' Wenjia agreed, more to her husband than the head of the team. Even though her face was partially concealed by the radiation suit's visor, Huabei could still clearly see the unease in his wife's eyes.

The boy was practically dancing in front of them. 'When they started, this hole was only as big as our basement. After just two blasts, it got gigantic! Think of the fireballs those blasts made – it was probably like there were huge *babies* under the ground having tantrums, kicking and screaming. It must have been amazing!'

Shen Huabei and Zhao Wenjia exchanged glances. He was grinning slightly, but the worry in her expression had only deepened.

'My boy, there were eight babies!' Professor Kavinsky said to Shen Yuan with a laugh. He turned to face Shen Huabei. 'Doctor Shen, this is what I meant to discuss with you. In the last blast, you detonated the warheads of eight Giant Wave submarine-launched ballistic missiles, each with a yield of one hundred kilotons. The warheads were on a rack, stacked in a cube—'

'What is the issue?'

'Before the detonation, I clearly saw on the monitor that there was a white sphere in the center of the cube.'

Shen Huabei stopped walking again. Looking squarely at Kavinsky, he said, 'Professor, the provisions of the Destruction Treaty prohibit us from detonating less than our mandated quota, but I do not believe they restrict us from detonating more. There were five independent observations that verified the size of the blast. Anything else is immaterial.'

Kavinsky nodded. 'That is why I waited until after the detonation to raise this issue with you. I am simply curious.'

'I imagine you have heard of "sugar coating".'

Shen Huabei's words fell like a curse over the site. The cavern went silent as everyone stopped walking, and the beams of light from their headlamps became still, shining in every direction. They conducted their conversation over a wireless intercom system in their radiation suits, so even the people far ahead had heard Shen Huabei's words. The silence ended as the members of the inspection team walked over and gathered around Shen Huabei. Everyone in this select group, no matter what part of the world they hailed from, was a luminary in the field of nuclear weapons research, and they had all clearly understood.

'It really exists?' an American asked, gawping at Shen Huabei. The latter just nodded his head.

There is a story claiming that after receiving news of China's initial nuclear test in the middle of the last century Mao Zedong's first question was: 'Was there a nuclear explosion?' Whether he knew it or not, this was an excellent question. The key to designing fission weapons is the ability to apply compression. When a nuclear bomb goes off, a package of conventional explosives detonates around a mass of fissile material, compressing it into a dense sphere. When that sphere reaches critical density, a violent chain reaction begins, which results in a nuclear explosion. All of this takes place within a millionth of a second, so the pressure on the fissile core must be calibrated with extreme precision, as even a minuscule imbalance can easily result in the core failing to reach critical density. If that happens, the weapon will only produce a normal chemical blast. Since the inception of nuclear weapons, researchers have used complex mathematical models to design a variety of compression charge arrays. New technologies developed in recent years had enabled researchers to design compression mechanisms with groundbreaking accuracy, and 'sugar coating' was one of the techniques that allowed them to achieve this.

A 'sugar coat' was a kind of nanomaterial that was used to encase the core of a nuclear weapon. Once applied, it was, in turn, covered in a layer of conventional explosive charges.

'Sugar coating' had the function of automatically balancing compressive stress, so even if the outer layer of explosives did not produce uniform pressure the 'sugar coat' would balance its distribution, resulting in the precise compression necessary to bring fissile material to critical density.

'The white sphere you saw between the warheads was an alloyed material wrapped in a "sugar coat",' Shen Huabei said. 'It ought to have undergone extreme compressive stress in the explosion. This is part of a research project we plan to continue throughout the process of weapon destruction. Once all the nuclear weapons on Earth have been destroyed, it will be difficult to produce momentary compressive stress of this magnitude – for a while, at least. It will be interesting to see what happens to the test material under such pressure – to see what it will turn into. We hope this research can help us find some promising uses for "sugar coating" in civilian hands.'

One UN official, considering the possibilities, said, 'You should encase graphite in "sugar coating", so we could produce a large diamond with every explosion. Maybe this costly project of nuclear weapon destruction could turn a profit.'

Laughter erupted in their headphones. Officials without technical backgrounds were often the butt of jokes in situations like this. 'Let's see, eight hundred kilotons... How many orders of magnitude greater is that than the pressure needed to turn graphite into a diamond?' someone asked.

'Of course it didn't make a diamond!' Shen Yuan's bright voice crackled in their earphones. 'I bet it made a black hole! A tiny black hole! It's going to suck us in, suck the whole world in, and we'll wind up in a prettier universe on the other side!'

'Haha, the explosion wasn't quite that large, my boy. Doctor Shen, your son has a fascinating mind!' said Kavinsky. 'So, what were the test results? What did the alloy turn into? I assume you could not find most of it.'

'I don't know yet. Let's go see,' said Shen Huabei, pointing ahead. The explosion had blasted an enormous, spherical cavity into the Earth, and its curved bottom formed a small basin. In the basin's center, the lights of several headlamps flitted around. 'Those are people from the "sugar coating" research team.'

They walked down the gentle slope towards the center of the basin. Suddenly, Kavinsky stopped. He then laid his hands flat against the ground. 'There's a tremor!'

The others felt it too. 'It couldn't have been induced by the explosion, could it?'

Zhao Wenjia shook her head. 'We have carried out repeated surveys of the geological structure of the area around the destruction site. There is no way for an explosion to cause an earthquake here. The tremor began after the explosion and has continued uninterrupted since. Doctor Deng Yiwen said it has something to do with the "sugar coating" experiment, though I don't know the details.'

As they approached the center of the basin, the tremor became stronger, emanating from deep below the ground. Soon it was strong enough to send a tingling sensation up their legs, as if a giant train was rumbling wildly in the Earth beneath them. Upon reaching the center, a suited researcher at the bottom of the basin rose to greet them. It was Doctor Deng Yiwen, the scientist responsible for the experiments involving the compression of materials with nuclear explosions.

'What's that you're holding?' Shen Huabei asked, pointing at a large, white ball in Doctor Yiwen's hand.

'Fishing line,' said Doctor Yiwen. Around him, a ring of people crouched on the ground, peering into a small hole in the surface of the rock that had melted and re-condensed in the explosion. The hole's rim was a near-perfect circle, around ten centimeters in diameter, and its edge was quite smooth, as if it had been bored with a drill. One end of the fishing line in Doctor Yiwen's hand was in the hole, and he unraveled more line in a continuous stream.

'We've already fed more than ten thousand meters of line into the hole and we're nowhere near the bottom. Our radars say it's more than thirty thousand meters deep and getting deeper.'

'How did it form?' someone asked.

'The compressed test alloy sank into the Earth like a stone in the sea. That's what made this hole. The alloy is passing through dense layers of rock as we speak, which is what's causing the tremor.'

'My God, that is astonishing!' Kavinsky exclaimed. 'I assumed the alloy would be vaporized in the heat of the blast.'

'If it had not been "sugar coated", that would have been the result.' Doctor Yiwen agreed. 'As it was, it didn't have time to evaporate – the "sugar coat" redistributed the force of the blast, compressing the alloy into a new state of matter that ought to be called a super-solid-state. That name was taken, so we are calling it "new-solid-state".'

'Are you saying that this thing's density, compared to the density of the earth below, is analogous to the density of a stone dropped into water?' Professor Kavinsky asked, still somewhat incredulous.

'It's much denser than that. The main reason stones sink in water is unrelated to either material's density; it's the fact that water is a liquid – when water freezes its density doesn't change considerably, but if you place a stone on ice it won't sink through it. New-solid-state matter, however, actually *sinks through* rocks, so we can only imagine how dense it must be.'

'You mean it turned into something like neutron-star material?'

Doctor Deng Yiwen shook his head. 'We haven't determined its precise density yet, but just by looking at the speed of its descent we can be certain that it's not as dense as the degenerate matter of a neutron star. If it were, it would be falling as fast as a meteorite through the atmosphere, and it would cause volcanic eruptions and large earthquakes. It's a state of matter somewhere between ordinary solid-state and degenerate matter.'

'Will it sink to the center of the Earth?' asked Shen Yuan.

'It is possible. Below a certain depth, the rock strata of the Earth's crust and mantle give way to the liquid core, where it will be even easier for the thing to sink.'

'Awesome!'

While everyone's attention was on the hole, Shen Huabei and his family quietly parted from the group and walked off into the darkness. Except for the hum of the tremor, it was silent away from the hole. The beams of their headlamps dissolved into the immense darkness around them, and their presence was subsumed into the vast, featureless void. They turned their intercoms to a private channel. Here, Shen Yuan was to make a choice that would determine the course of his life: would he follow his father or his mother?

Shen Yuan's parents faced a problem worse than divorce: his father had terminal leukemia. Shen Huabei did not know whether his work in nuclear research had caused the disease, but he knew he had no more than six months to live. Fortunately, the technology existed to induce artificial hibernation. Shen Huabei would enter a state of suspended animation until there was a cure for leukemia. Shen Yuan could either enter hibernation with his father or continue his life with his mother. The second choice seemed more prudent, but it was hard for a child to resist the idea of following his father into the future. Shen Huabei and Zhao Wenjia each tried once again to win him over.

'Mom, I'm going to stay with you. I won't go to sleep with daddy!' said Shen Yuan.

'You changed your mind?' asked Zhao Wenjia, overjoyed.

'Yes! I don't need to go to the future to have fun. There is plenty of fun stuff around now, like that thing – the one that's sinking into the ground. I want be around to see that!'

'That's your decision?' asked Shen Huabei. Zhao Wenjia glared at him, worried her son might change his mind again.

'Yeah,' said Shen Yuan. 'I'm gonna go try to see what's down that hole.' He took off running towards the basin, where the others' headlamps flickered.

Zhao Wenjia watched her son run off. 'I worry I won't be able to give him what he needs. He's just like you – lost in his dreams. Maybe the future would suit him better.'

Shen Huabei put his hands on his wife's shoulders. 'No one knows what the future will be like. And what's wrong with him being like me? The present needs dreamers, too.'

'There's nothing wrong with being a dreamer. That's why I fell in love with you. But you must know he has another side to him – he was chosen as class head of two of his classes!'

'Yes, I heard. I don't know how he managed that.'

'He has a thirst for power, and he knows what it takes to achieve it. In that way, he's nothing like you at all.'

'Yes. How can he reconcile that with his fantasies?'

'I'm more worried about what will happen when he does.'

Shen Yuan had arrived at the basin, his headlamp indistinguishable from the others. His parents stopped watching him, turned off their headlamps and sank into darkness.

'No matter what, life will continue. They may develop a cure next year, or it might be a century, or... they may never develop one. Without question, you'll live at least another forty years. I need you to promise me something: in forty years, if there is still no cure, I need you to wake me up. I want to see you and our son again. This can't be our final goodbye.'

'You want to see an old woman and a grown man ten years your senior in the future? But it is as you said, life goes on.' In the dark, Zhao Wenjia managed a miserable smile.

In that giant cavern hollowed out by nuclear blasts, they spent a final, silent moment together. The next day, Shen Huabei was to enter into a dreamless sleep. Zhao Wenjia would be left to live with Shen Yuan, whose life was consumed by his dreams. Together, they would continue down the treacherous road of life, toward an unknown future.

Chapter 2
Awakening

It took a day for him to wake up fully. When he first opened his eyes, he saw only a white mist from which blurred, white figures gradually emerged over the next ten hours. After a further ten hours, he was able to recognize them as doctors and nurses. People in suspended animation are unaware of the passage of time, and Shen Huabei initially thought that his weak consciousness was part of the process of entering hibernation, that perhaps the hibernation systems had suffered a malfunction as he was going under. As his vision continued to improve, he examined the hospital ward around him, which was softly lit by sconces on its white walls. This place was familiar, which confirmed to him the idea that he had not yet entered hibernation.

In the next moment, it became clear that he was mistaken. The white ceiling of the ward began to glow blue, and against this backdrop, sharp, white letters emerged.

Greetings! Living Earth Cryogenics, your suspended animation provider, filed for bankruptcy in 2089. Responsibility for your care was transferred to Jade Cloud Corporation. Your hibernation serial number is WS368200402-118. You retain all rights and privileges granted to you in your contract with Living Earth Cryogenics. You underwent medical treatment before being awoken, and you are successfully cured of all disease. Please accept Jade Cloud Corporation's congratulations on your new life.

You have been in hibernation for 74 years, 5 months, 7 days, and 13 hours. Your account is paid in full.

The current date is 16 April 2125. Welcome to the future.

His hearing gradually began to return, and three hours later he was able to speak. After 74 years of deep sleep, his first words were, 'Where are my wife and son?'

A tall, thin doctor stood next to his bed. She handed him a folded piece of paper. 'Doctor Shen, this is a letter from your wife.'

Shen Huabei cast a strange glance at the doctor. *Even before I went under, people hardly ever wrote paper letters*, he thought to himself. He managed to unfold the letter, though his hands were still half-numb. Here was more proof that he had traveled through time: the paper, blank at first, began to emit an azure light that formed letters as it traveled down the page. Soon, the page was full of writing.

Before entering cryo-sleep, he had on countless occasions imagined the first words his wife might say to him as he woke up, but he could never have imagined what was written on the paper:

Huabei, my love, you are in great danger!

By the time you read this letter, I will no longer be alive. The person who gave you this letter is Doctor Guo. You can trust her; in fact, she may be the only person left on Earth you can trust. Follow whatever directions she gives you.

Forgive me for breaking my promise. I did not wake you in forty years. You cannot imagine the person Yuan has become, the things he has done. As his mother, I felt unable to look you in the eye. My heart is broken. My life has been wasted. Please take care of yourself.

'My son – where is Shen Yuan?' shouted Huabei, rising with great effort onto his elbows.

'He died five years ago.' The doctor's answer was icy, utterly indifferent to the heartache this message inflicted. As if realizing this, she softened and added, 'Your son was 78 years old.'

Doctor Guo took a card from her coat pocket and handed it to Huabei. 'This is your new identity card. The information it contains is explained in your wife's letter.'

Huabei examined the paper, checking it back and front. There was nothing on it except for Wenjia's brief note. As he turned it over, the creases in the paper seemed to ripple, like the LCD screens of his day did when touched. Doctor Guo reached over and pressed on the letter's lower right corner, and the paper's display switched over to a spreadsheet.

'Sorry about that. Paper as you know it no longer exists.'

Huabei looked at her quizzically.

'There are no forests anymore,' she explained, shrugging. She then returned to the spreadsheet. 'Your new name is Wang Ruo. You were born in 2097. Your parents are deceased, and you have no close family. You were born in Hohhot, Inner Mongolia, but you now reside here,' she said, indicating a cell on the spreadsheet. 'It is a remote village in the mountains of Ningxia. It was the best place we could find, considering. You won't attract attention there. Before you depart, you will need to undergo plastic surgery. Under no circumstances should you talk about your son. Do not even express an interest in him if someone else mentions him.'

'But I am Shen Yuan's father! I was born in Beijing!'

Doctor Guo stiffened and became cold again. 'If you say that publicly, your hibernation and treatment will have been for nothing. You'll be dead in an hour.'

'Whatever happened?' Huabei needed to know – *now*.

The doctor smiled coldly as she began. 'There is much in this world that you probably don't know.' She shook her head ever so slightly. 'Well, we should hurry. You should first get out of bed and learn to walk again. We then need to get you out of here as quickly as possible.'

Just as Huabei opened his mouth to ask another question, a loud banging erupted from behind the door. It crashed open, and six or seven people rushed in and surrounded Huabei's bed. They were all of different ages and they had different clothes, except for a strange sort of hat that some of them wore and some carried. The hats had brims wide enough to cover their wearers' shoulders, like the straw hats farmers used to wear. Each of them also had a transparent oxygen mask, which some of them had removed when they entered the room. They all stared at Huabei menacingly.

'This is Shen Yuan's father?' one of them asked. He appeared to be the oldest member of the group, at least 80 years old, and he had a long, white beard. Without waiting for the doctor to answer, he turned to the rest of his group and nodded his head.

'He looks just like his son. Doctor, you've done your duty. He's ours now.'

'How did you know he was here?' asked Doctor Guo coolly.

Before the doctor could answer, a nurse spoke up from the corner of the room. 'I told them.'

Doctor Guo turned and glared angrily at the nurse. 'You betrayed a patient's confidence?'

'Happily,' said the nurse, her pretty face twisted into a grimace.

A young man grabbed Huabei's gown and dragged him off the bed. He lay paralyzed on the ground, still too weak to move. A girl kicked him in the gut so hard that the sharp toe of her boot almost pierced his stomach; the pain was excruciating, and he writhed on the floor like a fish. The old man took hold of Huabei's collar and hauled him to his feet with an unexpected strength. He held Huabei upright in a futile effort to make him stand. He released his grip and Huabei fell backwards, smacking his head on the floor. His eyes blurred with pain. Someone said, 'Great, that'll cover a small bit of this bastard's debt to society.'

'Who are you people?' asked Huabei weakly. From his position on the floor between their feet, he felt as if his captors were a menacing group of giants.

'You should know who I am, at least,' said the old man, sneering vindictively. Seen from below, his face appeared twisted and grotesque. Huabei shuddered. 'I am Deng Yang, Deng Yiwen's son.'

The name made Huabei's stomach lurch. He turned and grabbed the hem of the old man's trousers. 'Your father was my co-worker and close friend! You were my son's classmate! Don't you remember? My goodness, you're Yiwen's son? I can't believe it! Back then, you were—'

'Get your filthy hands off me!' shouted Deng Yang.

The young man who had pulled Huabei off the bed crouched down and leaned close to his face, his eyes full of malice. 'Listen. You aren't any older than you were when you went to sleep. This man is your elder, and you need to show him some respect.'

'If Shen Yuan were still alive, he'd be old enough to be your father,' said Deng Yang loudly, eliciting a round of laughter. He pointed at one of his companions. 'When this young man was four years old, both his parents died in the Central Breach Disaster,' he said to Huabei. 'And this young lady lost her parents in the Lost Bolt Disaster. She wasn't even two years old.' Deng Yang gestured towards two more members of his group. 'These people invested their life savings in the Project. When this man learned it had failed, he attempted suicide. And this man simply lost his mind.' He paused, then added, 'And as for me, I was tricked by your bastard son. I threw my youth and my talent into that goddamn hole, and the whole world hates me for it.'

Huabei still lay on the floor, shaking his head in confusion.

'Shen Huabei, this is a court, and we, the victims of the Antarctic Entry Project, are your judge and jury! Everyone in this country is a victim, but we have the special privilege of administering your justice. We could have sent you to a real court, but our justice system is even more convoluted now than it was in your day. Lawyers would have spent a year spewing bullshit about your case, and then you'd probably have been acquitted, like your son was. We won't take more than an hour to deliver our righteous judgment, and believe me: once we have, you'll wish the leukemia had taken you 70 years ago.'

They began jeering at Huabei. Two people lifted him by his arms and hauled him towards the door. He was too weak to struggle, and his legs dragged on the floor.

'Mr Shen, I did what I could,' said Doctor Guo as Huabei neared the door. He wanted to look back at her, the only person he could trust in these vicious times, according to his wife's letter, but the position he was held in made it impossible. She spoke again from behind him.

'Don't despair too much. Living in these times isn't easy, either.'

As he was dragged out the door, Huabei heard Doctor Guo call out, 'Close the door and turn up the air purifiers! Do you want to choke to death?' Her tone was urgent, and it was clear that she was already indifferent to his fate.

Once they got out of the hospital ward, Huabei understood Doctor Guo's last words: the air was acrid and hard to breathe. He was dragged out through the hospital's main corridor. As they exited the building, the two people dragging him put his arms over their shoulders and began to carry him. He took a deep breath, relieved to be outside of the hospital, but what he inhaled was not the fresh, outdoor air he expected; instead it was a gas even more noxious than the air in the hospital. His lungs erupted in pain, and he was racked by a sudden, violent cough that did not stop. As he began to suffocate, he heard someone say, 'Give him a respirator. We don't want him to die before we can administer justice.' Someone fitted a device over his nose and mouth. The air it provided had a strange taste, but at least he could breathe. Someone else said, 'You don't need to give him a screen hat. He won't be alive long enough for the UV to give him leukemia again.' This drew a burst of cruel laughter from the group. Huabei's breathing became somewhat more regular, and the tears caused by his cough began to dry, restoring his vision. He raised his head and took his first look at the future.

The first thing he noticed was the people on the street; all of them were wearing transparent respirator masks and every head was covered by one of those large straw hats his kidnappers had just called a 'screen hat'. He also noticed that despite the warm weather, everyone was swaddled in clothes, without an inch of skin showing. The street was lined with enormous skyscrapers on both sides, so tall that he felt like he was in a deep valley. 'Skyscraper' was an apt term for these buildings – they literally stretched into the gray clouds overhead. In the narrow strip of sky between the buildings, the sun shone indistinctly behind the clouds. Streaks of smoke passed in front of the sunlight, and he soon realized that the clouds themselves were in fact plumes of pollution.

'A great time to be alive, isn't it?' asked Deng Yang. His friends laughed heartily, as if they hadn't laughed for ages.

They carried him towards a nearby car – similar in size to a sedan and able to accommodate four or five people. As they approached it, two people passed by them, walking with purpose in another direction. They wore helmets, and though their uniforms were unfamiliar to Huabei, he could guess at their profession. He called out to them.

'Help! I'm being kidnapped! Help me!'

The two police officers abruptly turned around and ran over to Huabei. They looked him up and down, taking special notice of his hospital gown and bare feet. One of them asked, 'You're just out of cryo, aren't you?'

Huabei nodded weakly. 'They're kidnapping me...'

The other police officer nodded at this. 'Sir, this sort of thing is common. Many people have been waking from cryo-sleep recently, and getting them established in society takes a lot of resources. People are resentful and angry, and they often lash out.'

'That's not what's happening here—' began Huabei, but the officer cut him off with a wave of his hand.

'Sir, you're safe now.' The police officer turned toward Deng Yang and his co-conspirators. 'This man obviously still requires medical attention. Two of you have to take him back to the hospital. We will investigate this matter thoroughly, but for now, all seven of you are under arrest on suspicion of kidnapping.' He lifted the radio on his wrist to his mouth and called for reinforcements.

Deng Yang rushed over and interrupted him. 'Officer, wait a moment. We aren't anti-cryo thugs. Look closely at this man. Doesn't he look familiar?'

The police officers peered at Huabei's face for a long time. One of them pulled down his respirator for a moment to see him better.

'It's Mi Xixi!'

'He's not Mi Xixi, he's Shen Yuan's father!'

Mouths agape, the two policemen looked back and forth between Shen Huabei and Deng Yang. The young man whose parents had died in the Central Breach disaster pulled the policemen over to him and whispered to them. As he spoke, the policemen glanced occasionally over at Huabei, and with each glance their eyes grew colder. The last time they looked at him, his heart sank. Deng Yang had two more accomplices.

The policemen walked over, avoiding Huabei's eye. One of them stood sentry and the other approached Deng Yang. In an urgent whisper, he said, 'We saw nothing. Whatever you do, don't let anyone figure out who he is – there'd be a riot.'

It wasn't just the policeman's words that terrified Huabei, but the way he said them. He spoke without regard to whether Huabei heard, as if Huabei were part of the landscape. The members of Deng Yang's gang quickly pushed Huabei into the car and entered behind him. As soon as the car's engine revved up, its windows grew darker, preventing the sun from shining in and Huabei from looking out. The car was self-driving and completely devoid of any visible means of manual control. No one spoke as they took to the road.

At last, Huabei ventured a question, if only to break the ominous silence.

'Who is Mi Xixi?'

'A movie star,' the Lost Bolt orphan sitting next to him said. 'He is famous for playing your son. Shen Yuan and alien monsters are the media's villains of the day.'

Huabei squirmed in his seat, trying to move away from the girl. As he did, he inadvertently brushed his arm against a button beneath the window. The window's glass immediately turned clear again. Through it, Huabei saw they were driving on an enormous, complex highway overpass. The structure was packed with vehicles separated by no more than two meters. Alarmingly, the cars were not stopped in traffic, as their proximity suggested they should be – they were all moving at full speed, at least one hundred kilometers per hour. The whole overpass looked like an unsafe amusement park ride.

Their car sped ahead towards a junction in the road. As they approached the junction, their car turned to change lanes, and just as it seemed they would crash into another car, a gap opened in the lane beside them, allowing them to merge. In fact, a gap opened for every merging vehicle, with an action so quick and so smooth that the two lanes seemed to meld into one. Huabei had already realized that the car was self-driving; now, he realized that the AI operating the car enabled an extremely efficient use of the highway.

A person in the back seat reached over and hit the button to darken the window again.

'I don't know anything that's going on, and you still want to kill me?' asked Huabei.

From his seat in front, Deng Yang turned to face Huabei. After a pause, he unenthusiastically said, 'Well, then I guess I'll just have to tell you.'

Chapter 3

The Antarctic Doorstep

'**P**eople rich in imagination are usually weak, and most strong people – the people who make history – lack imagination. Your son was a remarkable exception: a man with imagination and the strength of will to bring his visions into being. To him, reality was just a small, remote island in a vast ocean of fantasies; but when he wanted to, he could reverse the two, making his fantasies into an island and reality into the ocean. He navigated both oceans with incredible skill—'

Huabei interrupted him. 'I know my own son. Stop wasting my time.'

'No matter how well you knew him, you could never have imagined the status that Shen Yuan attained, the power he held. He was in a position to bring his darkest visions to life. Unfortunately, the world did not recognize how dangerous this was until it was too late. Perhaps there have been others like him in history, but they were like asteroids that flew by the Earth. They never made impact – they just flew off into the vastness of space. History gave Shen Yuan the means to realize his twisted vision. His asteroid made impact, to our great misfortune.'

'In your fifth year of cryogenic hibernation, the world took a preliminary step towards resolving the problem of who should

control Antarctica. The continent was declared a shared region
of global economic development. Strong nations circumvented
this declaration and carved out large areas of the continent for
their own exclusive benefit. Each of those nations wanted to
exploit the resources of its own region as quickly as possible.
Doing so was their only hope to escape the economic depression
that resource depletion and pollution had brought about. There
was a saying back then – the future lies at the bottom of the
world. It was then that your son proposed his insane idea. He
claimed that implementing it would turn Antarctica into China's
backyard, that he could make it simpler to get from Beijing to
Antarctica than to Tianjin. This was not a metaphor – it actually
was faster to get to Antarctica than to Tianjin, and the trip
used fewer resources and created less pollution. When he began
announcing his plan in a televised press conference, the whole
country laughed, as if they were watching a ludicrous comedy.
But before the conference was over, we had all stopped laughing.
We realized it really was possible! Thus began the disastrous
Antarctic Doorstep Project.

Deng Yang abruptly stopped talking.

'Well, what is the Antarctic Doorstep Project?' asked Huabei,
urging Deng Yang to continue.

'You'll know soon enough,' said Deng Yang icily.

'Can you at least tell me what I have to do with any of this?'

'You are Shen Yuan's father. What else is there to say?'

'So we've regressed to genetic determinism now?'

'Of course not, but by your son's own admission, bloodline
is relevant in this case. After he became internationally famous,
he said in countless interviews that his way of thinking and
his personality were already largely formed by the time he
was eight years old and that it was his father who had formed
them. He said that all his work over the years was meant only
to supplement the knowledge his father gave him. He even
declared outright that his father was the original innovator of
the Antarctic Doorstep Project.'

'What? Me? Antarctica? That is simply—'

'Let me finish. You also provided the technological foundation for the project.'

'What are you talking about?'

'New-solid-state matter. Without it, the Antarctic Doorstep Project would have been a pipe dream. It made it possible to turn this twisted fantasy into a reality.'

Shen Huabei shook his head in confusion. He was completely unable to imagine how super-dense new-solid-state matter could enable such fast travel to Antarctica.

Just then, the car came to a stop.

Chapter 4

The Gate of Hell

They got out of the car, and Huabei saw a strange, small hill in front of them. It was the color of rust and completely barren, without even a single blade of grass on its surface.

Deng Yang nodded towards the slope, 'That's an iron hill.' Seeing the surprise on Huabei's face, he added, 'It's a single, huge piece of metal.' Huabei looked around and saw there were several more 'iron hills' nearby, jutting out from the ground at odd intervals, their color strange against the large plain on which they stood. It looked like an alien landscape.

By now, Huabei was able to walk again, though shakily. He staggered along behind his captors, towards a large structure in the distance. The structure was a perfect cylinder, more than three hundred feet tall, and its surface was completely smooth, with no visible entrance. As they approached, a heavy iron panel slid open in the side of the structure, allowing them to enter. It closed tightly behind them.

Shen Huabei saw that he was in a dimly-lit room that resembled an airlock chamber. On the smooth, white wall hung a long row of what looked like spacesuits. Each person took one off the wall and put it on, and two people helped Huabei into one. He looked around the room and saw another sliding door on the far wall. Above the door glowed a red light, and next to the light was a digital display that showed the current atmospheric pressure in the room. When his heavy helmet was tightened into place, a transparent liquid crystal display appeared in the upper right corner of his visor, showing a string of numbers and figures in quick succession. He recognized that it was the suit's internal diagnostic system. Then, he heard the deep drone of machinery start up. The number on the atmospheric pressure display above the door was falling fast. In less than three minutes, it hit zero. The red light turned green and the door slid open, revealing the dark interior of the airtight structure.

Huabei's guess had been correct: the room they were in was an airlock chamber that enabled passage between an area with atmosphere and one without any. The interior of the huge cylinder was a vacuum.

The group walked through the door, which shut behind them, leaving them in pitch darkness. The lights on a few people's helmets turned on, sending feeble shafts of light into the void. A feeling of déjà-vu came over Huabei, and he shivered with dread.

'Walk forward,' crackled Deng Yang's voice in Huabei's headphones. His helmet light illuminated a small bridge ahead of them, no more than three feet wide. Its far end was obscured by darkness, so he couldn't see how long it was. Beneath the bridge was blackness. With trembling steps, Huabei walked on. The heavy boots of his airtight suit produced a hollow clang against the metal surface of the bridge. He walked a few yards out onto the bridge and turned his head to see if anyone had followed him. As he did, everyone's helmet lamps suddenly turned off, and all was engulfed in darkness. A few seconds later, a blue light suddenly began to glow beneath the narrow bridge. Huabei looked behind him and saw that he was the only one on the bridge – everyone else had gathered at its foot, and they were all looking at him. Lit from below by the blue light, they looked like ghosts. Tightly grasping the bridge's railing, Huabei looked down, and what he saw made his blood run cold.

He was standing above a deep well.

The well was around thirty feet in diameter. Rings of light were evenly spaced along its interior wall; it was only by their glow that was he able to discern the well's presence. The bridge spanned the mouth of the well, and he stood in its exact center. He couldn't see the well's bottom. He saw only countless rings of light on the wall of the well, shrinking with perspective into the distance and finally coming to a point. It was like looking down at a glowing blue target.

'Your judgment is at hand – you will pay your son's debt!' shouted Deng Yang. He grabbed hold of a wheel at the foot of the bridge and began to turn it, muttering, 'This is for my stolen youth, my wasted talent...' The bridge tilted to one side, and Huabei tightly gripped the higher railing, trying with all his might to keep his footing.

Deng Yang gave control of the wheel to the Central Breach orphan, who turned it forcefully. 'This is for my mother and father, for their melted bodies...' The incline of the bridge increased.

The girl whose parents died in the Lost Bolt Disaster stepped up. She turned the wheel, her wrathful gaze on Huabei. 'This is for vaporizing my parents...'

The man who had attempted suicide after losing his fortune took the girl's place at the wheel. 'This is for my money – my Rolls Royce, my Lincoln, my villa on the beach, my swimming pool. This is for my ruining my life, for making my wife and son stand in that long, cold welfare line...'

The bridge was now tilted on its side, leaving Huabei hanging on to the top railing as he desperately caught a foothold on the railing now below him.

The man who had lost his mind joined the man who had attempted suicide at the wheel, and they turned it together. He was clearly still ill, and he said nothing – he just looked down into the well and laughed. The bridge flipped over completely. Huabei clutched the railing with both hands and dangled over the pit.

His fear had actually subsided somewhat. As he gazed through the gate of hell into the bottomless pit beneath him, Huabei's life flashed before his eyes. His childhood and youth had been a drab and joyless time for him. He had found success as a student and a researcher, yet even after inventing 'sugar coating' technology, he still felt ill at ease in the world. Personal relationships had always felt to him like a spider's web whose strands bound him more tightly the more he struggled. He had never known true love; he had married out of obligation. As soon as he decided never to have children, a child came to him and his wife. He was a man who lived in a world of dreams and fantasies, the sort of man most people despise. He had never found his place among other people. His life was one of isolation, of going against the current. He used to put all his hope in the future. Now, the future had arrived: he was a widower whose son was the enemy of humanity, in a polluted city, surrounded by hateful, twisted people... He was nearly overcome with disappointment in the era in which he found himself and in his own life. He had once resolved to learn the true nature of things before he died; now, that no longer mattered to him. He was simply a weary traveler whose only desire was to rest.

Cheers rose as Huabei's grip finally failed and he plummeted towards his fate, towards the glowing blue rings beneath him.

He shut his eyes and gave himself over to weightlessness. It felt like his body was dissolving away, and with it, the crushing burden of existence. In these, the last few seconds of his life, a song suddenly popped into his mind. His father had taught it to him – an old Soviet tune, already forgotten by the time he had entered cryogenic hibernation. He had once gone to Moscow as a visiting scholar, and while there, he tried to find someone who knew the song. No one had heard of it, so it became his own, private song. He would only have time to hum a note or two in his head before he hit the bottom of the well, but he was sure that after his soul left his body, it would enter the next world humming.

Before he knew it, Huabei had already hummed half of the song's slow melody to himself. He suddenly became aware of how much time must have passed. Opening his eyes, he saw himself flying past ring after ring of blue light.

He was still falling.

'Ha ha ha ha!' Deng Yang's maniacal laugh came through his headphones. 'You're about to die – what a feeling that must be!'

Huabei looked down at the row of concentric rings glowing blue beneath him. They whizzed by him, one after the other, and each time he passed through the largest circle a new one emerged at its center, tiny at first but growing rapidly. He looked up at the concentric rings of light above him, whose expansion off into the distance mirrored the sight below.

'How deep is this well?' he asked.

'Don't worry, you'll hit the bottom soon enough. There's a hard steel plate down there, and you're going to splat against it like a bug on a windshield! Ha ha ha ha!'

As Deng Yang spoke, Huabei noticed that the small display in the upper right corner of his visor had flickered back to life. In glowing red letters, it read:

You have reached a depth of fifty miles.

Your speed is 0.86 miles per second.

You have passed the Mohorovičić discontinuity.

Having passed the crust, you are now entering the Earth's mantle.

Huabei shut his eyes again. This time, there was no music. His mind was like a computer, dispassionate and quick, and after thirty seconds of thought he opened his eyes. Now he understood everything. This was the Antarctic Doorstep Project. There was no steel plate at the end. This well was bottomless.

This was a tunnel straight through the Earth.

Chapter 5

The Tunnel

'Is its path tangential or does it go straight through the Earth's core?' wondered Huabei aloud.

'Clever! You figured it out!' exclaimed Deng Yang.

'As clever as his son,' someone added – the Central Breach orphan, by the sound of his voice.

'It goes through the Earth's core, from Mohe to the easternmost part of the Antarctic Peninsula,' said Deng Yang, responding to Huabei's question.

'The city we were just in was Mohe?'

'Yes, it experienced a boom once the tunnel was constructed.'

'As far as I know, a tunnel from there straight through the Earth would reach the southern part of Argentina.'

'That's correct, but this tunnel curves slightly.'

'If that's the case, won't I hit the wall?'

'No – in fact, you would hit the wall if the tunnel went to Argentina. A perfectly straight tunnel would only be workable between the Earth's poles, along its axis. To make a tunnel at an angle to the axis, you must consider the rotation of the Earth. This tunnel's curvature is necessary for smooth passage.'

'This tunnel is a remarkable achievement!' exclaimed Huabei sincerely.

You have reached a depth of 185 miles.

Your speed is 1.5 miles per second.

You have entered the Earth's asthenosphere.

Huabei saw that he was passing through the rings of light at an increasing rate. The concentric circles of light above and below him now appeared considerably denser.

Deng Yang spoke. 'Digging a tunnel through the Earth isn't exactly a new idea. As early as the 18th century, at least two people had already considered it. One was the mathematician Pierre Louis Maupertuis. The second was none other than Voltaire. After them, the French astronomer Flammarion raised the idea again, and he was the first to take into account the rotation of the Earth.'

Huabei interrupted him. 'So how can you say the idea came from me?'

'Because those people were just doing thought experiments, while your idea influenced someone – someone talented, with vision, who went on to make this outlandish idea a reality.'

'I don't remember mentioning anything like that to Shen Yuan.'

'Then you have a poor memory. You had a vision that changed the course of human history, and you forgot it!'

'I honestly can't recall.'

'Surely you remember a man called Delgado, from Argentina, and the birthday present he gave your son.'

You have reached a depth of 930 miles.

Your speed is 3.2 miles per second.

You have entered the Earth's mesosphere.

Huabei finally remembered. It was Shen Yuan's sixth birthday, and Huabei had invited the Argentine physicist Doctor Delgado, who happened to be in Beijing, to his home. Argentina was one of the two South American nations that emerged from the struggle for Antartica as a superpower. It had vast territorial claims on the continent, and large numbers of Argentine citizens had gone to live there. Argentina had also begun rapidly augmenting its nuclear arsenal, to the great alarm of the international community.

In the subsequent process of global nuclear disarmament, it was natural that Argentina, as a nuclear-armed state, should join the UN's Nuclear Eradication Committee. Shen Huabei and Delgado were both serving as technical experts within that committee.

Delgado had given Shen Yuan a globe. It was made of a novel kind of glass, one of the products of Argentina's rapid technological development. The refractive index of this glass was equal to that of air, so it was entirely invisible. On the globe, the continents appeared as if they were floating in space between the Earth's poles. Shen Yuan loved his gift.

As they chatted after dinner, Delgado took out a prominent Chinese newspaper and showed Huabei a political cartoon. It was a drawing of a famous Argentine soccer player kicking the Earth like a soccer ball.

'I don't like this cartoon,' said Delgado. 'China knows nothing about Argentina except that we play soccer well, and this limited understanding affects international politics. The Chinese see Argentina as an aggressive nation.'

'Well, Doctor, Argentina is the furthest nation from China on Earth. We are at opposite ends of the globe,' said Zhao Wenjia, smiling. She took the transparent globe from Shen Yuan and held it up. China and Argentina overlapped through the perfectly clear glass.

'I know a way to improve communication between our countries,' said Huabei, taking the globe. 'We'd just need to dig a tunnel through the center of the Earth.'

'That tunnel would be more than 7,500 miles long. That's not much shorter than a direct flight path,' said Delgado.

'But the travel time would be much shorter than flying. Think about it – you'd pack your bags, hop into one end of the tunnel, and...'

Huabei had only raised this idea to turn the conversation away from politics. It worked. Delgado's interest was piqued, and he said, 'Shen, your way of thinking is truly original. Let's see – after I jumped into the hole, the speed of my fall would continuously accelerate. The deeper I fell, the slower my acceleration would be, but I would continue to accelerate all the way to the center of the Earth. At the center, I will have achieved my maximum velocity, and my acceleration would be zero. Then, as I began to ascend the far side of the hole, I would decelerate, and my rate of deceleration would increase the further I ascended. When I arrived at the surface of the Earth in Argentina, my speed would be exactly zero. If I wanted to return to China, I could simply jump back into the hole. I could continue this sort of travel forever, if I wished, moving in simple harmonic vibration between the Northen and Southern hemispheres. Yes, it's a wonderful idea, but the travel time...'

'Let's calculate it,' said Huabei. He turned on his computer.

Completing the calculation took only a moment. Based on the planet's average density, if you jumped into the tunnel in China, traveled 7,917 miles through the Earth and emerged from the tunnel in Argentina, your travel time would be forty two minutes and twelve seconds.

'Now that's what I call fast travel!' said Delgado, clearly pleased.

You have reached a depth of 1,740 miles.

Your speed is four miles per second.

You are passing the Gutenberg discontinuity and entering the Earth's core.

As Huabei continued to fall, Deng Yang spoke. 'You certainly didn't notice it at the time, but clever little Shen Yuan hung onto

425

your every word that evening. You also wouldn't know that he didn't sleep a wink that night. He just stared at the transparent globe next to his bed. Your influence on his thinking was enormous. Over the years, you planted countless seeds in his imagination. This one happened to bear fruit.'

The wall of the tunnel was around fifteen feet from Huabei, and he watched it fly upwards. The rings of light now sped by so rapidly that they appeared as a blur on the wall.

'Is this wall made of new-solid-state material?' he asked.

'What else could it be? Is there another material strong enough to construct a tunnel like this?'

'How did you produce such an enormous quantity? How can you transport and operate a material so dense that it sinks through the Earth?

'The short answer is this: new-solid-state material is produced in a continuous series of small nuclear explosions, using your 'sugar coating' technology, of course. Producing it is a long and complex process. We can produce new-solid-state material in a range of densities. Lower-density material does not sink into the ground, so it is used to build large foundations that can bear the weight of high-density material without sinking, by dispersing its pressure. The same principle can be applied in transporting the material. The technology used to machine the material is more complex; you don't have the background knowledge to understand it. Suffice it to say that new-solid-state material is an enormous industry, larger in scale than steel production. The Antarctic Doorstep Project is not the material's only application.'

'How was this tunnel built?'

'I'll tell you first that the basic component of the tunnel's structure is a wellbore casing. Each section of casing is around 320 feet long, and the tunnel is made of around 240,000 sections linked together. As to the specific construction process, you're a smart man – you figure it out.'

'A caisson?'

'Yes, we used a caisson. First we sank the wellbore casing

from sites in China and Antarctica. Linked together, the sections of casing formed an unbroken line through the Earth. The second step was to excavate the material from inside the casing, forming the tunnel. The metal hills you saw outside the entrance to the tunnel are made of excavated material, iron and nickel alloys from the core of the Earth. The actual work of linking the casing was carried out by 'subterranean ships', machines made of new-solid-state material that are capable of travel among and between the strata of the Earth. Some models are able to operate at core depth. We used these machines to maneuver the sinking sections of casing into place.

'By my calculation, the process you describe would only require 120,000 sections of casing.'

'Super dense solids are able to withstand the high pressures and temperatures found in the interior of the Earth, but the movement of liquid matter within the Earth is more problematic. There is magma at relatively shallow depths, but the real danger is in the core, where the flow of liquid iron and nickel produces enormous shearing force against the tunnel. New-solid-state matter is strong enough to withstand these forces, but the joints in the casing aren't. Therefore, the tunnel is constructed out of two layers of casing, one wrapped tightly around the other. By staggering the joints of the two layers, we were able to achieve sufficient resistance to the shearing forces.'

You have reached a depth of 3,350 miles.

Your speed is 4.8 miles per second.

You are approaching the Earth's solid core.

'I suppose you'll tell me next about the disasters that this project caused.'

Chapter 6

Disaster

'Twenty-five years ago, the Antarctic Doorstep suffered its first disaster, just as the project entered the final phase of survey and design,' Deng Yang continued. 'This stage required substantial underground navigation. On one exploratory voyage, a ship called *Sunset 6* experienced a malfunction while in the Earth's mantle and sank down to the core. Two members of the three-person crew were killed. Only the young, female pilot survived. She is still down there, sealed off in the core of the Earth, doomed to live out her remaining days encased in that subterranean ship. The neutrino communication device on the ship is no longer able to transmit messages, though it might still receive ours. Oh, that's right – her name is Shen Jing. She is your granddaughter.'

Huabei's heart skipped a beat.

At this speed, the rings of light on the wall of the tunnel were completely indistinct, making the wall itself appear to glow with a harsh, blue light. Huabei felt as if he were falling into a tunnel through time, into the recent past, the past he had not known.

You have reached a depth of 3,600 miles.

Your speed is 4.8 miles per second.

You have entered the solid core and are approaching the center of the Earth.

'In the sixth year of construction, the tragic Central Breach Disaster struck. As I mentioned before, the tunnel's wall is composed of two staggered layers of casing. Before installing a section of the inner layer, it was necessary to join the adjacent outer sections and extract all material from inside them, as any debris could have compromised the seal between the layers. This was time-sensitive work, especially in the liquid core. After two sections of the outer ring were coupled and before the inner section was inserted, the outer layer had to hold on its own against the force of the nickel-iron flow. The riveting used to join the rings was exceptionally strong. Its design was projected to be able to withstand the force of the flow almost indefinitely. Three hundred miles into the core, two sections of outer ring that had just been coupled were struck by an aberrant surge in the nickel-iron flow, five times more forceful than anything observed in prior surveys. The force of the surge dislocated the sections, and in an instant, high-temperature, high-pressure core material rushed through the breach, into the caisson, and up the tunnel. As soon as the breach was detected, Shen Yuan, as general director of the project, immediately ordered the closure of the Gutenberg Gate, a safety valve located at the Gutenberg Discontinuity. More than 2,500 engineers were working in the five hundred miles of tunnel beneath the valve at the time. These workers boarded high-speed freight elevators to evacuate the tunnel as soon as they became aware of the breach. The final elevator departed around twenty miles ahead of the crest of the nickel-iron flow. In the end, only sixty-one elevators made it through the Gutenberg Gate before it closed; everyone else was trapped on the wrong side, swallowed by torrents of the core flow, burning at over seven thousand degrees. One thousand five hundred and twenty-seven people lost their lives.

'News of the disaster shook the world. There was a consensus that Shen Yuan was to blame, but people disagreed about how he should have responded. One group asserted he had had time to wait for all the elevators to pass through the Gutenberg Gate before closing it. The last elevator was twenty miles ahead of the flow – it would have been a close call, but possible. Even if the flow had overtaken the Gutenberg Gate before it could be closed, there was still the Moho Gate, another safety valve at the Mohorovičić discontinuity. Outraged members of the victims' families accused Shen Yuan of murder. His public response was a single sentence: I had to act fast. He wasn't wrong – hesitating might have caused a cataclysm. There was a whole subgenre of disaster films about the Antarctic Doorstep. The most famous, Metal Fountain, was a nightmarish depiction of what would have happened if the core material had breached the surface. In it, a column of liquid nickel and iron shot out of the tunnel into the stratosphere, where it blossomed outwards like a flower of death. It glowed with a blinding white light that illuminated the whole Northern hemisphere, and a rain of molten metal began to fall over the Earth, turning all of Asia into a furnace. Humanity met the same fate as the dinosaurs.

'This wasn't artistic license; it was a probable outcome. Because of this, Shen Yuan faced another line of accusation that contradicted the first: he should have closed the Gutenberg Gate immediately, without waiting for sixty-one elevators to ascend. This was the more popular view, and its adherents labelled Shen Yuan's crime 'criminal negligence against humanity'. There was no proper legal basis for either accusation, but Shen Yuan resigned from his leadership position on the Project. He refused to be reappointed elsewhere, and he continued his work on the tunnel as an ordinary engineer.'

The light on the wall of the tunnel suddenly turned from blue to red.

You have reached a depth of 3,900 miles.

Your speed is five miles per second.

You are passing through the center of the Earth.

Deng Yang's voice came through Huabei's earphones once again. 'Your current speed would be fast enough to carry you into orbit, but your location at the center of the planet means that the world is revolving around you. The continents and oceans of Earth, its cities and people, are all orbiting you.'

Bathed in the solemn red light, another piece of music came to Huabei, this time a magnificent symphony. He was traveling at first cosmic velocity in a tunnel through the center of the Earth – a tunnel whose glowing, red walls gave Huabei the impression that the Earth itself was alive and that he was floating through one of its veins. His heart raced.

Deng Yang continued: 'New-solid-state material is an excellent insulator, but the air around you is still above 2,700 degrees. Your suit's cooling system is running at full power.'

After about ten seconds, the red light on the wall suddenly turned back to a tranquil blue.

> You have passed through the center of the Earth and begun your ascent and deceleration.
>
> You have ascended three miles.
>
> Your speed is 4.8 miles per second.
>
> You are in the Earth's solid core.

The blue light soothed Huabei. He had already gotten used to weightlessness, and he slowly turned his body so that he was moving head-first. In this position, he felt he was rising rather than falling. 'Wasn't there a third disaster?' he asked.

'The Lost Bolt Disaster happened five years ago, after the Antarctic Doorstep Project had been completed and officially opened for use. Core trains traveled through the tunnel nonstop. The cars of the trains were cylindrical, twenty-seven feet in diameter and 165 feet long; a single train was made up of as many as two hundred cars that could carry twetnty-two thousand tons of freight or nearly ten-thousand passengers. A one-way trip through the center of the Earth took only forty-two minutes and required no resources besides gravity.

'At the Mohe Station, a repair technician carelessly dropped a bolt into the tunnel. It was no thicker than five inches in diameter, but it was made of a new material that is able to absorb electromagnetic waves, so the radar safety system was unable to detect it. The bolt fell down the tunnel, through the Earth, and arrived at the Antarctic Station, where it began to fall again. Near the center of the Earth, it struck a core train ascending to Antarctica. The speed of the bolt relative to the train was close to ten miles per second; its kinetic energy made it like a missile. It penetrated the first two cars of the train, vaporizing everything in its path, and the explosion sent the rest of the train off course. It crashed into the wall of the tunnel at five miles per second, tearing it to shreds in an instant.

'Debris from the crash oscillated back and forth in the tunnel. Some pieces rose as high as the surface, but most of the debris had lost momentum in the crash and simply swung around near the core. It took a month to clean the shards out the tunnel. We were unable to recover the bodies of the three thousand passengers on board – they had been incinerated in the heat of the core.'

You have ascended 1,360 miles from the center of the Earth.

Your speed is 4.6 miles per second.

You have re-entered the Earth's liquid core.

'The biggest disaster of all was the Project itself. The Antarctic Doorstep Project may have been an unprecedented feat of engineering, but from an economic standpoint, it was incredibly stupid. People still can't figure out how such a patently foolish project could ever have made it off the drawing board. Shen Yuan's reckless ambition certainly played a role, but the true reason it succeeded was people's frenzied desire for new lands to claim and their blind worship of technology. The economic benefits of the Project dried up on the day it was completed. It was true that the tunnel enabled extremely fast travel through the Earth and consumed almost no resources – people used to say 'just toss it in the tunnel' or 'just hop in the tunnel'. But it had been a huge investment, and the transport fees on core trains were astronomical. Despite its speed, the high cost of using the tunnel eliminated its competitive advantage over traditional modes of transport.'

'Humanity's Antarctic dream was soon shattered. The last pristine land on Earth was overexploited and destroyed in a swarm of industry, and Antarctica became like everywhere else: used up, covered in refuse – a landfill. The ozone layer over Antarctica was completely destroyed, which affected the whole world. Even in the Northern hemisphere, strong UV rays made it necessary for people to cover their skin outdoors. The melting of the Antarctic ice sheet accelerated sharply, causing a dramatic rise in sea levels across the globe. In the midst of these crises, human reason once again prevailed. Member States of the United Nations unanimously signed a new Antarctic Treaty that mandated an immediate, complete withdrawal from the continent. It is once again a wilderness, and we expect its environment to recover gradually. The treaty caused a sudden, sharp drop in demand for shipping to Antarctica, and after the Lost Bolt Disaster, all core train operations ceased. The tunnel has now been closed for eight years, but its effects on the economy still linger. Thousands of people who had bought stock in the Antarctic Doorstep Company lost everything, which caused serious social unrest. The tunnel was a black hole for investors, and it brought the country's economy to the brink of collapse. Even today, we are still mired in the troubles and pain it caused.

'That is the story of the Antarctic Doorstep Project.'

As Huabei's speed decreased, the blur of blue light on the wall of the tunnel began to flicker, and soon he was again able to distinguish each ring as it passed. In each direction, the lights appeared once again as the dense, concentric rings of a target.

You have reached a height of 2,980 miles above the Earth's core.

Your speed is 3.1 miles per second.

You are passing through the Earth's mesosphere.

Chapter 7

The Death of Shen Yuan

'What became of my son?' asked Huabei.

'After the tunnel was closed, Shen Yuan stayed on as part of a skeleton crew at the Mohe Station. I called him on the phone one day; he said he was "with his daughter" and hung up. I didn't learn the truth behind those cryptic words until several years later. It nearly defies description. He spent all his time in an airtight suit, falling back and forth through the tunnel. He slept in the tunnel. He only returned to the station to eat and recharge his suit. He passed through the Earth roughly thirty-two times each day. Day after day, year after year, he traveled from Mohe to the Antarctic Peninsula and back again, in a simple harmonic wave with a cycle of eighty-four minutes and an amplitude of 7,830 miles.'

You have ascended 3,730 miles from the center of the Earth.

Your speed is 1.5 miles per second.

You are passing through the Earth's asthenosphere.

'No one knows exactly what Shen Yuan did during his endless fall. According to his colleagues, each time he passed through the center of the Earth, he used a neutrino communicator to hail his daughter. He often had long conversations with her as he fell – one-sided, of course. But Shen Jing, trapped in the *Sunset 6* as it drifted in the nickel-iron flow of the Earth's core, was probably able to hear him.

'He subjected his body to long periods of weightlessness, interrupted by two or three exposures each day to the normal force of Earth's gravity when he returned to the station to eat and recharge his suit. He was an old man, and the constant change in gravity weakened his heart. His heart gave out as he fell. No one noticed. His body continued to travel through the tunnel for two days until his sealed suit exhausted its charge. The tunnel was his crematorium. His final pass through the center of the Earth burned his body to ashes. I believe your son would have been satisfied with this fate.'

'That will be my fate as well, won't it?' asked Huabei, calmly.

'It should satisfy you, too. You saw everything you wanted to see before your death. We had originally planned to throw you into the tunnel without a suit, but in the end, we decided that you should get a thorough look at the thing your son made.'

'Yes, I am satisfied. This life has been enough. I am sincerely grateful to each of you.'

There was no answer. The hum of Huabei's headphones abruptly disappeared as his executioners, standing on the other side of the world, cut off communications.

Huabei looked up. The concentric rings of light above him were quite sparse now. It took two or three seconds to pass each one, and the interval was getting longer. A beeping sound came through his headphones, and words appeared on his visor:

You have reached a height of 3,850 miles above the Earth's core.

Your speed is 0.9 miles per second.

You have passed through the Mohorovičić Discontinuity, and are entering the Earth's crust.

Attention!

You are approaching the Antarctic Terminal.

At the center of the rings above him there was only emptiness, which grew as he approached the final ring of blue light. He passed it and rose slowly towards a bridge spanning the mouth of the tunnel, identical to the bridge on the other end. On the bridge stood several people in airtight suits. As he ascended through the mouth of the tunnel, they reached out to grab him and pulled him up onto the bridge.

The interior of the Antarctic station was also dark, lit only from below by the glow of the blue rings. Huabei looked up and saw a huge cylindrical object suspended above him. Its diameter was slightly smaller than that of the tunnel. He walked along the bridge to the rim of the tunnel and looked up again. There was a whole row of cylinders hanging above the mouth of the tunnel. He counted four of them and guessed that there were more in the darkness above those. This, he knew, had to be the decommissioned core train.

Chapter 8

Antarctica

Half an hour later, Huabei walked out of the tunnel's Antarctic Terminal station, accompanied by the police officers who had saved his life. He stood on a snowless expanse of Antarctic plain. There was an abandoned city in the distance. The sun hung low over the horizon, casting its weak rays over the vast and otherwise uninhabited continent. The air here was cleaner than on the other side of the Earth, and no respirator was necessary.

A policemen told Huabei that they were members of a small police force left to guard the empty city. They had rushed to the station after receiving an alert from Doctor Guo. The tunnel's mouth was sealed when they arrived, so they immediately contacted the tunnel's management department and lodged an urgent request to remove the cover. Huabei was approaching the mouth of the tunnel just as it opened, and they saw him rise towards them in the blue light, like something floating up from the depths of the ocean. If it had opened a few seconds later, Huabei would have certainly perished. The tunnel's seal would have blocked his ascent, and he would have begun falling again towards the Northern hemisphere. His suit would have run out of power before he reached the core, and he would have been burned to ashes, just as his son was.

'Deng Yang and his co-conspirators have been arrested and will be charged with attempted murder. However...' The police officer paused and glared at Huabei. 'I understand what drove them.'

Huabei was still dizzy from the weightlessness of his fall. He looked off towards the sun at the edge of the sky and sighed. 'This life has been enough,' he said.

'If that's how you feel, you'll find it easier to accept your fate,' said another officer.

'My fate?' Huabei's senses came back to him and he turned his head to face the second officer.

'You can't live in these times or this sort of thing will happen again. Fortunately for you, the government has a 'temporal emigration program' aimed at reducing population pressures on the environment. Under this program, a portion of the population is obliged to enter cryogenic hibernation, to be awoken at some future date. We have already received our orders – you will be a temporal emigrant. I don't know how long it will be until you are awoken.'

It took Huabei a long time to fully comprehend what he had been told. Once he did, he gave the police officer a deep bow. 'Thank you. How am I always so lucky?'

'Lucky?' asked the officer, clearly confused. 'Temporal emigrants from this era will have a hard enough time adapting to the society of the future. There is no hope for someone from the past like you!'

A faint smile crossed Huabei's face. 'That doesn't matter. What matters is that I will have the chance to see the Earth Tunnel restored to glory!'

The policemen scoffed. 'I wouldn't bet on it. The Project was a catastrophe! It will stand forever as nothing more than a monument to you and your son's failure.'

'Ha ha ha ha!' Huabei burst into laughter. He was still weak from weightlessness and could barely stand straight, but his spirit soared. 'The Great Wall and the Pyramids were utter failures, too. The Mongols invaded China from the north, and the pharoah's mummy never came back to life. But is that how we think of these colossal projects now? No, we think of them as glorious monuments to the human spirit!' He pointed behind him, at the towering cylinder of the tunnel station. 'This tunnel is a Great Wall through the center of the Earth itself, and here you are at its edge, weeping like Lady Meng Jiang! How pitiful! Ha ha ha ha!'

Huabei opened his arms to embrace the cold Antarctic wind. 'Yuan, our lives were enough,' he said happily.

Epilogue

The next time Huabei awoke half a century had passed. His experience was almost identical to the last time: he was taken by a group of people to a car, which drove to the tunnel's Mohe Terminal station. He was put into an airtight suit – for some reason, much heavier than the one he had worn 50 years before – and was thrown, once again, into the tunnel. After fifty years, the tunnel looked much the same as it did before – a bottomless hole, lit by an endless series of blue, ring-shaped lights on its walls.

This time, however, someone had jumped in with him. She was young and beautiful, and she introduced herself as his tour guide.

'A tour guide? So my prediction was right – the tunnel has become a wonder of the world, like the Great Wall or the Pyramids!' Huabei said excitedly as he fell.

'No, not like those places. The tunnel has become...' She was holding Huabei's hand, to ensure that they fell at the same speed, and her speech trailed off as she carefully adjusted her grip.

'What has it become?'

'The World Cannon!'

'What?' Huabei looked again at the walls of the tunnel as they flew by, trying to understand.

The tour guide explained, 'After you entered hibernation, the environment became even worse. Pollution and the destruction of the ozone layer killed what little vegetation remained on Earth. Breathable air became a commodity. At the time, we were left with one option if we wanted to save the Earth: shut down all heavy energy industries.'

'That may help the environment, but it would also mean the end of civilization,' Huabei interrupted.

'Many people were willing to accept that as a side effect, given the size of the problem. However, some continued looking for another way out. The most feasible alternative was to move all the planet's industrial operations to the moon and to outer space.'

'You built a space elevator?'

'No, though we tried. It turned out to be even harder than digging the Earth Tunnel.'

'Did you invent anti-gravity spacecraft?'

'No. In fact, that has been proven to be theoretically impossible.'

'Nuclear-powered rockets?'

'Those we have, but they're not much cheaper to operate than traditional rockets. Using them to move all industry to space would have been an economic disaster of the same scale that this tunnel was.'

'So you weren't able to move anything to space in the end.' Huabei smiled grimly. 'Has the world entered... a post-human age?'

The guide did not respond. Together they fell in silence into the abyss as the rings of light flying past them grew denser and blended together into a single, luminescent surface on the wall of the tunnel. Ten minutes later, the light turned red, and they wordlessly passed through the center of the Earth at five miles per second. The walls soon turned blue again, and Huabei's guide deftly turned her body 180 degrees, so that she ascended head-first. Huabei followed her motion clumsily.

'Oh!' Huabei shouted in surprise. The display in the upper

right corner of his visor said their current speed was 5.3 miles per second.

They had passed the center of the Earth, but they were still accelerating.

Something else alarmed Huabei: he felt the force of gravity. The process of falling through the Earth was supposed to take place entirely in weightlessness, but he distinctly felt his own weight. His scientist's intuition told him that what he felt was not in fact gravity – it was thrust. Some force was thrusting them forward and causing them to continue to accelerate, even as gravity should have been slowing them down.

'I take it you've read *From the Earth to the Moon*, by Jules Verne?' asked the guide suddenly.

'When I was young. It was the dumbest book I'd ever read,' Huabei answered, absent-mindedly. His attention was on his surroundings as he tried to figure out what strange force was acting on them.

'It's not dumb at all. To implement large-scale, fast transportation into space, a cannon is ideal.'

'Unless the speed of the launch squashes you flat.'

'The reason you'd get squashed would be if you accelerated too quickly, and you'd only accelerate too quickly if the barrel of the cannon was too short. With a long enough barrel, the payload could accelerate gently, just as we are right now.'

'So we're in Verne's cannon?'

'As I said, it's called the World Cannon.'

Huabei looked up at the blue tunnel and tried to imagine it as the barrel of a cannon. At this speed, the wall appeared as a single, uninterrupted object, so he had no sense of movement. He felt as if they were motionless, hovering in a glowing, blue tube.

'In your fourth year of hibernation, we developed a novel type of new-solid-state material. It possesses all the properties of the previous material, but it is also an excellent conductor. A thick wire made of this material is wrapped around the exterior of the Antarctic half of the tunnel, making it function as a four-thousand-mile-long electromagnetic coil.

'What powers the coil?'

'There is a strong electric current in the core of the Earth. It's what produces the Earth's magnetic field. We used core ships to assemble more than one hundred thousand-mile-long loops of conductive solid-state wire in the core. These loops collect the current in the core and transfer it to the coil around the tunnel, filling the tunnel with a powerful electromagnetic field. In the shoulders and midsections of our suits are two superconducting coils that produce the opposite magnetic field. That's how we achieve thrust.'

Continuing to accelerate, they quickly approached the end of the tunnel. As they did, the walls again began to glow red.

'Our speed is 9.3 miles per second, well above escape velocity. We're about to be fired from the World Cannon!'

The towering Core Train Station above had long been dismantled, replaced with nothing but a sealed gate, covering a simple opening right up into the sky.

A recorded message played over their headphones:

Attention passengers: the World Cannon is about to commence today's forty-third launch. Please put on your protective eyewear and insert your earplugs. Failure to do so will cause permanent damage to your eyesight and hearing.

Ten seconds later, the sealed mouth of the tunnel slid open loudly, revealing its thirty-foot-wide mouth. Air roared into the vacuum of the tunnel's interior. With a noise like thunder, a long tongue of flame leapt out of the mouth of the tunnel, so bright that it outshone the weak, low-hanging Antarctic sun. Instantly, the sealed gate slid closed again, the tunnel's air pumps roaring to life. Soon they had removed all the air that had rushed into the tunnel during the three seconds that the gate had been open; then the cannon was ready for the next launch.

People looked up to see two shooting stars, trailing tails of fire as they streaked upwards and disappeared into the deep blue Antarctic sky.

Huabei looked back to see the ground receding beneath his feet. He recognized the city next to the tunnel's terminal, which soon appeared only as big as a basketball court. He saw the color of the sky quickly transitioning from blue to black, as if a screen were being dimmed. Turning his gaze below, he saw the long arc of the Antarctic Peninsula surrounded by ocean. A long tail of flame trailed behind him, emanating from the red-hot surface of his suit. He was enveloped in a thin cloak of fire.

He looked over at his guide, some thirty feet away. She was also wrapped in flames, like some fantastic creature of living fire. The air resistance felt like a giant hand pressing relentlessly down on his head and shoulders. As the sky grew darker, this giant hand was conquered by another, more powerful, force and the pressure subsided. Looking down, he saw all of Antarctica, noticing with joy that it was white once again. In the distance, the curvature of the Earth became clear. The sun appeared to move upwards from the arc of the horizon, scattering its resplendent light throughout the planet's thin atmosphere. Once more, Huabei looked up and saw the constellations spread out above him. He had never seen the stars shine so brightly.

The fire surrounding his body was extinguished as they shot out of the atmosphere. They were now floating through the vast silence of space.

Huabei felt as light as a feather. His sealed suit, or spacesuit, was much thinner than before, as its top layer of heat-dispersing material had burned off in the friction of the atmosphere. Their communications had been interrupted by atmospheric disturbance, but now they were back online. Huabei's guide spoke: 'Atmospheric resistance slowed us down a bit, but we are still traveling at escape velocity. We're leaving the Earth. Look over there.'

She pointed beneath them at the Antarctic Peninsula, which was now tiny. Huabei saw a flash of light from the spot where the tunnel emerged, and a shooting star shot upwards into the sky, trailing fire behind it. As it exited the atmosphere, the fire dimmed and went out.

'That was a spaceship leaving the World Cannon. It's going to pick us up. At every moment, five or six "payloads" are traveling through the barrel of the cannon, firing off at eight-to-ten minute intervals, so getting into space is as fast and easy as taking the subway. It fired even more rapidly when the great industrial migration began twenty years ago. There were often more than twenty ships accelerating through the barrel at a time, with two- or three-minute intervals between shots. Back then, the spaceships shot into the sky like a never-ending shower of meteors. The job was enormous, but humanity's fate hung in the balance. It was truly magnificent!'

Huabei spotted numerous streaking stars, easy to see against the stillness of the stars in the background, and Huabei realized that they were in fact objects in orbit around the Earth. Squinting, he was able to make out some of their shapes: some were ring-shaped, others were circular and some appeared to be irregular assemblies of many different shapes. They looked like jewels against the deep blackness of space.

'That one is Baoshan Iron & Steel Company,' said Huabei's guide, pointing towards a glowing, ring-shaped object. She pointed out several other bright objects. 'Those are Sinopec which, of course, no longer handles oil. Those cylindrical ones are the European Metallurgy Association. Over there are solar power stations – they collect solar energy and send it to the surface using microwaves. The shining parts are just their control centers; their panels and transmission arrays are invisible from here.'

Huabei was enraptured by the sight. He looked down at the lush, blue orb of Earth, and tears flowed from his eyes. His heart went out to everyone, living or dead, who had participated in the Antarctic Doorstep Project. He wished that all of them could see this. And one of them especially – a certain young woman, who would remain forever young in his heart.

'Did they find my granddaughter?' he asked.

'No. We don't have the technology to conduct long-range scans in the core. The search area is vast, and no one knows where the iron-nickel flow has carried her.'

'Can we send this image to the core as a neutrino transmission?'

'We already are. I believe she can see it all.'

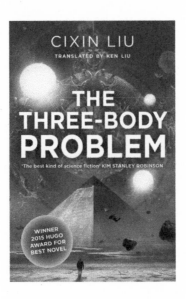

1967: Ye Wenjie witnesses Red Guards beat her father to death during China's Cultural Revolution. This singular event will shape not only the rest of her life but also the future of mankind.

Four decades later, Beijing police ask nanotech engineer Wang Miao to infiltrate a secretive cabal of scientists after a spate of inexplicable suicides. Wang's investigation will lead him to a mysterious online game and immerse him in a virtual world ruled by the intractable and unpredicatable interaction of its three suns.

This is the Three-Body Problem and it is the key to everything: the key to the scientists' deaths, the key to a conspiracy that spans light-years and the key to the extinction-level threat humanity now faces.

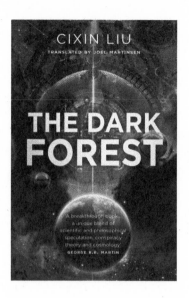

Imagine the universe as a forest, patrolled by numberless and nameless predators. In this forest, stealth is survival – any civilisation that reveals its location is prey.

Earth has. Now the predators are coming.

Crossing light years, they will reach Earth in four centuries' time. But the sophons, their extra-dimensional agents and saboteurs, are already here. Only the individual human mind remains immune to their influence.

This is the motivation for the Wallfacer Project, a last-ditch defence that grants four individuals almost absolute power to design secret strategies, hidden through deceit and misdirection from human and alien alike. Three of the Wallfacers are influential statesmen and scientists, but the fourth is a total unknown.

Luo Ji, an unambitious Chinese astronomer, is baffled by his new status. All he knows is that he's the one Wallfacer that Trisolaris wants dead.

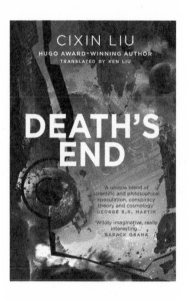

Half a century after the Doomsday Battle, the uneasy balance of Dark Forest Deterrence keeps the Trisolaran invaders at bay.

Earth enjoys unprecedented prosperity due to the infusion of Trisolaran knowledge and, with human science advancing and the Trisolarans adopting Earth culture, it seems that the two civilizations can co-exist peacefully as equals without the terrible threat of mutually assured annihilation. But peace has made humanity complacent.

Cheng Xin, an aerospace engineer from the 21st century, awakens from hibernation in this new age. She brings knowledge of a long-forgotten program dating from the start of the Trisolar Crisis, and her presence may upset the delicate balance between two worlds. Will humanity reach for the stars or die in its cradle?